The DEVIL in the MARSHALSEA

The DEVIL
in the
MARSHALSEA

Antonia Hodgson

MARINER BOOKS

HOUGHTON MIFFLIN HARCOURT

BOSTON   NEW YORK

First U.S. edition

For information about permission to reproduce selections from this book,
write to Permissions, Houghton Mifflin Harcourt Publishing Company,
215 Park Avenue South, New York, New York 10003.

www.hmhco.com

First published in Great Britain in 2014 by Hodder & Stoughton

Library of Congress Cataloging-in-Publication Data
Hodgson, Antonia.
The Devil in the Marshalsea / Antonia Hodgson. — First U.S. Edition.
pages cm
ISBN 978-0-544-17667-6 (pbk.)
I. Title.
PR6108.O335D48 2014
823'.92 — dc23
2013045482

Printed in the United States of America
DOC 10 9 8 7 6 5 4 3

For Joanna, Justine and Victoria, with thanks

'Conscience makes ghosts walk, and departed souls appear
. . . it works upon the imagination with an invincible force,
like faith.'

— Daniel Defoe, *The Secrets of the Invisible World Disclos'd,* 1729

'Arose about four. In the Park I saw half a Dozen Crows in
very hoarse conversation together, but not understanding
their Language I cou'd not devise what they were upon, but
believe they was agreeing how to divide the Corps of those
unhappy wretches that Dye so briefly in this Place.'

— John Grano, *A Journal of My Life while in the Marshalsea,* 1728–9

HISTORICAL NOTE

The Devil in the Marshalsea is set in the autumn of 1727 in London and Southwark, which was generally regarded as a separate town at the time. King George I had died in June. His son, George II, was now king, although he was not crowned until October. People were curious to discover what sort of a monarch he would turn out to be. (A philistine and a buffoon, if we are to believe Lord Hervey, the waspish chronicler of court life.)

The Marshalsea of 1727 is not the same prison that Dickens depicted so brilliantly in *Little Dorrit*. This second gaol was not opened until the turn of the 1800s and was situated further down Borough High Street. The original prison had existed since at least the fourteenth century and was set between Mermaid Court and what is now Newcomen Street.

In 1720 Britain suffered its first great modern economic catastrophe – the collapse of the South Sea Company. Thousands were ruined when the company's stock plummeted and the devastating effects were still being felt seven years later. The *London Gazette* of 17–19 September 1727 was filled with commissions of bankruptcy and death notices calling on creditors to confirm any debts owed. (Not everyone was suffering. There was also a page with instructions to peers and peeresses on their coronation robes, detailing how much ermine they could wear.)

London's debtors' prisons were packed – which spelled misery for thousands and a splendid business opportunity for men such as William Acton, head keeper of the Marshalsea. Debtors' prisons had been common in England for centuries. While the gaols were ultimately owned by the Crown they were privately run for profit. Debtors who had satisfied their creditors would often languish in prison for years because they had run up further debts to the gaol keeper.

It may seem odd that there was so much money to be made from debtors – until we see adverts for pay-day loans and realise there are still plenty of ways to profit from someone else's misfortune. Many prisoners were supported by family and friends, or could pawn belongings while they looked for ways to pay off their creditors. Some even ran businesses from inside the prison walls – Sarah Bradshaw's coffeehouse and Mack's chophouse being two examples. 'Women of the town' were regular visitors. And there was indeed a barber called Trim and – exotically enough – a French fortune teller called Madame Migault living in the Marshalsea in 1727. Debtors' prisons were meant for containment rather than correction – if you could afford to pay for food, drink and company so be it, as long as the keeper got his cut.

Dinner and Supper

A small note to avoid confusion: in the early eighteenth century dinner was usually eaten at around 2 or 3p.m. followed by a light supper later in the evening if needed. All the meals referred to in the novel are based on dishes described in John Grano's diary written in the Marshalsea in 1728–9. And yes – they really did drink and smoke that much back then.

Swearing

They did an awful lot of this, too. All the words used in the book were in currency at the time – flagrantly so. César de Saussure, a Swiss visitor to London in the 1720s, commented: 'Englishmen are mighty swearers', and that 'not only the common people have this unfortunate habit'. And he was not referring just to 'damn' and 'by God'.

If these swear words seem in any way anachronistic, it is perhaps because they don't appear in the more familiar novels and plays of the time. A brief – or indeed a long – glance at 'libertine literature' such as *Venus in the Cloister* (1725) confirms that extremely strong language and graphic sex scenes are nothing new. In the coffeehouses of Covent Garden, the slums of St Giles and the debtors' prisons of the Borough, I think we can safely assume they did not say 'sugar' and 'fiddlesticks' when there were more colourful choices available.

PROLOGUE

They came for him at midnight. There was no warning, no time to reach for the dagger hidden beneath his pillow. They had moved as silently as ghosts, crossing the prison yard and stealing up the dank, narrow staircase while he slept on, oblivious.

A guilty man should not sleep so soundly.

He woke to find a cold blade pressed to his throat. They gagged him and bound his wrists before he had the wit to cry out; dragged him so hard from the bed to his knees that the floorboards split and buckled with the force.

A lantern flared into life, illuminating his attackers. Now, at last, he knew them, and why they had come. He tore frantically at the heavy leather purse tied about his neck for safe-keeping and flung it at their feet, gold and silver coins scattering across the floor.

The man holding the lantern reached down and plucked half a guinea from the dirt, turning it slowly between his fingers. 'D'you think this will save you?' He gave a thin smile and tossed the coin back to the floor. Nodded to his accomplice.

Then they sent him to hell.

The watchman found the body the next morning, hanging from a beam in the Strong Room, too high for the rats seething and scrabbling in the shadows below. The turnkeys cut him down and laid him out in the yard, away from three Common Side prisoners taken by fever in the night. The captain may have fallen on hard times, but he was still a gentleman.

The chaplain pointed to the dead man's battered face and broken body and insisted that the coroner be called at once to investigate. The governor, who'd been drinking with his cronies in the Crown for hours, spat in the dirt and called it suicide — and a pox on anyone who said otherwise. The coroner would rule the same; he'd make sure of it.

Up in the captain's room, his friends gambled hastily for his scant belongings before the serjeant took them. Clothes, tobacco, a pound of bacon. A small cooking pot smeared with the remnants of last night's supper. No money. But that was no surprise in a debtors' gaol.

A young maidservant paused on the landing, arms laden with fresh linen. She stood for a while in the shadows, watching the game and the men who played it. She'd learned a long time ago to keep her eyes and ears open. A good secret was better than gold in the Marshalsea — and more deadly than a blade if you used it right. Her eyes flickered to the floor. Strange. Someone had swept the floor clean in the night. She tucked the thought away, like a stray lock of hair beneath her cap, and returned to her chores.

The killers had swept the floor, but they'd missed one small thing. A coin had skittered across the room in the struggle, coming to rest in a dark corner beneath the captain's bed. And there it remained as the long months passed, hidden in the dust — a silver crown stained with blood. Waiting to tell its story.

Waiting for me to find it.

PART ONE

ROBBERY

One

'Y ou have the luck of the devil, Tom Hawkins.'

I grinned at the man across the bench. It was a warm September night, I had a full purse for the first time in months and we had just found a table in the most disreputable coffee-house in London. Life could not be better. 'It wasn't luck,' I replied, shouting over the din.

Charles Buckley, my oldest friend, shot me a look I had come to know very well over the years: exasperation, disapproval – and a flicker of amusement glowing deep in his eyes. I settled back, content, and lit a pipe. One of my greatest pleasures in life was making Charles laugh when he knew he shouldn't.

A serving maid passed close to our table – a pretty girl called Betty with tight black curls and skin the colour of roasted coffee beans. I beckoned her over and ordered a bowl of punch.

'A bowl of coffee,' Charles corrected. 'And then home. You gave me your word, remember?'

I slipped a shilling into Betty's hand. It felt good to have money again – and to spend it. 'Coffee. *And* a bowl of punch. We're celebrating,' I said, dismissing Charles' protestations with a lordly wave.

Betty arched an eyebrow. There were only two reasons to celebrate at Tom King's coffeehouse – a win at the tables or a full recovery from the clap.

'I took ten pounds at cards tonight,' I called out hastily, but she was already gliding through the crowds to the coffee pots hanging over the fire. When I turned back, Charles had his head in his hands.

'What am I to do with you?' he groaned through his fingers.

I looked out across the long, low room, breathing in the heady fumes of smoke, liquor and sweat. I would hang up my coat tonight and in the morning my little garret would be filled with the same familiar scents. 'One bowl of punch, Charles. Just one! To toast my skill at the tables tonight.'

'Skill?' He dropped his hands. Charles had a pleasant countenance, his features as neatly arranged as a well-proportioned drawing room. It was not a face created for outrage, but he did his best, widening his dark brown eyes a fraction. '*Skill? You risked everything on the turn of a card! Down to your very last farthing! That is not skill, it's . . .' He shrugged, helplessly. 'It's *madness.'

I didn't argue with him. Charles refused to believe there was anything more to gambling than blind luck – in part because he played so ill himself. No use explaining that I had known three quarters of the men in that hot, smoke-filled gaming room – had played against them so many times that I understood their strengths and failings better than my own. No use explaining that even half-drunk I could remember every card that had been played and work out the odds in a flash. To be fair there was some truth in what Charles said – I *had taken a terrible risk with that final bet, but I'd had no choice in the matter. My life had depended on it.

Early that morning my landlord and three other creditors had burst into my room and clapped an action on me for twenty pounds in unpaid rent and other debts. The warrant had given me just one day's grace to pay enough to satisfy them. If I failed I would be arrested at once and thrown in gaol.

Little frightened me in those days. I was five and twenty and death seemed a distant, hazy thing. But I knew three men who had been sent to a debtors' gaol in the last year. One had died of a fever, another had been stabbed in a fight and only just survived. The third had passed through the prison gates a fat, cheerful fellow and emerged six months later a grey, stuttering skeleton. He refused to say what had happened to him and there was a look in his eyes when we pressed him . . . as if he'd rather die than speak of it.

And so I'd flung on my clothes and run out into the brightening streets to call in every debt and favour I could think of. When that wasn't enough I'd pawned everything of value, until my room was stripped as bare as a maid on her wedding night. I saved only two items of any worth – my dagger for protection and my best suit for deception. (A little swagger and a few gold buttons will open most doors in London.) My creditors had demanded half what they were owed as proof they would see the rest in good time. As the sun set I counted out what I had made: two guineas and a handful of pennies. Hardly a quarter the sum I needed.

It was then that I was forced to do what I had been avoiding all day – I turned to Charles for help. We had been as close as brothers at school and at Oxford, but in the last few years our friendship had faltered. My old companion in mischief had become the Reverend Charles Buckley, a civil, sober gentleman who gave afternoon lectures to enraptured old ladies at St George's on Hanover Square. All of this was well and good, I supposed, until he'd started to lecture me on my own behaviour. I was not an enraptured old lady. I had not seen him for several months.

Charles lived with his patron, Sir Philip Meadows, in a large house near St James' Square. It wasn't a long way from my lodgings but my footsteps were slow and heavy as I walked along Piccadilly. I couldn't bear the thought of burdening him with my troubles, and worse – I knew he would forgive me for it in a moment. I was on the brink of being ashamed of myself – an uncomfortable feeling.

Luckily, when I explained my predicament to Charles he scolded me so hard that I quite forgot to feel ashamed and swore at him for being such a damned prig.

'Oh, for heaven's sake, hand me the warrant,' he snapped and began to read. He gave a grunt of surprise. 'This is for the Marshalsea. You must know that Sir Philip is Knight Marshal?'

Must I? I knitted my brows. I tended to drift off when Charles talked about his illustrious patron and his family, except when he mentioned Sir Philip's two eldest daughters. That always roused me. 'He owns the gaol?' I guessed.

'The king owns it,' Charles replied absently, reading further. 'Sir Philip administers it in his name. Well – he hires the head keeper . . . my God, Tom – twenty pounds? You owe these men *twenty pounds*? That's more than I earn in six months.' He peered at the warrant, as if hoping the numbers might rearrange themselves into something smaller if he squinted hard enough.

'London is a costly place to live.'

He gestured at the gold buttons on my waistcoat. 'It needn't be.'

Another lecture. 'Very well.' I snatched the warrant from his hands and stuffed it in my pocket. 'If I promise to dress in brown stockings and drab fustian breeches from now on, will you help me?'

Charles laughed, despite himself. 'Of course I'll help you.' He pulled an iron box from a high shelf, unlocked it and tipped out a small pile of coins. 'Will this be enough?'

I counted it quickly. A little under four pounds. Even if I took every last penny, it wouldn't save me from gaol.

'I can find more,' Charles said anxiously. He stole a glance at his belongings, assessing their worth with narrowed eyes. 'It may take a little while.'

Ah, now – there it was. *Now* I felt ashamed. 'I will borrow this and no more,' I declared, martyr-like. 'And you will have it back, Charles – you have my word. By the end of the evening, I hope.'

I hadn't been quite that fortunate. Over five straight hours at the gaming tables I had lost and won, won and lost, never quite reaching the ten pounds my creditors had demanded. Charles – who had insisted on accompanying me – paced about, or sat in a corner chewing his nails, left the room, came back, left it again. It grew late and I lost six times in a row, leaving me with a little over five pounds – less than I had arrived with. But I was playing Faro now and in this final game I had built up my stake one card at a time. If I bet on the right card last I would double my winnings.

But if I chose the wrong card . . . I would lose everything.

Charles appeared at my shoulder, whispered in my ear. 'Tom, for God's sake, come away.' He reached for the five pounds and began drawing it across the table. 'You will need every last penny of this in gaol.'

I stopped his hand, slid the coins across the table. 'One last turn. Five pounds for the queen. God bless her.'

The dealer smiled. Charles covered his face. 'You'll lose it all, he groaned.'

'Or double it,' I said. 'Have faith, Mr Buckley.'

The other players placed their bets. The dealer touched a finger to the pile and slid two cards free. My heart hammered against my chest. My God, how I loved this – the thrilling sensation of hope and fear bound together in one single moment. Waiting for the revelation, good or ill. The dealer turned the first, losing card. The five of hearts. The gambler sitting next to me gave a low curse.

And now for the winning card. I held my breath. The dealer flipped the card over on the table.

The queen of diamonds.

I breathed out, then laughed in relief. I was saved.

Betty returned with our coffee and behind her came our good hostess Moll King herself, carrying a small bowl of punch. The sign carved above the door said this was Tom King's coffeehouse, but it was Moll who ran the place. She supplied the girls, fenced the goods, sold the secrets and even – once in a while – poured the coffee.

She waved Betty away then settled herself close to me on the bench, kissing my cheek as her thief's fingers slid up my thigh. Charles, sitting across the table, watched her open-mouthed. With her wide, square face, long nose and sallow complexion, Moll was not a great beauty, and at thirty her jawline had begun to soften and sag. But she had a sharp wit and clever, dark eyes that could read a man's thoughts in a heartbeat. I loved her – when I could afford to.

'I hear you won at cards tonight,' she murmured. 'Let me help you spend it . . .'

Another night I might have played along, but not tonight. I needed the money in that purse. I pulled away, with some reluctance. Moll's hand was back above the bench in a flash. 'And who's this?' she asked, tipping her chin across the table.

'This,' I said with a flourish, 'is the Reverend Charles Buckley.'

'Honoured,' Moll said, taking in his well-tailored black coat and crisp white cravat. An empty pocket, though – I could have told her that. 'Tom often speaks of you.'

Charles lowered his bowl of coffee in surprise. 'Indeed?' He smiled at me. 'What does he say?'

Moll poured herself a glass of punch. 'He says, "Thank God Charles isn't here to see me doing this."' She raised her glass, chinking it with mine.

The coffeehouse was full tonight and boisterous with it. As it was every night. 'Fights, fucking and fine coffee' – that's how Moll described it, like a proud merchant listing his wares. What happened in the darkest corners of most coffee-houses was on full display here: plots hatched, purses snatched and breeches unbuttoned. God knows what happened in the dark corners at Moll's – what was left? In a little while the men would stagger home or head out across the piazza to a discreet bagnio if they wanted company. The girls would go back to work – in a rented room close by if they were lucky, or back to the dark, stinking passages off the Strand if they were not.

'Tom,' Charles said in a low voice as Moll pulled a pipe from her pocket. 'We should leave.'

He was right. Sitting here with ten pounds in my purse was reckless. 'We should finish the punch first.' There was still half a bowl left and it was high time I learned not to waste my money.

Charles rose and took his hat down from its hook on the wall. 'Well, I must go. Sir Philip locks the house at midnight.'

Moll flashed him a smile as she lit her pipe. 'Oh, there's men here can help you with locks, sir—'

'Thank you, Charles,' I interrupted hurriedly. I stood up and grasped his hand. 'I will pay back the money I owe you. I swear it.'

He put a hand on my shoulder and looked deep into my eyes. 'God has given you a sign, Tom. He saved you from gaol today. You have a chance to start your life afresh. Come to the house tomorrow morning. I will talk with Sir Philip, see if we can find you a position . . .'

'Tomorrow.'

He beamed at me, then bowed to Moll and left. I watched him weave his way through the chairs and tables and had the sudden urge to leave with him as he'd asked. All my life Charles had given me good advice. For some reason I could not fathom, I never took it.

'*Tomorrow*,' Moll said.

I frowned at her absently.

'Always tomorrow with you, Tom.' She studied me closely, her chin propped in her hand. I was one of her favourites, I knew; I was handsome enough, I suppose, and a good customer when I had the funds. And when I didn't, I could still pick up a wealth of information at the gaming tables, sitting between lords and thieves and politicians. Idle gossip in the main, but Moll knew how to sift it for gold. 'I'm glad you've escaped gaol,' she said. 'The Marshalsea most of all. The warden's a monster . . .'

There was a loud crash, then louder jeers from the next bench as a large bowl was sent flying, smashing into a hundred pieces and spilling punch across the floor in a red, sticky pool. A gang of apprentices, stockings splattered and ruined, shouted at one of the girls for knocking it over. 'You silly slut, you'll pay for that,' one of them sneered, grabbing her by the hair.

'*Gentlemen.*' Moll rose from her seat. There were fights here most nights, but they never lasted long; Moll had men she could call and a vicious long blade tucked under her skirts. I'd cut my hand upon it once, reaching for something softer. The apprentices bowed their apologies and ordered another bowl.

'You can't work for a nob like Sir Philip,' Moll declared, settling back down. She took a long pull on her pipe. 'Come and see *me* tomorrow. I'll find you an occupation.'

'What did you have in mind?'

Moll had plenty of suggestions, most of which could get me transported or hanged. Still, I had to admit that I had been drifting for too long, relying on charm and luck in the main. Perhaps I *should* work for Moll. For all the day's troubles, I had enjoyed having a purpose for once. Life or death, on the turn of a card; irresistible stakes for a gambling man.

'I'll think on it tomorrow,' I said. 'With the new king there will be new opportunities, new patrons . . . I thought I might try my hand at writing.'

She stared at me, alarmed. 'There's no need to panic, sweetheart.'

I finished my punch and rose to leave. Moll came with me, flinging her spent pipe on to the table. It bounced and clattered to the floor. 'I need a lungful of clean air,' she said, and we both laughed. There was nothing clean about Covent Garden, especially at this late hour.

At the door, she leaned her back against the frame and gazed out across the piazza; a queen surveying her hunting grounds. There was a kind of alchemy to Moll, I thought, watching her. Her coffeehouse was not much more than a tumbledown shack. But when you were inside, and Moll was holding court, it felt like the centre of the world.

She tilted her face up to the sky. 'Black as the devil's arsehole. You'll need a link boy.' She gave a sharp whistle and a lean, ragged creature raced from the shadows, dark locks spilling out from beneath a battered little tricorn. He skidded to a halt in front of us, holding an unlit torch in his hand.

'All on your own, mischief?' Moll asked. She grabbed his chin to get a better look at him. 'I don't know you, do I?'

Some boys would have stuttered out their life story under that formidable gaze. This one stared straight back, undaunted. 'They're waiting on Drury Lane. Play's almost finished. Where to?'

'Where to, *Mistress King*,' Moll corrected him sharply, then smiled. She'd worked the streets herself as a girl. 'Light this gentleman to Greek Street.'

She turned the shack. On a whim I grabbed her arm and pressed my lips to hers, tasting smoke and brandy and a trace of sweet oranges. She giggled and kissed me back as the blood thrummed hard in my veins. *This* I would tarry for, even with a hundred warrants for my arrest. I remembered the last time we'd kissed, the night we heard the king had died. Three months ago now. I'd thought the world would change. It didn't, of course. Moll's hand moved lower.

Around my purse.

I seized her wrist and pulled her hand away. She gave a lazy smile. 'Just testing. Wouldn't thieve from one of my own, now would I, *Reverend*?' She slipped back inside before I could answer.

The link boy rubbed his mouth to cover a grin. I frowned and tossed him a penny. 'Light your torch.'

He did as he was told, holding it to the lantern burning at the door. As the pitch caught light it illuminated his face with a soft orange glow.

'Why'd she call you Reverend?' he asked. He crinkled his nose. 'You a black-coat or something?'

Or something. Reverend was a nickname Moll liked to tease me with, knowing my history. I gestured to my blue silk waistcoat, cinnamon-coloured coat and breeches. 'Do I look like a black-coat?'

He shrugged, as if to say he would believe anything of anyone. It was a weary gesture, and sat strangely on such young shoulders. This was what happened to boys who guided rakes and whores back to their beds in the dead of night. Knocked the innocence clean out of them. Well; there were worse ways to earn a penny in this city. He turned and trotted towards Soho, holding the blazing torch high. I settled my tricorn on my head and hurried after him, a ship following the north star home.

And I wondered, fretfully. Beneath my fashionable clothes, did I still have the look of a clergyman? I turned this unhappy thought over in my mind. Ever since I was a boy – younger than this little imp running ahead of me – I had been told that I was destined to join the Church just like my father, the Reverend Dr Thomas Hawkins. (There. He had even given me his name, so I might more easily become him one day.) Things had not gone to plan. I had always known, deep within my soul, that I was not suited to the clergy. The trouble was, I had no idea what I *was* suited to. Have you ever seen a child refusing to be fed? It turns its face away – *no, no, no.* That was how I felt about joining the Church. It didn't matter how many times my father lifted the spoon to my lips. How many times he tried to force-feed duty and honour and decency down my throat. *No, no, no.*

I was so caught up in my thoughts that I took little notice as we crossed Long Acre. The streets were quiet – too late an hour for some, too early for others. We turned, then I suppose we must have turned again a few times, into a dark, narrow alley. Old timber houses sagged wearily against one another, their top storeys leaning out and almost touching across the street. One had collapsed entirely. Most of the wood had been scavenged, leaving just a rotting frame like a skeleton poking up into the night sky.

A sharp breeze blew down the alley, and a butcher's sign creaked on its hinges. I stopped, startled, then cursed softly. I didn't recognise this street. There was a scent of turpentine in the air – the sharp tang of a nearby gin still. A burst of drunken laughter sounded in the distance. St Giles. We had reached St Giles.

I spun about wildly, panic flaring in my chest. Somehow, instead of heading west for Soho, we'd blundered into the most infamous slum in London. Only a fool walked alone here at night. I pulled my dagger from my belt; thank God I'd had the sense not to pawn it.

The link boy had run on ahead but now he stuttered to a halt, and shot me a curious look.

'What's your name, boy?' I called.

He cupped his hand over the torch, shielding it from the wind. 'Sam.'

'You a moon-curser, Sam?' Moll had warned me about them when I'd first arrived in town – link boys who lured their victims away from the safe streets to be set upon in the shadows.

He smiled. '*Do I look like one?*' he mimicked.

The little bastard. I strode towards him, footsteps loud in my ears, a thousand eyes on my back.

'We must leave here. At once.'

I was just five paces from him now. He was standing quite still and silent; a stone cherub on a tomb. And then he glanced over my shoulder – a quick, furtive look.

The light tread of footsteps close behind me. Too close – much too close. An arm around my neck. My dagger was ripped from my hand and pressed to my throat.

'*Don't move.*'

My gambler's mind whirled and raced. Should I fight? Run?

The blade bit deeper. '*Your purse.*'

Sam held up his torch, illuminating the scene as if we were on the stage.

I should do as I was bid. *Hand him the purse*. My fingers slipped to the leather bag tied below my waist.

No.

Before I even knew what I was doing I reached up and shoved his arm from my throat, pushing him off balance. I spun round to face him, backing away slowly. Let him stab me if he must. But I would look him in the eye as he did it.

We circled each other warily. He wore his hat low across his face, and he'd wrapped a black cloth about his nose and mouth. Only his eyes were visible, dark and steady.

I took another step back, gaze fixed on the long, keen dagger in his right hand. My own dagger, damn it, sharpened by my own hand. One quick slash would be enough to rip me open.

'Come, sir, don't be a fool,' he said, in a calm, reasonable tone. And then, under his breath, '*I'm not alone.*'

He stretched out his free hand for the purse. The blood pounded in my ears.

I ran.

The world spun as I fled past the boy who was grinning now, thrilled by the action and his part in it. The street began to narrow even further, and a high brick wall loomed up ahead. It was too dark to see if there was another way out. I would have to clamber over it. I lengthened my stride, ready to spring at it when a black figure flew out of the shadows and knocked me to the ground.

For a moment I lay dazed. He began to grope for my pockets, hunting for my purse. With a loud curse I pushed him from me, kicking and punching my way free and back on to my feet, but there were others now, scurrying down from the roofs and balconies and dropping softly to the ground, calling out to one another in low voices. I fumbled in the darkness, searching for a brick or a piece of wood to defend myself, but I knew what was coming. I had gambled, and I had lost.

A hand grabbed my shoulder and I whirled about, frantic. And then another, and another, tearing and snatching, pulling me down like devils dragging me to hell. I fought them off, terrified now, but there were too many of them. I fell heavily to the ground again.

'Hold him there, lads!' their chief called out.

They pulled me to my knees and pinned my arms behind my back as he strode towards us. He ruffled the link boy's hair as he passed and somehow I realised – strange! the clarity that comes to you in such a moment – this was the boy's father. And I thought there was more affection and pride in that gesture than my father had shown me in a lifetime.

He came closer, crouching down in front of me, dark eyes skimming my face. 'I told you not to run,' he said, his voice muffled by the cloth.

I glared at him.

He signalled to one of his men.

'Wait . . .'

Too late. I felt a sharp blow on the back of my head. The world flashed white, and then it was gone.

Two

I woke. For a moment I thought I was home, in my little garret room on Greek Street. Then I tried to move. Pain shrieked through my head and I almost passed out again.

Slow, Tom. Careful.

Gently, this time, I sat up. The world pitched about me then settled, enough for me to raise a trembling hand to the back of my head. A large, tender bump. The warm, sticky feel of blood on my fingers. Memories flashed like sparks from a tinderbox: hands grabbing; laughter and shouts; the press of my own blade at my throat.

I reached for my purse, though I knew what I would find. Cut. Gone.

My stomach lurched. I was lost. Ruined. I lay back and closed my eyes. Then let me rest here. What use was fighting now? Let the spirit leak from my bones into the cold street; flow away with the filth and rubbish and leave my body in peace.

. . . No, no, I would not be food for the rats of St Giles. I was lucky to be alive. Didn't feel lucky. Didn't feel alive, for that matter. But damn every one of those cutpurses to the deepest pits of hell – I would get to my feet.

Or to my knees, at least.

I was lying in a dank, deserted side passage that stank of piss and vomit and other fluids, as all such places do and no doubt always will to the end of time. The ground was littered with broken gin bottles, bloody rags, spent pipes. They must have dragged me here through the filth in order to rob me the better, the link boy holding his torch high and proud as they worked. My jacket was gone, my wig and tricorn dashed from my head in the struggle. My breeches were torn; my knees and fists scraped raw. They'd cut the gold buttons from my waistcoat, emptied every pocket. I pulled myself to my knees, groaning softly with the effort. I couldn't risk being heard – couldn't risk calling the alarm. There were gangs in St Giles that would do far worse to a gentleman than merely beat and rob him, if he were foolish enough to stumble on to their patch. I was not out of danger yet.

I crawled back towards the alley, inch by inch, feeling my way blindly in the darkness, fingers flinching as they touched broken glass or the slip and slither of foul, stinking mud. When I reached the alley I collapsed in the shadows of the nearest porch, back pressed hard against the wall, panting with exhaustion. Each breath drew a fresh throb of pain. I ran my fingers beneath my shirt, prodded each rib. Bruised but not broken.

The moon escaped from behind a cloud and the world turned a soft silver in its light. I gazed up at the maze of ramshackle galleries and balconies above my head, planks slung from roof to roof, ladders and ropes connecting one mean hovel to the next. A secret city in the rooftops, mapped out by thieves. *Rooks*, they called themselves, and St Giles was the greatest rookery of them all. Were they back in their nests above me, laughing to themselves as I dragged myself through the filthy streets, battered and bloody? I searched every roof, every shadow, with an anxious eye. No – long gone, surely. Busy emptying my purse in the nearest brothel.

I staggered to my feet, almost welcoming the pain that stabbed the back of my head. Pain kept me sharp, kept me alert. I pressed my shoulder to the nearest wall and scraped my way slowly down the alley.

You have the luck of the devil, Tom Hawkins. Is that right, Charles? I couldn't go home, not without money. Benjamin Fletcher, my landlord, would have me clamped in irons in a flash. No point asking friends for help – I'd used up every remaining favour. Charles had no money left to lend – I had taken his last last penny. And family . . . I cut the thought dead.

As I reached the end of the alley I heard the unmistakeable hiss of hot piss plattering into the mud ahead. I turned the corner to find an old whore squatting in the middle of the street, illuminated in the moonlight, a small puddle spreading about her feet. The street was still and empty – and it felt in that moment that we might be the only two living souls in the city, God help us. As she saw me she raised her skirts higher, a thin trickle of piss still rolling down her leg.

'Farthing for a fuck,' she said, weaving a little on the spot.

A farthing to catch the pox? It was a bargain, I suppose – men have paid finer whores a great deal more for the privilege. I shook my head, then winced as the pain smacked against my skull. 'Which way to the Garden?'

She took in my tattered clothes; the blood stains on my shirt . . . and held out her hand. 'A penny and I'll show you.'

'I was set upon. They took my purse.' I opened my arms wide. 'Have pity, madam.'

'Pity?' She chuckled, and wiped herself dry with her dirt-streaked petticoat. 'Can't afford it.'

She stumbled away, back towards the dark heart of St Giles.

I found my own way back to Covent Garden in the end. I kept to the shadows, hiding in porches when other men strode by. Perhaps someone would have helped me, if I'd dared to ask. One hears of good Samaritans, even in London. But I couldn't risk it. I limped slowly through the streets alone, no doubt turning in circles half the time. Sometimes I felt eyes upon my back, and swore I heard the soft tread of footsteps behind me – but when I turned and peered into the darkness, there was no one there. *Follow me all you wish*, I thought. *There's nothing left for you to take.*

At last I stumbled upon the Garden – the reassuring feel of cobbles beneath my feet; the neat, solid silhouette of St Paul's church and the glow of lights burning even now in the bagnios, shrill cries of false passion spilling from their windows. Out in the piazza, market traders set up their stalls by torchlight, calling and laughing to one another as they worked. An old woman in a red cape sat huddled on the steps of the Shakespeare Tavern selling hot rice milk and barley broth. I stumbled past them all, feeling like an old soldier returned from a war no one knew we were fighting. A nightwatchman held up his lantern and I shrank away – in my tattered, filthy state he might decide to sling me in the lock-up on suspicion of something . . . anything . . . and then discover there was a warrant out for my arrest with a nice plump fee attached.

Moll's coffeehouse was open – always open – but empty save for Betty, sweeping softly around an old lawyer lying dead drunk beneath a table. She took one look at me then ran and fetched Moll, who was sleeping in the shack next door – maybe with her husband and maybe not. I collapsed on a chair by the fire, my head in my hands, and started to shake. Relief that I was safe. Terror that I was not. As soon as the sun rose my creditors would call the alarm. How long before a warrant officer found me here, my favourite haunt? I had to run – but I was so battered and exhausted I could barely think, never mind move.

Moll was still lacing up her dress as she arrived. 'Well, now, Tom. What's all this?' Then she saw the state of me and gave a low curse of surprise. She prodded Betty towards the door. 'Hot water, fresh clothes.' She sat down beside me, touched her fingers to a scrape on my cheek. 'What happened?'

'They took my purse, Moll. They took everything.'

· · ·

There was only one thing for it, Moll decided. I must leave town at once. 'Run to the Mint, before dawn.'

I sighed bitterly. A few short hours ago I had succeeded in turning my fortunes around. Now my only hope was to flee to the old debtors' sanctuary across the river. The Mint's tight maze of streets was so violent, so riddled with disease, that bailiffs refused to set foot across its borders. One tried it, a few weeks back. They beat him bloody and pushed his face down into the thick, stinking river of filth that ran through the streets. He died a few days later.

'Better the Mint than the Marshalsea,' Moll insisted, wiping the blood from the back of my neck with a wet cloth. 'You can leave again on Sunday. They won't arrest you on the Lord's day.' She brought her hands together in mock-piety.

'And after that? What shall I do on Monday, Moll?'

'*Monday?*' She rubbed harder at the dried blood, making me gasp with pain. 'Since when have you planned that far ahead?' Then she stopped, and pressed her lips to my ear. 'My offer's still open, Tom. Come and work for me. I could use a boy of your talents . . .' And she set off upon a story about a new venture she had in mind, involving a trip to France. I can't remember the details now and could barely understand them then. My head was throbbing and it was hard to follow her. I remember it sounded dangerous and reckless. And tempting.

I considered my choices while Moll rinsed my blood from the cloth, wringing the water into the bowl with a sharp twist. I could stand and face my fate with honour, like a gentleman, and meet some squalid end in gaol. Or I could escape to the Mint and be lost from good society for ever. It was easy enough for Moll to advise the latter course. She was born in the stews and had spent most of her life working the streets for profit, one way or another. She knew when to run and where to go. She had escaped prison and transportation, been called a whore and a thief and worse. Somehow she always came back, brighter and braver than before.

It was not the same for me. As the eldest son of a Suffolk gentleman, my life had been set along an old, straight track from birth: I would join the clergy like my father, and – in time – inherit his position. Three years ago – following an unfortunate incident in an Oxford brothel – I had abandoned that path. Now here I was, five and twenty, with no family, no prospects and no money. True, I had Greek and Latin and could dance a passable gavotte, but a man cannot survive on such things, even in London.

I glanced through a copy of the *Daily Courant* that had been left upon the table, hoping for some clue to what I should do. Amidst the advertisements for horses, houses and an 'infallible cure for scurvy', I noticed that the South Sea Company had announced a three-month extension on borrowing. When the stocks collapsed seven years ago some investors had arranged to pay their debts in instalments – with interest, naturally. Perhaps Mr Fletcher might consider a similar scheme.

Betty appeared with a clean change of clothes and a bowl of hot punch, God bless her. My waistcoat could be cleaned and mended, but my breeches and stockings were torn beyond repair. I stripped by the warmth of the fire, wincing from the bruises along my ribs. I pulled on the fresh stockings and a pair of old, snuff-coloured breeches, then eased myself into a match-ing waistcoat and jacket. Clean and dressed, I felt more myself again – but when I glanced in the tarnished mirror above the fireplace, I was startled by my reflection. I didn't look like a man of honour – if I ever had. I looked like a man who would run.

I shivered. So – this was my choice now. Gaol or a life of crime. A life that would most likely end with a rope around my neck. I touched my hand to my throat.

'Mr Hawkins.' A soft, low voice behind me. Betty's reflection joined mine in the mirror, my ruined clothes gathered in her arms. She stole a glance towards the front door, where Moll was slopping out the blood and water into the piazza. 'There is another way,' she whispered.

I turned, hope rising in my chest. 'Tell me.'

She smiled, gently. 'You could go *home*, sir. Go home and ask your father for help.'

My shoulders sagged. I poured myself a glass of punch and knocked it back. 'I'd sooner ask the devil.'

'What's this?' Moll asked sharply as she returned, but Betty had slipped away with my clothes and we were alone.

'*There's the scoundrel! Arrest him!*'

Benjamin Fletcher, my landlord, stood in the doorway, hands on his knees as he caught his breath. He must have run all the way from Greek Street. As he limped forward he was followed by a warrant officer, a huge ox of a man, carrying a large wooden club in his fist. His nose had been squashed about his face a few times and a large white scar ran through one brow. A long loop of chains hung over his shoulder like a sash. Our eyes met and he smiled, quite cheerful, as if he had come to escort me to the theatre, not prison. His gaze dropped to the blood-soaked cloth in Moll's hand. 'Run into some trouble, sir?' he asked, in the slow, steady voice of a man with very quick fists.

'Seize him, Mr Jakes!' Fletcher wheezed, tearing the hat from his head and fanning his sweaty face.

'Mr Fletcher,' I said, holding my hands out wide in apology. 'I swear to you I had the money . . .'

'No more lies, Mr Hawkins,' he cried. He pulled a note from his waistcoat and thrust it at me, his hands shaking. 'You have played me for a fool, sir.'

The note was short, and written in a neat script that reminded me of my own. A gentleman's hand.

Sir.
As a good Christian it is my Duty to report that yr Tenant that vile Dog Hawkins is engaged in relations of the most sordid

Nature with your Wife and that the whole World speaks of their Infamy. Your kind Patience and Tolerance of his Debts to You, sir, he repays in this monstrous Manner to his own Shame and your Wife's Ruin.
A Friend.

Beneath it was a crude drawing of a man sprouting horns from his brow – the unmistakeable sign of a cuckold.

I frowned at the note, quite confounded. Mrs Fletcher was a pinched, mean-spirited woman with a shrill temper and the look of a shaved ferret. The very notion we were 'engaged in relations' was beyond contempt, but Fletcher believed it. This was calamitous. As my chief creditor, he alone could show mercy and grant me more time to pay my debt. He was not a cruel man; in truth he had been more patient than I deserved. But above all other things, he doted upon his wretched wife. His anonymous 'friend' had played a clever game upon us both. I must answer this with great care.

'Mr Fletcher, sir. We are men of reason, are we not?' I waved the note limply. 'You must see that this is no more than malicious gossip? I mean no dishonour to your good wife, but . . .'

Behind me, Moll gave a little cough. 'But he'd rather fuck his own sister.'

The chains lay heavy across my chest as Jakes led me through Covent Garden towards the river. I walked with my gaze upon the ground, the manacles tight about my wrists, hands clasped together as if in prayer. Too late for that, now. I doubt I was much of a spectacle. I had seen dozens of men led through Soho on their way to the Fleet or the Marshalsea or some other rotten lock-up, and given them little more than a moment's thought. At least I didn't have a wife or children trailing at my heels, lamenting their sorry fate. And that, I realised, was the best I could say for myself in that moment.

We pushed our way through the busy market, past stalls laden with bright bunches of flowers and ripe fruit fresh in from the suburbs. I breathed in the sweet scent of herbs and the dusty rich tang of spices and wished I could linger, disappear into the bustling confusion of the crowds – traders shouting their wares; young maids selling nosegays, handkerchiefs, anything to keep them from the brothel; livestock bleating and lowing and snorting and stinking to the heavens; actors and tumblers, footmen and chairmen; gossiping madams and rock-faced bullies – just let me join you all, let me slip into this mass of bodies and disappear . . .

Jakes kept pace beside me, one hand firm upon my shoulder, steering me down Southampton Street to the Thames. 'Nice day,' he observed, squeezing my shoulder in a friendly manner that almost buckled me to the floor. 'Shame.'

When we reached the river a crowd of watermen all dressed in doublets of red or green clamoured for our business at the Worcester stairs shouting 'oars! oars!' and 'scullers!', their boats knocking hard against each other as they fought to claim us. Jakes pointed to one dressed in green with the Lord Mayor's arms picked out in silver. He rowed towards us while the rest jeered and cursed his good luck. When he reached the steps he glanced up at my chains. 'The Borough?'

'Aye,' Jakes nodded. 'Tooley steps. But threepence, no more.'

'It's double past the bridge, Mr Jakes,' the boatman called up, then grinned. The Tooley stairs were only a few feet beyond the bridge.

'I'll take you for three, sir!' another man cried from his sculler.

Our waterman rounded on him. 'Selling yourself cheap, Ned – you learn that from your mother?' He turned back to us. 'Fourpence.'

'Three,' Jakes replied, stubbornly. He gestured to the fifteen or so other boats we could choose. Our man sighed and waved us aboard, muttering in an unconvincing fashion about his poor starving wife and children.

Jakes nudged me aboard then settled his impressive bulk at the other end of the sculler, facing the south bank. His thick knees pressed hard against the sides of the boat, but he seemed content enough, tilting his head to catch the sun. The waterman, sitting between us with his oars raised, looked anxious as the boat rocked under our combined weight – but my chains balanced out Jakes' muscles and we settled soon enough. As we pushed off into the river, I watched the city drift slowly away from me like an inconstant lover, already forgetting me, turning its attentions on some new, sweeter diversion.

Jakes leaned forward and the boat began to rock back and forth again, water slopping up and over the side. 'Do you have much coin, sir?' he called over the boatman's shoulder.

I held up my manacled wrists by way of answer.

He traced a scar that cut through his left brow, considering this unfortunate situation. 'Well, you'd better find some pretty sharp, Mr Hawkins. D'you not have friends? Family?'

I shook my head. Jakes and the boatman exchanged a look. *No friends. No family. No money.* I might as well tip myself overboard and save everyone the trouble. Well, damn them both – I might not have much, but I did have my wits about me, and I was not as innocent as I seemed.

We passed Somerset House, almost derelict, its golden days of masquerades and court intrigue long past. I caught the high, pungent scent of manure on the air; the Horse Guards had sequestered the old stables a few years back. These were the days we lived in since the South Sea Bubble burst: houses abandoned half-built or half-falling down; money flowing in and out of people's lives, harder to keep hold of than quicksilver.

The boatman rowed on, whistling quietly to himself, oars cutting smoothly through the water. Jakes reached past him and tapped my knee, making me jump. 'I might look the other way, when we reach Southwark,' he said in a low voice, rubbing his thumb against his fingers in an unmistakeable gesture. 'Not something I do as a rule.'

The bridge loomed up ahead, the windows of the houses upon it glinting in the mid-morning sun. A queue of boats waited to ride the churning waters below. 'Why would you help me, Mr Jakes?'

A sad, distant look came into his heavy-lidded, sea-green eyes. 'You remind me of my old captain.'

The river was flowing faster now as we reached the narrow arches of the bridge. I had to shout above the roar. 'You were in the army?' I should have realised from his battered, weather-beaten face.

'Nine years,' he called back. He paused, lost in memories, then shook his head. 'Captain Roberts was just like you. A rake and a gambler. And a drunk.'

I opened my mouth to protest, then closed it again.

'You look the spit of him, too. Odd, that. You could almost be brothers.'

'Indeed?' The closest I had to a brother was Edmund, my step-mother's son – and we were both delighted to be nothing like each other.

'John was not what you'd call respectable,' Jakes said, frown-ing at the memory. 'Not always square. But he was a good friend to me. Saved my life once.'

I could tell by the way he was talking that Roberts was dead. 'What happened to him?'

He looked away, down into the swirling waters. 'The Marshalsea killed him.'

The boatman steered towards the arch closest to shore, hold-ing tight to the oars. It was crowded with traffic, boats slamming against one another, shouts and curses filling the air. And above it all, the rush of the Thames, surging hard beneath the bridge. The river could be dangerous here, forced between the narrow arches; the waterman had to use all his strength to hold the little scull steady. One slip and it would be smashed to pieces. I didn't fancy my luck in the water – not with twenty pounds of iron chains wrapped about me.

'Coroner called it suicide,' Jakes continued, oblivious to the drama unfolding behind his back. 'But it was murder, no doubt of it. I've seen better corpses on a battlefield. There's a rumour in the Borough that his spirit haunts the gaol, begging for justice.' The boat pitched and turned against the swirling waters as we reached the arch. 'Fat chance,' he snorted, then leaned closer. 'D'you know, there's some that say the devil lives in the Marshalsea. And – forgive me, sir. I'm not sure you're ready to meet him.'

I wanted to ask him what he meant but at that moment the boatman steered us into the rush of water and we plunged full force beneath the arch, shooting through as though fired from a pistol. Jakes gripped the sides of the scull while I clung hard to my seat. The roar of the river echoed against the stone, white water frothing about us, spraying our faces. And then we were through, riding out into slower currents.

I drew back, heart thudding against my chest, grinning with relief. Now we were through and safe, I had a fancy to go again, as I always did – but the boatman drew up hard against the Tooley stairs. As I left the boat and clambered up the green, slippery steps, it struck me that perhaps Jakes told this story of his old captain to all his charges, in the hope of being paid off. Ghosts and devils, indeed.

We left the river behind and headed for the Borough's High Street. Back among the throng, I grew conscious of my chains again, clinking together with every laboured step. Only a week before I had come to Southwark Fair with a group of friends and walked down this street a free man. Now the fair, and my friends, were gone. We passed St Saviour's and the long line of taverns stretching out of town, laughter and shouts from every window, every doorway. The scent of cooked meat and beer cut through the noisome stench of the street. As we passed the White Hart a man staggered out from the alley and spewed a thick gush of vomit across the pavement then collapsed into it. A young boy raced across the road, scavenged the drunkard's purse then scampered away, back into the shadows.

'Here we are.' Jakes gripped my arm and guided me between two boarded-up shop fronts.

We turned into the narrow, sunless alley. The clamour and life of the High Street bled away into a chill silence. Ahead of us, at the end of the alley, stood a high stone lodge – the entrance to the gaol. It looked like an old castle keep, flanked by twin turrets looming forty feet into the sky. I half-expected men in armour to appear at the top and throw burning oil on our heads.

The Lodge gate comprised two large doors studded with iron, wide enough for a carriage to pass through when both were flung open. A hand-written sign had been nailed into the wood, paper curling at the edges:

MARSHALSEA GAOL
and COURT PALACE
Southwark
Under the Charge of His Majesty the Knight's Marshal: Sir
Philip Meadows
Head Keeper: William Acton

Underneath the keeper's name, someone had scrawled *BUTCHER* in fresh ink.

Jakes pounded upon the door with his club, the sound ringing back down the passageway. After a long moment there was a harsh scraping sound and an iron grate opened in the door. A pair of mean, bloodshot eyes glared at me contemptuously through the bars.

'Who's this son of a whore?' a rough voice called through the gate.

Jakes leaned down and whispered urgently in my ear. 'Are you sure there's nothing, Mr Hawkins? *Nothing* you can pawn?'

And all of a sudden I remembered that there was, indeed, something: my mother's gold cross, set with a small diamond at its heart. I had worn it about my neck for so long that I had almost forgotten it. It was the only thing I had left of her and I'd vowed to wear it always. But I had been a boy then, and boys make all sorts of foolish plans before they learn better. Shuffling beneath the chains I touched my fingers to my throat. By some miracle it was still there, unrobbed. I loosened my collar. 'Will this do?'

Jakes unclasped the fine gold chain and held it up to the light. 'There should be some capital in it. Enough to keep you from the Common Side for a few nights, at least.'

The turnkey slid back the bolts and flung open the door. He looked me up and down, taking in the mean cloth of my borrowed clothes and the low slump of my shoulders. He snorted, and shook his head at Jakes. 'He'll last a week if he's lucky,' he said, then laughed nastily and pushed me through the door. 'Welcome to the Marshalsea, *sir*.'

PART TWO

MURDER

THURSDAY. THE FIRST DAY.

Three

Jakes abandoned me at the Lodge gate with a promise to return that afternoon. I watched him stride away towards the freedom of the High Street, my mother's chain tucked in his pocket. Should I trust him? The truth was, I had no choice.

The turnkey slammed the door shut, the sound echoing down the corridor ahead. My heart sank. No chance of escape now. The corridor walls seemed to press closer and closer while the chains tightened about my chest, making it hard to breathe. I gasped for air, my head spinning.

The turnkey's face loomed in front of mine. 'Feeling a little sick, are we, sir?' he asked gleefully.

I fought back my fear and stood taller. 'I'm perfectly well,' I lied. It would not do to show weakness in here. At the end of the corridor lay another set of double doors to match the Lodge gate. One had been propped open with a barrel of ale – I could just make out the entrance to the prison yard beyond. Without thinking I began to shuffle towards the light and open air, but the guard grabbed me roughly by the arm and shoved me back towards a small, overheated room next to the Lodge gate. This was where the turnkey on gate duty would sit, waiting for the next poor devil to come along. I saw now why this one was in such a foul temper – I'd interrupted an early dinner; a bottle of sack and a bowl of greasy mutton broth balanced precariously on a stack of papers. He tipped the last of the wine down his throat, examining my arrest warrant with a sour expression. Then he slammed open a black ledger filled with names and debts and scratched a fresh line on to the page.

Thomas Hawkins, Greek St. Thurs. 21st September, 1727. 20l. 10s. 6d. Gent.

'Soho,' he grunted, narrowing his eyes as he wrote the address.

'You know it well?' I guessed.

'*Joseph Cross Wardour Street Tuesday 6th February 1725 ten pounds seven shillings Bricklayer.*'

All said in one breath, as if it were his full name.

'Pleased to meet you, Mr Cross.'

'Oh. *Pleased* are you,' he snorted. 'Well, fuck me.'

Joseph Cross. I had never met a man more well-named; he was like the cauldron hanging over the fire at Moll's, bubbling and roiling in a constant fury. He had the red, bloated face of a seasoned drinker and his thick brows met across the bridge of his nose, as if years of aggressive scowling had knitted them together.

'So you're a debtor too?'

'Trusty,' he corrected. 'I work for the governor.'

'I see.' *But you're still a debtor, aren't you?* 'Did you know someone's written "butcher" under the governor's name on the gate?'

Cross shrugged. 'They wrote "cunt" yesterday. Well, Thomas Hawkins, *Gent*. What are we going to do with you, eh?'

I gazed longingly at the low chair by the fire. My chains felt so heavy now I was struggling to stand. 'Perhaps I could wait in here until Mr Jakes returns?'

'Oh, of course!' Cross trilled, clapping his hands. 'And perhaps sir would like a sugar cake and a pot of tea while he's waiting . . . ?' He dragged me back out of the room. 'No money and no warning,' he grumbled as he led me down the corridor. 'Mr Acton won't like this. He won't like *you*,' he added, with obvious relish.

We headed towards the yard doors, sunlight glinting up ahead. Deep grooves ran down towards the yard where the carriages had rattled through, bringing in food and drink. And taking out the bodies. The ancient stone floor had been worn smooth by centuries of debtors trudging wearily through the gate. And now here I was to join them – just one in an endless line of wretched souls stretching on and on for ever, to the end of days, all pressed and pushed and prodded by men like Cross.

Before we reached the yard he opened a door to the right and pointed up a set of dank stairs that smelled violently of piss and beerish vomit. I could hear laughter coming from the floor above, and music. 'Tap Room,' Cross said. He leaned down beneath the stairs and pulled open what looked like a cellar door, revealing a narrow coffin-shaped space below. A foul, rotten smell wafted up, even worse than the stairs. Cross grimaced and put an arm across his face. 'The Hole. Punishment room. I've seen a man last three days in there. Couldn't remember his own name when we pulled him out.' He watched my face fall with a satisfied air.

At the end of the corridor he unlocked a door to the left and pushed me into a small cell. 'The Pound. You can wait here until the governor gets back.'

The Pound was not as bad as the Hole – that much I was grateful for. But it was not much better. The air felt suffocatingly close and damp and the walls and floor were filthy, with just one tiny, barred window too high to look through. A line of chains and manacles of different weights hung from the ceiling, clinking softly in the breeze from the door.

Cross gestured to a ghoulish collection of torture implements fixed to the far wall: thumbscrews, iron collars and whips. 'D'you like our display, Mr Hawkins? The governor put those up himself.' He turned to me with a straight face. 'Mr Acton takes a keen interest in the history of the gaol.'

I stared at them in horror. 'They're not used on the prisoners?'

'Of *course* not.' Cross pulled down an iron skull cap and gave it an affectionate pat, as if it were a child's head. 'That would be against the law, wouldn't it?' He scraped his thumbnail slowly against a thick crust of blood that had dried along the rim. 'Well, then. Shall I remove your chains before I go, sir?'

At last. Jakes had promised they would come off once I was inside. 'If you would,' I said, holding out my hands.

Cross took a key from the ring at his belt and slotted it into the lock at my chest. Then he pushed his face up close to mine, his breath reeking of bad gums and worse liquor. 'Oh. That'll be sixpence, sir.'

And then he laughed.

I had been beaten. I had been robbed. I had lost everything and now I was trapped in the most notorious debtors' gaol in London. Anything would have provoked me in that moment; his laughter was more than enough. Without thinking, I raised my fists and swung them hard against his jaw, the iron cuffs about my wrists adding weight to my punch. He staggered back, blood bursting from his mouth, then leapt at me in a fury, hands tearing at my throat.

'Mr Cross!' A voice cut the air between us. 'Stop this at once!'

A small, slender woman stood in the doorway – a widow, dressed in deep mourning. Her husband must have left her rich, judging by her fine black bombazine gown and hood. I lowered my fists.

'Mrs Roberts.' Cross gave an ill-tempered bow. 'Didn't see you there. *Madam*,' he added, forcing the word from his lips with great effort.

'Evidently,' she murmured. She was turned from me, hood shielding her face, but I could tell from her voice and bearing that she was a gentlewoman. I could not imagine what she was doing here in the Marshalsea of all places.

'My apologies, madam,' I said, and bowed as best I could while wrapped in chains. 'I fear we have startled you.'

'I'm not easily startled, sir,' she replied, tilting her head towards me.

My heart jumped. She was still young – close to my own age of twenty-five – and exceptionally pretty, with a fair complexion and delicate features. Her eyes were most striking – a clear grey, fringed with dark lashes – but there were deep shadows beneath them, from grief and lack of sleep I supposed. Her husband's death must have been recent; she was still wearing a pair of dull black shammy gloves. Beneath her hood and cap, her hair was dark brown, laced with auburn that burned bronze in the light from the window. I caught myself wondering how it would look tumbling about her shoulders.

She did not seem as pleased by my appearance. Her gaze flickered over the shabby coat Moll had lent me, my mud-spattered stockings and patched breeches. She pursed her lips, nostrils flaring in disapproval. *You would make a fine abbess*, I thought; *chilly and severe*. A shame. I was rather fond of widows, in the main. Especially rich ones.

'Why is this man still in chains, Mr Cross?' she demanded.

I smiled to myself. I had misjudged her – it was my chains she disapproved of, not my tattered clothes.

'He hasn't paid the fee,' Cross growled, fists clenching impatiently at his side. Then he leered at me. 'He can't afford it.'

I felt my face grow hot. It was shaming to be unmasked as a man without six pennies to his name. I had the sudden urge to explain my story – to make her understand that I came from a good family, the eldest son of a respected gentleman. (The disgraced and disinherited eldest son, admittedly, but there was no need to trouble her with such trifling details.) 'I can assure you, madam, I'm expecting the money at any moment—' I began, then stopped in surprise. There were tears shimmering in her eyes.

'I have heard those words before,' she said, her voice tinged with grief. She took three pennies from her purse and handed them to Cross, who pocketed them at once. The low, cheating bastard had tried to rob me of double the fee.

I thanked Mrs Roberts profusely, promising to return the money as soon as I had it.

She waved a black-gloved hand. 'I have heard that many times as well,' she said, wearily. She gestured to Cross to unchain me. He muttered something under his breath but did as he was told, shoving the key into the lock then pulling hard at the chains that ran about my chest. Whoever Mrs Roberts was, she was used to being obeyed. She nodded with a satisfied air as the iron links slid to the floor. 'What is your name, sir?'

I stepped neatly from the pile of chains and bowed again. 'Thomas Hawkins, madam. At your service.'

A sparkle of amusement lit her grey eyes. 'And what service might that be, I wonder? Do you mean to pummel another turn-key for me?'

'If he punches me again I'll hang him up here until he chokes,' Cross snarled, slinging the chains over a hook on the ceiling. He pointed to his cut lip. 'The governor will hear of this.'

'Indeed?' Mrs Roberts raised an eyebrow. 'And what will you tell him, I wonder? That his head turnkey was bettered by a chained, unarmed prisoner? Well, well. I'm sure Mr Acton will find that most . . . *diverting*.'

Cross scowled and unlocked the manacles, pulling them off so sharply he scraped my wrists. He glowered at me as he left, as if to say, *we are not done yet*. I stared back as evenly as I could, cursing my hot temper. I had not even stepped out into the yard and I'd already made an enemy of the head turnkey – and doubtless every guard who served under him.

Still, at least I was free of my chains. I rubbed my wrists and stretched out my back, my body aching and sore from the heavy irons and the night's rough beating.

Mrs Roberts gave a little gasp, and covered her mouth.

'Madam – are you well?' I took a step towards her.

She gave a start, then looked down, smoothing her skirts. 'Quite well, thank you. It is just . . .' She cleared her throat. 'You remind me of my late husband. You have . . . the way you . . .' She stumbled to a halt, blushing with embarrassment.

I remembered the story Jakes had told me on the river about his old friend Captain Roberts, who'd died in the gaol. *You look the spit of him.* But Roberts had been a penniless debtor. Where had his widow found the money for such fine clothes, cut in the latest fashion – and why the devil would she be haunting the Marshalsea now that her husband was dead?

'Forgive me – are you visiting friends inside the gaol?' I asked. 'I can see you are not a prisoner here.'

'Oh, but I am, sir,' she replied, and gave a bitter laugh. 'You cannot see *my* chains, but they are wrapped about me even now.' She moved closer, the hem of her dress brushing softly against the stone floor. 'My husband was murdered in here a few short months ago. Whoever killed him is still hiding within these walls. I have vowed never to leave until he is discovered.' Her lips tightened to a thin, determined line. 'I shall see the devil hanged for it – if I must do it myself.'

I stared at her in alarm. It was hard enough to be slung in prison – harder still to learn I was trapped in here with a murderer.

'So, Mr Hawkins,' she said with a small smile. 'Do you still wish to be of service?'

I groaned inwardly. That was the trouble with gifts, even thrupenny ones. They always landed you in debt. 'Of course.'

She laughed – and for a moment her face was transformed, the cares and sorrows of her life dissolved away. 'I don't believe you. But perhaps I'm wrong. Perhaps you are more than you seem.'

I frowned at the insult. 'You don't know me, madam.'

She lifted her chin and studied me for a moment. 'Oh, I think I do. I think I know you *very* well, sir.' She pulled her hood low over her face and stepped back, shoulders high. It was as if she had slammed a door in my face. 'May God protect you in this wretched place,' she said, a stranger again, then turned and left.

I stood alone, astounded by the exchange. What right did she have to judge me when we had just met? Very well, I was not the most reliable of men, but she didn't know that. And it was true – I liked to drink and gamble and spend time (and money) with accommodating women of the town. What of it? From what Jakes had told me, I was no worse than her husband.

Ah. So there it was. I reminded Mrs Roberts of her husband – and not just because of my looks. How had Jakes described him? A rake, a gambler and a drunk. Still, she'd married him all the same. I rubbed my jaw. Perhaps it was not so bad to be mistaken for Captain Roberts after all . . . except that someone in here had murdered him. Both Jakes and Mrs Roberts had been moved to help me because I reminded them of a dead man – a man who had been killed here within the prison grounds. I gazed about the Pound, at the thumbscrews and skull caps and iron collars hanging from the wall. And then I turned and left, as fast as I could.

I was grateful there was no one to see me enter the prison yard for the first time. As I stepped out of the Lodge my father's last words came to me unbidden; the Reverend Thomas Hawkins' final sermon to his prodigal son. Three years ago he had summoned me to his study and forced me to stand there, waiting like a child, while he sat gazing into the fire.

'The path you have chosen leads but one way,' he said, eventually.

'At least I have chosen it, sir,' I replied, frowning at the familiar lecture. We had been locked in this same argument for years – ever since I had first dared to challenge him.

He propped his head in his hand, rubbing his forehead. 'Foolish boy,' he murmured, almost to himself. 'This is not *your* choice. It is the devil guides you now; you have let him into your soul, with your drinking and gambling and debauchery. With your *lies*. I thought . . . I thought you had changed. You deceived us all, Thomas.' He turned from the fire at last. He looked exhausted, his face gaunt and grey. For a moment I felt sorry for him – and ashamed for what I'd done. If I could just explain. If he would only listen.

'Father . . .'

'I thank God your mother is not alive to see this day.'

My mother. He should have known not to mention her. I don't know how I stopped myself from striking him. We fought with words instead; accusations that left no chance for forgiveness, no possibility of return. *I* was a selfish, wilful child, set upon a one-way path to damnation. *He* was a cold-hearted hypocrite who dared to lecture me when he had married his own mistress. And worse. We both said much worse. The accusation that had always lurked in the shadows of every conversation, brought into the light at last. Which one of us was responsible. Which one of us had broken my mother's heart.

'Go, go, live your godless life,' he called down the stairs as I stormed out of the vicarage for the last time, my sister Jane watching silent and ashen-faced. 'And when you're alone and penniless, rotting in a debtors' gaol, do not come begging to me.'

And now his prediction had come to pass. I cursed the memory, spat the bitterness away and walked out into the prison.

The Marshalsea is an old gaol – centuries old. Its buildings are a peculiar hodgepodge, some brick, some timber, set in a quadrangle around a cobbled yard close to an acre in size. There were perhaps two dozen prisoners outside that first morning, men and women, some walking up and down in a distracted fashion, others talking and smoking and laughing, as if they had chanced to meet in the street. I watched them quietly in the shadow of the Lodge, settling my nerves and waiting for the best moment to step into the arena.

The Lodge gate was the only way in and out of the prison, unless you were suicidal enough to try scaling the walls. To my left was a two-storeyed timber house with bright yellow curtains and a low wooden fence about the door – the governor's house, I discovered later. A tree shaded the windows – the only one in the prison and a mangled, sickly thing at that. Beyond the governor's lodgings this west side of the prison was given up to a high wall crowned with iron spikes, where men played rackets.

The north wall was much longer and began with a terrace of three rundown houses. These, I learned, were the prison wards, with twenty large rooms in all. Most cells were occupied by at least three men – often twice or even three times that. The best rooms were at the front on the first floor; they were larger, and looked out into the yard. I could see a few pale faces at the windows, men smoking and drinking or staring dejectedly into thin air.

At the end of these three terraced buildings was a tall, narrow house, kept in a much better state than its neighbours. The turn-keys' lodgings took up all of the ground-floor rooms while the prison chapel lay on the floor above, with a large window facing the yard. What God made of the view below I couldn't say.

At the end of this north row stood a handsome brick building, five storeys high and wider than all its neighbours put together. It seemed to look down its nose at the rest of the prison, like a duke forced to live cheek by jowl with his peasants. A small crowd sheltered beneath its long, colonnaded porch, watching a game of backgammon.

On the far east wall lay a final block of prisoners' quarters, meaner than those by the governor's lodgings, with a sagging roof and cracked windows.

In short, it was not St James' Palace; it was not even Soho. But there was a tree, and a game of backgammon, and no one was being murdered, as far as I could see. Indeed it reminded me of my old college, save for the iron spikes, and the hot stink of sweat and shit in the air. (Not that Oxford had been *fragrant* – all those old dons and lazy students cramped together, with no women to remind them to wash.) I straightened my jacket, stood a little taller, and strode into the yard with as much confidence as I could muster.

Then I turned to the south wall.

It stood twenty paces to my right, towering high above my head and stretching all the way down the long southern side of the yard like the armoured spine of some terrible beast. I had assumed it was the edge of the gaol, but now I looked more carefully, I was not so sure. There was a small, heavily barred door a little way down its flank and I had the sudden, intense suspicion that I was lucky to be on this side of it.

As I moved closer I found myself caught within its chill shadow and the hairs on the back of my neck began to rise. Unlike the rest of the prison this wall was kept in excellent repair, solid and sheer. It would be near impossible to climb without a rope. I placed my hand against the stone; it felt smooth beneath my fingers, and cold as a corpse. I shivered. Was it my imagination, or was there another scent here, beneath the general filth of the prison? A thick, rotten stench, almost like . . .

I staggered back, my hand across my mouth.

'You've smelled death before, then?'

I spun round to see a man of middling age sitting on a bench by the Lodge, smoking a pipe. There was a bottle resting at his side, and a tattered leather journal stuffed with loose papers and tied with a black ribbon. He was well-featured – handsome, even – but he cut an eccentric figure, still dressed in his banyan and a matching red velvet cap. The nightgown trailed along the cobbles as if it had been cut for a taller man, and he had been forced to roll up the sleeves. At first glance the effect was almost comical: the absent-minded gentleman scholar, unshaven, unkempt, wrapped up in his thoughts. I had met enough of those at Oxford; he had the clothes and bearing just right but his expression was too sharp – dark eyes watchful and alert under heavy black brows. He must have been sitting there for some time, studying me. Indeed, now I thought of it, he could well have heard my argument with Cross, and my exchange with Mrs Roberts.

I bowed, cautiously, and introduced myself.

He plucked off his cap and gave a deep, satirical bow in return. 'And what a pleasure to meet you, Mr Hawkins,' he said, the way a wolf might declare itself pleased to meet a small, trembling fawn. 'Samuel Fleet.'

I blinked. His name seemed familiar somehow. 'Do I know you, sir?'

A secretive smile spread slowly across his face. He stuffed his journal and his bottle somewhere deep within his robe, and tapped the stem of his pipe against my chest. 'You need a drink,' he said. And then he clapped me round the shoulder and pulled me away from the wall and its long, cold shadow.

The Tap Room stood to the right of the Lodge, as if it knew a man would always need a drink as soon as he entered the prison, and had decided to lie in wait for him there. It sold all the drink you would find in a regular tavern for twice the cost and half the taste. Wherever the profits had gone, it was not on the furnishings; the cane chair backs needed mending and the tables were infested with woodworm. One sharp sneeze and the entire room would collapse into splinters. The floor was sticky with spilt beer, the air tainted with the stink of cheap candles – pig fat, by the smell of it. Thank God for the thick fug of pipe smoke or it would have been unbearable.

It was only just past one o'clock but the room was already filled to the brim with drunken debtors and their guests. Most had gathered at the bar, where a young woman with butter-blonde hair was pouring drinks and holding court. The ribbons on her stomacher had come loose and she was almost spilling out of the top; artfully so, I thought. A snuff-pinch too respectable for Moll's place, but playing the same game – just enough soft, creamy flesh on display to keep the customers happy and buying. Everyone seemed in excellent spirits; there was a great deal of laughter and singing and shouts for more punch, more wine, more of everything. How it was all paid for, I couldn't tell.

Samuel Fleet weaved his way through the crowd, nimble as a thief. I followed him, against my better instinct – I didn't like the ugly, hostile looks he was drawing from the other prisoners, or the suspicious glances they awarded me as his companion. As he neared one group, two of the men – clearly brothers – gave him a black look, as if they would like to reach over and rip his head from his shoulders. The older one – a big man, solid as a prison wall – muttered a curse, and spat at his feet.

Fleet stopped sharp. He turned towards the man who'd cursed him and studied him silently. There was no anger in his eyes, only the cool, deadly concentration of a snake about to strike. The threat hung heavily in the air between them. In a moment there would be knives drawn – I could feel it.

'Harry,' the younger man hissed, breaking the spell. He put a hand on his brother's shoulder. 'Come away for God's sake.' They left together, pushing their way through the crowds. Harry looked back once, over his shoulder. He was a head taller than Fleet and almost twice as broad – but there was fear in his eyes.

Fleet watched them go. Then he turned his gaze on me. 'Do you wish to join them, Mr Hawkins?' His lips curled into a smile, baring his teeth.

My mouth turned dry. My mind screamed *run! run while you have the chance!* But my feet stubbornly refused to move. He was dangerous company; that much was clear. But I knew in my bones that running from him would be a mistake. Turn your back on a man like Fleet and you could find a knife in it. I swallowed hard. 'You promised me a drink, sir.'

Fleet laughed, pleased. He slapped me on the arm. 'So I did.'

The other men fell back, relieved to return to their drinks without any trouble. As I passed them I heard one mutter, '*Harry's a fool. The devil's killed a man for less.*'

All the tables were filled bar one, positioned next to a narrow balcony overlooking the yard. It seemed odd that no one had taken it when the Tap Room was so full. Fleet settled into his chair with a proprietorial air.

'They call it the Park,' he said, tilting his chin towards the window. 'The yard and these rooms by the Lodge. The gaol's known as the Castle.' He waved his pipe in a circle, as if taking in the whole prison. 'Weak men often give foolish names to the things they fear. Makes them feel safe, I suppose.' He smirked at me as if to say, *but you and I, we are above such nonsense, are we not?* He lit his pipe and took a deep draw. 'They've given *me* a name,' he muttered, smoke trailing from his lips. He had a strange, conspiratorial way of speaking, like a villain coming front of stage to let the audience in on his schemes.

I barely heard him. I should have been listening more carefully; I should have paid a lot more attention to Samuel Fleet that first day. But I was too busy peering out of the window. 'I can see over the wall from here,' I said, opening the window and slipping out on to the balcony to get a better view.

'That,' murmured Fleet, 'is why no one sits here.'

On the other side of the wall was another yard and more buildings. More iron spikes, too – and bars at the windows. A prison within a prison. The yard was long and narrow – scarcely a quarter the width of the Park – and packed tight with prisoners, thin, tattered souls stumbling slowly round and round as if in a stupor. More still peered out of the windows or lay stretched out in the dirt.

A gust of wind blew up and I caught the sweet, sickly smell of rotting meat again. And then I realised why. Some of the figures laid out in the far corner were wrapped in sheets. Corpses, left out in the autumn sun. I counted four in total. One was half the size the rest. A child.

Behind me, at the bar, they were singing a drinking song. Someone had brought out a fiddle. They all had their backs to the window.

'The Common Side,' Fleet called from his seat, making me start and draw back. 'Hell in epitome. Does it interest you, Mr Hawkins?'

I closed the window with a firm click. I thought I could still smell the corpse stink on my clothes – but it was just my imagination. 'How can they live in such a foul way?'

'They don't. Not for long.'

'Do you not care, sir?'

'Not if I can possibly help it.' He yawned and removed his cap, running his fingers across the short bristle of his scalp. I noticed with surprise that he was wearing what seemed to be a gold poesy ring on his left hand. Did this man have a wife? A family? Somehow this did not seem possible. 'I'll tell you what interests *me*, sir,' he said. 'I've been trapped in this . . .' he drummed his fingers, searching for the right word '. . . cesspit for eight months. I've seen a man flogged to death for sport. I've seen bodies left to rot for days in the heat of summer. And I've sat on that bench by the Lodge and I've watched every new prisoner arrive on the Master's Side. Not one of them walked up to the wall on the first day. Not one. Most of them never go near it. So what I'm wondering . . .' He leaned forward, his eyes fixed on mine. 'Are you brave? Foolish? Or just curious? Because any one of those can get you killed in here . . .'

'Here you are, gentlemen.' The barmaid placed a large bowl of punch on the table and smiled down at me. 'I hope it's to your taste, sir.'

'Well, well.' Fleet leaned back. 'Served by the lady of the Castle herself. What an honour.'

They exchanged a look. It was not friendly.

I introduced myself quickly, hoping she would not judge me by my company. Our hostess was not quite as young nor as beautiful as Mrs Roberts, but she was a fine-looking woman and her ribbons seemed to have come loose still further since I last checked.

'Pleased to make your acquaintance, sir.' She had a high, girlish voice and an accent that seemed to be at war with itself: part lady, part fishwife. She poured herself a glass and looked me up and down, cheeks dimpling as she smiled. 'Tell me, Mr Hawkins, do you like to dance?'

'I do, madam. When the mood takes me.'

'Well, then.' She gazed at me wantonly over the rim of her glass. 'You must come and find me, sir. When the *mood* takes you.' She sucked a drop of punch from her bottom lip.

Fleet cleared his throat. 'Mr Hawkins has been asking of the Common Side.' He gestured to an empty chair. 'Perhaps you'd like to join us? Tell us a tale of life on the other side of the wall? You must have heard a few.' He paused, savouring the taste of the next words before he said them. 'From your father.'

Her expression changed so fast I could scarce believe it. It was as if we were at a masquerade, and she had whipped off her mask to reveal a Medusa, cold-eyed and dangerous. Fleet – quite unruffled – flashed her a wide, triumphant grin and poured himself another glass of punch. She glared at him so hard I thought, surely he will turn to stone in front of my eyes. When he stubbornly refused to do so, she rounded on me.

'You should choose your friends more wisely, sir,' she hissed. Then she gathered her skirts and skipped towards the bar with a smile, the mask neatly back in its place. 'I'll hold you to that dance, Mr Hawkins,' she called gaily over her shoulder, loud enough for the whole room to hear. A few of the drinkers nudged one another and laughed.

Fleet raised his glass. 'Well. To your good health, sir. While it lasts.'

I frowned. 'What the devil do you mean?'

'You've just promised to *dance* with Mary Acton. The governor's wife.'

I excused myself with a short, irritable bow. Fleet seemed unsurprised by my sudden departure, drawing the punch closer to him with the tenderness of a mother drawing her baby to her breast. I left him scribbling something in his journal with a short pencil, pipe clenched between his teeth. People shook their heads at me as I passed. I could hardly blame them.

When I reached the yard, I was relieved to find Jakes waiting for me. It was only two hours since he'd left me and yet it seemed as if a lifetime had passed. We headed back into the Lodge where he handed over the receipt for my mother's cross and a small pile of silver and copper coins. They hardly covered my palm.

Jakes did his best to look encouraging. 'There's more than two guineas there. Enough to live on for a good while.'

'Not on the Master's Side it's not,' Cross said, emerging from his room by the gate. He must have heard the chink of the coins. His lip was swollen from where I'd hit him with the manacles. I couldn't say I felt too bad about it.

'What's your cheapest room?'

He shrugged. 'That's down to the governor. He'll take a week's rent in advance from an honest debtor.' He grinned, his eyes glittering with malice. 'He'll want more from *you*, I'd say.'

Jakes stepped closer, towering over him. 'How *much*, Joseph?' His tone was measured, but there was a hint of steel beneath.

Cross folded his arms and rocked back on his heels. 'Two shillings and six a week. That's if you share a bed, of course. With two or more chums.'

Two and six a week? I could get the best room in a good tavern for less. Or a brothel, come to think of it. I glanced anxiously at Jakes. 'I have enough for that, at least.'

'Then there's food,' Cross added, counting it off on his fat red fingers. 'Bedding. Tobacco. Coffee. Coal for the grate. You'll want someone to wash your linens. And that's before you start on court fees. Fourpence here, threepence there; you know how lawyers are. And clerks. Then your chums will demand you pay garnish, of course. That's another six shillings. Oh dear.' He held up his hands. 'I seem to have run out of fingers.'

Jakes prodded him hard in the chest. 'It's not Christianlike to revel in a man's misfortune, Joseph.'

Cross snorted. 'It's not Christianlike to punch a man in the face, is it now, Mr Hawkins?'

I ignored him. 'What's this about a garnish?'

'You have to stand your new ward mates a drink the first night,' Jakes explained. 'It goes to the Tap Room.'

And straight into the warden's pocket. No wonder Mary Acton was happy to play mistress of the bar. I clinked my small handful of coins together and felt the floor shift beneath my feet. How long could I survive on so little? How long before I was thrown over the wall on to the Common Side to rot? I thought of the corpses lying out in the yard. *I must stay on this side of the wall*, I thought, desperately. *Whatever the cost*.

Jakes settled his hat back on his head. 'Best of luck, Mr Hawkins,' he said, shaking my hand. 'I'll pray for you.'

Cross sniggered. In a flash, Jakes spun round and slammed him against the nearest wall, fixing an arm across his throat hard and heavy as an iron collar. 'I lost a good friend in here,' he snarled, blue-green eyes blazing with a furious intensity. 'I will not let this damned place destroy another man the way it destroyed John Roberts. *Never again*.' He pressed his arm harder against the turnkey's throat, making him choke. 'Is that clear?'

Cross nodded, veins bulging as he tried to breathe. Jakes let go and he slid to the floor, panting hard.

Jakes bent down to whisper in my ear. 'If there's trouble ask the Ranger to send a message. I'll come if I can.' He patted my shoulder then stomped back down the corridor, slamming the Lodge gate closed behind him.

Cross pulled himself back on his feet. We glared at each other for a moment, a pair of tom cats fighting over . . . what, exactly? Then Cross sighed, deflated, as if he'd had the same thought.

'Oh, bugger off,' he said, and limped away back to his room.

I pressed my hand to my chest, gave a deep bow, and did as I was told.

Four

I needed money.

Hardly a startling revelation in a debtors' prison, but it was true and it was urgent, nonetheless. I had seen enough of the Common Side – even that brief glimpse from the Tap Room balcony – to know I could not survive it. The certainty of it was like a blade at my throat.

I sat down on Fleet's bench beneath the Lodge and stared hard across the cobbled yard, weighing my choices. No, not the yard, I corrected myself – the *Park*. This was the same as school, or college; the sooner I learned the language of the Marshalsea the better. I could see now why Fleet favoured this bench. From here I could watch the whole of the Master's Side go about its business, like old King Henry watching a tournament. It was the perfect place to gather information, and information was valuable currency in a prison.

Thinking of Fleet made me wonder if I'd been too hasty in rejecting his company. Even here on the Master's Side I would need a friend to watch my back, and he'd frightened the wits out of a man without lifting a finger. For some reason he had taken an interest in me. An unsettling interest – but perhaps one I could turn to my advantage.

In the middle of the Park, beneath the lamppost, a debtor in a threadbare coat was deep in conversation with an older man of near sixty; a porter, I supposed, or perhaps another turn-key, given the set of keys at his belt. His clothes were mud-brown from his wig down to his stockings, save for a bright red neckerchief at his throat, which gave him the appearance of a giant robin. His brows, and the stubble on his cheek, were a mix of soft ash and honey, as if he were fighting his age bristle by bristle. He slipped a letter to the prisoner then waited, hands clasped behind his back, gnarled fingers twitching in anticipation.

There was money being made here; I could smell it. I left the bench and approached softly.

The prisoner tore open the letter with trembling fingers and read swiftly, his expression collapsing from hope to despair within a few lines. He groaned and crumpled the letter in his fist.

The robin cleared his throat in a theatrical manner. 'Bad news, sir? Very sorry to hear it. These are hard times, sir. Hard, cruel times . . .' He cleared his throat again.

'Indeed.' His customer sighed, and pulled a ha'penny from his purse. 'Well, Mr Hand. I suppose you must be paid the same, whether the news is good or ill.'

Mr Hand inclined his head. 'Regrettably, sir. Regrettably.' His eyes, the colour of old pennies, opened wide in sympathy. 'Hard times . . . We're all suffering together, sir.'

The man gave Hand a sour look as he handed over the coin and trudged away, head bowed, still clutching the crumpled letter in his fist. As soon as he had limped from sight, Hand flicked the coin jauntily in the air, caught it, and slipped it into some deep crevasse of his jacket.

'Business goes well, sir?'

He gave a start, then smiled broadly, presenting a small collection of ruined teeth. I introduced myself and he gave a bow so low it bordered on the sarcastic. 'Gilbert Hand, sir. Ranger of the Park.' He told me what I had already guessed,

that he ran errands for the other prisoners. 'Among other
things,' he added. There was a glint in his eyes that told me
exactly what – or who – those things were. Mr Hand was a
pedlar of gossip and sex. No wonder he seemed so cheerful;
he'd made such a good profit he'd decided to stay even now his
creditors were paid off. 'I've a dozen boys working for me,' he
said, pitching his chin towards the Common Side wall. 'Helps
keep their families from starving.'

'Charitable of you.' I hoped the boys just ran errands. Not a
safe bet with a man like Hand.

He grinned. 'And how may I help you, sir?'

'I need to send a letter. To Reverend Charles Buckley.'

Hand gave a sharp intake of breath. 'Sir Philip's curate?' An
avaricious look crossed his lined, lean face. 'Friend of yours?'

'My oldest friend.'

'That so.' I could see his mind whirring, calculating the ways he
might make a profit from such a connection. He gave a sharp whistle and three boys came racing from the other end of the yard,
kicking up the dust as they ran. He sent two of them back, leaving
a boy of about ten standing alone. His clothes were poorly patched
and his skin was streaked grey with dirt, but he had the same restless energy as Hand, as if he had a hundred places to be at once.

'Benjamin.' Hand leaned down. 'Chandler's shop. Paper, ink,
quill.' He held his finger in front of the boy's face. 'No charge,
d'you hear? The Careys owe me. Bring them to Mr Hawkins.'

Benjamin nodded, gaze flickering over Hand's shoulder to
where I was standing. He was young, but life had already knocked
him about – worse than that wretched little moon-curser by the
looks of it. His head was shaved for lice and one of his front teeth
was chipped. I smiled at him and he pursed his lips, brows
furrowing with suspicion. 'Which room?' he asked.

I glanced at Hand. 'That's for Mr Acton to decide.'

Hand snorted. 'Governor's in the Crown. Won't be back for
hours. Suppose I could talk to Mr Grace for you. Acton's clerk,'

he explained, and pulled a face. 'Usually charge a hog for *that* pleasure.'

I shrugged and smiled. If he thought I would pay him a shilling just to talk to some wretched clerk he could think again. Benjamin ran off towards the Lodge to the little chandler's shop beneath the Tap Room. As I turned to watch him I caught sight of Samuel Fleet standing on the balcony, smoking a pipe. Watching. Hand cursed and grabbed my elbow, pulling me away towards the north side of the gaol.

'He couldn't hear us from up there,' I protested.

Hand's expression had turned grim. 'Wouldn't put anything past that tongue-pad. I hear he's taken an interest in you.' He looked me up and down and snorted. 'I'll give you this advice for free, boy. No matter what happens, you stay away from Samuel Fleet.' His lips curled in disgust as he spoke the name, but it wasn't disgust I saw in his eyes. It was fear.

While Hand left to speak with Acton's clerk about a room, I continued my tour of the Master's Side, heading for the grand brick building at the far end of the north wall, beyond the men's wards – and a long distance from the Tap Room balcony. A crowd was still gathered beneath its porch, watching another game of backgammon. I propped myself against a column and studied the players for a while, noting their flaws for later use, then tapped my neighbour's arm.

'Forgive me, sir. What's the purpose of this building?'

The man smiled politely. 'This is the Palace Court.' He pointed to the long row of windows above the porch, stretching two storeys high. 'They hear our cases up there in the Court Room. Are you visiting, sir?'

I shook my head. 'I arrived this morning . . .' I said – and found I could say no more, confronted with the truth of my imprisonment. I would spend the night in this place. And the next night.

And the next . . . my God. How would I endure it? How would I survive?

'I'm sorry for your misfortune,' the man said quietly, as if he had read my thoughts, and turned back to the game.

I drifted away from the crowd, feeling out of sorts and quite sorry for myself. Beyond the porch, the Palace Court had been built further out into the yard; more living quarters, I presumed, from the trails of grey smoke wafting up from the chimney. At the end of the building stood a sentinel's box that I never once saw used save for pissing behind. It was quieter in this corner of the gaol, far away from the Tap Room and the Lodge. I could hear voices on the other side of the wall, the sound of hammering, men whistling and laughing as they worked. I felt a sudden crush in my chest at the thought of all those free men standing just a few paces away. Life flowed fast around this prison, like a river flowing round a boulder. I longed to jump the wall and swim away but it was no use – I was trapped. If I did not find some money soon I would die in here.

'Mr Hawkins!'

I turned to see a plump, silver-haired woman leaning out of a window on the ground floor of the Palace Court. She whisked off her cap and flapped it at me. '*There* you are!'

I offered her a short bow, wondering how she knew my name. 'Madam.'

'Ahh, bless you.' She laughed and gave a mock-curtsey in return, pulling up her coarse woollen skirts and twirling them about. 'Moll said you were a gent.'

I drew closer. She had a broad, pleasant face but her complexion was poor, and her cheeks were pitted with old pox scars. It was a face one could read in a moment – guileless and open, but not foolish, with clever, greyish-blue eyes that missed nothing. 'You're a friend of Moll's?'

She fixed her cap back on. 'Does Moll have friends . . . ? Come on in, my dear; I'll serve you a pot of coffee on the house.'

. . .

Sarah Bradshaw's coffeehouse was tiny, with rickety, mismatched old chairs and tables, but the floor was swept clean, the fire was blazing in the hearth and there were pots of fresh flowers on each table. Prisoners sat talking and drinking idly, wrote letters or read the paper. Gilbert Hand's unlucky customer sat in one corner, weeping quietly. No one paid him any mind.

Over by the fire, a young maid in a light blue calimanco gown tended the cauldron, sleeves rolled up to the elbow. Her face was flushed from the flames and damp straggles of red hair stuck to her cheeks. She paused, and poked them back beneath her cap, frowning with irritation. A chubby boy of about three years of age sat at her feet, gazing up at her in unfocused adoration, holding tight to a corner of her apron with one dirty little fist. I smiled, watching the girl for a moment. She was in a foul temper, clanging the pots and muttering curses under her breath. But she had a quick, capable manner I liked very much; she reminded me of the young maids who worked at the vicarage when I was a boy. I'd whiled away many happy hours in their company. A memory I'd buried long ago suddenly came back to me. *Lizzie Smith.* I was home from school, trying to keep out of my stepmother's way. Lizzie followed me into the woods one day. Pushed me up against the nearest tree and kissed me, took my hand and slid it beneath her skirts . . .

The girl must have felt my eyes upon her. 'I'm not for sale,' she warned, glaring at me.

'I've no interest in hiring you, hussy!' I snapped back, annoyed by her cheek.

She raised an eyebrow, gaze dropping to my breeches. 'Then you should tell your cock, sir,' she muttered, and turned back to the fire. A couple of men at the nearest table sniggered into their coffee bowls.

'*Kitty Sparks* . . .' Mrs Bradshaw tutted, bustling me away from the girl towards a seat near the window. 'I *do* apologise, Mr Hawkins.'

I laughed and shook my head; she had caught me fair and square. 'Moll would hire her in a flash, would she not?'

'Aye, she might. But she'd have to slit my throat first.' There was a hard tone to her voice; had Moll *really* told her I was a gentleman and left it at that? A sin of omission if ever I'd heard one.

Once I was settled, Mrs Bradshaw eased herself down into a chair by the door, resting her feet on a low footstool. A clever spot, where she could keep watch on her customers and still observe all the comings and goings on the stairwell. She took up a half-made quilted cap and began stitching with a neat, practised air, casting glances into the passage beyond whenever someone walked by. When Benjamin – Gilbert Hand's boy – came by with paper and ink for my letter, she watched us sharply from beneath lowered lids, never missing a stitch.

I had just begun my letter to Charles when Kitty appeared with my coffee, slopping half of it upon the table. She mopped it up with her apron, cursing to herself. She was younger than I had first thought, eighteen at most, with a pale complexion and freckles all across her face and arms, as if God had flung them at her in a rage. I smiled at her and she responded with a complicated look, as if to say – what the devil have *you* to smile about?

I leaned back in my chair. Her ill-humour was intriguing, like the sharp tang of lemon in a syllabub. 'Tell me. Are the rooms above us here for prisoners?'

'This is the Oak ward.' She shifted her weight to one leg; the familiar tilt of a girl humouring a man against her wishes. 'This floor and the two above us. The women's quarters are on the next landing.'

'Indeed . . .' Several delicious, indiscreet questions began to form in my mind. *How many women were housed there? What were their ages? Their circumstances? How many were there to a bed?* I shifted in my seat. 'And why is it called the Oak?'

She met my gaze, green eyes steady and shrewd. 'There's thick oak doors off each corridor.' She mimed the doors with her hands, fingertips touching in the middle. 'The ladies close them when they don't want visitors. But they're spread *wide open* most of the time,' she added, parting her hands. 'And then a gentleman can enter as often as he likes. If he's wanted.'

Behind me, men were coughing into their drinks again. 'I *see*. Well, thank you, Miss Sparks, I'm obliged to you.'

She offered me a half-smile, pleased I'd taken her teasing well. 'What you in for?'

The question caught me by surprise. The Marshalsea was a debtors' prison, with only a handful of prisoners in for other crimes. 'What do you *think* I'm in for?'

She shrugged. 'How should I know? Sedition? Piracy? Sodomy—'

'Debt. I'm in for debt.'

'If you say so.' She winked and headed back to the fire.

I finished my letter to Charles, explaining what had happened to me. What he could do to help I wasn't sure; the money he'd lent me was now being spent somewhere in St Giles – and not in a way he would approve, I was sure. I asked if he might speak with his patron, though I doubted Sir Philip would feel inclined to help. Once I was done I called to Benjamin through the window and paid him a ha'penny to deliver the letter to St James'.

After that there was nothing I could do but wait for Gilbert Hand to return with news of my living quarters. As I waited the prison chaplain appeared at the door and greeted Mrs Bradshaw in a vague fashion before limping breathlessly to a seat by the fire. He was a large man with a goutish look about him that made it hard to guess his age, even more so as he wore a long wig in an old-fashioned style. Fifty, I decided. A large roll of fat wobbled over the edge of his white neckerchief, which had yellowed with age and sweat. His black waistcoat and jacket were badly faded and in need of a tailor's needle – more through absent-mindedness than poverty, I guessed, as his hat and cane were both new and well-made. He reminded me of my old divinity tutor at school; he had the same kind but distracted air and – by the look of him – the same quiet devotion to port wine.

I was about to introduce myself when he pulled out a Bible of all things, settled a pair of glasses on his nose and began scribbling his thoughts down in a little notebook. A Bible in a coffeehouse? Very bad form. I frowned at his offence and returned to my coffee. After a little while Mrs Bradshaw put down her needlework and joined me in a fresh pot, squeezing her way between the tables to reach me. She might have been in debt but she certainly wasn't starving. In fact she didn't seem like a prisoner at all. She laughed when I told her this.

'I've been here six years,' she said, rolling the little vase of flowers on the table round and round in a wistful fashion. 'Came in with a debt of fifty and I'll leave in a box still owing it, no doubt.' She shrugged. 'It's home to me now. I'm free to come and go as I please, as long as I'm back for lock-up. The Careys are the same, and the McDonnells. They run Titty Doll's, the chop-house upstairs. Tell Mack you know Moll and he'll give you the better cuts. Oh! I forgot!' She magicked an envelope from her voluminous skirts and tipped a half-guinea into my palm. 'She must like you, Mr Hawkins. I've never known Moll give money freely to anyone.'

I tucked the coin away. I doubted it was given freely – Moll would call in her debt sooner or later – but I was grateful for it all the same. I nodded at the envelope. 'What does she say?'

Mrs Bradshaw held the letter out in front of her, leaning back and narrowing her eyes. '*Please keep watch for a friend of mine, an honest gent fell on hard times,*' she read, mimicking Moll's low, commanding tone. '*He's a tall, fine-looking boy with dark brows, blue eyes and good calves.*'

We both studied my legs for a moment, then laughed together.

'What do you make of that, madame?' Mrs Bradshaw called out to a dusty old woman muttering to herself in a dim corner. She was dressed all in black and white like a living chessboard: white hair stabbed with black combs and tied up in a series of tiny black ribbons; face powdered bone-white, black velvet patches only half-covering old pox scars. Flecks of spittle clung to the corners of her thin grey lips.

She tilted her head, studying me with the cold black eyes of a raven about to tug a worm from the ground. And then she shuddered, flapping her black lace shawl tighter about her bony frame. '*Pas beau*,' she sneered. '*Il est trop pâle. Comme un fantôme.*'

Well, that's rich coming from you, you old baggage, I thought.

Mrs Bradshaw leaned back and raised her eyebrows at Kitty, who was sitting by the fire, bouncing the little boy violently on her knee while he squealed in a mixture of delight and alarm. To my surprise, she translated at once. 'Too pale. Like a ghost.'

'A ghost? Well, now . . . she would know, I suppose.' Mrs Bradshaw glanced about anxiously, as if the air might be alive with spirits with nothing better to do than listen to her chatter. 'Madame Migault is a fortune teller, Mr Hawkins. She'll read your future if you like.'

'No, thank you, madame,' I said. I preferred to make my own future, not have it spat at me in riddles by a bony old witch. 'I'm afraid I don't hold with fortune telling.'

'Well said, sir.' The chaplain, still sitting by the fire, closed his Bible with a snap. 'Only the Lord Himself knows our path through this world. The rest is devil's work.' He removed his spectacles and peered across the room – then gave a startled cry when he caught sight of me. 'Good heavens!' he exclaimed, heaving himself up from his chair. The blood had drained from his face, turning it a sickly tallow colour. 'Is it . . . are you . . . ?'

'Captain Roberts, returned from the dead? No, sir.' I smiled, but this only served to heighten his alarm. I hurried to give him

my name before the poor man expired from shock, explaining
that I had arrived only this morning.

The chaplain pulled a handkerchief from his pocket and
patted the sweat from his face. His hand was shaking. 'Of
course. Forgive me.' He gave a weak little laugh, the flesh about
his neck jiggling softly. 'Now I look closer . . . it is just a passing resemblance.'

Madame Migault cackled to herself. '*Pauvre* Monsieur
Woodburn. Thinks he sees a ghost.'

Mrs Bradshaw threw her a sharp glance as she pulled out a
chair. 'Sit yourself down here, sir,' she said, pushing the window
wide in a vain attempt to bring fresh air to the room. 'You've
given him quite a shock, Mr Hawkins.' I started to apologise but
Mrs Bradshaw patted my shoulder. 'Not your fault you look like
a dead man,' she said generously. 'You've heard the story, then,
have you?'

'I met his widow.'

'Hmm.' A pinched expression fixed upon Mrs Bradshaw's
face, the look of a woman failing – quite intentionally – to hide
her dislike. 'Poor Catherine,' she said.

'She told me her husband had been murdered.'

Mrs Bradshaw nodded. 'Terrible business. There was uproar,
wasn't there, Mr Woodburn? A man dragged from his bed and
killed – and no one caught. Who's to say it won't happen again?'
She took the opportunity to place a hand on my knee. 'You must
sleep with a blade in your hand in here, Mr Hawkins.'

Good advice, I was sure, but my blade had been taken from
me last night. And for a moment I could feel the cold hard
bite of it against my throat again, and the weight of my purse,
the smooth leather pressed to my skin. I had been so close to
freedom . . . Still – at least I was alive, which was more than
could be said for Captain Roberts. 'The coroner called it
suicide, I believe?'

'He was murdered,' Woodburn muttered, almost to himself.

'Well, it's a shame the court didn't agree with you, sir,' Mrs Bradshaw replied. 'And do you know what they did with his body, Mr Hawkins?'

'Yes, indeed.' Everyone knew what happened to the corpses of those who committed self-murder. It was not pleasant. 'In truth I'd really rather not—'

'They buried him at a crossroads, with a stake plunged in his heart,' Mrs Bradshaw said with some relish, pounding a fist to her huge chest. 'Not even a bier to keep the worms from his poor body. And now his spirit haunts the gaol, never to rest. Mr Jenings the nightwatch saw him standing by the governor's house in the middle of the night, all pale and grim with a noose still wrapped about his neck. And Mrs Carey swears she heard footsteps and a *terrible groaning* beneath the chandler's window but when she looked out there was no one there. I'm scared to walk the yard at night in case he looms up out of the dark—'

'*Enough!*' Woodburn bellowed, making Mrs Bradshaw flinch and stutter to a halt. He gave a low moan. 'Forgive me,' he muttered. 'I cannot bear to think of it . . .'

Mrs Bradshaw patted his shoulder, clearly thrilled by the drama. 'Mr Woodburn saw the body,' she mouthed in a stage whisper over the chaplain's shoulder. 'They found it hanging in the Strong Room over on the Common Side, all beaten and bloody. Barely recognised him, did you, sir?'

Woodburn gave a little sob and pressed his handkerchief to his lips. 'God rest his soul,' he whispered.

Mrs Bradshaw patted his shoulder again. 'A man doesn't beat himself black and blue before hanging himself, does he, Mr Hawkins?'

I frowned. 'I hope Mrs Roberts discovers the truth, for her own sake.' As the widow of a suicide, she would be shunned by all decent society. I felt a surge of pity for the proud young woman who had saved me from Joseph Cross earlier that morning. Her reputation had been ruined through no fault of her own. 'Does she suspect someone in particular?'

Mrs Bradshaw laughed. 'Oh, we all *suspect* someone in particular.' Her laughter died away and she glanced about her with an anxious expression. For a moment her gaze settled on Kitty, her maid, who was still playing with the little boy by the fire. She lowered her voice. 'Captain Roberts had a roommate. He was there the night of the murder, lying in the very next bed just a few paces away. He *says* he didn't hear a thing – claims he slept through it all. But the devil never sleeps, does he? How does it go . . .'

The words of St Peter rose to my mind unbidden. *'Be sober, be vigilant: because your adversary the devil, as a roaring lion, walketh about, seeking whom he may devour.'*

When I looked back the chaplain was staring at me, his mouth a little 'o' of surprise.

'A roaring lion?' Mrs Bradshaw sniffed. 'A hissing snake's more like it, slithering about the place, studying you with those nasty black eyes of his.'

Samuel Fleet. It had to be. I shifted uneasily in my chair.

'Mrs Bradshaw,' Woodburn tutted. 'You cannot accuse a man of murder just because—'

'He's not a man,' she cried. 'He's a demon!'

'What's this?' Kitty called from across the room. 'Do you speak of Mr Fleet?'

'Mr Woodburn,' I said quietly. 'Do you believe it?'

He sighed and shook his head. 'I cannot say, sir. But I fear he *is* capable of the very worst crimes.' He held my gaze. 'The very worst.'

I was about to reply when a terrible cry rose from the yard. A second later one of Gilbert Hand's boys rushed into the room.

'What news, Jim?' Kitty asked sharply.

'They've took Jack Carter!' the boy replied, hopping from foot to foot in a mix of fear and excitement. 'He fell off the wall trying to escape!'

Kitty pushed past us to reach the window. I joined her, more curious than alarmed, and saw Joseph Cross dragging a small heap of rags into the middle of the yard. A tall, broad-shouldered man in black breeches and a bright red waistcoat strode behind them, holding his jacket in one meaty hand. Prisoners and guards leapt out of his way, scurrying to the far corners of the yard. Within a few moments, the Park was empty.

Only one person could command such power in a prison. I glanced at Kitty.

'Mr Acton,' she muttered, her face twisted with hatred.

Woodburn rose a little from his chair and put on his spectacles before peering out into the yard. 'Drunk.' He sighed and returned to his seat, pocketing his spectacles. 'This will go badly for Jack.'

Kitty turned and glared at him. 'Then *do* something.'

The chaplain rubbed the back of his neck. 'He won't listen to me,' he muttered, looking shamefaced.

Out in the Park, Cross threw the prisoner to the ground. He gave a sharp scream of pain, and clutched his ankle. It looked broken. 'Oh, please! Oh, God,' he sobbed in a cracked voice, dragging himself along the ground and staring desperately at all the windows. 'Please! Someone help me!'

Acton said something to Cross and they both laughed.

'He's just a boy,' I said, shocked.

'Thirteen,' Woodburn whispered to the floor. 'He's thirteen.'

Acton threw his jacket at Cross and began to roll up his sleeves. I knew then what would come next. 'Dear God,' I said, my voice shaking. 'He can't . . ., he *won't* . . .'

Acton took a short, hard whip from his belt, a savage thing made to drive cattle. Enough to tear flesh from a young boy's bones.

Kitty clutched my arm so tight I almost cried out, but she didn't look away.

Acton grabbed the boy's shoulder and hauled him to his knees. He raised the whip in the air.

One silent moment.

The whip came down. Then again. And again.

The boy screamed, holding up his hands to shield himself.

A ripple of sympathy spread across the room, but no one moved. The beating went on and on, relentless. I could hear Acton grunting softly with the effort. Sometimes he would pause, and wipe the sweat from his brow with his sleeve. Plant his feet a little wider. And then he would begin again. Woodburn covered his face with his hands.

The boy's cries faded to whimpers, then silence, as the blows came down.

Slowly, without a word, people moved away from the window. Only Kitty remained, still clutching my arm, her fingers digging in with every lash as if she could feel it ripping her own skin. A tear slid down her cheek.

You must act, a voice spoke in my head. *You must do something, for pity's sake. He's just a boy, and they're beating him to death in front of your eyes.*

He was on his knees, now, crawling through the dirt. Acton raised his boot and stamped down hard on his back.

'Henry. Oh God, *no!*' Kitty cried, bringing me to my senses. Her tiny charge – forgotten in all the confusion – had wandered out of the coffeehouse and was now toddling across the yard towards Acton and the whip, arms outstretched and giggling.

Before I could even think to stop her Kitty dropped my arm and ran after him. Mrs Bradshaw flung herself in front of the door. 'You can't stop it, sweetheart,' she cried in a panic. 'You'll only bring trouble on yourself.'

'He's just a baby, Sarah,' Kitty hissed. 'He thinks it's a game, don't you see? He thinks they're playing a game!' She pushed her way past Mrs Bradshaw and darted outside.

A moment later I found myself chasing after her.

What possessed me? To this day, I still wonder. One moment I was standing in the coffeehouse, the next I was outside, the prison buildings spinning about me like a carousel, the blood roaring in my ears. Kitty ran out and I followed her, as if there were a chain tying us one to the other.

Some men are wise. Some men are cowards. In dangerous times, both stand back and think hard before they act. A coward would have let Kitty stand up to Acton alone and swallowed down the shame of doing nothing. A wise man would have realised that Kitty didn't need his help – all she was trying to do was catch Henry before he witnessed a bloody, violent act no child should see.

Prison taught me many things about myself, and here was my first lesson, something I had not suspected. I could not stand back and let things happen. I *had* to act, no matter the consequences. Those few steps from the coffeehouse into the yard sent a pulse through my life and nothing would be the same again. I had moved out of the audience and taken my place on the stage. Or on the gallow steps. Perhaps that is a better way to put it.

Every eye in the prison was upon us.

Little Henry was only a few short steps away from Acton, who was still bringing his whip down hard on the boy as Cross watched. Kitty shouted for Henry to stop, to come back inside and play with her, but he just carried on toddling towards them, chattering to himself, his feet pattering on the cobbles.

Kitty would never reach him in time. I leapt forward and snaked my arms about her waist, dragging her away. She gave a scream and kicked at my shins, beat my arms with her fists. 'Let me go. Let me *go*, damn you!'

'Close your eyes,' I whispered hard in her ear. 'Don't look.' She slumped against me, defeated, but she didn't turn away.

I was close enough to see Acton clearly now. This was not a man to reason with. He was beating a child to death, and yet there was no expression on his face, no malice, no pleasure, just the dogged concentration of a man doing his job.

Henry tottered closer, then stretched out his arms. I held my breath.

'Papa!'

Acton spun round, whip raised high in his fist. For a moment I thought he would bring it down upon the little boy. But then his face transformed, brightening with pleasure. 'Henry!' he exclaimed. 'Bless my soul! Where did you spring from?' He tossed the whip to the ground and swung his son up into the air, setting him firmly on his shoulders. Henry squealed and laughed, grabbing at his father's wig with chubby fingers.

'That's his son?' I whispered.

Kitty bowed her head. 'I didn't want him to see,' she whispered. 'He's too young to understand. He won't remember this.'

'I pray to God you're right.'

I took her hand and backed away quietly towards the coffeehouse.

'Stay where you are, sir,' Acton barked, lifting his son from his shoulders. He glanced at his deputy. 'Who's this?'

Cross scowled. 'Hawkins.' He touched a hand to his swollen jaw. 'The one I told you about.'

Acton pulled a handkerchief from his pocket and wiped the blood and sweat from his hands. He had the fleshy, pock-marked face and heavy jaw of a brothel bully, but his piercing blue eyes were sharp and clever as they looked me up and down. He swaggered closer, until I could feel his breath upon my face, hot and tangy with liquor. There were spots of blood on his shirt. 'Hawkins.' He spat my name out as if he didn't like the taste of it. 'Why did you punch my head turnkey?'

Behind us, his last victim was curled up on the ground, shuddering softly. Still alive; just. I swallowed hard. The wrong answer would kill me, I knew it. I took a deep breath. 'Because he's an arsehole, sir.'

Acton blinked in surprise. And then – thank God – he roared with laughter. 'Aye, that's the truth!' he agreed, and laughed again.

I almost sank to my knees with relief.

'Why did you come after my boy?'

Henry was throwing pebbles at the ground, oblivious to the drama playing out above his head. I could see his father in him now. The same square face, the same wide, full lips. 'I thought he might hurt himself, Mr Acton.'

He grunted, pleased. 'Henry's always safe in the Marshalsea,' he said, rolling down his sleeves and picking up his whip. 'But I'm obliged to you, sir. Always happy to welcome a proper gent to my Castle.' He grabbed my hand and shook it vigorously.

I looked at my hand in his and felt my stomach turn. 'Thank you, sir.'

Acton gestured to the house next to the Lodge. 'You must join me and the governess for supper tomorrow night.'

Cross started to protest, thick brows drawn in fury. Acton silenced him with one glance. He pointed at the body on the ground. 'Lock young Carter here in the Strong Room. Chains and the collar. Tighten the screws, Mr Cross. Let's remind our little pigeons what happens when they try to fly away.' He looked up at the prison quarters, at all the white faces peering down upon the spectacle, and gave a low chuckle. Then he took Henry's hand and strode towards the bar.

As soon as Acton had left, Kitty ran over to Jack Carter and cradled him in her arms. His face was swollen, his shirt shredded and drenched with blood. His ribs would be broken, I was sure of it – there was barely any flesh on him to cushion Acton's blows. It looked bad, very bad. He raised his head weakly, eyes flickering open.

Cross pushed me aside and stood over Kitty, his shadow falling across her face. 'Move, hussy. You heard Mr Acton, he's for the Strong Room.'

She gripped the boy tight. 'Just you try it, Joseph Cross,' she snarled. 'I'll rip your eyes out their sockets and shove 'em up your arse.'

Cross blinked, then shot her a grudging look of respect.

Woodburn appeared from the coffeehouse, eager to help now that Acton was gone. 'Come now, Joseph,' he said, gently. 'Let's clean the lad up first, eh? Fetch the nurse, perhaps . . . ?'

'Thoughtful of you, sir,' Cross sneered. 'Will you pay her fee?'

'*I'll* tend him,' Kitty said firmly. She was already checking her patient, fingers prodding and testing along his sunken ribcage.

Cross glanced back towards the Lodge. 'Governor won't like it.'

'*Governor won't like it,*' Kitty mimicked. 'You wouldn't rub your own prick without asking him first, would you?'

The turnkey laughed, despite himself. 'Oh, go on, take him if you must,' he said with a shrug. 'We'll sling him in the Strong Room once he's cleaned up.'

I lifted the boy to his feet, wrapping his arm about my shoulder for support. As he stood up he gave a scream of pain.

'His ankle's broken,' Kitty said. 'What were you *thinking*, Jack?'

He sank hard against my side. 'Acton saw me climb the wall. He made them cut the rope.'

'We can tend to him in the chapel,' Woodburn said, gesturing to the house next to the Palace Court. 'Run and fetch water, Kitty.'

'Oh, am I your servant now, sir?' she muttered, but she did as she was told.

Woodburn took Jack's other arm and we lifted him together. The boy was so thin I could have easily carried him on my own, but now that Acton was gone the chaplain seemed almost desperate to help.

'That was brave of you, Mr Hawkins,' he said, as we made our way to the chapel.

I frowned, remembering Samuel Fleet's observation up in the Tap Room. *Had* I been brave? Or just foolish? Was there much difference in a place like this?

Thinking of Fleet, some instinct made me look back at the Tap Room window. And there he was, watching us from above, leaning over the balcony. As I caught his eye he grinned and clapped his hands, as if this had all been a play for his benefit. The applause echoed around the empty yard.

'*Look* at him.' Woodburn clenched his jaw. 'The black-hearted fiend. God forgive me, but I'd wring his neck if I had the chance.'

Five

The chapel was quiet and clean, with smooth-plastered white walls and a large window facing on to the yard. Woodburn threw a fresh blanket on the floor by the altar and I settled Jack down carefully. I could feel him trembling in my arms as I laid him down.

'Poor boy,' Woodburn sighed. He heaved himself into the nearest pew and bowed his head in prayer.

Jack shuddered softly and coughed. A thin trickle of blood slid from his lips. I hoped Woodburn was praying for Jack's soul – it was too late for the rest of him. The shock of it brought tears to my eyes. *Thirteen years old.* I blinked them back and kneeled down next to him, wondering how on earth I had become entangled in all of this. On a different day, in a different mood, Acton could have clapped me in irons or beaten me just as he'd beaten Jack – and who would have come running to save *me*?

Jack reached for my hand. 'Ben. Where's Ben . . . ?'

Kitty arrived with a bowl of hot water and a cordial. She shooed me away, loosening Jack's grimy rags and examining his injuries with a speed and skill that surprised me. He was so dirty that it was hard to see where the bruises lay, but once the hot water had washed him clean the violence of Acton's attack was clear enough. Thick red weals crisscrossed his body, deep, savage wounds that had torn almost to the bone.

Kitty cleaned them as best she could and put the bottle of cordial to his lips. 'Just a few sips, Jack.' She touched his hair softly.

'Is he a friend of yours, Kitty?'

She nodded, setting the cordial to one side. 'He cleaned bed sheets on the Master's Side till he caught a fever. Then they threw him back over the wall.' She ran her fingers across the boy's battered body then glanced at Woodburn, still praying with his head down. 'Look,' she murmured, touching a large spread of green and yellow bruises running across his chest like countries on a map. 'These are old beatings.'

I studied the boy with new eyes. Kitty was right; the bright red wounds from Acton's whip were merely the climax to a brutal story that had played itself out for many weeks. Jack had been battered and beaten so badly that there was barely an inch of clear skin left. No wonder he'd tried to escape.

'Why did they do this to him?'

'He got himself into trouble with John Grace, Acton's clerk,' Woodburn said. He was slumped back in his pew, almost as grey as the boy.

'Trouble?' Kitty rounded on him. 'His mother was starving to death on the sick ward! They left her lying in her own filth, no blankets, no bed. *Nothing*. Jack only asked for what he was owed. Just a bit of *charity*.'

Woodburn flinched, then turned a deep red. 'Watch your tongue, girl,' he cried, rising from the bench. 'I did everything I could to help Jack and his family. I spoke with Mr Grace and Mr Acton on countless occasions.'

'Little good it did them,' Kitty snapped back.

Woodburn glowered at her. 'This is Samuel Fleet's influence,' he said, narrowing his eyes. 'Mrs Roberts tells me you've been spending far too much time in his company . . .'

Kitty pressed a hand to her chest. 'I'm so sorry, sir,' she said, her voice catching with remorse. 'It's just . . . the shock of . . . of seeing poor Jack . . .'

I almost laughed, it was so poorly acted. But Woodburn fell for it. He patted her head, all thoughts of Fleet forgotten. 'You're a good-hearted girl, Kitty. We just need to calm that temper of yours, eh? And my thanks to you, sir,' he said, giving me a short bow. 'If you would stay here I'll have a quiet word with Acton about the Strong Room. Perhaps I can change his mind.'

He waddled down the aisle, closing the door softly behind him. The chapel fell silent for a moment.

'Sanctimonious cock,' Kitty said, rinsing her hands.

Even Jack cheered up at that.

I nodded at the boy's bandaged ankle. 'You've done a fine job there.'

'My father was a doctor,' Kitty said, without thinking, then gave a start, as if surprised by the confession. She turned away and began scrubbing the blood from the chapel floor.

With Jack cleaned and bandaged there was little more we could do for him, but we were loath to call for assistance. As soon as he left the chapel he would be clapped in chains and locked in the Strong Room, over on the Common Side. Kitty wouldn't say much about it, except that Mr Acton was a bastard for sending him there.

We sat side by side on the front pew, not saying much. I felt numb with shock, the force of what I had witnessed only now hitting me. Kitty was trembling a little, fighting off the tears. Jack had fallen unconscious again.

'He might live,' I said.

'No. He won't.' She pulled off her cap and shook her hair loose, red locks tumbling down about her shoulders.

'He was asking for someone called Ben.'

'His brother. There's just the two of them. Their mother died of gaol fever a month back.' She covered her face with her hands.

• • •

I headed down the stairs and back out into the yard. It was late afternoon and the sun hung low above the Lodge gate, casting long shadows. Woodburn was sitting on a bench by the chapel door, prodding at the weeds growing up around the cobbles with the end of his cane. He looked miserable and distracted; clearly his talk with Acton had not gone well. As for the rest of the Park, it was as if nothing had happened. A game of ninepins had resumed beneath the Court's porch and Gilbert Hand was back at his station by the lamppost in the middle of the yard.

'What a parish, eh?' Woodburn said, rubbing his temples. 'Do you think if I prayed *very* hard the Lord would take pity and transfer me to Mayfair?' He stuck a finger through a hole in his jacket. 'The truth is I wouldn't change it for the world. There's so much good work to be done here. So many souls to save.' He glanced up, shyly. 'Does that sound foolish to you, Mr Hawkins? I fear it's not the fashion for clerics to talk about souls these days.'

I smiled, understanding better than he realised. I had spent three years at Oxford studying to join the clergy. Three years of rising at dawn to pray, daily seminars in classics, divinity and logic. Long hours hunched over my desk translating Greek into Latin and Latin into English before rushing back to church for evening prayers . . . and finally to bed. Unfortunately, it was in that gap between 'evening prayers' and 'finally to bed' where I was tested; and failed magnificently. If only God had put fewer hours in the day. And not invented twins.

'Well, well. I must call for a chair to take me home,' Woodburn said, heaving himself up from the bench with the help of his cane.

I rose and bowed. Lucky man, to come and go as he pleased.

He cleared his throat. 'And will I see you at chapel on Sunday, sir?'

'Naturally,' I said, and watched as his face glowed with delight. I had not attended church in months, but there was no harm in keeping the chaplain on my side. 'As a matter of fact, I studied divinity at Oxford . . .'

'Indeed?' Woodburn's eyes shone, as I thought they might. 'That was always a great dream of mine. Alas, the fees . . . But you did not take the cloth?'

I hung my head. 'I'm afraid I was led astray.' *By myself.*

'Ah.' Woodburn nodded his understanding. 'Well — there is still hope for you, sir. The good Lord loves a prodigal son.'

Yes . . . and so do good-natured old chaplains. I'd hooked him with it; I could see it in his eyes. There is nothing more irresistible to an honest clergyman than a penitent sinner. Even more so a penitent student of divinity. He was doubtless already dreaming of long nights by the fire discussing the finer points of theology as he dragged my soul slowly but steadily from the brink of damnation. I almost felt guilty for deceiving him. *Almost.*

Woodburn clapped his hat to his head. 'D'you know, I believe you have been brought here for a reason,' he said, in a quiet, earnest voice. 'God has plans for you, Mr Hawkins. I am sure of it.'

The chaplain left me frowning in suspicion at the darkening sky, grey clouds drifting slowly by. 'Well, He can choose some-one else,' I muttered.

After my encounter with Mr Acton, I longed to retreat to some quiet spot to recover, but there were no private places in the Marshalsea; no escape from the curious gaze of others. I returned to Fleet's bench by the Lodge and closed my eyes, reaching out beyond the prison walls, a bird released from its cage. It was a trick I had learned as a boy and I did it now with-out thinking. For a moment I was not sealed up in gaol — I was in Suffolk, running along the coast road towards Orford and the sea, the wind fresh and cold on my skin, the taste of salt in the air.

'Mr Hawkins.' I opened my eyes. A thin, pallid face loomed over me, cold blue eyes peering over a pair of spectacles. 'Twenty pounds, ten shillings and sixpence?'

I blinked, not sure how I was expected to reply.

He pushed his spectacles up his nose with a long, bony finger. 'Twenty pounds, ten shillings and sixpence is your debt, is it not?'

'Well . . . yes. Thank you for reminding me, Mr . . . ?'

'John Grace.'

'Ah!' I jumped up. 'Mr Acton's clerk, of course. Do you have a room for me, sir?'

'*Head* clerk to the *head* keeper. And chief steward,' Grace replied and turned sharply on his heel.

I followed him across the Park, passing the main prison quarters nearest the Lodge. He was leading me towards the east wall – and the poorest lodgings.

We walked by the coffeehouse, where Acton had beaten Jack Carter just an hour before. Fresh spots of blood glistened on the cobbles. Grace walked through them.

'You went to that Common boy's aid,' Grace called over his shoulder. He had a flat, empty way of speaking, as warm and human as a creaking door. 'A waste of time and money.'

I glared at his back. 'I doubt he'll last the night.'

'Indeed,' he said, without a trace of interest. And then, 'His mother owed five pounds, three shillings and fourpence. She's dead.'

Grace had – no doubt with a good deal of pride and effort – managed to find me a bed in the meanest room in the filthiest ward in the worst building on the Master's Side. The landings were filled with rubbish, full chamber pots still waiting to be collected by each door, fouling the air. As we passed one room I heard the familiar sound of a bed slamming against a wall, followed by a long, guttural grunt of release. Grace's mouth tightened to a thin line. 'O'Rourke. Nine pounds, twelve shillings.' A final grunt. 'And tuppence.'

'We take our pleasures where we may, Mr Grace,' I said, skirting round a pool of dried vomit on the top-floor landing.

'As long as we *pay* for them, Mr Hawkins,' he replied, pulling out a silk handkerchief and clamping it to his nose and mouth. He gestured to a door at the end of the corridor. 'Your room,' he said, his voice muffled through the cloth, then left without another word.

I thought this was a little odd, but I had already prepared myself for what lay behind the door. Sharing a small, close room with four or five other men would never be a pleasant experience but I had boarded at school and I knew what to expect. I needed a bed, and a place to be locked up for the night, but for the rest of the time I could always sit in the Park, or Mrs Bradshaw's coffeehouse.

There was no answer to my knock so I opened the door slowly. A hideous, sour-sweet smell poured out into the corridor. Unwashed linen, shit, sweat . . . and underneath that something much worse. Meat. Decay – as bad as the Common Side. I gagged, the stink catching in my throat.

If I breathed through my mouth it was almost bearable. I would just find my bed and go; the next time I came up here I'd make sure I was too drunk to care about the stench.

As I stepped into the room something stirred in the furthest bed. It was hard to see through the gloom: the window was covered with a tattered, grime-smeared sheet and the candles were unlit. The hearth was cold. I made my way across, squeezing past three other beds covered in filthy linen. Teeming with lice, no doubt. I shuddered, and scratched at my skin.

When I reached the final bed I saw that a man lay curled on his side under a thin blanket, his face to the wall. As I edged closer he coughed and shook, phlegm rattling deep in his chest.

I stood over him for a moment, not certain what to do. Something was not right here – I could feel it in my bones. I cleared my throat to get his attention.

Slowly, painfully, like a figure in some fevered nightmare, he turned towards me. A thick, raw mass of oozing yellow pustules covered his face and spread down his neck across his body. His lips, his eyelids – every inch was infected.

Smallpox. I gave a jolt of terror and staggered back, flinging my arm up to cover my nose and mouth.

'Please . . .' He reached out his hand, delirious with pain and fever. 'Who's there? Oh, God, have pity, sir. Don't leave me. Don't leave me, I beg you . . .'

I fled the room, stumbling back along the corridor, down the stairs and out into the yard. I ran so fast that I almost collided with Grace, who was walking back to the Lodge with a firm tread and a straight back. I grabbed hold of his coat and spun him round to face me. 'Smallpox! There's a man . . . dying . . .'

Grace flinched and knocked my hand away. 'Did you touch him?'

'No.' I thought of his hand, reaching out for mine. Oh God. 'No, of course not.'

Grace straightened his coat. 'Well, then, what of it, sir?'

'What of it?' I stared at him in horrified disbelief. Grace shrugged, indifferent, and began to turn away. I seized his jacket again, this time with both fists, and pulled him closer. He was a good head shorter than me, and very light. Hollow. '*What of it?* You must find me another room!'

Grace pursed his thin lips. 'That is the room you have been given. It is the room you can *afford*.'

I let go of his coat. There was not a shred of fellow feeling in him. He would let me die in that room without a thought – without a flicker of conscience.

'Mr Grace.' Samuel Fleet leaned over the balcony of the Tap Room, a glass of punch in his hand. 'What's the matter?'

Grace frowned up at him. 'Mr Hawkins is not satisfied with his accommodation.' As if I'd been complaining of the view.

'My roommate is dying of smallpox,' I called up, though I was sure he had heard every word. 'I am being charged two and six a week to murder myself.'

'How unfortunate.' He leaned his chin on his hand, coal-black eyes fixed upon mine. Smiled slowly. 'There is a bed free in my room. You are welcome to it, sir.'

A shiver of dread ran through me. Lock myself in a room each night with a man who killed his last cell mate? I might as well share a cage with a tiger. 'I . . . I thank you sir, but I—'

'*I insist.*'

I had never heard such menace in two short words. Fleet had not taken his eyes from mine for a moment. Had not even blinked. I swallowed hard, then bowed my agreement. What else could I do?

Well, Mr Woodburn, you were quite right, I thought bleakly. *God does have a plan for me. I am to be murdered in my bed on my very first night.*

'No, no, this will not *do*,' Grace tutted.

'There must be another room,' I said, seizing my chance. 'If I might just speak with Mr Acton . . .'

'There are procedures. There are rules.'

Fleet raised an eyebrow. '*Money* is the only rule in here, Mr Grace.' He held his hand over the balcony and poured a stream of coins on to the ground by the clerk's feet. 'That should cover the shortfall.'

Grace blinked at the coins for a moment before scooping them up, wiping each one clean with his handkerchief and then pocketing them. He studied me for a long moment with a puzzled expression, as if I were a sum he had added up incorrectly and even now could not make work. 'Well. It seems you are in Mr Fleet's debt, sir,' he said at last, and stalked off.

I stared up at my unexpected benefactor. It was hard to feel grateful, given his reputation. 'Mr Fleet,' I said, offering him a short bow. 'How am I to repay you?'

Fleet grinned. 'By staying alive, Mr Hawkins. And keeping me entertained.' Then he drew back from the balcony into the shadows.

A few moments later I felt a tug on my coat tail. It was Benjamin, Gilbert Hand's boy, returned with a large parcel of items wrapped in an old blanket and a hastily written note from Charles.

'*My dear Tom,*' he wrote. '*Do not despair. I will find a way to help you. Until then I have given the boy some spare clothes, a cooking pot and a few other small items. For God's sake be careful. I will pray for you. Your loving friend, Charles.*'

I tucked the letter in my pocket. Benjamin had already crossed the yard towards my new quarters. Fleet's room was in the first of the prisoners' blocks, in the northwest corner of the gaol. As I strode after him I realised this must be Jack Carter's brother. He'd been asking for Ben and now I looked I could see the resemblance. I stopped him at the main ward door and tried to take the parcel from him.

'You should go to your brother,' I said. 'He's asking for you.'

He snatched the parcel back and kicked the door open. 'I'm working.'

And proud of it, too. Proud to be earning his keep. Benjamin had no need to climb the wall to escape the gaol like his brother Jack – he had found himself an occupation. But he couldn't afford to stop working, even though he knew Jack would die tonight. Before I could stop myself, I pulled out half a shilling, vowing this would be my last good deed in this rotten place. The boy's eyes widened and he went very still, holding his breath.

'Here,' I said, placing the coin in his hand. 'You're working for me tonight. Go to your brother, I'll square it with Mr Hand. Go on, run, damn you! Before I change my mind.'

Fleet's quarters were on the first floor. The room was bigger than the one I had just fled, with two beds and a large window overlooking the rackets wall and Acton's house beyond. But it was so cluttered that I could scarce move without treading on something. It was more like a pawnbroker's than a living space – a pawnbroker's ransacked by lunatics. Towers of books teetered alarmingly against the walls, and the floor was a tussle of abandoned clothing jumbled with old wigs, dented tankards, spent pipes and what appeared to be an ivory tusk protruding from beneath a pair of leather breeches.

I picked my way across the room to what I decided must be my bed and cleared it of a small library of chapbooks, broadsides, novels and even – to my surprise – a bound and printed sermon. I had not taken Fleet as a man of faith. There was a short, hand-written message on the inside cover:

> *This usefull Discourse is*
> *given to be seriously perused*
> *and to be lent*
> *about to other persons*
> *gratis but must not*
> *be sold, pawn'd or kept*
> *too long nor be ill used*
> *by any Reader*
> *Rev'd Andrew Woodburn, 1725*

The next several pages had been torn out, with some force.

I took out the coins Jakes had secured for me along with Moll's half a guinea and laid them out upon the bed. I had walked out into the Park with the urgent intention of increasing my funds and two hours later was short almost a shilling. No more good turns, I warned myself again sternly. I couldn't afford them.

I pulled off my jacket and lay down, closing my eyes. When I came to, the sun was setting, and a bell was ringing somewhere out in the Borough. I swallowed painfully, mouth dry and heavy.

My head was pounding and my body ached from my beating the night before.

I ran my fingers carefully along my ribs. I had been lucky – there was no serious damage. At times the night's attack felt like a fevered dream, so much had happened in the hours since I'd walked down that cursed alley. But now it felt close again, the memories playing round and round in my head, my cuts and bruises tingling and throbbing as if freshly made. If I had not gone with that link boy. If I had paid more attention to where we were going . . .

I made myself a pipe and limped across to a chair by the window. Outside, the nightwatchman was lighting the lamp in the middle of the yard while the prisoners wandered past in the long shadows. For the first time since my arrival, a kind of peace descended on the Marshalsea.

I was just beginning to doze off again when there was a smart rap at the door. I sat up, startled, to find a fit, dapper man of about thirty leaning against the doorway, studying me in a friendly way. He was well turned out, with a spotless lace-trimmed shirt and good wool breeches. He stepped like a dancer through the piles of Fleet's belongings and offered his hand, his small, soft brown eyes shining with good humour. Some men one likes at once. I liked Trim at once.

'How do you do, sir.'

'How do you do, Mr . . . ?'

'Trim. Just Trim,' he smiled. 'The barber.' He jerked his thumb towards the ceiling. 'We're neighbours.'

Trim's cell was on the next landing, directly above mine. He'd rented a large, well-proportioned room with two neatly made beds tucked against the far wall, though the second lay empty. The last of the sun's rays gleamed off the spotless floor and large bunches of herbs hung from the ceiling, the clean, fresh scent of marjoram and meadowsweet masking a faint trace of tobacco and the fusty smell of damp wood that clung to all the prison quarters.

Trim placed a chair in the centre of the room, and motioned for me to sit down. I walked over, the floorboards creaking and bowing underfoot. It was clear that he took pride in his business – the room was as neat and clean as a barber's in Mayfair, but he could do nothing about the general rottenness of the wards. He brought over a copper bowl of steaming hot water scented with lavender, laying it carefully on a small table next to a block of soap and a mirror with an ebony handle. He tied an apron about his waist and pulled a silver razor from its case.

Remembering my vow not to lose any more money, I leaned forward. 'This is kind of you . . . but I'm not certain I can afford . . .'

He stopped me with a wave of his hand. 'On the house. We'll be drinking at your expense tonight, Mr Hawkins,' he said, throwing a sheet across me and tucking it into my collar. 'You should look your best for the occasion.'

He washed my face with the scented water and began working the soap into my skin with firm, expert fingers. I closed my eyes and settled back, relaxing for the first time since stepping through the Lodge gate that morning.

And then he put the blade to my throat.

'Mr Hawkins . . . ?'

I opened my eyes. My hand was squeezed tight about Trim's wrist, the blade shoved violently away from my neck. For a second I fought the urge to dash the razor to the ground and strike him hard.

'Mr Hawkins,' he said again, softly. Carefully. 'Is all well, sir?'

I blinked, and took a deep breath. Dropped my hand. 'Forgive me,' I said. My face flushed with embarrassment.

'Nothing to forgive,' Trim smiled, his eyes flickering with a mix of curiosity and concern. 'You've had a shock, I think?'

My fingers reached for the bump on my head. 'I was set upon, last night. A cutpurse put a knife to my throat.'

'Ah.' He put the razor down with a soft clatter. 'I'm sorry to hear that.'

My story tumbled out – everything that had happened to me since I'd left Moll's for home the night before. A great deal, it transpired.

Trim shook his head in sympathy. 'You are bearing up remarkably well, under the circumstances. Admirable. But here, I have something that may help.' He poured some wine into a small pan and placed it on the stove, then stepped over to a set of shelves filled with glass bottles and stone pots. He ran his fingers over the jars then began tipping ingredients into a pestle and mortar. 'What bad luck you've had,' he commiserated over his shoulder.

'It was my own fault. I should have been more careful.'

He added the ground-up powder into the pan. A warm, spiced aroma filled the room. 'You shouldn't blame yourself. You weren't to know the boy would trick you.'

'Perhaps God is punishing me,' I muttered, surprising myself. Those were my father's words falling from my lips.

'Punishing you . . . ?' Trim ladled the wine into a wooden bowl and handed it to me with a frown. 'What on earth for?'

I breathed in the steam, caught the soothing scent of cloves and cinnamon. I smiled. 'For having too much fun.'

'Hah!' He eyed me appraisingly. 'I can imagine.'

Whatever Trim had mixed into the wine it did me good, as he'd promised, and I was soon relaxed enough to bear the touch of his razor against my skin without flinching. Once I was shaved he trimmed my hair close to my scalp to keep away the lice and then he washed and dressed the worst of my cuts and bruises, applying a soothing balm of his own recipe. For all this he wouldn't take a farthing. No wonder he was in a debtors' gaol.

Trim was busy sweeping the floor when a porter arrived with his supper carried over from Titty Doll's, the chophouse above the Oak. Trim asked me to join him and I accepted gratefully, mouth watering as the porter slapped down dishes of dressed mackerel with gooseberries, boiled beef and artichokes and cold ham with salad. The meat did not look in its prime but I hadn't eaten all day – and it had been a very long day.

While we were eating I asked Trim about some of the people I'd met in the gaol. After all, who knows more about a man's true character than a barber? Who sees a man at his most vulnerable and yet his most relaxed? This is the way stories are spilt – drowsily, in a scented room.

Perhaps because they *were* his customers, Trim was more charitable in his observations than I might have been. The Reverend Andrew Woodburn was a good man who did his best for the Common Side. A little weak? Oh . . . (a tilt of the head, a gentle prodding of the mackerel) *perhaps*, but his heart was in the right place. Widow Roberts – you found her proud, Mr Hawkins? Aloof? But then she *had* suffered a great loss. And the stain of the poor captain's suicide . . . one had to admire her for holding her head high. Joseph Cross was unruly and coarse, yes – but that was the drink. If he were ever sober he might be a different man altogether; who could say? And of course Gilbert Hand was as slippery as an eel but what energy! what industry! As for Acton, well, there was no denying the man was a bully, and could be vicious, yes – truly vicious. A short pause. A large swig of beer. But . . . another pause. Well, they say Bambridge up at the Fleet gaol is worse still.

'You're a generous man, Trim,' I said, helping myself to a sugar cake. 'And what of Mary Acton? Is she . . . *cheerful* company?'

'She's . . .' Trim thought for a moment. 'Spirited.'

I licked the sugar from my fingers. 'Indeed.'

'Her father was a prisoner here some years back. On the Common Side.'

'Yes, Mr Fleet told me.'

Trim's shoulders stiffened. He pushed away his plate. 'Mr Fleet . . . Yes.'

I waited, the silence hanging in the air. When Trim didn't elaborate I leaned forward. 'I've heard a great deal of my cell mate.' *None of it good.* 'What sort of a man is he, Trim? Can I trust him?'

Trim picked up his knife and cleared his throat. 'Mr Fleet is a fine gentleman,' he said loudly, while jabbing his knife towards the floor in a pointed fashion. 'Most agreeable.' And then, under his breath, 'With excellent hearing.'

Of course. I had forgotten Trim's room was directly above my own. And the floorboards were rotten.

Supper over, we scraped our chairs back from the table. Trim patted his stomach with a contented air. 'Not bad for Mrs Mack,' he conceded, and burped behind his hand. 'Good preparation for a night's drinking.'

'Will my six shillings cover the whole ward?' There were twenty men at least in my building, and the garnish was meant to buy a drink for every one of them.

'It will add nicely to the pot,' he smiled.

'And if I refuse to pay?'

Trim rose and stretched. 'Then I'm afraid we let the black dog walk.'

'The black dog . . . ?'

'Old gaol tradition. Your ward mates grab hold of you, pin you to the ground, tear all your clothes off and, well . . .' He grinned. 'Then you pay your garnish.'

'Ah.'

'Funniest one I ever saw was your new chum, Mr Fleet,' he added.

'He refused to pay?'

Trim shook his head. 'Refused to call it garnish. Stood in the middle of the Tap Room, stripped himself naked then strode up to the bar and ordered two guineas' worth of drinks for the whole room.' He paused. 'I must say, for a man of his years, he's kept himself in good order.'

. . .

I promised Trim I would join him shortly in the Tap Room and returned to my room to change my shirt. Fleet was lying stretched out upon his bed, thankfully still dressed in his banyan, though his stockings and breeches lay in a crumpled heap on the floor. He was smoking a pipe and reading a dog-eared pamphlet called

A TREATISE on the USE of
FLOGGING
In Venereal Affairs
Translated into English
By a PHYSICIAN
To which is Added
A TREATISE OF HERMAPHRODITES.

He had made notes in the margin, with exclamation points.

I could feel his eyes upon my back as I stripped off my shirt and took out the clothes Charles had sent.

'You've taken a nasty beating, Mr Hawkins.'

'I was attacked last night.' I turned to face him, buttoning up the plain white shirt. 'They took my purse. That's why I'm here.'

'Is that so.' He breathed out a long stream of smoke. There was no surprise in his voice; no question. 'Fate can be cruel.'

'I don't believe in Fate,' I said, crossly.

My response – or perhaps my ill-temper – seemed to please him enormously, but he said nothing, just stared at me in that strange, intense way of his. I felt a sudden desire to strike him, or run from the room. I had never met a man who could provoke so easily, with just a look, or a knowing smile. But I had brewed up enough drama for one day. I held up the suit Charles had sent over. The coat was a little worn but the breeches and waistcoat were new and all were a better quality than the clothes Moll lent me. They were also black – without a gold button or silver stitch to be seen. I slipped them on and was confronted with a terrible truth.

'My God. I look like a country parson.' I fixed my wig and hat and turned away from the glass before I saw my father in it. 'Will you join us in the Tap Room, Mr Fleet?'

'And ruin your evening? No, I think I shall stay here and work.' He gave me a sly smile and returned to his pamphlet.

Six

It was dark as I crossed the Park towards the Tap Room and I didn't see Kitty until she called out to me. She was standing hidden beneath the tree outside Acton's house.

'How's Jack?'

She pulled her shawl closer about her shoulders and gave a tight shake of her head.

'Are you heading for home? When do the turnkeys lock the gates?'

'Soon,' she said, her glance sliding towards the Lodge. 'But I sleep here in the prison. Mrs Bradshaw lets me bed down in the coffeehouse.'

'Oh! Are you a prisoner? Locked in with your family?' I had assumed Kitty had family in the Borough, and only worked in the gaol during the day.

'I have no family. Mr Fleet takes care of me.' She caught my expression. 'Not in *that* fashion. Ugh! He's my guardian. And five and *forty*,' she added, sticking out her tongue in revulsion. 'He's providing me with an education. Oh, stop looking at me like that,' she said, smacking my shoulder. 'A proper education. History, natural philosophy, languages. *Trade*. He's promised that when we're done there won't be a single man in England who'll marry me.'

It took me a moment to catch her meaning. 'You don't wish to marry?'

'Of course not. I shall take lovers and—'

The door to Mr Acton's lodgings opened and Mrs Roberts stepped out, her hood thrown back from her face. She flinched when she saw us together then frowned in disapproval, drawing herself straight. 'Kitty. How many times must I scold you for this? You should not be out here alone, speaking with strangers. It's not seemly.'

I bowed. 'Good evening, madam. Thomas Hawkins. We met this morning.'

She stared at me as if I were an ill-made suit she would like to return to its tailor. 'I know who you are, sir. And *what* you are, more to the point. Kitty, run along. I have something I wish to say to Mr Hawkins. Run *along*, child.'

Kitty rolled her eyes at me then ran off towards the Oak ward, lifting her skirts out of the dirt and showing a fine pair of ankles.

'She's a lively girl,' I said.

Mrs Roberts narrowed her eyes. 'She's not as worldly as she pretends. And still a maid,' she added, sharply. 'I hope to make something of her, if I can keep her unspoiled.' She took a step back as if to view me better. 'Are you a gentleman, sir? I hear wildly differing reports. Mr Woodburn seems quite taken with you, and yet you've been seen with that . . .' She glanced up towards my cell window. 'Mr Fleet is a poor choice of companion. It does not reflect well upon you.'

I gave a sigh of frustration. 'I have little choice in the matter, madam. We're not all rich widows. In any case, I'm sure you are wise enough to ignore idle gossip.'

'I am also wise enough to see beyond surface charm, sir,' she replied. 'One day, when I am free of this place, I hope to take Kitty with me. She will make an excellent lady's maid.' She set her jaw. 'But not if she is ruined by some unscrupulous rake who will toss her aside like a spent pipe the moment he's done with her.'

I laughed in astonishment. 'Mrs Roberts. I can assure you . . .'

'You do not fool me, sir,' she snapped.

'And you should not judge me by your husband's poor standards, *madam*.'

She slapped me hard across the cheek.

We stood there for a moment, staring at each other. And then she flung her hands to her face. 'Oh! Why did I do that? It is just . . . you are so . . .' She backed away, then turned and fled across the yard, her black silk skirts trailing behind her.

I was still rubbing my cheek when I heard a low, mocking laugh cut through the darkness. I peered into the gloom. Something rustled quietly – a whisper of a noise – then fell still. The hairs rose along my neck.

'Is someone there? Fleet? Mr Hand?'

Silence. A cold breeze swept through the yard, lifting clouds of grit and dust into the air. Perhaps I had imagined it. I turned on my heel and walked quickly to the Tap Room. If someone was there, let them play their games alone in the shadows.

I was greeted with a loud cheer as I entered the Tap Room, Trim slapping my back and drawing me inside with a flourish as if to say, 'Here he is! The man of the moment.' Anyone might think I had passed an exam, or won some profitable new position, not been thrown into one of the most notorious gaols in London. *Yes indeed. Well done, Mr Hawkins*, I thought wryly to myself. *You have excelled yourself.*

I went straight up to the bar, where Henry Chapman, the tapster, was waiting for me. He was by no means as pleasing on the eye as Mary Acton – he had a low, surly manner and a piggish face. And he was Acton's man; I could tell just by the swagger of him. A 'trusty', like Cross – prisoners who worked for the governor. I slapped down my six shillings garnish and he slid it quickly into his palm as if it might dissolve before his eyes.

As I settled down in a chair near the fire, Trim introduced me to the two other men at the table. Richard McDonnell was a quick-witted, garrulous Irishman known by all as Mack. He'd been a painter before he ran into debt. Now he ran Titty Doll's, the prison chophouse, with his wife. He was already merry and red-cheeked when I arrived, his fine, musical voice carrying across the Tap Room. He spent much of the evening with an unsteady hand upon my shoulder, trying to persuade me I should buy all my meals from him. 'Best meat in the Borough,' he insisted, while Trim made a choking gesture over his head, eyes crossed, hands clutching his throat.

The second man was Mr Jenings, the nightwatchman, a thin, long-limbed, fretful man of few words. 'Did I pass you in the yard just now, sir?' I asked. 'I thought you might have started your rounds.'

Jenings bit his lip. 'I've been here a half hour, sir. Did you see something?' He glanced nervously towards the window.

'Oh, no more of that nonsense, I beg you.' Mack yawned and stretched his arms above his head. 'He thinks the prison's haunted, Mr Hawkins. He'll fill your head with ghosts and devils if you'll let him.'

Jenings frowned across the table. 'I know what I saw. It was the captain, back from the grave.'

Mack snorted. 'Well, next time you see him, remind the old bastard he still owes me three guineas. I've asked Widow Roberts several times with no luck.' He pulled a sour face. 'Penny-scrimping harridan.'

'Mrs Carey swore she heard something, a few nights ago,' Trim said, scratching his jaw.

Mack groaned. 'For God's sake, will you let it rest, the pair of you! John Roberts is *not* haunting the Marshalsea. He *hated* this damned place – wouldn't come back if the angels themselves begged him . . . Ah! Here's the punch.'

And with that, the talk of ghosts was forgotten. Trim pulled out a set of dice and we played a few rounds of Hazard. As we played I recounted the adventures and misfortunes of my life and how they had led me to a cell in the Marshalsea. As the punch flowed and the rest of the ward joined us the stories grew wilder. I was part way through a somewhat intimate explanation of how to tell identical twin sisters apart when Jenings stood up, scraping back his chair.

'Mr Jenings is a little out of sorts,' Trim observed, settling down his punch with a slow, weaving hand. I was glad he'd offered to shave me at the beginning of the evening.

Mack snorted. 'Wouldn't do for our church warden to approve of such things, now would it?'

'Forgive me, sir,' I said. I hadn't realised he was Woodburn's assistant. 'I trust I haven't offended you.'

Jenings loomed over me. 'It is God's forgiveness you should seek, Mr Hawkins. But I think you know that, in your heart. I should start my rounds.' He picked up his hat and club and gave us all a short bow. 'Gentlemen.'

With my story told I sat back and let the rest of the company take over. Everyone was keen to offer advice and I was happy to take it – the more I understood about the running of the gaol the better. All was cantering along merrily enough until I mentioned my new roommate. The conversation stumbled to a halt.

'Tell me,' I said, searching their faces. 'What sort of a man is Mr Fleet?'

The men looked at one another, hoping someone else might answer.

'He's . . . not as bad as he's painted,' Trim offered, eventually. The rest of the table groaned its protest. 'Mischievous, perhaps.'

'*Mischievous?*' Mack's eyebrows shot up his forehead. 'Would you call the devil *mischievous*, Mr Hawkins?'

The table laughed along with Mack, though I noticed some of the men checked over their shoulders first. I cursed myself for mentioning Fleet at all. It had been a pleasant enough evening. I had almost forgotten that once it was over I would be escorted back to my cell and locked in with a man most of the prison feared and hated in equal measure.

'I'll tell you this,' Mack said. 'I wouldn't share a cell with him. Not for a single night. Not if you paid off my debts twenty times over.'

'For pity's sake, Mack,' Trim said, nudging him in the ribs. 'No need to scare him . . .'

'A pox on it, Trim – he has a right to know!' Mack shouted, banging his fist upon the table. He was very drunk. He leaned in, and wrapped an arm about my neck, liquor breath warm on my face. 'Your new chum murdered Captain Roberts. Everyone knows it.'

The other men were all nodding now, apart from Trim. 'I don't believe a word of it,' he declared. 'Fleet isn't capable of such a thing.'

I took a fortifying swig of punch. 'I'm glad to hear that, sir.'

'He's too *short*,' he continued, oblivious. 'Think on it for a moment, Mack. *How on earth* could Samuel Fleet carry a man as tall and heavy as the captain all the way down the stairs, across the yard, over to the Common Side and then hang him from a beam in the Strong Room *by himself*? And don't forget, Roberts would have been a dead weight by this time.' He held out his arms as if he had a body in them, then shook his head. 'No, I'm quite certain he couldn't have done it. Well.' He paused. 'Not on his own.'

I pulled out my tobacco and lit a fresh pipe. Around us, all was bright, good cheer, men singing and shouting above the din, whores brought in from the local brothels calling for more drinks. But here, at this table, the air seemed to have turned cold. 'You don't really believe Fleet murdered Captain Roberts, do you, Mack?'

'Of course he doesn't,' Trim answered hastily. And then, to Mack, 'They're sharing a room tonight, for God's sake . . .'

Mack ignored him. 'What you must understand about Mr
Fleet is, he never sleeps. He's known for it. But the night Captain
Roberts died, he slept right through till morning, so he says.
Dead to the world. Convenient, eh? As far as I can see, either
Fleet is lying, which he has been known to do *every time he opens
his mouth* ... *Or*, he slept right through, while another man burst
into the room, beat Roberts to a bloody pulp and dragged him
away to be hanged like a dog.' He leaned back. 'Which sounds
most likely to you, Mr Hawkins?' He smiled grimly. 'And that's
where you'll be sleeping tonight. "Belle Isle", Fleet calls it. His
idea of a joke, I suppose. I'll tell you something for free. You
should have taken that first room Mr Grace gave you. Better to
die of smallpox than be murdered in your bed by that devil.'

It was not easy to lighten the mood after such a conversation, but
Trim did his best and most of the men rallied soon enough. Talk
turned to money and creditors and legacies – the same refrain
running back and forth across the table, that they would be free
any day now ... that a friend had promised them faithfully ...
that their lawyer was quite certain ...

I sat quietly, letting all their hopes and schemes wash over me.
Unlike these men, I had no expectations, no promise of inheritance to come. Three years ago, I had returned home to Suffolk
to take up my position as curate in my father's church. This had
always been his dream: for his son to join him and – in time –
become vicar of the parish in his place.

Sometimes I had been able to convince myself it was my
dream, too. Other times I had wanted to scream the truth – that
I was not my father. That I did not want to spend my life serving
a quiet Suffolk parish, being dutiful and steady and good. That
the very thought of such a life put an ache in my chest as if someone had placed a giant rock upon my heart. I buried this truth as
deep as I could; tried to convince myself that I could change;
swore that once I took my vows everything would be different. I

would – miracle of miracles – transform myself and become the man my father wanted me to be.

A month before my ordination, I sat among the congregation while my father warned that if any man knew why I ought not to be ordained, 'by reason of any vice that he is addicted to, or any scandal he has given', he must speak out. There was a soft hush as he looked about the church. Neighbours and friends smiled at me. For a moment my father's gaze met mine, and I saw the tiniest flicker of pride. *I have pleased him*, I thought. *For once in my life, I have done something right in his eyes.*

Then Edmund, my stepbrother, shifted a little in his seat next to me. And before I could stop him, he rose to his feet and in a high, tremulous voice told them all about my scandalous life at college, painting me as the most debauched and infamous rake who'd ever set foot in Oxford. In a few short sentences, he tore my reputation to shreds in front of the whole parish. Then he sat back down, his hands linked neatly in his lap.

'Forgive me, brother,' he whispered, the ghost of a smile on his lips. 'I have a duty to Father. And to God.'

His mother reached over and covered his hands fondly with hers.

My father had no choice but to pass the matter on to the bishop. An investigation was made. Edmund's claims were discovered to be exaggerated . . . but not unfounded. On the day the bishop's letter arrived at the vicarage my father called me to his study. He had not spoken two words to me until then – conducting all necessary communication through my poor sister Jane, caught between us as ever. I stood with my head high, jaw clenched, as he told me that I had brought shame upon the family. 'I have worked ceaselessly for this parish all my life,' he said, with a trembling voice. 'Now they laugh at me behind my back.'

'Father, that is not true . . .'

His eyes flashed with rage. 'And what would you know of truth?' he cried. 'Your whole life is built on shame and deceit.'

As I walked away from my father's house, Jane ran after me and collapsed in my arms, tears streaming down her face. She had suffered more than anyone under my stepmother's subtle tyranny, and now I was abandoning her for ever.

'Promise you'll write, Tom. Send word that you're safe and well.'

I smiled and kissed her softly on her forehead. 'I promise.'

But I never did. God forgive me, I broke my promise. When I arrived in London I vowed that I would never contact my family again. My father had disowned me; well, then, I would disown him too. I would make my own way in the world. And that – I decided – meant abandoning Jane, too. I forced myself not to think of my beloved sister, or the man I might have become if my stepbrother had not spoken out against me. I made new friends, and fell in love with London, and told myself it was all for the best.

Now that I was here, locked up in the Marshalsea, it was harder to convince myself of that. The thought of my father discovering my wretched condition filled me with a sort of bleak horror. I would rather die, I realised, I would rather be murdered in my bed by Samuel Fleet than be revealed to him as such a miserable failure. But Jane . . . thinking of her now, I felt ashamed of myself. She couldn't run away, as I had – she had no choice but to stay and suffer. She'd been a prisoner long before I passed through the Lodge gate.

I felt a light tap on my arm. Trim was peering at me with a worried expression. 'Are you well, Mr Hawkins?'

'Yes, thank you,' I said, shaking myself from my thoughts. 'A little tired, perhaps.'

He smiled gently. 'The first night is always hard. Things will seem much better in the morning, I'm sure.'

I thanked him, and bowed to the company, who bid me good-night before returning to their drinks and their dreams of freedom.

. . .

If I had not been so out of sorts I might well have stayed in the Tap Room all night rather than return to my lodgings and confront Samuel Fleet. I took a turn about the yard in the moonlight, trying to clear my head and delaying the moment I had to return to my cell. Belle Isle indeed. How on earth would I sleep tonight?

This morning, in the daylight, the prison had reminded me of my old college. But now I knew the walls were steeped in blood. Only a few hours ago I had watched the governor beat a boy almost to death in this yard. Now he sat behind the yellow curtains of his lodgings having supper with his family. The apparent order and respectability of the Master's Side now seemed sinister and unsettling, especially in the dark. A thin veneer hiding the violence and corruption beneath. I could only guess at this on my first night in the gaol, but I would experience the truth at first hand soon enough.

As I reached the lantern in the centre of the Park a short, sturdy figure stepped into its warm glow. I gave a start. 'Mr Hand. I thought you were a ghost.'

He chuckled. 'Have they been filling your head with stories in the Tap Room? It's not ghosts you have to worry about in here, Mr Hawkins.'

We talked for a while and he offered to light me to my room. As we walked towards the prison block a sudden scream rent the air.

'God have mercy!'

I stopped dead, chilled to the bone. The cry had come from the other side of the wall. In all my life I had never heard such a desperate sound. The man cried out again, joined by another voice, and another – a hundred or more shouting their grief up into the night sky. I caught a few distinct voices. *'Spare me, Lord!'* *'God help a poor sinner!' 'Save us! Oh, God – save us!'* But the rest was just a heart-shredding din, that seemed to shake the very walls of the prison – the lamentation of souls trapped in a hell on earth.

'My God,' I said. 'What ails them?'

Gilbert Hand spat on the ground. 'It's lock-up, poor devils. Acton has 'em packed so tight they can scarce breathe. It's worse in the summer heat; I've seen 'em pull out a dozen each morning.'

'A dozen sick?'

'A dozen *dead*.'

I followed him in a daze as he led me back up to my room. Twelve prisoners dead each night? Surely that was not possible. But why would Hand lie? I felt sick to my stomach, and had to press my hand against the wall as we mounted the stairs so as not to fall. It was the thought of all those men and women dying for no good reason. And the thought that I could so easily find myself among them. In the lurching good cheer of the Tap Room I had forgotten for a moment how easy it would be to find myself thrown over the wall. I must *not* forget.

When we reached Fleet's room I staggered to my bed and buried my head in my hands.

'How's business, Mr Fleet?' Hand asked, cheerfully.

Fleet's voice drifted across the room. 'What ails the boy? Drink?'

'Nah. Just the evening chorus.'

'I see.'

I heard the chink of coins and Gilbert Hand's light footsteps as he left the room. I looked up, dizzy with shock. Fleet was pouring cordial into a fine crystal glass. He crossed over to my bed and pressed the glass into my hand saying nothing, for once. He watched me carefully as I drank.

'Thank you,' I said, when I had finished. I rubbed my forehead slowly, my hands still shaking. 'Does it become easier?'

'That's up to you, Mr Hawkins.' He poured a glass himself, knocked it back in one gulp like medicine. 'Your heart will break in here, or it will turn to stone. It's your choice.'

'And what happened to *yours*, sir?'

'Oh . . .' He drummed his fingers against his chest. 'I don't have one. Did they not tell you in the Tap Room?'

We were both quiet after that. I could still hear the cries from the Common Side – carried on the wind at first and then just in my head, churning round and round. *That could be my voice*, I thought. *A few shillings less and I could be locked away with them*. I stayed awake for as long as I could, afraid to sleep with Fleet so close by. Afraid to sleep in a dead man's bed. And when at last I slept my dreams were cruel and filled with dread. A dark alley. A man in black stepping out of the shadows. A blade gleaming blue in the moonlight.

I awoke to the pungent scent of good tobacco. The room was dark, and there was a stillness in the air that only comes at the very dead of night. Fleet sat crouched like a hobgoblin in his chair by the window, clutching his journal to his chest and staring intently out into the yard. I moved softly under the sheets, heart hammering hard against my chest. He glanced at me, his face shadowed by the candle burning beside him. He pulled the pipe from his lips.

'Go back to sleep, Mr Hawkins. You're safe enough,' he said, smoke wreathing about his face. And then he smiled. 'For tonight.'

II) *FRIDAY. THE SECOND DAY.*

Seven

The next morning dawned bright and cold; so cold my breath clouded the air. I lay on my hard, thin mattress, scarcely able to move. It was as if a dozen horses had ridden across me in the night: the beating in St Giles playing out across my body.

Up. I must get up. I could not afford to lie here. I would not fall to the Common Side; I would not join those voices crying out in the dark. I dragged back the blanket and sat up slowly, rubbed my hand across my face. Sunlight sliced bright lines across the bed.

'*Awake, thou that sleepest, and arise from the dead.*'

Fleet: already up and standing sentinel at the window, wrapped in his banyan. The *open* window. No wonder the room was so cold.

I shivered, then groaned as my bruised ribs protested. 'Close the damned window and light a fire, for God's sake.'

Fleet gave a low chuckle. 'I don't remember that in Ephesians. But you're the student of divinity, Mr Hawkins. Best to stay cold. Keeps you moving. Keeps you thinking. Alert.' He clapped his hands and rubbed them together. 'We have much to do today.'

We?

There was a light rap at the door.

'Come in, Kitty, come in! We are unlocked,' Fleet called and before I could make myself decent she had done just that, bucket and brush in hand, a couple of books tucked under one arm. She gave a little scream at the sight of me – half-naked and only half-awake – and covered her face with a dictionary of thieves' cant.

I cursed and swung my legs back under the cover.

Fleet laughed to himself as I pulled my breeches on under the sheets. 'And so we continue your education, Kitty,' he declared, sweeping his arm in my direction. 'Behold: Noble Man in his natural state.' He tilted his head. 'More like a wild boar than a man, hmm? Snores like a pig, too – I can vouch for that. How much did you see? Perhaps a drawing lesson is in order . . .'

Kitty threw her bucket and brush to the floor and stormed over to the cold hearth, averting her gaze from my side of the room. She took a tinderbox from her apron pocket and began striking the flint very hard against the steel.

Fleet gave a wicked grin. 'Excellently done, Hawkins. I'll wager you've warned Miss Sparks off men and marriage for two years at least. A good thing too, Kitty. I have greater plans for you than a life of drudgery surrounded by squalling brats.'

'Drudgery?' Kitty was on her hands and knees building the fire. She held up her palms, covered in greasy dark ash. 'Perhaps I have my *own* plans.'

I slid from the bed, every muscle screaming in protest, and stood at the window, stretching as best I could. The yard was empty save for Jenings the nightwatchman finishing his shift, narrow shoulders hunched against the cold. The wind must have whipped through his old, thin bones last night. Joseph Cross appeared in the Lodge gate, swigging from a tankard. From this distance he looked small enough to squash beneath my thumb and fingers – a satisfying thought. He shouted something coarse at Jenings while grabbing at his cock, his baying laughter echoing off the walls of the gaol.

I watched for a moment longer but no one else came out into the yard though I could see from the sun that it must be past eight o'clock. I turned back from the window. 'Are we not free to leave our rooms?'

Fleet was leaning against the wall by the hearth, watching Kitty as she worked. He behaved quite differently in her company, his expression lighter, indulgent even. Kitty had called him her guardian and he did seem protective of her, in his own fashion. But if she were indeed his ward, why keep her working here in the Marshalsea? Fleet was clearly not in prison for debt – he could afford to send her somewhere safe.

'What news from the night?' he asked her.

She paused in her work, leaning back on her heels. 'Three pulled dead from the sick ward. And Jack . . .' She turned back to the fire.

Jack Carter. Woodburn had said the boy would not last the night, but still the shock of it ran through me. He had been murdered in front of my eyes. The whole prison had stood and watched . . . and done nothing. 'How does his brother fare, Kitty?' I asked.

She blew softly on the kindling, the flames flickering and dancing along the wood. 'He stayed by Jack's side in the Strong Room all night. It shook him. Very bad.' She glanced up at me for the first time. 'But he is grateful to you.'

Fleet looked startled. 'Benjamin Carter . . . grateful to *you*? What on earth for?'

'There's no mystery,' I replied. 'I gave the boy half a shilling to watch over his brother in the Strong Room last night.'

'But . . .' He stared at me across the jumble of the room, brows furrowed. 'What on earth did you hope to gain from it?'

'It was for charity, sir. To give them both some comfort before the end.'

Fleet scrunched up his face, as if he had just bitten hard into an unripe lemon. 'Half a shilling? For *charity*?' he yelped. 'What the devil were you thinking, flinging your coins about in such a fool- ish manner? Fuck the stars and all the heavens . . . If I'd wanted a condescending idiot for a roommate I would have asked Mr Jenings.'

'Well. Forgive me if I've caused offence, sir,' I muttered.

Fleet grunted, irritable, as if he might *consider* it.

Kitty clapped the coal dust from her hands and rose from the fireplace. 'Ben saw the ghost last night.'

'What's this?' Fleet rounded on her at once. 'When? Where?'

'The stroke of midnight.'

'The *stroke of midnight*. Impeccable timing.'

'It walked right past the Strong Room, Ben said. Knocking on the walls and crying out for vengeance.' She rapped her knuckles on the wall, *knock . . . knock . . . knock*. 'Don't *laugh*,' she said, glaring at Fleet. 'Poor Ben half-died of fright.'

'Indeed? Which half?'

Kitty ignored him. 'He ran out into the Common yard and there it stood, all pale and terrible in the moonlight, with a noose hung about its neck. It cried out, "Murder! Oh, dreadful murder! Avenge me!"' (She acted this part very well, with her hands outstretched.) 'And then it vanished in front of his eyes.'

'*In front of his eyes*, Kitty?'

'He called the alarm and Mr Jenings searched the whole Common yard. He found a handkerchief dropped by the wall, embroidered with the initials J.R. It was wet with blood.'

Fleet snorted, then began pacing the room in a restless way, kicking aside books and clothes in his path. 'Captain John Roberts, returned from the grave.' He stuck his hands in his banyan pockets. 'I should like a word or two with him.'

I frowned. 'You don't believe this nonsense, surely?'

'It isn't nonsense,' Kitty said, wounded.

'Belief is not the issue,' Fleet said. 'Facts — we must have facts.' He clapped his hands together sharply, as if summoning them to him. 'Where's Benjamin now, Kitty?'

'Next door in the chapel. Mr Woodburn is saying prayers for Jack's soul.'

Fleet curled his lip. 'Damned meddlesome fool. We must bring the boy here at once, before the memory fades.'

I thought of Acton, his bloody fist wrapped about the gaol. 'Before he's silenced.'

'Aye, indeed,' Fleet grunted. 'Kitty. Run and fetch him for me. Tell him I'll pay if he comes to me right away.' He raised an eyebrow. 'I believe half a shilling is the current *extortionate* rate.'

With Kitty gone I summoned the courage to defy Fleet and closed the window, shutting out the icy chill at last. I soon realised my mistake. Fleet's gentle, indulgent side had left the room along with Kitty. I swear I could feel his anger burning my skin even before I turned to face him.

'Open it,' he said, in a low, dark voice.

For one foolish moment I considered challenging him – just to see what he would do. I was twenty years younger and almost a head taller. Then I caught his expression and I thought, *he'll murder you, Tom. That's what he'll do.*

I opened the window.

Fleet grinned.

I picked up the black coat Charles had sent me and stalked to the door with as much dignity as I could muster. 'Well. I will not sit here and freeze to death. I shall take a turn in the Park.'

'You're half-frozen so you'll take a turn outside? Hardly rational, sir.' He shook his head like a disappointed tutor. 'You can't go out; it's Friday. Sit yourself by the fire, smoke a pipe and I'll call for breakfast. And stop *sulking*. Can't abide it.'

'Friday?' I sat down by the hearth, pointedly rubbing my hands and holding my palms up to the flames.

'Court day. No prisoners allowed in the yard. Upsets all those delicate gentleman lawyers. Poor, sensitive fellows.' He stuck his head out of the window and called down to a porter to fetch us some rolls, milk porridge and coffee, then began prowling the room again. Once in a while he would pause, pick up some discarded shirt or tankard or letter and stare at it for a moment, before dropping it somewhere else. His idea of housekeeping, I supposed.

During one turn of the room he upended a boot and an old pistol clattered out on to the floor. He held it up by the barrel. '*Here* you are.' He kissed it fondly, then dropped it back in the boot and returned to the window. 'I am awake,' he pronounced, stretching out his arms and yawning in an extravagant fashion. 'I have been asleep these past weeks. Hibernating like a great, wild bear.'

'Or a hedgehog.'

'Indeed. Like a great, wild hedgehog.'

The porter arrived with our breakfast and Fleet joined me by the fire. I cupped the dish of coffee in my hands and blew gently on the surface, recognising its rich, bitter aroma; this came from Sarah Bradshaw's coffeehouse. The scent transported me back to the day before, standing by the window as Acton raised his whip for the first time. His boot crunching down upon the boy's back.

Fleet nudged my plate. 'You should eat, sir.'

I picked up my porridge and ate slowly while my roommate lit a pipe and settled back in his chair. He'd said we had much to do today, but I chose not to ask him what he meant by it. I did not work for Mr Fleet and he did not own my time, no matter what he thought. But I was curious to hear Ben's ghost story and until then we were trapped together. After that I thought I might take myself upstairs and spend the day with Trim – I couldn't leave the ward building but our rooms were left unlocked, at least.

I glanced up to find Fleet studying me in that strange way of his. It really was the most uncomfortable experience. Something about those peat-black eyes, almost unnatural in their darkness. They were not truly black, of course – no man's are. They would be brown, the darkest brown if you stepped close enough to look. But what sane man would do such a thing? There were secrets hiding in those eyes; private jokes and sharp observations. They were not the eyes of an innocent man.

The eyes of a killer, then . . . ? Perhaps – but not a reckless one. Not a bold and vicious bully such as Acton. Fleet was not a hot-tempered killer. If he wanted a man dead he would plot and plan and wait patiently for the perfect moment to strike. This is what I believed of my cell mate after one night in gaol. And in this – if nothing else – I was proved right.

'Why are you locked away here, Mr Fleet?' I asked, if only to break the spell of his stare. 'Not for debt, clearly.'

'Clearly,' he acknowledged, through a stream of smoke. He scratched his jaw, fingers rasping against days-old black and grey stubble, before selecting a book from the floor. He opened it at the frontispiece:

THE TRUE AND GENUINE
ACCOUNT OF
MATTHEW DANCE
HIGHWAYMAN AND THIEF

After a short passage expounding upon Dance's infamous life and death, came the following words:

LONDON:
Printed for, and Sold by, S. FLEET in *Russel-Street, Covent-Garden;* MDCCXXV.

'You're a printer.'

'Printer, bookseller, translator. Scribbler.' Fleet tossed the book back on the floor. 'Purveyor of obscenity, murder and perversion in the main.'

And then I remembered the little shop with the green door at the far end of Russell Street, only a short stride from Moll's. Books and pamphlets piled high in the window and strewn across the floor, just as they were here. 'The Cocked Pistol!' I exclaimed, recalling the sign above the door. *Proprietor, S. Fleet*. 'You have an excellent shop, sir.'

Fleet inclined his head in regal acknowledgement.

'How did it lead you here?'

He paused, recalling some painful memory – or composing a fresh lie. 'I printed a pamphlet for a friend last winter. It was regarded as somewhat . . . *inflammatory*. When I refused to give up his name I was charged with seditious libel and slung in here to rot.'

A pretty story, I thought, and probably no more than that. I was not sure I believed in Fleet's loyalty to anything save himself. 'Libel? Against whom?'

Fleet shrugged. 'Parliament. The Church. The king.' He sucked his pipe with a thoughtful air. 'It was my own fault. Gave them the excuse they'd been waiting for. I know too much, Mr Hawkins. Too many years spent taking down confessions from murderers and thieves and whores . . . and hearing all about the fine ladies and gentlemen who crossed their paths and their beds. It's not wise, to know so many secrets.' He smiled. 'But it keeps life interesting.'

At nine o'clock the doors to the Lodge were pushed open and carriages and horses began to stream through the gates, clattering into the cobbled yard. Turnkeys and porters rushed about as the lawyers chattered idly to one another, black robes billowing in the sharp September wind. Acton strolled among them in his bright red waistcoat, patting shoulders, shaking hands and laughing, the very image of a genial host – though I saw a couple of men turn away to avoid his greeting. John Grace, Acton's head clerk, followed stiffly behind his master, clutching the black ledger from the Lodge and snapping orders to the servants. There was something thin and bloodless about him that turned my stomach; or perhaps it was just the memory of him sending

me into that pox-infected room the day before – his cold indif-
ference to another man's fate.

A few minutes later a gentleman of about thirty years of age
rode through the gates on a fine black stallion, grinning and
waving cheerfully at those he passed. The whole gaol seemed
to sit up straighter as he jumped down from his horse. His
clothes were well-cut and of the latest fashion, with good lace
cuffs and fine stitching at the pockets. He carried a gold-topped
cane, which he used to get the attention of a nearby lawyer,
prodding him in a playful way. They talked for a moment, the
lawyer whispering in the other man's ear. Then they laughed
and shook hands.

Fleet had joined me at the window. 'Edward Gilbourne.
Deputy prothonotary.'

'What the devil does that mean?'

'Glorified clerk.'

I frowned. 'I thought John Grace held that position.'

'Grace is head clerk of the *gaol*. Gilbourne works for the
Palace Court. Process must be followed, Mr Hawkins. You can't
just throw men into prison and let them rot. That would be
cruel. They must have their time in court. Their case must be
heard, their creditors must be called to account . . .' He gave a
mirthless grin. '*Then* they can rot.'

Men were crowding round Gilbourne now, eager to secure his
attention. He nodded politely to them all, but seemed anxious to
leave the yard. 'He's popular with the lawyers.'

'Powerful,' Fleet corrected. 'He controls the order of the day.
Which he can change, if he chooses. For a fee.'

'He's young for such a post.'

'A prodigy,' Fleet shrugged, sarcastic, and sat back down by
the fire. He had seen enough, it seemed. A few moments later
Mrs Roberts crossed the yard, weaving her way through the
huddles of clerks and lawyers straight towards Edward Gilbourne.
They spoke briefly, urgently, Gilbourne's face filled with concern.

For a moment he touched her arm and Mrs Roberts placed her black-gloved hand on his. Then Acton joined them, clapping Gilbourne hard on the back. Gilbourne dropped his hand at once, but I noticed he and Mrs Roberts shared a brief, knowing glance before she bowed and moved away. Were they lovers, I wondered? I touched my cheek, remembering the sharp slap she'd given me the night before.

The lawyers and clerks were drifting towards the Palace Court when a large, gilded carriage raced into the yard, followed closely by a gentleman in a black suit and hat, riding a chestnut colt. As the carriage rolled to a halt, liveried servants jumped down and opened the door, pulling the steps to the ground and clearing a path to the Court. Acton stood to one side, bowing deeply as a heavily wigged and powdered gentleman squeezed his way out, the carriage tilting with his weight as he stepped down. Flunkies hovered about him, ready to be flattened if he fell.

'Sir Philip Meadows,' Fleet intoned from the fireplace. 'Knight's Marshal.' How he knew this without looking I couldn't say. Perhaps he recognised the rattle of the carriage.

I was so preoccupied with Sir Philip's grand entrance that I barely noticed the gentleman in the black suit as he swung down from his horse. It was only when he removed his hat and peered up at the prison windows that I realised who it was.

'Charles!' I cried, leaning out of the window.

He grinned when he saw me, and waved his hat, hand shielding his eyes from the sun. And then he paused, and I watched his smile vanish, as he remembered where we were. 'One moment,' he called, holding up a finger. 'I will speak with the governor.'

I nodded, unable to speak. Charles was my friend and my brother. His good opinion mattered to me more than anyone else's in the world. For him to see me like this, reduced to a common debtor, trapped in his patron's gaol, was so shaming it was as if I had been grabbed by the throat and shaken.

Charles and I had taken different paths in life but until today I had considered us as equals. Indeed I had thought myself the luckier soul – living by my wits and free from the stultifying life of a curate. I could never be the man he was – I didn't have his patience or his even temper – but I had always planned to turn my fortunes around one day. Well, *planned* is perhaps too strong a term. I had *dreamed* of turning my fortunes around. *Talked* of it. *Swore* I would do it. But planned it? That would have required time and concentration and *work*, God help me. It would have meant making a decision one day and keeping to it the next. How was that to be achieved? I couldn't fathom it.

And so here I was, a prisoner in a debtors' gaol – relying on the kindness of an old friend who had already given me all his savings. Savings I had lost and had little hope of returning. Standing at the cell window, watching as Charles pleaded with Acton to let me out into the yard, I understood at last how far I had fallen. How deeply I had failed.

'Sir Philip's curate,' Fleet said, startling me. He had slipped behind me without making a sound. 'You know him?'

Charles was gesturing up at the window while the warden shook his head and shrugged his apology. Even Sir Philip himself paused and frowned up in my direction for a moment, before lumbering away with a fat pout of disapproval on his face.

There was a dance of silver from Charles' hand to Acton's and suddenly the warden was nodding and smiling. 'Mr Hawkins,' he boomed, and beckoned me down.

I needed no further encouragement. I sprang from the window and gathered up my jacket.

Fleet nodded his consent. 'Very well, run along. I shall interrogate the boy alone.'

I had almost forgotten Benjamin Carter and his ghost story. I was sure it would be diverting, but it could not compete with seeing Charles, and escaping my cell. I grabbed Fleet's hand, suddenly grateful now that I was free to leave his company.

'Don't be too long,' he warned. There was a sharp edge to his voice, a reminder of the debt I owed him. 'This talk of Roberts coming back from the dead is foolish prattle. But someone is using it to play a game with us – and a clever one at that. Things are moving at last, Mr Hawkins, I can feel it. We shall stir this hornet's nest together, you and I!'

I laughed and raced down the stairs towards Charles and freedom. It was only later that I questioned the wisdom of stirring a hornet's nest. As for clever games, I should have guessed that Fleet was the master of those. But by the time I realised that, it was much too late.

Eight

When I reached the yard Charles threw his arms about me. 'Tom. My God, what ill luck. I can scarce believe it. Are you hurt?'

'I'm fine,' I said, though in truth I was bruised from head to foot, and the bump at the base of my skull still throbbed whenever I turned my head. 'Thank you for these,' I added, sweeping a hand over my black suit. 'I look almost respectable.'

'Almost,' Charles smiled, but his eyes were sad. 'Mr Acton.' He turned to the warden and gave a polite incline of his head. 'Would you permit me to take Mr Hawkins out into the Borough – perhaps to the George?'

Pleasure sparked in Acton's cunning blue eyes, quickly dampened. Oh, to be asked a favour by a man of true standing and good reputation! To have the power of yea or nay over him! 'My regrets, Mr Buckley.' He widened his hands as if the decision were not of his choosing. 'Mr Hawkins was only brought in yesterday and I don't yet have his measure. I'm sure he's an honest gentleman . . .'

Charles looked offended. 'There is no doubt of it,' he shot back, which was good of him under the circumstances, and not entirely accurate.

'. . . but I can't permit him to wander in and out of my Castle as he pleases, especially on court day. The other prisoners . . .'

Acton gestured at the men and women peering out from the windows above us. Many of them were indeed glowering in envy at my release into the yard. But this was not the real reason for Acton's refusal. This was about exercising his control over Sir Philip's man. Reminding everyone who was truly in charge of the Marshalsea.

Charles, however, seemed oblivious to this. 'Would a donation to the prison reassure you, Mr Acton?' he asked, pulling half a crown out of his purse. My fingers began to itch. 'I will vouch for him.'

'And will you vouch for his twenty pounds of debt, Buckley? If he runs?' Acton tilted his head, genuinely interested.

Charles sighed – in truth his whole body seemed to sigh in upon itself, so that he appeared to shrink a good few inches before my eyes.

Acton bared his teeth, amused. 'Perhaps not such *great* friends, after all . . . ?'

I suppose it was too much to dream – to be allowed to walk out of the Lodge gate and back into the Borough on my first day in gaol. Trim had explained to me the night before that Acton allowed some of the more trusted prisoners out into the town – with a guard – so they could manage their affairs and keep enough money flowing into their pockets to pay him their rent. It made good sense in other ways – gave him a reputation for gentlemanlike behaviour to counter all those rumours in the Southwark bars of cruelty and sickness and worse. And it kept the prisoners on their best behaviour, on the Master's Side at least. No one wanted to lose their privileges.

On the other hand, if a prisoner escaped from the Marshalsea then as governor Acton would be held responsible for their debts. And to be fair he was right to mistrust me. Now I had spent a night in his Castle I would have fled to the Mint or back to Moll's . . . anywhere, given the chance. I was only one small stumble away from the Common Side. If Acton took against me. If Fleet grew tired of me. I had not forgotten those pitiful cries rising up into the sky last night – the screams of the damned. So yes, I would have run if Acton had let me out of the prison that morning. My God, I would have run and never looked back.

As all the wards were locked and the Tap Room closed, we had no choice but to head for the Palace Court building. Passing beyond the Court porch we found that Sarah Bradshaw's coffee-house was also closed, so we carried on upstairs towards Mack's chophouse, Titty Doll's, squeezing past lawyers and clerks and creditors waiting to be called back to court, arguing on the land-ings, papers clutched to their chests or waved as weapons in each other's faces. Their voices echoed from the walls and all said the same thing. Money. Who has it, who owes it, how can we make some more? *Your client owes me three pounds and ten shillings. We were promised three guineas last month. To sign this document? Threepence, sir. He expects his aunt to leave him twenty pounds and I have it on good authority she is taken ill, very ill indeed.* One would think there were no other conversation to be had in the world, no other thought in a man's head. And there wasn't – not here.

'Mr Hawkins!' Mr Woodburn called, peering down from the highest landing. He waved his broad-brimmed hat over the banis-ter. 'And is that the Reverend Charles Buckley I spy with you? Bless my soul! You are acquainted, sirs?'

Charles gave a low curse then called out, pleasantly, 'Why, Mr Woodburn! A good day to you, sir.'

We pushed our way towards him, up the stairs and past the Oak – the women's ward. I cast a longing glance towards the thick double doors. I had yet to meet the more genteel women debtors – the Tap Room was too low a place, fit more for ladies of the town. I didn't expect them to visit Fleet for afternoon tea, either. Sadly the entrance to the Oak was locked tight while court was in session.

I supposed at some point my own case would be heard and I would be forced to throw myself on the mercy of Mr Fletcher, my landlord, who was furious with me for fucking his wife – or for not fucking her. Either way, I did not expect him to be in a forgiving mood. I wondered again who could have written that poisonous note to him . . . but then it slipped my mind, and I did not think of it again. It was foolish of me to forget it.

'My dear sirs,' Woodburn sighed when we reached the final landing. He had an arm about young Ben Carter's shoulder, clutching him tight as if he might slide to the floor. I didn't recognise the boy at first, he was so hunched in upon himself. They made quite a pair: the old, well-fed cleric in his wilfully shabby clothes and the boy, too thin, too serious, too wary for his age.

Woodburn clasped both of Charles' hands in his, releasing Ben who swayed on the spot, exhausted.

'I'm sorry about Jack,' I said in a quiet voice. 'He was a brave lad.'

He gazed up at me, with red-rimmed eyes. I had the impression he did not share my opinion of his brother. 'I've a message for you.'

'From Mr Hand?'

'No, sir.' There was a slurred, vacant tone to his voice, as if shock and grief had wrung all the life from him. 'From the ghost. From Captain Roberts.'

'Indeed?' I stared at him, astonished, and started to smile.

A flash of anger. 'I swear it! On my soul!' His fists bunched at his sides.

'Very well, Ben,' I said, gently. The poor boy had been through enough – it cost nothing to humour him. 'And what did he want with me?'

His fists unclenched a little. 'He said he must speak with you tonight. Midnight – beneath the Court porch. Alone. You mustn't tell a soul.'

'What's this?' Woodburn glanced over, curious.

'We were just speaking of poor Jack,' I said, remembering Fleet's description of the chaplain. *Meddlesome*. 'I'm sure he was glad to have his brother there, at the end.'

Woodburn's expression softened. 'Aye, and all thanks to you, sir.' He turned to Charles. 'Your friend understands the true meaning of charity – a rare gift in this wicked world.'

'Indeed.' Charles coughed back the laugh forming in his throat. 'Tom's a veritable Lot in Sodom.'

Woodburn nodded absently. 'Well, I'm afraid we must leave you,' he said, pushing the boy towards the stairs. He lowered his voice. 'We are to visit Mr Fleet. He insists on hearing this business about a ghost and I will not have Benjamin see him alone. The man's wicked. Wicked to the core.'

'My cell mate,' I explained to Charles.

He stared at me in alarm. 'You're sharing a room with *Samuel Fleet*?'

'Do you know him, Charles?'

He shook his head a fraction, as if to say, *not here*.

Woodburn was fidgeting with his collar, ill at ease. 'What do you make of this ghost story, gentlemen? I can scarce believe it, but it is not like the boy to lie.' He gave an anxious frown. 'Perhaps he *did* see something. Scripture teaches us—'

'He has just spent the night watching over his dying brother, all alone in the dark,' Charles interrupted mildly. He patted the chaplain's arm. 'We would all see ghosts, would we not?'

Woodburn did not look convinced, but he nodded all the same. 'Aye, I'm sure you're right. Well, best not keep the devil waiting, eh?' He bowed and excused himself, pulling Ben along silently in his wake.

Titty Doll's was a large, dingy, smoke-filled room at the back of the Court Palace, on the top floor. Sarah Bradshaw's coffeehouse made the yard its own theatre. The Tap Room offered views – wanted or not – of the Common Side. But the windows in Titty

Doll's were high up by the ceiling, granting only snatches of sky and the occasional bird wheeling and swooping far in the distance. Of all the places to dine in the Marshalsea, this was the place to hide, to forget where you were. For that reason alone the prices were higher. Luckily for me, Charles was paying.

With most of the prisoners locked up in their rooms the chop-house was quiet, just the soft murmur of court business and low gossip passed among a straggle of customers. A fat, sweating lawyer was slobbering over a late breakfast of glistening, fricas-seed tripe and calves' feet, while a pale-faced clerk ordered raw milk and bread from Mrs Mack.

'Long night,' he explained, rubbing his forehead with inky fingers. 'I'm paying for it, Mrs Mack.'

'No sympathy,' she replied cheerfully. 'Lord and master's groaning into his pillow this morning, same reason. *Every* morn-ing,' she corrected herself and smiled at us. 'Settle yourselves, gents. With you in a moment.'

As we moved towards a quiet table by the fire we passed a trio of young whores recovering from a night locked in with the turnkeys, ladling out glasses of punch and miming scenes from the night to one another. They nudged each other and stifled giggles as Charles passed by in his black suit and white neck scarf, but he just smiled and raised his hat.

'Ladies.'

They laughed more warmly at that and called out a menu of services, prices discounted for kind-hearted clerics such as himself. He shook his head politely. I bowed to them with a flourish once his back was turned.

Mrs Mack returned to take our order. She was, in essence, Not Mack — tiny, round, calm, sober. Short on words. We ordered a bottle of wine from her, after which Charles lapsed into silence.

I lit a pipe and waited. He had grown into his looks these past few years. I always thought of Charles as he was at school:

plump-cheeked and bashful, brows drawn into an anxious expression, as if he were afraid of the things he did not know. But he was a man now, certain of himself and his place in the world, all his childhood worries smoothed away. Or buried, perhaps.

The wine arrived. Charles poured himself a glass and stared into its red velvet depths. 'I have spoken with Sir Philip.'

Ah. I took a long gulp of wine and waited.

'I'm sorry, Tom. He refuses to help.' Charles pushed his wine away. He looked wretched. 'I begged him . . .'

'Please, Charles.' I touched his arm. 'I understand.'

'I'm afraid he remembers you. A little too well.'

I frowned in confusion. I was sure I had never spoken with Sir Philip in my life . . . And then I remembered – a warm spring morning a few months before. I'd been weaving my way home via Mayfair when I saw Charles from a distance, standing outside Sir Philip's house with a boy of about sixteen, about to step into a fine carriage. I had spent the night drinking out on the river and it had seemed a tremendously good idea to shout his name down the street.

'The Reverend Charles Matthew Buckley!' I yelled heartily, just as Sir Philip puffed his way down the path.

Charles had turned, startled. I held up my hand, and a bottle, in greeting.

'Oh, Lord,' I said now, groaning at the memory. 'What on earth did I say to him?'

'Nothing,' Charles sighed. 'I rather foolishly introduced you to his son. He told you he would be attending Oxford shortly. You asked if I had furnished him with a list of the cleanest brothels.'

'A practical question.'

Charles did not smile. 'I bundled him into the carriage before you could do any more damage, but Sir Philip heard you. It took a long time to convince him I had *never* attended a brothel in my life.'

'But you—'

'That is not the point,' he hissed. 'I was a student then. A foolish boy.' And then he chuckled, despite himself. 'And you led me astray.'

'Willingly, as I recall.'

'But I could have lost my position, Tom,' he added, softly. 'D'you know, I swore I would have nothing more to do with you after that.' He threw up his hands in mock despair. 'Yet here I am.'

'You're a good friend, Charles.'

'And you're a wretched one,' he said, then laughed and took a swig of wine. 'But heaven help me, I've missed your company.' He huddled closer. 'So. What is to be done? How are you to pay your debts?'

'I have plans . . .' I replied, sounding vague even to myself. 'They play backgammon under the porch here . . .'

'No,' Charles sighed, drawing the sound out until it transformed from a word into a low, exasperated moan. 'No, no. That will not do, Tom. You cannot live in such a desperate, haphazard fashion — look where it has brought you!'

I looked about me and caught the eye of one of the turnkeys' whores. She winked and raised her glass.

'There is nothing else to be done,' Charles was saying, oblivious. 'You must write to your father.'

My eyes snapped back to his. 'I will do no such thing.'

'He would forgive you in a heartbeat . . .'

'Would he indeed,' I muttered, glaring at Charles across the table. 'How *generous*. You have stayed in touch, I suppose? He always loved you best.'

'For pity's sake!' Charles cried, exasperated. 'Listen to my advice for once, I beg you! Don't you understand? Your *life* is in danger! You are hanging by a *thread*.' He pinched his thumb and forefinger together. 'If we do not pull you to safety now you will fall so far and so fast you will be lost for ever.' He swallowed hard, then continued, more quietly. 'Write to your father. Apologise for your mistakes and I promise you, he will welcome you back with open arms.'

'My mistakes?' I pressed my hand to my chest. '*Mine?* And what of his mistakes? My mother was not cold in her grave when he brought that woman into our home and that wretched son of hers, that venomous snake in the grass . . .'

'Yes, yes,' Charles groaned. 'I remember. But you are the one locked in prison, not your father. Forgive me, Tom – but you can't afford to be proud.'

I scowled but said nothing. Charles should have known better than to mention my father. I fiddled grumpily with my pipe, packing the tobacco as he gave me his well-meaning advice. It took me a moment to realise he had stopped speaking. I glanced up to see him watching me, tears in his eyes.

'I should not have abandoned you. You looked after me at school.' He looked away. 'I should look after you now.'

'Nonsense,' I shrugged, lighting my pipe. 'You're not my keeper. We chose different paths, that's all; you mustn't blame yourself for that.'

'But I'm afraid for you, Tom. Men die so quickly in this place and you have a knack for trouble. You must watch yourself with Acton; he can turn like *that*.' He snapped his fingers. 'Do you know what he was, before he came to the Marshalsea? A *butcher*! Fine training for a governor. You have no idea, the blood on that man's hands.'

I poured myself another glass of wine and drained it quickly. 'So why does your dear patron employ such a monster?'

A delicate flicker of shame crossed Charles' face. 'He keeps the peace.'

I raised an eyebrow.

'And makes a profit,' he admitted, reluctantly. 'More than you can imagine.' He was about to say more when Mrs Mack arrived with a fresh bottle of claret. He waited until she was out of earshot before continuing. 'Sir Philip did have one suggestion on that score.' He bit his lip. 'But are you *sure* you will not write to your father, Tom?'

I scowled at him through the pipe smoke.

'Very well,' he sighed. He looked about him and lowered his voice. 'You have heard about Captain Roberts?'

'I am sleeping in his bed, Charles.'

He shivered. 'Yes, of course. Well. Sir Philip is under a great deal of pressure from his widow to look into the matter.'

'The matter of his murder.'

Charles hushed me with a look. 'It's not wise to speak of this in here,' he muttered. 'But yes, he would like the business resolved. All this talk of ghosts and murder . . .'

'Bad for profits?' I suggested in a sour tone. 'Poor Sir Philip.'

Charles blushed. 'You're right. I should not have mentioned it—'

'No, no,' I interrupted hurriedly. 'If there is a deal to be made I'll hear it. Tell me. What does he want of me?'

'He . . . he wants you to unmask the killer.'

I blinked, surprised. '*Unmask the killer?* How in God's heaven would I do that?'

'I have no idea,' Charles confessed. 'But I would start with your roommate.' He pursed his lips in disgust. 'Of all the men to share a cell with . . .'

'And if I succeed?'

Mrs Mack returned to the table again, this time with our dinner: a plate of oysters and a shoulder of lamb with cauliflowers. She must have noticed that we stopped talking whenever she appeared but she paid us no mind.

'It's no good speaking in here,' Charles said, after she'd gone. 'I will send a letter through Gilbert Hand tonight. Be sure the seal isn't broken.' He chewed unhappily on a bit of gristle then washed it down with a mouthful of claret. 'I still think you should write to your father.'

'I swear to God, Charles – if you mention my father again I will push your face in those oysters.'

We stayed in Titty Doll's for another two hours, sharing a pint of sherry and recalling happier times as the clouds rolled past in the high chophouse windows. Then Charles reached for his hat and declared it was time he called for a chair. I had the sudden urge to grip his wrist and beg him to stay. The truth was, I was afraid of spending another night locked up in here, at the mercy of Fleet and Acton and Cross. Some men seemed able to navigate these dangers – men like Trim and Mack. But Charles was right; I had always had a knack for trouble. Still, I could not cower in Titty Doll's for ever.

The court was still in session as we stepped outside and the yard was empty save for Jenings, the nightwatch, lighting the lamp in the twilight. The darkening sky reminded me of what Ben Carter had promised – that Captain Roberts' ghost would visit me tonight at midnight under the Palace Court. A very punctual ghost, as Fleet had observed. I told Charles. 'I do hope he'll tell me who murdered him. That would be tremendously helpful.'

Charles looked puzzled. 'What the devil would Roberts' ghost want with you?'

'Perhaps he wishes to apologise for his widow. She slapped me across the face last night for no good reason.'

We had reached the Lodge. Charles paused, and considered me for a moment. 'How long have you been locked in the Marshalsea, Tom?'

'A day. And a half.'

'*A day and a half* . . .' he murmured, wonderingly. 'I think you should go to your room. Hide under the bed for the rest of the night.'

'I can't. I'm invited to supper with the governor. And his wife, Mary.' I grinned, peering up at the governor's lodgings. The yellow curtains were closed, but there was a light glowing behind them. 'Have you seen her . . . ?'

'For God's sake, don't tell me you have designs on her? The governor's *wife*?' Charles spluttered. 'Well, it would speed your way out of gaol, I grant you. Straight through the gate in a coffin . . .'

'Well, then . . . Perhaps you should smuggle me out in your chair tonight? No one would blame you for it, surely.'

The blood drained from his face. 'Tom,' he said, gripping my arm as if I might jump up and run through the Lodge gate at that very moment. 'If you escape, Acton will hold me responsible for your debt. I would lose everything. I could be thrown in gaol myself.'

'Ah.' If Moll were here, I knew what she would say: *What of it? He'd find his own way out. You owe no debt to him; not really. Perhaps Sir Philip would take pity on him. Perhaps God would save him; he'd be more likely to save Charles than you, Tom Hawkins.*

'I'd best set off for home,' Charles said sharply.

We paused at the Lodge gate while Cross grumbled out of his room, jangling his keys and spitting on the floor. Whatever he'd paid those whores, it wasn't enough. While he was unlocking the door Charles drew me back a little way and whispered in my ear. 'Watch for my letter tonight.' He squeezed my arm then walked out to freedom.

Cross turned to face me. There were bruises blooming at his throat where Jakes had half-throttled him on my behalf, and his lip was split where I'd punched him. For a moment, I almost felt sorry for him.

'D'you think your friend will save you, Hawkins?' he asked.

I shrugged, determined not to let him bother me. 'Perhaps.'

He grinned. 'Well, don't count on it. No such thing as friends in here.'

Nine

Back in the yard, Gilbert Hand was standing sentinel beneath his lamppost, stamping on the ground to keep warm. Waiting to squeeze me for information, I thought, from the knowing grin on his face. 'You're to meet the ghost tonight, I hear,' he said.

'Ben told you?'

'Ben tells me everything, Mr Hawkins. He's my boy.'

'He must have dreamed it.'

Hand shook his head slowly. 'He's not a dreamer.' He grabbed my shoulder and pulled me close, bringing his lips to my ear. I felt the scratch of his grey and gold stubble against my skin. 'If you see Roberts, ask him what happened to the money.'

'Money? What money?'

But Hand was already walking away to share a pipe with one of the court clerks.

I was feeling a little out of sorts from all the drink I'd taken with Charles, so I headed to Bradshaw's for a bowl of coffee. Mrs Bradshaw herself was asleep in her chair, leaving Kitty in charge at the hearth, her back to the room. A couple of elderly court lawyers were seated by the window, picking at an unsatisfactory late dinner, lifting the gristle up with their forks as if expecting to find a choice cut of steak hiding shyly beneath. Otherwise the coffeeshop was empty, the prisoners still locked in their wards even now at the end of the day. I wondered if it were the same for the Common Side – after all, there was no need to keep them locked in as all the court business was conducted on this side of the wall. No need except spite – and Acton was full of that.

I felt something press on my foot and discovered little Henry, Acton's son, crawling along the floor, chubby fingers slapping against the boards. He dribbled a long trail of spit at my feet then took himself exploring through the forest of chair legs, chattering to himself.

Kitty smiled brightly when she saw me then covered her mouth, feigning a coughing fit.

'A pot of coffee please, Kitty.'

That stopped her coughing. She glowered at me. 'Am I your slave, then?'

I looked about me. 'This is a coffeehouse, is it not? And you do work here?'

'I *suppose*,' she conceded, grudgingly, and began fixing a fresh pot. When it was ready she poured a bowl for herself and joined me. 'So. Are you ready for tonight?'

'Tonight?' I stared at her over my coffee. Had she heard about the ghost too?

'Oh, have you forgotten?' She tapped her forehead. 'Supper with the governor? Dancing with the governor's wife?' She drew a line across her throat. 'You're in for it.'

'Well, thank you, Kitty. You're a great comfort.'

'Why, sir, do you need *comforting* . . . ?' She fluttered her eyelashes saucily. 'I'm sure Mrs Acton would oblige.'

'Should Henry be that close to the fire?'

She leapt up at once and pulled him roughly away from the hearth. Henry screamed in protest, mouth wide, tears streaming down his face. Mrs Bradshaw woke with a loud snort and stared about her, blinking. 'Oh Lord, Henry,' she groaned, and rose wearily from her chair. She plucked the boy from Kitty's arms and cuddled him until he was half-smothered, his cries stifled in her ample bosom.

In the midst of all this chaos Mrs Roberts stepped into the room. I supposed she could come and go as she pleased even on court day, as she wasn't a prisoner. She nodded at Mrs Bradshaw who gave a chilly smile in return, and pulled off her black shammy gloves. 'A bowl of coffee, Kitty.'

Kitty scowled but turned back to the fire, slamming together a fresh pot with the delicacy of a blacksmith hammering a horseshoe.

I expected Mrs Roberts to snub me, but instead she walked straight up to my table. 'Mr Hawkins.'

I rose and bowed. 'Madam.'

'May I . . . may I join you?'

I reeled back in mock fear. 'Do you promise not to strike me?'

A half-smile. 'No, indeed. Do you promise not to provoke me?'

'No, indeed,' I smiled back, gesturing for her to sit down.

She did so, smoothing her skirts and sitting with her back quite straight as if she were at court and not a modest coffee-house in a debtors' prison. 'I must apologise for my behaviour last night, sir.'

'I'm sure I deserved it.'

'I'm sure you did not,' she said, then laughed, eyes brightening for a moment. 'We are quarrelling again.'

'So we are.' I smiled back at her. 'But let me set your mind at ease; I have no designs upon Kitty Sparks, and never will. I do not make a habit of chasing little servant girls about the place.'

'No, of course not.' She put her hand to her cheek, embarrassed. 'I was too quick to judge you. It's a failing of mine. And you were right; I fear I *was* thinking of my late husband. There is a resemblance, you see . . .' She pulled a gold locket from her skirts and opened the clasp before slipping it into my hand. On one side was a miniature of a young boy, no more than four.

On the other was the portrait of a man in a black coat, a short wig and a mustard waistcoat. 'It was commissioned after his death, when I came into my fortune and could afford it. But it is a fair likeness.'

Captain Roberts. I had always imagined him in uniform. I squinted at the portrait, holding it up to the light. There was a resemblance, it was true. We shared the same clear blue eyes and dark brows, the same pale, Scots complexion that I had inherited from my mother. But his jawline was weaker, his forehead too high, and he seemed to enjoy his dinner a good deal more than I. The honest truth was that of the two of us, I had been blessed with the better looks. I did not make this observation to his widow.

I touched the other side of the locket. 'Who is the little boy?'

She lifted the chain from my palm and stared tenderly at the picture for a long moment. 'That is Matthew,' she said, softly. 'My son.'

'Was he . . .' I faltered. There was a pain in her eyes, so deep I feared she must be mourning not one death but two.

'Yes, he was taken from me.' She clipped the locket closed. 'But not in the way you are thinking, Mr Hawkins.'

Kitty arrived with a pot of coffee. Mrs Roberts acknowledged it with a slight nod then waved her away again.

'I was very young when I married John,' she began again, after a short pause. 'My father was furious. He had promised me to a friend; it was all arranged. It would have been an *advantageous* match; there was land, property. A title, even. I was seventeen. His friend was close to sixty.' A frown of distaste. 'I ran away. My family disowned me, of course. I didn't care. I was in love.'

She shut her eyes and laughed mockingly at the notion.

'It is not a crime to fall in love,' I said.

'Not a crime, no.' She frowned at me, as if I were a child, but then her expression softened. 'No, you are right,' she murmured, almost to herself. 'After all that has happened – it is easy to forget that we *were* happy for a time.'

'Did he . . .' I cleared my throat. 'Betray you?'

'Oh, no doubt!' she laughed bitterly, tossing back her head. 'Isn't that what men do?' I began to protest but she stopped me, touching her fingers softly to my wrist. 'Please, Mr Hawkins, I know what you would say but forgive me. I have learned to judge a man by his actions, not by his words.'

The touch of her hand sent a spark through me and I was seized with the desire to take it in mine, to press it softly to my lips. I wonder what would have happened if I had? Another slap, I shouldn't wonder. She moved her hand away and the moment passed.

'So. You fell out of love with your husband.'

'No!' She frowned, suddenly defiant. 'We ran out of money. Some men have a knack for making it; John had a talent for losing it. By then I was with child. I wrote in secret to my mother. She sent me what she could; what would not be missed.' She swallowed hard. 'My father would have been very cruel to her, if he had found out.

'I thought things might improve once the baby was born, that John would want to do his duty as a father. Matthew was so sweet; such a good boy. John doted on him, but . . . he was a reckless man. In truth he was all the things I had been warned about before I married him. And yet I loved him. Always. Even at the end, when I had every reason to hate him. We survived for a couple of years, while John was still in the army. Then his battalion was disbanded and we lost everything, very fast.' She looked up, her clear grey eyes haunted by the memory. 'You know how it is, Mr Hawkins.'

'When did you come to the Marshalsea?'

'In January. I had written to my mother begging for help but had heard nothing for weeks. And then at last I received a letter, a few days after we arrived here. It was from my father.' She paused, this time for much longer, and stared off into the distance. When she continued her voice was flat and drained of feeling, as if she were telling someone else's story and not her own. 'My mother was dead from a fever. When she fell sick, her maid brought my letters to my father and confessed we had been in contact for several years. She was afraid for her position, I suppose; or perhaps she hoped for some reconciliation before it was too late. If so, she did not know my father at all.' She gave a bitter smile. 'He waited until my mother died and then he wrote to me with a proposition. I will never forget his words, Mr Hawkins, even though I burned the letter. *You are ruined by your own hand. I have no pity for you or that damn'd scoundrel you call a husband. But I will not have you disgrace the family name by dying in gaol like some common slut.*' She stopped, and covered her mouth with her hand. Those last words had brought her back to herself, back to the coffeehouse.

'A wicked thing to say.'

'Yes . . .' She rallied herself. 'He offered to grant us a small allowance. Just enough to keep us locked up here, safe on the Master's Side. His offer came with one condition. I was his only child, you see. He had no heir. He would send us the money, but in return, we must give him Matthew.'

'He took your son.' I frowned, struck by the cruelty of it – to break the bond between a mother and son out of spite and vengeance. Or perhaps he thought he was being generous. I could imagine my own father offering something similar, and convincing himself it was all done out of charity.

She nodded, face drained of colour. 'We refused at first. But what choice did we have? We would have starved to death, all three of us. I couldn't let that happen. John and I argued about it for days. So I told him to visit the Common Side to see how they lived. How they *died.*' She shivered. 'And then he agreed. But it broke him, Mr Hawkins. And he blamed me, for changing his mind. Things were never well between us again. Everything was ruined. Lost.' She covered her face with her hands, just for a moment. 'My father sent his land manager down to collect

Matthew. As if he were livestock, not a boy of three. I have not seen him since. My boy. My son.' She touched the closed locket, resting on the table between us.

'But . . . forgive me. Are you not wealthy, now? Could you not go to him?'

'My father refuses all contact.' A single tear slid slowly down her cheek. 'He is Matthew's legal guardian now; I cannot even write to him. Oh! It was all planned so *cleverly*. Do you not wonder how I came by my fortune? It was an inheritance bestowed upon me by an aunt on my mother's side. She died last December; a few short weeks *before* we came to the Marshalsea. If we had known of the money, we would have been spared all of this. John would be alive. I would never have let my son go.' She clenched her jaw. 'My father bribed my aunt's executor. He only came forward with the will after John's death. And now my son is being raised by that . . . *oh!*' she shuddered.

'Can nothing be done? If you put this to the courts, surely there would be great sympathy for your story?'

She sighed wearily. 'My lawyer believes I have a case. But I know my father. He is powerful and ruthless and he always gets his way. He would do anything to keep me from my son. He is still punishing me, you see, for running away. After all these years . . . He would use the shame of John's death.' A wince of pain and grief. 'His lawyers would say I drove my husband to it. That I am not fit to take care of Matthew. The disgraced widow of a man who took his own life.'

'That's why you've stayed here,' I said, understanding at last. 'Not for your husband. For your son.'

'Yes.' She gazed out of the window. The court had ended for the day, the last of the carriages rumbling out through the Lodge, the turnkeys opening up the wards at last. 'Lord knows I loathe every brick of this foul place, but the truth is buried somewhere here. John was not perfect, but he did not hang himself. He was murdered by someone in this prison.' She narrowed her eyes at all the debtors rushing out into the yard. 'And I will prove it.'

Outside, everyone was making the most of their late release, stretching their legs and catching up on the news. Trim and Mack took up a game of rackets against the wall next to Acton's lodgings, Mack all arms and legs and cursing as Trim won. A reminder that I should always bet on Trim, given the opportunity. I nodded to them both then stuck my hands in my waistcoat pockets and strolled over to the Tap Room, thinking about Mrs Roberts. *Catherine.* I was glad we were on good terms again.

If I could only discover the truth about Roberts' death! Not only would I fulfil Sir Philip's task, but surely I would earn Catherine's respect and gratitude. And love . . . ? The thought crept stealthily into my mind. Love and freedom – a tantalising prospect. Mr Woodburn believed I had been thrown in gaol for a reason. (*Aye*, a snide voice sounded in my head. *For owing twenty pounds.*) But what if he were right? What if this were my fate – to find the murderer and begin my life afresh, with Catherine at my side?

I ordered a glass of beer from the ever-surly Chapman and smoked a pipe out on the balcony, looking down upon the two yards divided by the high brick wall. It seemed more brutal from above – a long thin line separating hope from despair, life from death. Jenings had found Roberts hanged in the Strong Room over on the Common Side. Belle Isle – the room I shared with Fleet – was way over by the northwest corner, close to where Trim and Mack were playing rackets. I let my gaze travel across the yard. The two points could hardly be further apart. I saw now what Trim had tried to explain the night before in the Tap Room; Fleet could not possibly have carried or even dragged Roberts all the way across the gaol by himself.

'Fine puzzle, isn't it?'

It was Fleet, appearing as if by magic at my side and making me jump in alarm. He was still dressed in his banyan and cap; in fact I was beginning to suspect this was his daily uniform. He had the smell of a man who washed irregularly. He gestured across the yard, pipe clamped between his teeth. 'Must've been two of 'em, wouldn't you say?'

I frowned, thinking it through. 'One man could do it, if he were strong enough.'

'Are you thinking of our dear governor . . . ?' He shot me a sidelong glance. 'Acton could manage it alone, I suppose. But he likes his cronies about him for the dirty work. Bullies are just men who don't know they are cowards, of course.' He pointed the stem of his pipe at the door in the wall. 'Whoever it was, they would need a key to get through to the Strong Room.'

Out in the Common Side yard a fight had broken out, two men pushing each other to the ground and rolling in the dirt. A woman screamed at them to stop, a baby crying on her hip. A thin rabble gathered round to watch, jeering and shouting encouragements.

'Perhaps they picked the lock.'

'Aye,' Fleet said, then chuckled. 'You are determined to contradict me, aren't you?' He spread his hands out, assessing the wall's height. 'Perhaps there were ten of them, all clambered upon each other's shoulders like tumblers.'

Four of Acton's men tore out into the Common yard, cudgels raised high. They pulled the two men apart and clubbed them about the back and shoulders before dragging them away. The woman ran after them, yelling curses. One of the guards cuffed her as she reached him, knocking her hard in the mouth. She fell heavily to her knees, the baby sliding from her arms into the dirt.

'There is another possibility,' I said. 'Perhaps Roberts really did hang himself.'

'Nonsense,' Fleet snorted. 'He was a bloody mess when Jenings cut him down. Poor bastard.'

'But he could still have taken his own life, *after* his beating.'

Fleet considered this for a moment, brows furrowed. 'I hadn't thought of that,' he murmured. 'Not likely, but possible. So tell me . . . why would he kill himself?'

Down in the yard, the baby was screaming. The woman gathered it up and staggered away, sobbing into her apron. 'Guilt? Shame? Despair? I can think of a dozen reasons.'

'Guilt . . . ?' Fleet's fierce black eyes fixed on mine. 'For what?'

'For giving up his son. Catherine said he was never the same again.'

'Ah.' He waved his hand, dismissing the whole notion. 'No, no. Roberts loved himself far too much to end his own life. I've never known a man spend so much time staring at himself in the glass. With good reason, I suppose; he was a handsome enough fellow.' He gazed at me for a long, uncomfortable moment, then grinned. 'Catherine . . . ?'

'She's a fine woman.'

'She's a *rich* woman.'

'She's a fine, rich woman.'

Fleet laughed. 'We are agreed on this, at least. But I'm surprised you haven't yet asked me about Ben Carter. Are you not curious to learn what he saw?'

I kept my expression guarded; the same look I used when I had a pair of aces to play. 'About the ghost . . . ? It's all nonsense, isn't it?'

Fleet tossed the spent pipe to the floor. 'I'm afraid none of this is nonsense, Mr Hawkins. It is deadly serious. You would be wise to remember that if you wish to survive in here.' He stepped closer. 'There are two killers on the loose in this prison. And I believe you will be dining with one of them tonight.'

Ten

Fleet's words unsettled me, but they also confirmed what I had guessed: that Acton could well have been involved in Roberts' death. Once one dismissed the idea that Fleet had killed Roberts (and I was not sure I had *entirely* done that), then Acton was a natural suspect. He had the freedom of the prison — and the strength and temperament to commit a murder. If it was Acton, I presumed that money was involved. Perhaps Catherine's father had paid Acton to kill his troublesome son-in-law. Whatever the reason, I had seen enough of Acton to know he was capable of just about anything if there was profit in it for him. Supper was becoming less and less appealing.

Back in Belle Isle, Fleet was in a strange mood, even for him. He seemed determined to cheer me up, scavenging through the driftwood of his belongings to find me a suitable costume for the evening. When I saw the quality of the suit he was proposing I was happy to oblige him: a well-tailored black coat with matching breeches, much finer than Charles' old suit; a fresh pair of white silk stockings; good shoes with mirror-bright buckles and a blue silk waistcoat embroidered with silver thread. I caught myself in the glass and almost laughed. I had never been so poor in my life, and yet here I was, the very picture of an eligible young gentleman. I would marry myself if I could.

'It's a shame Mrs Roberts won't be there tonight,' I said, fiddling with my cravat.

'Hmm. . . .' Fleet was staring at me in a very peculiar fashion, even for him. 'D'you know,' he said, changing the subject with a speed I did not think to find suspicious until later, 'Ben Carter said that Roberts' ghost was dressed in a mustard waistcoat and good leather boots last night. Carrying a lantern that cast strange shadows upon his face . . .' He held up an imaginary light and pulled a suitably ghoulish expression. 'Does that not strike you as odd?'

'Which part?'

Fleet dropped the invisible lantern impatiently. 'The *waistcoat*, of course . . .'

I was about to ask him why this detail in particular bothered him rather than, say, the fact that a dead man had risen from the grave and was floating about the prison terrifying young boys when there was a knock at the door. It was one of the porters, carrying Fleet's supper and a letter from Charles. I abandoned my roommate to his odd fancies and headed out to the yard. The Park was quieter – almost peaceful – now the last of the sun had gone, and a warm light spilt out from the rooms on the Master's Side as prisoners lit their fires and started their suppers. I had no money, the governor was a brute and I was sleeping in a dead man's bed – but I had survived my first full day in gaol, at least. A small triumph to celebrate. One flight up from Belle Isle, Trim was at his window smoking a pipe. I saluted him before settling down on the bench beneath the lantern to read Charles' letter.

As I removed the note I spied something glinting at the bottom of the envelope. I pulled it out and stared at it in wonder. My mother's cross. Charles must have seen it in the pawnbroker's window on the High Street and recognised it from its shape and the diamond at its heart. I touched her initials etched into its back: M.H. My heart lifted at Charles' generosity – but my gratitude was tinged with shame. He knew more than anyone what the cross meant to me. He slept in the next bed to mine at school and had heard me crying softly into my pillow in the months after my mother died. He'd never told a soul – boys were bullied without mercy for much less – but he reached out once, in the night, and touched my wrist. That was all – one brief moment – but it was enough.

What must he think of me now and the wreck I had made of my life, that I had been forced to pawn the one thing I had left of her? Holding it now in the palm of my hand it seemed an impossible piece of luck that it had returned to me so soon – as if she were looking down on me. My God, what a thought. I slipped it back around my neck vowing never to part with it again. But even as I did so, a cold whisper ran through my head. *You have promised that before.*

The letter began with a few kind words renewing our friendship. *'You are more a brother to me than my own flesh and blood, Tom; and always will be.'* There was also rather a lot about divine providence and another request for me to write to my father, which I ignored. The second page offered more tangible hope, expounding on Sir Philip's offer.

Sir Philip is most concerned about these Rumours of a Spirit haunting the Prison. There were tales of a Ghost appearing in the Fleet gaol this summer that sparked such Terror that Bambridge, the Governor, feared a Riot. Acton in his Arrogance believes he has his prisoners on a tighter Leash, but Woodburn and others tell Sir Philip otherwise. In truth, it would take very little for the Common Side to erupt into Revolt and Violence. If it does – God help us all.

Tom: I will be frank with you – Sir Philip makes a great Profit from the Marshalsea, ever more so with Acton in charge. He does not wish to see those profits drop by one farthing. An ugly truth, but there it is. He has also grown tired of Mrs Roberts and her friends petitioning him day and night for an Investigation into Roberts'

death. *Affairs of State keep him busy and he dislikes being troubled
with what he sees as trifling matters.*

*As you know, I have spoken with him on your Account; if you
prove able to resolve this matter of Roberts' death and put an end
to these Dangerous Rumours then your Release is assured. But you
must be quick about it, Tom; Sir Philip is not a patient man.*

*A word of Caution: Sir Philip would be most reluctant to believe
in Acton's involvement. To be blunt — a confirmation of Suicide or
proof of Samuel Fleet's guilt would be the preferred outcome. You
must follow the Truth where it leads you, of course, and if it leads
you towards the Governor, so be it.*

*I will not pretend this task is without risks — but as I cannot
afford to pay your Debts I believe this is the best way I can help
secure your Release. I have also taken the liberty of hiring Jakes, the
warrant officer, to help you. He is anxious to discover his friend's
killer and will assist you in any way he can. He visits the Prison
tomorrow and will meet with you then.*

*My Dear Friend: I Pray this opportunity gives you Hope in a
Dark hour. I only wish I could do more — it breaks my Heart to see
you confined in such a miserable way. When you are released — and
you will be released, Tom — we must find you a good Position. It is
not right that a man of your Talents and Education should find
himself in such a Woeful Condition and I will do everything in my
Power to rectify this.*

*Until that Cheerful day, I will pray for you and offer all the help
at my Disposal to ensure your Freedom.*

I am yours, sir, etc

Charles Buckley

*Postscript: I enclose your Mother's cross. If you pawn it again I
will never forgive you.*

'Good news I hope, Mr Hawkins?' The tall, lean figure of Mr
Jenings emerged from the gloom, lantern lit ready for the
nightwatch.

I thought of Fleet, acting the ghost, and stifled a smile. 'Mr Jenings. Would you light me to the governor's rooms?'

He led the way, lantern swinging. As we reached Acton's quarters next to the Lodge I thought of the strange, mocking laughter I'd heard the night before. 'Mr Jenings, sir. Tell me. Was it here you saw the ghost?'

Jenings pointed into the gloom with a long, bony finger. 'Right there,' he whispered shakily. 'Terrible thing, it was; all pale and grey like a corpse. Moaning and wailing as if the hounds of hell were on its back . . . Then it vanished.'

'Vanished?' I peered into the darkness. 'How so?'

'Disappeared into the shadows. I searched for it for an hour or more, up and down the Park and all, but it was gone. They can walk through walls, of course.' He gave me a sharp look. 'You saw something last night, didn't you? Right on this spot.'

'I thought I *heard* something . . . It had been a long day.' I touched the back of my head; there was still a large bump where I'd been knocked senseless by the footpads in St Giles. 'The mind can play tricks in the dark.'

'No,' Jenings said, firmly. 'There's something out there; watching us. Watching everything we do. Good and bad.'

He gave me a short bow and returned to his rounds, abandoning me in front of Acton's door. A touch of habit made me reach for my mother's cross, finding comfort in the familiar shape beneath my fingers. I wondered what my mother would have made of Jenings' story. She had been raised a Catholic and though she converted when she met my father, she had clung to some of the old beliefs. Miracles and wonders, mysteries and spirits; these were things she had whispered to me at night when I couldn't sleep. Popish nonsense, my father would have called it, if he'd known; but I'd loved her ghost stories as a boy. And now . . . ? I straightened my shoulders and rapped on Acton's door. Now I should forget all about them. The real world was dangerous enough.

. . .

'Mr Hawkins! Welcome, sir, welcome!' Acton's rough, powerful voice boomed out across the Park, bouncing from the prison walls. He had opened the door himself, in high spirits, a mug of ale in one hand. I could hear music and chatter coming from next door, Mary's girlish laugh cutting through it all. Acton clapped an arm about my shoulder and pulled me inside. He was already loud and unsteady with drink – 'in his fucking altitudes', Moll would have muttered had she been there – and restless as a bull, roving us down the hall and kicking out at a chair that dared get in his way.

'Thank the devil you're here,' he growled, grabbing me tight as if I might jump his grasp like a frightened hare. To be fair, the thought had crossed my mind. 'Here he is!' he said, thrusting me into the room. 'Fresh meat!'

Acton's parlour was warm – stifling, even – crowded with too many people and too much furniture. The air was heavy with tobacco and sweat and smoke from the fire. A pair of half-drunk musicians – debtors from the Master's Side brought in for the night and without question *honoured and delighted* to play for free – were playing a fiddle and pipe in a hectic manner, changing the tune whenever Acton shouted for it. In one corner an older couple finished their supper; the woman was plump and merry, sucking on a chicken leg and clapping her hands along to the music, while the man seemed sick and ill at ease, glancing at the door from time to time as if to assure himself it were still there and still working.

At the centre of it all was Mary Acton, dancing gaily with little Henry at her feet, a glass of punch raised high above her head. I was glad to see Mack standing by the fire, talking with Edward Gilbourne, the young Palace clerk I'd spied earlier in the yard with Catherine Roberts. Gilbourne seemed good company – he had a pleasant, easy manner about him. He caught my eye and nodded politely. I made my way towards them in such a hurry that I cracked my shin against a low table.

'Mind yourself, Hawkins,' Acton cried, shoving it away with his foot. 'Can't have you going lame. Not when you've promised to dance with Mary.' He caught my alarm and roared with laughter. 'Dance with her all you want, sir,' he snorted, beckoning Mary over. 'Can't stand the damned business myself.'

A servant pushed past me with a fresh bowl of punch, liquor slopping over the brim on to the floor. Acton grabbed two glasses and plunged them into the bowl before it was even set down, handing one to me as Mary danced up to us, swishing her skirts.

'Well now, hussy,' Acton grinned, pulling her close. 'What do you make of Mr Hawkins in his fine gentleman's outfit?'

Mary smiled up at her husband, arms wrapped tight around him. Her gaze flickered over my clothes from the ribbon in my wig to the buckles of my shoes. 'I know that waistcoat . . .' she frowned, narrowing her eyes.

'It's on loan from Mr Fleet,' I explained.

'Ugh,' she sneered, mock-shuddering in Acton's arms. 'Horrible little toad, sliming about in other people's business. William . . .' She stroked her husband's chest and put on a high, babyish voice. '*Surely* we can find a better roommate for our guest.'

Acton kissed the top of her head. 'That's up to his purse, my love, isn't it?' A sudden gleam entered his eyes. 'So. You're a friend of Buckley's, eh? I'll wager Sir Philip pays him well enough . . .' He licked his lips, already stained red with punch. 'Did he offer to help with your fees?'

It was at this very moment that the musicians put down their instruments to rest and take a glass of punch, leaving Acton's question to fall heavily upon a quiet room. It was also at this moment that I spied Acton's clerk, John Grace, sitting by himself in the darkest corner of the room, far away from the fire. He did not eat or drink, just sat, silently, still clutching the black ledger, bony hands stroking the surface as if it were a purring cat. He leaned forward to catch my response, wintry blue eyes unblinking behind his spectacles.

To my great relief, Edward Gilbourne slipped across the room to join us. 'Mrs Acton, would you introduce me to our new guest?' he said, darting a friendly glance in my direction. Acton, seeing the conversation move away from money, wandered off in search of more punch. John Grace sat back, stiff as an old hinge, glaring at Gilbourne with unguarded hatred. So – it would appear that the two clerks were not on good terms. Another reason to like Gilbourne.

'This is Mr Gilbourne, our deputy prothonotary,' Mary trilled, announcing him as if he were some foreign diplomat new at court.

Gilbourne rolled his eyes. 'Palace clerk,' he muttered in my ear. 'You don't have to kneel.'

'This is Mr Hawkins,' Mary continued, quite oblivious. 'He's a . . .' She paused, lips pouted in thought. 'What is it that you *do*, Mr Hawkins?'

'I'm a gentleman, madam. I do as little as possible.'

Gilbourne laughed. 'An excellent ambition,' he said, with mock solemnity. 'But I don't believe a word of it. You seem an industrious fellow to me, Hawkins. You've only been here a day and the whole prison speaks of you. Kindly, of course,' he added swiftly. 'Mr Woodburn has been singing your praises to the skies.'

Mary puffed out her cheeks with irritation and stormed over to the poor musicians to harangue them for stopping. They put down their drinks and took up their instruments again with a dejected air.

Gilbourne winked, mischievous. 'Our dear governess finds the chaplain tedious company,' he smiled. 'Too many sermons and not enough dancing. Just the mention of his name is enough to rile her. Perhaps that was wicked of me . . .' he pondered, taking a small sip of punch. 'But at least we are free to talk for a while.'

As the music resumed Mary twirled about the room searching for a partner. Acton and Grace were hunched over the clerk's ledger, plotting, while Mack suddenly found that he needed to send out for more food, so she settled for the thin, elderly gentleman sitting at the table. She pulled him to his feet and shuffled him into a reluctant, doddery minuet.

'Mr Wilson. Mary's father,' Gilbourne explained. 'His daughter has danced circles round him for years.'

'He was a prisoner on the Common Side, I hear.'

'Astonishing!' Gilbourne stepped back a little, marvelling at me. 'So newly arrived and yet you have the measure of every man here.' He waggled his finger at me. 'You're a capable man, Mr Hawkins. Observant.'

Mary's father was clutching his side and mopping the sweat from his brow with a silk handkerchief. 'It must be hard for Mr Wilson,' I said. 'Returning again and again to the place where he suffered such misery and disgrace.'

'I had not thought of it,' Gilbourne frowned. 'But now you say it, I see you are quite right. But then . . . perhaps he has forgotten his time as a debtor here? It was many years ago.'

I cleared my throat. 'From what I've heard of the Common Side, it is not an experience easily forgotten, Mr Gilbourne.'

'That is true. And it's worse under our host's rule.' He shook his head. 'I only wish there were more I could do to help the poor wretches.'

'I am sure you do your best, sir,' I said, sorry to have brought the conversation to such a gloomy turn. 'Shall we sit down together and try Mack's feast?'

We settled ourselves at the table and fell quickly into deep conversation. Gilbourne told me his family were farmers from Kent, but he had come to London as a lad to live with his uncle, a lawyer, who had no children of his own.

'I can't imagine you tending the fields,' I said, nodding at his clothes. His suit was plain but expertly stitched to fit his lean frame and he wore a brand-new brown wig, lightly powdered. The warm, chocolate-coloured cloth of his jacket and waistcoat matched his eyes precisely and there was a crispness to his appearance that could only come from the very best tailoring.

'And I cannot imagine you tending your flock in a Suffolk parish,' he replied with a smile. 'It seems we are neither of us cut out to be our fathers.' He held up his glass and chinked it against mine. 'Praise the Lord.'

Gilbourne was a good companion, witty and perceptive for all his insistence to the contrary. It seemed to be a trait of his to admire other men's talents while dismissing his own. And yet he had risen to the post of deputy prothonotary in just a few short years – a position which, I soon realised, was blessed with a good deal of power and reward. Every court case, every arrest or release for every debtor, came through his office to be ordered and approved. Every prison fee, every change in the rules or hiring of a new turnkey must be signed and agreed with Edward Gilbourne. He wore his position lightly and with a humble shrug of the shoulders but I saw now I had underestimated him. He was not just excellent company; he could be a powerful ally. Charles might have Sir Philip's ear, but Gilbourne understood the inner workings of the Marshalsea better than anyone; save perhaps its governor.

With Mary's mother still grazing her way through the supper dishes we kept our conversation light, though she seemed more interested in her large slice of pound cake than our talk. Mary had trapped poor Mack in a dance while Acton was singing and swaying to the music, his arms about his father-in-law, squeezing him like a wet cloth on laundry day. Henry had somehow managed not to fall into the fire amidst all this chaos and had now reached the more dangerous destination of Mr Grace's feet. The clerk was glaring impatiently at Acton, lips twisted in annoyance, the ledger now open and waiting on a table by his side. I watched in alarm as the boy attached himself to Grace's stick-thin calf, perhaps mistaking it for a chair leg. Grace gave a shiver of revulsion, as if he had seen not a boy but a diseased rat clutched to his stocking. His gaze flickered to his master. When he was sure Acton wasn't looking he gave a sudden, violent shake of his leg, kicking the boy into the middle of the room.

Henry paused for a moment, as small children do when they are shocked and hurt and want the world to know it. He took a deep breath. And then he screamed. He screamed with such a piercing intensity that the musicians flinched and stopped playing. Mack clapped his hands to his ears.

'Henry!' Mary wailed, scowling at her young son. 'Stop your caterwauling! Mama! Make him *stop*. Oh!' She stamped her foot and then again, louder. 'He's *ruining* the party.'

Mrs Wilson rose from the table and gathered her grandson in her arms, who shrieked and reached for his mother. Mary shooed them both away.

'Take him for a walk about the Park. Hurry about it!' she snapped. Then she caught my eye, and pressed a hand to her chest. 'I cannot bear to hear him cry, Mr Hawkins,' she sniffed. 'It breaks my heart.'

Mary's father looked worried. 'It's a cold night, dearest . . .' he ventured, timidly.

'Take him to the Tap Room and give him some whisky,' Acton commanded his mother-in-law. 'And tell Chapman to send over two more bowls of punch, damn it; we're almost dry.'

Mrs Wilson did as she was told and took the screaming child away, his cries growing fainter as they headed across the yard. The party resumed, though Mack was now so drunk he had surrendered command of his flailing limbs and Mary was still sulking over her son's selfish behaviour.

Grace cleared his throat. 'The ledger, Mr Acton . . . ?'

Acton scowled at him. 'Very well, very well. No rest for the wicked, eh?' He prodded a line in the book with a thick finger. 'He can go.'

'Very good, sir . . .' Grace took up his quill and marked some-thing on to the page.

Gilbourne watched them with a hand propping up one cheek. 'And so a life is scratched out,' he murmured.

'What are they doing?' I asked him.

'Marking the Black Book. Grace keeps tally of each prisoner's debts to the warden. It's rent day tomorrow so they're checking to see who has fallen behind. They'll grant a week's respite to the lucky ones, if they think they can squeeze more from them later. The rest will be flung over the wall. Monstrous. But what can one do?'

Grace dipped his quill and put a mark in the margin with a satisfied smile. The nib squeaked as it scraped across the paper, making my stomach turn. I'd heard enough about the Common Side to know that he was signing a death warrant for most of those unlucky prisoners. Worse still − it could so easily be my own name he was scratching out. Samuel Fleet struck me as a fickle friend − the moment he tired of me I would be discarded, tossed aside like the rest of his belongings.

I couldn't afford another week's rent on the Master's Side, not even for the poorest room. For all of Acton's good cheer and back-slapping, once he'd squeezed me of my last farthing he would throw me over the wall and leave me to rot with the rest of the poor Common Side wretches. How long before I caught a fever, or a blade in the ribs? How long before they were pulling my corpse out into the yard?

There was only one chance of escape. I had to solve Captain Roberts' murder − as soon as possible. But where to start? Perhaps I should ask Gilbourne for help; he seemed a sharp, astute man and he would know more of the prison's secrets than most, given his occupation. But could I trust him? Could I trust anyone?

John Grace drew a line through another name, sharp and straight. And then he looked up from his book and gazed at me for a long moment. The glass in his spectacles was shining in the candlelight so that I could not see his eyes – just the reflection of the flame.

The room grew hot, and I found it hard to breathe. I fumbled at my cravat, loosening the knot with trembling fingers.

'Mr Hawkins.' Gilbourne touched my arm, his dark brown eyes filled with concern. 'Let's step outside for a moment. You need fresh air, I think.' He lowered his voice. 'And there is a private matter we must discuss.' He gave a discreet nod towards Acton and Grace. When Mack obligingly trod on Mary's foot we used the distraction to slip outside.

'Peace . . .' Gilbourne sighed. He leaned against the tree outside Acton's door and closed his eyes for a moment.

I lit a pipe and took a long draw of tobacco. My hands were still shaking. There were moments when I forgot the danger I was facing. It was an easy thing to forget, with all the drink, the music and the cheerful company of debtors like Trim and Mrs Bradshaw who had somehow made the Marshalsea their home. But that was just a thin layer of ice glittering across the lake. One false step and I would plunge into the black, freezing waters beneath. Charles was trying his best to protect me, and I loved him for it – but he was outside the prison walls. A man needed friends *inside* if he were to survive. For now, Acton had decided to like me, but I had made enemies of both his head clerk and his chief turnkey. Joseph Cross was an ill-tempered, mean-spirited bastard, but at least he attacked with his fists. John Grace was another matter. I wasn't even sure why he disliked me so much, but I could sense it all the same; a cold, unwavering hatred that bided its time, waiting for the perfect moment to strike. The thought made the hairs rise on the back of my neck.

There was a light fog in the air, softening the gaol and leaving a damp trace upon the skin. The moon was still rising in the sky, shimmering behind the mist, and I could just make out the weak glow of the lantern in the middle of the Park. Out in the Borough, a clock struck ten, very faint. I peered out across the yard. The Palace Court, way down at the other end of the Park, was barely visible in the fog. Sam had said the ghost would meet me there at midnight. *Well, it can wait all it wants*, I thought, irritably. *I shan't be there.* I had enough to worry about without chasing after phantoms.

'Has Mr Buckley written to you yet, sir?' Gilbourne asked quietly.

I gave a start. Charles' letter was still tucked in my jacket pocket.

'Sir Philip sent a message,' he explained. 'He's ordered me to assist you in any way I can.' He smiled at this, and gave a little bow. 'I'm at your service.'

I returned his smile, but the news made me anxious. Gilbourne seemed honest and his position and power in the gaol could be helpful. But the fewer who knew about my investigation the better – news travelled fast around this prison. 'Have you mentioned this to anyone?'

Gilbourne looked affronted. 'Not a soul. Upon my honour.'

'Forgive me, I meant no offence. It's just . . . this is my only chance to escape this place. I can't afford to fail.' I swallowed hard. 'My life depends on it, sir.'

'I understand.' His face was hard to read in the mist, but he sounded perfectly sincere. 'And you are wise to be cautious. *If* Roberts was murdered, his killer is most likely still here in the prison. And should he discover that you're hunting for him . . . Well. It's all too easy to murder a man in the Marshalsea.'

I frowned and took another draw from my pipe. There was a burst of laughter from the Tap Room and a small drunken gang scuffled their way out into the yard; dark, murky shapes in the fog. 'Light us, Mr Jenings!' one of them called through into the Lodge and a moment later a lantern light appeared. The men weaved behind it, singing and sniggering to one another. A group of Acton's trusties, heading for the turnkeys' room under the chapel, with a couple of girls from the town. They didn't notice us as they stumbled past. Jenings tipped his hat, silently.

'There are men who would sell this information without hesitation,' Gilbourne continued quietly, after they were gone. 'They wouldn't think or care about the danger to your safety. Mr Hand, for example. Your roommate for another.' His gaze slid to the room I shared with Fleet. A dull light glowed from the window, but it was too dark and misty to see if Fleet were at his usual post. 'D'you know, I happen to like Mr Fleet. He's a queer, unpredictable fellow, but he's decent company when he's not in one of his dark moods. But he is not to be trusted. Not this much.' Gilbourne pressed his thumb and finger together, leaving no space between them. 'Belle Isle . . .' he said, then laughed. 'Have you caught the joke yet? Run the words together.'

I thought for a moment. Belle Isle. I had assumed it was merely a sarcastic reference to a shabby room. Belle Isle. BelleIsle. '*Belial*,' I muttered. Of course. Belial, hell's most worthless, lascivious, sin-drenched demon. *A spirit more lewd fell not from Heaven.*

'Clever, eh?' Gilbourne said. 'But I would take it as a warning, if I were you. He's a clever man, and good company in his way . . . but don't rely on him for help. He's just as likely to betray you.'

I frowned, uneasy. 'He doesn't need the money.'

'He wouldn't do it for the money. He'd do it for the sport.'

I sighed and tapped the spent tobacco from my pipe. *For sport.* Yes, that sounded like Fleet.

'Work quietly on this case, Mr Hawkins,' Gilbourne murmured. 'And work fast. All this talk of murder and spirits haunting the gaol; it frightens people.' He tilted his chin towards the Common Side wall. 'There's trouble in the air. I can almost taste it. You do not want to be sleeping on either side of the wall if the Common Side erupts.'

'How bad is it over there?'

'I've never visited.' He caught my surprise. 'It's not safe. I've heard the tales, of course. Shocking. They stabbed a man to death last week for nothing. A crust of bread. Gentlemen like us wouldn't last the night.'

A broad, squat figure emerged from the mist, startling us both.

'Chapman,' Gilbourne snapped. 'Damn you, skulking up in such a weaseling manner.'

Chapman leered at us. 'Just delivering the punch, *gentlemen*. No law against that, is there?' He strode past us into Acton's lodgings.

'Insolent brute,' Gilbourne grumbled. 'But this is what happens when a prison is run by a butcher. We'd better head back before we're missed.'

'Gilbourne.' I clutched his arm to stop him. 'Do you believe Roberts was murdered?'

He hesitated for a moment. 'I suppose I do. Yes.'

'Who was it killed him, do you think?'

He stepped back and stared at me in surprise. 'Acton, of course. Who else?' Then he turned and headed back into the warden's house.

Back in the parlour, the evening rolled along in its lurching, drunken fashion. I danced with Mary under the red-eyed, stony gaze of her husband while Mack vomited in a chamber pot and Mary's father dozed fitfully by the fire. The musicians played on, raising their voices when the time came for lock-up and the Common Side prisoners cried out their nightly song of misery and dread. We played cards – 'let him win,' Gilbourne hissed in my ear as we sat down, so Acton won every game and I lost the half-guinea Moll had sent me. Just after eleven Cross came in to remind Acton the Master's Side was ready for lock-up and should he escort Hawkins to his room? Acton belched and cursed his turnkey for insulting his wife's guest and shoved him out of the door, then fleeced me of another half a crown. Several times I suggested I should return to my lodgings and was shouted down and mocked for my womanish mewling. And all the while Mr Grace watched from the corner, eyes narrowed, watching the flow of drink and money and conversation and saying not a word.

'Smile, damn you, Hawkins,' Acton shouted as he won another game. 'You're not on the Common Side yet.'

Mary begged another dance and I agreed readily enough. Another hour of playing this new game of Let Acton Win and my pockets would be empty. I drank another glass though I had already drunk too much; I could see no other way of making the night end faster short of passing out, which Mack appeared to have done beneath the table. We danced and the room seemed to dance with us, the candles sputtering low and Acton banging his fist in time to the music, making the punch glasses jump and judder and waking his father-in-law with a start. He bellowed something at Gilbourne, who smiled politely and nodded before glancing at the clock. Mary was telling me something about her husband, about his hands and how rough and cracked they were from years of butchery.

'Not like your hands, Mr Hawkins,' she breathed, her fingers rubbing against my palm. She stared unsteadily into my eyes. 'We make quite the pair, don't we? A pair of aces,' she giggled, tossing back her yellow locks. 'D'you know, I think you are the handsomest man in the prison. I liked Roberts . . .' She twirled her skirts coquettishly. 'But I like you better.'

'*Mary.*' Acton's low voice rumbled across the room. He had stopped pounding the table, but his hand was still curled into a fist.

Mary jumped, then pouted like a child and flounced to a chair by the fire. I found myself alone, abandoned in the middle of the room. The governor's eyes were cold, his face set in a deep frown. The song came to a hurried end and still Acton studied me beneath heavy lids. 'Some reward for my hospitality, sir,' he said, voice heavy as stone. 'Taking liberties with my wife. Do you think she's a common slut you can ride behind my back?'

I swallowed hard, mouth dry. The air between us seemed to thrum with violence, the way it had in the yard the day before, Jack Carter curled like a baby on the cold ground as Acton raised the whip. By the fire, Mary's father was clutching his hands together as if in fevered prayer.

'Forgive me,' I stammered. 'I meant no . . .'

'*Hah!*' Acton jumped up, pointing a finger at me. Then he clapped his hands, threw back his head and roared with laughter. 'Oh, that was good.' He wiped the tears from his eyes. No one else in the room was laughing. 'Did you see him, Gilbourne, whimpering like a dog? Well. Perhaps we should send him back to his kennel, what do you say?'

Gilbourne gave a weak smile and poured himself another drink while Acton swaggered towards me. He hugged me tight to his chest. 'I like you, Hawkins,' he announced. 'You're a good sport. We're friends, eh?' He brought his lips close to my ear. 'And you have some powerful friends, don't you? Lucky boy. Do you think they can protect you without my blessing . . . ?'

I shook my head tightly. My heart was still racing and I could feel myself shaking beneath his grip. He could feel it too, of course. I was not a coward but Acton was playing with loaded dice. Let him win, Gilbourne had said. It was good advice.

The party broke up soon after that. Jenings arrived with his lamp and the two musicians hurried away with him, with a lightness of step rarely seen in prisoners returning to their cells. Acton kicked Mack awake and the two of them staggered off to the Crown, singing tunelessly up into the night air. Grace followed them like a wraith. Mary was still in a sulk, glaring petulantly into the fire, even when Mrs Wilson arrived with a sleeping Henry on her shoulder. The evening had not gone as

our dear governess had planned and she made sure we all
understood that and shared the blame between us. Her parents,
who seemed used to this, kissed their grandchild, bid their
daughter goodbye and ordered a carriage to take them back
into town.

'It's a long ride back,' Mary's mother said wearily. 'But Mr
Wilson won't stay the night, will you, my dear?'

Mr Wilson winced at some long-buried memory. He touched
my arm as they left. 'God spare you, sir.'

Which left Gilbourne and me. 'Well done, Mr Hawkins,' he
murmured as the door closed behind us. 'You're still alive.'

I collapsed weakly against Acton's tree. 'Am I?'

Gilbourne chuckled. 'Near enough.' His smile faded. 'I'm not
sure Mr Buckley understands the danger he's put you in. I'm
sure he meant kindly, but . . .'

'. . . But if I accuse the warden of Roberts' murder I'll be
signing my own death warrant. Yes, I see. Do you think Acton
knows?'

'Mr Hawkins.' He touched my shoulder lightly. 'If Acton even
suspected you were conducting a murder investigation in *his*
Castle, he'd have you whipped and tossed in the Strong Room. If
you were lucky. But for now, you have some value. You're a friend
of Charles Buckley, and Buckley has Sir Philip's ear. Acton's a
clever man, don't let him fool you. One doesn't become warden
of the Marshalsea through brute force alone. He was a butcher
for twenty years; he knows when to bludgeon and when to fillet.'

I rubbed my jaw. The night had left me tired and uneasy – and
I was afraid of where my suspicions were leading me. I had no
doubt that William Acton was capable of murder. I'd seen the
look in his eyes when I was dancing with Mary. He had made it
into a joke, but the menace was still there, just beneath the
surface. Perhaps Roberts had owed him money, or insulted him
or beaten him at cards. Perhaps he'd tried to escape like poor

Jack Carter. Acton could easily have beaten Captain Roberts to death in a fit of anger. But Roberts was a gentleman, he had friends, a wife. They might have asked questions, insisted on an investigation. So Acton hanged Roberts in the Strong Room and bribed the coroner to call it suicide. How simple it would be, a murder in his own Castle. The Marshalsea was not a place for justice, for honest dealing. The only question was why Acton allowed Mrs Roberts to stay in the gaol, causing trouble. Surely if he had murdered Roberts he would want to keep her as far from the prison as possible. But then, Acton was an arrogant man. This was his Castle. He wouldn't be threatened by a woman, not even one as clever and determined as Mrs Roberts. Perhaps it amused him to take her money, knowing all the time that she would never discover the truth. If Catherine was prepared to pay a high rent on her room in the Oak, Acton was prepared to take it from her.

'I'll tell you something,' Gilbourne said quietly. 'If you could find enough proof to hang him I'd pay your debt myself. The man's a monster. Worse than that – an *unpredictable* monster. Lets his feelings run away with him. It's bad for the gaol, bad for profits. Things are much smoother at the Fleet prison, you know. Bambridge was a stockbroker; earned a fortune from the Bubble. That's what the Marshalsea needs.' Gilbourne nodded to himself. 'A man of business.'

'If I could prove it was suicide,' I pondered, not really following Gilbourne's thrust. 'If I said Acton beat him for some perfectly sound reason, but then Roberts killed himself . . . perhaps that's the safest path through all this.'

'Who's there? Who is that?'

The voice was muffled but I recognised the clear, commanding tone at once. Catherine Roberts. Had she heard me? Shame burned in my chest. A verdict of suicide might save me, but it would also keep Catherine and her son apart for ever.

'Is someone there?' she called. 'Mr Jenings?'

I breathed a sigh of relief. She hadn't heard us. 'Catherine,' I said. 'I'm here.'

Her small, dark figure glided towards us. Candles still flickered up in Acton's lodgings, throwing just enough light for her to find us. I could see her face now as she emerged from the mist. The damp air had left a light dew upon her skin and her cheeks were tinged pink from the cold. She looked softer and more beautiful than anything I had ever seen in my life – and too perfect for such a place as this.

'Catherine,' I said again, and reached out my hand.

For one sweet, heart-thrilling moment her eyes lit up with pleasure and recognition. But then her expression collapsed into grief and terror. 'Oh!' she cried, flinging a hand up to her chest. 'Oh! What is this?' She stepped back, overcome, tripping over her skirts and half-falling, half-sinking to her knees.

Before I could move, Gilbourne had stepped forward and kneeled before her. 'Madam, pray don't be startled.' 'You are quite safe.'

She looked up into his face, dazed and fearful. 'Mr . . . Mr Gilbourne?' Her shoulders sagged with relief as she recognised him. She let him lift her to her feet, leaning heavily against him. 'Oh, Mr Gilbourne, what is that creature?' she whispered, staring at me in horror. 'Do you see it?'

Gilbourne laughed in confusion. 'Why, there's nothing to fear,' he said, gently. 'It's only Thomas Hawkins. See?'

She stared at me for a long moment as I stood like a statue, afraid to move in case I startled her again. I supposed in the fog she must have mistaken me for her dead husband, returned to haunt the yard – just as Jenings and Ben Carter had said. And yet, did I truly look like Captain Roberts, so much that his own widow could be fooled? From the portrait she had shown me it had seemed a passing resemblance at best.

'Why . . . why is he dressed like that?' she asked, her voice high and trembling with shock. 'Some cruel trick?'

I looked to Gilbourne but he just shook his head, astonished. I reached out and touched her hand. 'Catherine . . .'

'Oh! Don't touch me!' she shuddered, backing away as if her skin were scorched. And now, in a moment, the fear and surprise turned to a cold, bitter anger. She glared at me, eyes burning with contempt. 'You *scoundrel*! How *dare* you wear my husband's clothes! The clothes he wore when he was *murdered*! I thought . . . Oh, God!' Her voice wavered, and a single tear slid down her cheek. 'It's so cruel. I thought he had come back. I thought he'd come back to me.' She turned away.

Gilbourne glowered at me, furious, all his earlier warmth and friendship vanished in a moment. 'What devilish foolery is this, sir?' he hissed under his breath. 'Did you hope to trick us all with this wicked nonsense?' He flicked his hand at my borrowed clothes, disgusted.

I held up my hands in dismay. 'Mr Gilbourne, please, I beg you . . . I had no idea. I swear upon my life.'

He gazed at me, cold and distant. 'This is a dangerous place to play games, Hawkins,' he said. 'I thought better of you.' He gave Catherine his arm and led her away. For a brief moment she turned back and gave me a look that left me in no doubt of her feelings. And then they disappeared into the mist, leaving me alone.

I'd lost them both. The two people in this rotten, stinking place I had truly admired. And the two people best able to help me escape it. Gilbourne would have been a powerful friend and ally. And Catherine . . . a lump formed in my throat. It would be difficult to learn the truth about Roberts' death without the help of his widow, but in my heart I knew I had lost something much more important than that. After we had spoken in the coffee-house that afternoon I had dared to wonder about Catherine Roberts; dared to hope. She was not a woman I could ever deserve and yet . . . I could imagine a life with her – one where

I became a better man. And a richer one, for that matter. Now, in one moment, that hope had been extinguished and I knew precisely who to blame.

'Samuel Fleet,' I whispered to the night. 'I swear to God. You will pay for this.' And with that, the clock struck midnight.

Eleven

I had an appointment with a ghost. It seemed impolite not to attend.

And why not, I thought bitterly, as I edged my way through the fog towards the Palace Court. What more could this night do to me? The only other choice was to return to my lodgings and murder my roommate. I stared down at my clothes; clothes that must have been stripped from Roberts' cold and bloody corpse. Fleet had sent me to Acton's lodgings dressed in a dead man's clothes and I had been stupid enough to think he was being kind.

'I'll wring his neck,' I muttered, then stubbed my toe against a wall. I cursed hard, then reached out into the darkness and found a broad brick column. I must have reached the porch that ran beneath the Court. The dark and the mist were impenetrable here; if someone or something were waiting for me, they had discovered the perfect hiding place. I felt a shiver down my spine; a powerful sense of being watched. Studied. I backed away softly.

There was a moment's silence. And then, from the darkest corner of the porch, a light flickered deep in the fog.

I gasped in shock. 'Who's there?'

The light came closer.

'I have a knife!' I lied.

A moment's pause. And then a face loomed out of the shadows, grey as the mist, and streaked with dirt. A pale hand held the lantern higher and I saw . . .

Impossible!

'Roberts.' I stared at him in horror. It was the captain; there was no doubting it, he looked exactly the same as his portrait. But how could that be? I touched my mother's cross and whispered a hurried prayer.

The phantom shuffled closer, groaning softly. I began to shake, terrified by this apparition standing so close in the dark, almost near enough to touch. There was a rope still hanging about its neck, dark bruises on its face and blood stains upon its shirt. 'Murder . . .' it shuddered. 'Murder . . .'

And a waistcoat. A mustard waistcoat.

Samuel Fleet, I thought. *Damn you. You're a genius.*

The ghost gave a wild shriek. 'Avenge me . . . !'

'As you wish.' I folded my arms. 'Tell me. Who was it murdered you?'

The ghost paused, thought for a moment. 'Avenge me . . .' it said again, more hesitantly.

'Come now, Captain Roberts.' I leaned up against the porch column. 'Who killed you? You must remember, surely?'

The ghost cleared its throat. 'It was dark . . .'

'*Indeed.*' I remembered Gilbert Hand's request. 'And what happened to the money?'

'Money? There was no money. Was there . . . ?' The ghost looked hopeful.

I lost patience. Springing forward I grabbed hold of his perfectly corporeal body and swung him hard against the porch column. He gave a soft 'oof' as the wind was knocked from his lungs. The lantern crashed to the ground.

'Who are you? Who sent you?'

'Let me go!' he cried. 'Help! Help!'

I raised my fist to punch him but somehow he tore himself free, running blindly out into the fog. At the same moment another light appeared and I saw Jenings hurrying towards me with his lantern. 'Who goes there?' he called. 'Mr Hawkins?'

I grabbed his lantern and swung it out into the mists. 'I just saw the ghost.'

He staggered back on his spindle legs. 'Heaven spare us!'

'He's just a man, Jenings; he won't harm you. He must still be in the yard, we can catch him.'

We spent a good half hour searching for him through the mist. Jenings was terrified, despite my assurances that there was nothing spectral about our visitor. We brought another lantern out from the Lodge and even persuaded the turnkey on duty to hunt with us but Roberts – or whoever it truly was – had vanished into thin air. That much, at least, was a mystery.

'It must have escaped through the walls,' Jenings whispered. The turnkey gazed up at them with wide, terrified eyes.

'*Through the walls*,' he agreed, wonderingly.

'Nonsense,' I snapped. 'He must have a key to the Lodge.'

'We would have heard it go through the gate,' Jenings insisted.

'What about the Common Side? Could he have climbed over somehow?'

'Climbed *into* the Common Side?' Jenings frowned at the turnkey, who shook his head.

They were right; that made no sense. He'd been too well-fed to come from that side of the wall. And who would want to break *into* the Common Side? He must have slipped out another way, but I was damned if I could puzzle it out. And how was it he looked so much like the real Captain Roberts? I needed a sharper brain than mine to understand it all.

I swore quietly to myself. I needed Fleet.

Twelve

'Get up, damn you!'

I grabbed the collars of Fleet's robe and pulled him from the bed, pamphlets slipping and sliding to the floor. He grinned back at me, eyes blazing with excitement.

'Something has happened!'

I took a swing at him and he danced away, robe flapping and flashing parts of him I had no wish to see. 'Tie your banyan, man, for God's sake.'

He smirked. 'Do I distract you, sir? Here, let us fight like the Greeks!' And with that he shrugged off his robe and presented himself ready, fists high.

I turned my back, infuriated. I should have thumped him; he deserved a good beating after the trick he'd played on me. But I would not wrestle a naked Samuel Fleet, not for all the world, and he knew it. I tore off my wig and threw it in a corner. No – not mine, that was precisely the point. These were Captain Roberts' clothes – the very ones he was wearing when he was murdered. I shuddered in revulsion and tore the waistcoat from my back as if it were infested.

I stood in front of the mirror to untie the cravat and glimpsed Fleet in the reflection, slipping his robe back around his shoulders and tying it tight. Thank God. I snapped the strip of muslin between my hands. I could throttle him with it now. Half the prison thought he killed Roberts; if I called it self-defence who would doubt it? I could name him the murderer and be free by morning. My stomach lurched at the thought. Could I really kill a man without provocation, just to save myself? The cravat slipped through my fingers to the floor.

'A wise choice,' Fleet said, watching me through the mirror. He was holding a dagger in his hand.

I spun on my heels to face him, heart thudding in alarm. He stepped closer, blade high. His expression was calm – almost bored – but his eyes never left mine. 'Are you a fool, sir?'

I swallowed, staring at the tip of the blade, just a short step from my heart. 'No. I don't believe that I am.'

'Or lunatic?'

I shrank back. 'No, sir.'

Fleet considered this for a moment. 'Then why would you *think* of killing the man who can save you from the Common Side? No, no,' he snapped, as I started to protest. 'Do not deny it. I know when a man is contemplating murder, Mr Hawkins. I've seen it enough times in the mirror.' He frowned. 'And *do* stop ogling that boot over there. I removed the pistol from it hours ago. Tell me,' he persisted, his voice hard. 'Has someone approached you? Offered you money? I have plenty of enemies . . .'

'No. I swear—'

With a growl of annoyance he sprang forward, faster than a heartbeat, pushing me back against the wall with surprising force. Loose plaster crumbled from the wall, making me splutter and choke as the dust caught my lungs. By the time I was recovered, Fleet's dagger was hard at my throat. 'Tell me,' he hissed again. 'What do you have to gain from my death, Mr Hawkins?' I struggled to push the blade away but he was much stronger than he appeared. He pressed the blade closer. 'Well, sir?'

I took a breath, about to tell him of Charles' letter and the investigation, when I remembered Edward Gilbourne's warning.

If I told Fleet the truth, there was every chance he would betray me to Acton in the morning, for money or for sport. I forced myself to match his gaze and reminded myself of what I was, at heart. A gambler. I knew how to read a man's intent from the lightest expressions – even a man as strange and guarded as Samuel Fleet. And now I looked closer, I was surprised to see that there was no real anger or threat in those dark eyes of his. Just . . . anticipation. And curiosity.

He was testing me. And the trick, I realised, was not in telling him the truth. It was in keeping his interest.

I took a breath, the knife catching my skin. 'Did you kill Captain Roberts?'

He blinked. Then smiled. 'Deflection. Very good.'

I pushed the blade away. He would not kill me. Not here, not in this way. 'Did you murder him?' I asked again.

'No,' he replied simply.

No. And with that one word, I was sure of it. When one makes a living at the tables one learns to read a man's face as if it were the *London Gazette*. One glance in Fleet's eyes – and more than one glance was ill-advised – convinced me that he was either the greatest actor on earth or that he was telling the truth. More than that, I had the strangest feeling that if he had indeed killed Roberts, he would have replied, just as simply, 'Yes'.

What he would have done with me after that, I prefer not to contemplate.

I stepped away from the wall, brushing the plaster and dust from my shirt. 'But you must have seen or heard something.' I gestured to our respective beds. 'You were scarce six feet away. And don't tell me you slept through it all.'

A pained expression crossed Fleet's face. He turned the dagger in his hand, dancing it between his fingers as he considered his next move. 'Very well,' he muttered at last. 'I will share my secret. But let me warn you, sir.' He shot me an evil look. 'If you breathe a word of this to another soul . . .'

I nodded swiftly. 'Pain. Retribution. I understand. What happened?'

'I was . . .' He winced. 'I was outwitted.'

I bit my cheek, stifling a laugh. I think he would have confessed more willingly to murder if he could. 'Outwitted,' I repeated, enjoying myself for the first time all evening. 'Impossible, surely.'

He gave me a sour look. 'Someone tipped a sleeping draught in my punch.' He paused, scratched his stubble with the tip of his dagger. 'I'd shake the rogue's hand if I could. First time I've slept well in years.' He looked away, then poked about until he found a half-empty bottle of wine.

'Then why not tell people?' I asked, as he handed me a glass filled dangerously close to the brim.

'And ruin my reputation as a cold-hearted devil?' Fleet gestured to the window. 'It helps to be feared in a place like this. Better to be thought a murderer than a fool.'

'Whoever drugged the punch must have killed Roberts.' I peered into the glass and gave it a suspicious little sniff. 'Or perhaps you're lying. Perhaps you drugged yourself.'

Fleet blinked, incredulous. 'Drugged myself? For what possible reason?'

'Perhaps you knew Roberts would be murdered that night.'

'I see.' Fleet frowned. 'I drugged myself to avoid witnessing the terrible crime, is that it? Tell me – if you knew someone was planning to sneak into your room one night and murder your roommate, would you knock yourself unconscious?'

I felt my grand theory dissolving. 'Then who was it?'

Fleet gritted his teeth, as if he were trying to imprison the next three words that escaped his lips. 'I don't know.'

'But you must have some notion,' I protested. 'Perhaps—'

'I don't know,' Fleet hissed, then collapsed miserably on the bed. He sank his head in his hands. 'I have thought it over day and night for three months,' he said, wearily. 'It could have been anyone.'

'Have you not asked about the prison?'

He dropped his hands. 'And how might I do that, without explaining what had happened?' He rubbed his thumb deep into his palm. 'It would spread through the gaol in moments. And everyone would know that I could be tricked. Beaten.' He scowled. 'I would rather let a dozen murderers go free than that.'

'You jest,' I said, without thinking.

'No, Mr Hawkins,' he replied softly. 'I am quite serious. If you wish to survive in this gaol . . . in this *world*, then you must make people believe that you are the most ruthless, calculating, treacherous man they know. They must believe that you are capable of anything – the worst imaginable outrages. If your enemies learn that you are weak, they will destroy you. That is the way of the world.'

'I do not wish to be thought of as ruthless or trecherous,' I said. 'And I don't believe I have any enemies. Apart from Cross. And Grace.' I frowned. 'I suppose there may be others I don't know about.'

'Those are the most dangerous,' Fleet said, crossing to the fire.

I knocked back my wine then started unbuttoning the captain's shirt and breeches. The sooner I was out of these corpse clothes the better. I slung them in a dark corner with the waistcoat and hunted out an old nightgown, wrapping it close with a wide sash. It was not as fine as Fleet's banyan, though it was a good deal cleaner – and at least no one had died in it. 'Why did you put me in those damned things?' I asked, gesturing at Roberts' clothes.

Fleet was intent on building up the fire. 'I thought it might provoke a reaction.' He glanced up at me, waving the poker at my face. 'You share a resemblance, especially in candlelight. The same colouring, the same bearing.'

'What,' I snorted, pouring myself another glass. 'Are we in *Hamlet*? Did you think the killer would take one look at me and run screaming from the room, wracked with guilt?'

'Perhaps.' Fleet shrugged and turned back to the fire. 'In any case, it passed the time.'

'*Passed the time?* You warn me that I'm dining with a murderer and then you send me off in his victim's clothes, just to help you *pass the time*?'

He blew on the kindling. 'Passing the time is very important in gaol, believe me.'

I glared at his back, furious. 'Acton could have broken my neck, damn it. Thank God he didn't even seem to notice . . .'

'Acton?' He grunted to himself. 'No, I don't suppose he would.'

'And what must poor Catherine think of me, parading about in her dead husband's clothes?'

'Did Mrs Roberts see you? Oh dear. What a pity,' Fleet said, with a distinct lack of remorse.

'I doubt she will ever speak to me again,' I sulked. The thought of that struck me again, harder than before. I'd begun to care for her, more than I liked to admit. Fate had been cruel to her. I wanted to help her find justice and win back her son, not for her fortune but because she deserved to be happy after all the suffering she had endured. Well. Perhaps I was a *little* interested in her fortune, to be honest – but it was hardly my fault that I had fallen in love with an extremely wealthy woman. The heart must be free to fly.

'She near fainted with the shock,' I added. Fleet remained unmoved. 'It was lucky Gilbourne was there.'

'Gilbourne . . . ?' Fleet tipped a shovelful of coal on the fire, stoking it slowly. 'And how did he react to your costume?'

'He was angry on Catherine's behalf.'

Fleet thrust the poker deep into the fire. 'How *gallant* of him,' he muttered.

'You don't like him.'

'I can count the number of men I *like* on one hand. Without letting go of my cock.'

'I think he's a good man. He rather likes you.'

'Does he indeed . . . ?' Fleet blinked. 'How peculiar.'

'He also warned me not to trust you.'

'Quite right. You shouldn't trust anyone in here.' He picked up his old boot and pulled out his pistol, waving it in the air with a grin before slinging it on to his bed. 'Vile den of filthy liars. But this is all most interesting. *Fascinating!*' He beckoned me towards the fire. 'Sit down. Tell me everything.'

I put on a blue velvet nightcap then settled down in the chair nearest the hearth. 'I thought you said the mind worked better in the cold.'

'I don't need you to think,' he said. 'In fact I'd prefer it if you didn't. Just talk.'

I described the whole evening at Acton's in detail, which to my surprise was a good deal more enjoyable than the night itself. Fleet revelled in the horror of it, from Grace kicking Henry flying to Mack lying dead drunk under the table to Mary flirting and pouting and sulking her way through it all. When I came to our dance, Fleet jumped up and twirled about, capturing her perfectly. 'Why, Mr Hawkins, your hands are like silk!' he trilled, running his fingers down his chest and miming an indecent fit of ecstasy. Then he dropped back on the bed, fanning himself saucily with one of his pamphlets.

'I thought Acton would kill me,' I said, laughing despite myself.

'Oh no, not while you can pay your rent. He guards his profits more jealously than he guards his wife. And Buckley is a powerful friend; Acton wouldn't risk angering him. That's why I knew it was safe to send you over in Roberts' clothes.' He leaned forward, suddenly serious. 'I would not put you in real danger, Tom. You must know that.'

Of all the things Fleet had ever said to me, that surprised me the most. Stranger still – I almost believed him.

He thrust a hand into his banyan pocket and pulled out a piece of string, a half-eaten roll, a pair of aces of the same suit and a silver watch. He tossed the first three over his shoulder and held the watch up to the light of the fire. 'Almost two. What a day you've had. You must be tired.'

'A little.' I yawned and put my hands behind my head.

He studied me for a moment, and then a slow smile spread across his face. 'There's more, isn't there . . . ? What do you know, you dog? What have you been keeping from me?'

I grinned back at him. 'What's it worth?'

'Is it good?'

'*Very.*'

He rubbed his lip with his thumb, thinking, then reached out and dropped the solid silver watch into my palm. I stared at it, astounded. It was very fine, ticking quietly in my hand like a small, living thing. The outer case was intricately engraved with two birds and the initials J.H. Stolen, no doubt, or won in a cheat's game of cards. I opened it up, squinting at the workings in the candlelight. I couldn't find the maker's mark in such low light but I could see and feel enough to know that the whole piece must be worth two or three pounds at least. I snapped it shut. It was wrong, I knew, to take it from Fleet, whatever his reasons for giving it. But I was twenty pounds in debt and trapped in gaol. I couldn't afford to refuse a gift that could keep me from the Common Side for weeks. I slipped it in my pocket.

'I saw the ghost.'

He was thrilled. Jubilant. New drama to keep the boredom at bay; that was a better gift than a solid silver watch. He jumped up and began pacing the room as I described what had happened.

'It's not a real spirit.'

'Well, of course it's not!' he cried, waving his arms. 'That's why it only appeared in front of terrified young boys and credulous beanpoles like Jenings.'

'It had a noose round its neck and blood on its shirt . . .'

'. . . but it was wearing the wrong waistcoat!' Fleet finished, triumphantly. 'Roberts was murdered in those clothes.' He pointed at the blue silk waistcoat lying crumpled on the floor. 'Which I won – with great genius I might add – in a card game the next morning. More to the point, Roberts hated that mustard waistcoat. Wouldn't be seen dead in it. Literally.'

'There are two things I don't understand,' I confessed. 'Whoever that man was, he was real, flesh and blood. I picked him up and knocked the breath out of him.'

'Excellent!'

'But somehow he managed to disappear into thin air. He didn't go through the Lodge and he wasn't in the Park, we searched everywhere. Even in the fog, we would have found him. I thought perhaps he could be a prisoner who somehow managed to slip out of his cell . . . But he looked exactly like Roberts. Someone would have spotted the similarity by now. Which brings me to the other matter. Fleet – he didn't just look like Roberts. He *was* Roberts. Is it possible he has a twin brother? I can think of no other explanation.'

Fleet smiled. 'Can you not . . . ? Tell me, how do you know what Roberts looks like?'

'From his portrait. Catherine showed it to me this afternoon; she wears it on a locket round her neck.' And then I stopped, and thought, and the hard truth fell like a stone. The picture in Catherine's locket wasn't a portrait of Roberts. It was a portrait of the man hired to play his ghost. 'Oh God. I'm an idiot.'

'I've suspected her for a while,' Fleet admitted. 'But I thought it best to let the whole thing play itself out. Didn't see any harm in it.'

'But why did she do it? What on earth possessed her?'

'She wants justice. She wants her son back! She's desperate enough to try anything. What better way to keep everyone fretting about her husband's death than to have his ghost wandering through the gaol? Now it's in everyone's interest to find the killer, is it not? Who wants to be trapped in prison with an angry spirit? And perhaps she hoped to shock the killer into a confession. Just as I did tonight.'

I frowned, thinking back to my conversation with Catherine in the coffeehouse. She'd sought me out – to apologise, she'd said. I should have realised then that I was being tricked. Since when has a woman ever apologised for slapping a man about the face? It was just a trick to give her time to show me the false portrait. She had played me better than one of Moll's girls, damn it.

'Well. I'm glad she almost fainted tonight,' I said. 'Bloody woman.'

'Good for you!' Fleet cheered. 'But one has to admire her courage. And her perseverance.'

'No, one hasn't,' I grumbled.

'D'you know, it's strange.' Fleet cocked his head. 'I believe she loves him more in death than she ever did in life. They used to have the most appalling rows; I'd escape upstairs to Trim's and we could still hear everything through the ceiling. Ah, well. Now she's free to remember him the way she wanted him to be. A good, honest gentleman in an ugly waistcoat. Poor old Roberts. He's so *obedient* now he's dead. Not like him at all.'

III) *SATURDAY. THE THIRD DAY.*

Thirteen

I woke before dawn to the sound of a key grating in the lock. Fleet was already at the door, hopping from foot to foot in his impatience to be free. Did he ever sleep? As soon as the door swung open he was gone, trailing a musky scent of tobacco, sweat and stale wine. The turnkey slammed the door closed again without a word, moving on to the next room.

I sighed and groped for my new silver watch, enjoying the solid weight of it in my palm. Not yet six. I lay dozing a while, waiting for daylight in blissful silence. Fleet was such a restless heap of pacing and talking and twitching; I'd almost forgotten the peace and pleasure of my own company.

I also needed time to think. Today I would begin my investigation into Captain Roberts' death. I rolled on to my back and stared at the ceiling, wondering where to start – and was struck with the thought that Roberts had lain in this very bed the night of his murder. He had not shared a room with his wife. Mrs Roberts had kept a separate room in the Oak as she did now. What did that say of their marriage?

I was still angry with Catherine for tricking me, but I was half-asleep and the thought of her alone in her bed in the Oak sent my thoughts rolling far away from my investigation . . .

I was in a state of some disarray when there was a knock at the door. I had barely enough time to cover myself and turn to the wall before Kitty entered to clean the room, slopping water from her bucket.

'Mr Hawkins,' she hissed. 'Are you awake?'

I feigned sleep, silently cursing the interruption. Was there no privacy in this damned place?

'Lazy dog,' Kitty grumbled to herself and began to work about me. Once I had *settled*, I turned quietly as if in my sleep and watched her through half-closed eyes as she folded Fleet's clothes and sorted his papers, creating order from his chaos. I was struck again by the quick, capable way she went about things. I couldn't say why it appealed to me quite so much, only that I was happy to lie there as she whirled about the room. Catherine was right. She would make an excellent lady's maid, if she could learn to curb that tongue of hers. Perhaps Charles could find a position for her in Sir Philip's household. I would speak with him about it. Better that than staying Fleet's ward – hardly a suitable reference.

Kitty began to sweep the grate, sending a cloud of dust into the air. I made a show of coughing and yawning as if freshly wakened then pulled on my breeches and slipped a waistcoat over my shirt. The floor was almost clear of Fleet's clutter, his books and papers, clothes and curios stacked in neat piles against the walls. It would be scattered again by nightfall, but still, it was an impressive feat. 'You've done a fine job there, Kitty.'

She froze, back stiffening at the compliment, then carried on with her work. 'Will you need a fire, sir?' she said, without turning round.

'No, thank you. I'll take breakfast at Bradshaw's.'

'Very good, sir.' She knocked ash from her brush, smacking it hard against the grate. *Clack, clack, clack.*

I paused, frowning at her back. She seemed ill-tempered this morning, even for her. 'Is something wrong, Kitty?'

She dropped her brush with a loud clatter, wiped the ash from her hands. Then she rose and looked me up and down. 'And what is that to *you*, sir?'

'Well, indeed! Your welfare is of no consequence to me, I'm sure,' I snapped, irritated. 'And you should mind your tongue when you're speaking with a gentleman.' *Oh, good God in heaven. Why did I say that?* I sounded like my father.

Kitty pressed her lips together, swallowing the words she so clearly wished to say. She looked me straight in the eye, chin high. 'I beg your pardon, *sir*.'

It was such a churlish apology, so lacking in conviction, that I burst out laughing. 'An elegant apology, Miss Sparks. You are forgiven.' I bowed and left the room before she could answer. When I reached the stairs I glanced back and saw that she was staring after me, brows furrowed in confusion. I gave her a wink and was on my way.

A tempting smell of coffee, fried bacon and fresh-baked rolls wafted from the doorway at Mrs Bradshaw's but as I reached the threshold she hauled herself from her chair and laid siege to the room, arms folded across her wide bosom. 'There's no room,' she sniffed. 'Try upstairs at Titty Doll's.'

I peered past her to the empty chairs and tables and raised an eyebrow. 'Have I offended you, madam?'

'Oh! As if you didn't know! You should be ashamed of your-self! *Poor* Mrs Roberts, she was in *agonies* last night,' she scolded, looking pleased at the memory. 'She thought the captain had come back from the grave, God rest his soul. I had to give her a sleeping draught just to calm her nerves. How *could* you, sir? Dressing up in the clothes he was hanged in. Well. I am *vastly* disappointed, Mr Hawkins. I thought better of you, I really did. But I should have known. *A friend of Moll's*.' She shooed me out of the door and slammed it behind me.

I was about to try my luck upstairs with Mrs Mack when I caught sight of Jakes striding across the yard beneath heavy black storm clouds. I'd forgotten Charles' promise to send him over this morning. I stepped outside and met him beneath the Court porch.

'Mr Jakes,' I said, clutching a large paw. 'I'm glad to see you.'

'Mr Hawkins.' He grinned. 'Busy night, I hear.'

'Oh. I suppose it's all around the prison.' *Was that why Fleet rushed out this morning?*

Jakes shrugged. 'Mr Buckley says you have a talent for trouble. Asked me to give you this. You'll need to keep it tucked away or the turnkeys will take it.' He pulled a bundle from a bag at his side and handed it to me.

I unwrapped the cloth to find a short dagger, plain but well-made. I slipped it beneath my waistcoat. 'It's good of you to help me, Mr Jakes. I hope Charles is paying you for your time.'

'Glad to help, sir. Captain Roberts was a loyal friend. I owe him my life.' He looked down at the ground. Then he looked up and smiled again, eyes twinkling. 'And yes, Mr Buckley is paying me for my time.'

'From what I hear of Captain Roberts, he would approve of you making a profit.'

Jakes laughed. 'Aye, true enough.'

'So,' I said, clapping my hands together. 'Where shall we begin our enquiries? Is the Tap Room open?'

'You won't find answers there. I have a better idea.' He glanced over his shoulder, a soldier's instinct. 'You had breakfast?'

'Not yet.'

He fixed me with a sombre look. 'Good.'

Jakes was adamant. If we wanted to learn anything about Roberts' death, we must visit the Common Side. 'That's where he was found. That's where the secrets are kept. If someone knows something, we'll find him over the wall.' He gripped his club. 'You'll be safe with me, sir.'

I frowned. 'Acton's not a fool. If he hears I've been asking questions over there he'll suspect something.'

'Ah.' Jakes jerked his chin towards the Lodge gate. 'I've thought of that.'

To my dismay Woodburn bumbled into view, hand clamped to his hat against the blustering wind.

Jakes took one look at my expression and burst out laughing. 'His heart's in the right place, sir. And he can help us without knowing it.' Woodburn, it transpired, visited the Common Side regularly to comfort the sick, lead the prisoners in prayer and hand out food bought with donations from the parish. 'But keep that to yourself,' Jakes muttered. 'Or Acton will take it in a flash.'

'Mr Hawkins!' Woodburn limped over, breathless and gouty. 'My dear fellow. Jakes tells me you wish to help me in God's work this morning?'

I glanced at Jakes. He widened his eyes and nodded slowly. 'Ah . . . yes. Indeed.'

'Mr Hawkins was too shy to write to you in person,' Jakes explained. 'But he's most eager to join you on your visit.' He turned to me, face perfectly composed. 'You were inspired by the good reverend's example, isn't that right, sir?'

'Inspired, yes . . .' I echoed, as Woodburn's face puffed out with pride. 'I thought I might ease their suffering in some small way . . .'

'Through prayer,' Jakes added.

'Through prayer,' I agreed, miserably.

'Praise the Lord,' Woodburn beamed.

Joseph Cross sauntered over, twirling his ring of keys. 'So, Hawkins, I hear the governor had sport with you last night.' He sniggered. 'Says you almost shat yourself.'

Jakes crunched one heavy step towards him. 'You'll get your neck wrung for good one of these days, Joseph.'

'Gentlemen, gentlemen . . .' Woodburn cautioned.

Cross made a show of looking about him. 'Won't find any of those around here.'

Cross gathered together a half dozen of Acton's trusties, including Jenings the nightwatch and Chapman from the Tap Room, who was laden down with several bottles of liquor. When we reached the small wooden door fixed into the Common wall Cross turned and addressed the men. 'You know the rules, boys. Hands on your clubs. Don't take any damned nonsense from those sons of whores.' He slotted the key in the lock. 'And breathe through your mouth.'

I let the trusties go through first, then Woodburn. Jakes steeled himself, then squeezed through the door. I hesitated for a moment – every nerve screaming at me to turn back.

'Hawkins,' Jakes called, softly.

I took a deep, steadying breath and stepped over to the Common Side.

. . . And was it so very different, truly? I gazed about me, heart pounding. The sky – low, grey, heavy – looked just the same on this side of the wall. The worn and broken cobbles felt the same beneath my feet. But the air . . . the air felt different. Thick and cloying. Poisoned. I glanced at the other men and knew they all felt it – even Cross.

'God, I hate this place,' he muttered.

We walked towards the crumbling prison quarters – a raggle-taggle of ancient timber houses slumped, exhausted, against the far south wall. The Master's Side had been unlocked for more than an hour but here on the Common Side the prisoners were still trapped in their wards. Three hundred souls crammed thirty, forty, fifty to a cell all night, stifled and starving, forced to breathe in each other's filth. As we drew closer we could hear them banging on the doors, begging in broken voices to be let out, for pity's sake.

'Be quiet, you dogs,' Cross snarled as he passed, slamming his club hard against the doors. 'Or we'll leave you locked up in there all day.'

The cries turned to whimpers, then silence. Cross gestured to Chapman, who began pouring the liquor he'd brought with him into wooden cups. Jakes grabbed one and passed it over. 'Not yet,' he said, stopping me as I brought it to my lips. He passed me a neckerchief. 'Cover your nose and mouth.'

The other men were all doing the same, rinsing the cloth in the liquor before tying it tight.

Cross stomped to the building at the far southeast corner, battling hard against the bitter wind. 'Sick wards first today,' he called over his shoulder. He pulled a face beneath his neckerchief. 'Get the worst of it over.'

Behind me, Woodburn began to pray softly to himself behind his handkerchief.

The trusties positioned themselves by the door. Cross chose a key from the ring and slotted it into the lock. 'Stand back,' he shouted to the prisoners inside. Chapman and the others knocked back their liquor in one quick gulp.

The door swung free.

A foul, putrid stench poured into the yard – so thick and strong we all cried out as one, turning our faces away. It was the festering, heavy stink of disease, of rotting, infected bodies, of men forced to piss and shit and sweat together in an airless cell. There was no escape from it, it clung to my nostrils no matter how hard I pressed the cloth to my face. I began to heave uncontrollably, again and again. I stumbled away, collapsing helplessly to my hands and knees and vomiting across the cobbles until there was nothing left but a thin stream of acid bile.

I stood up at last, half-faint, eyes watering, stomach aching from being turned inside out. By now they had opened up both the men's and women's sick wards and were dragging the night's dead out into the yard, heels scraping the dirt. I clapped my hand across my mouth and looked away, but I could still see the grey, lifeless bodies lined up in a row, even when I closed my eyes. My stomach heaved again.

Cross walked over – to mock me, I thought, but he just picked up my cup and filled it to the brim with liquor.

'Drink,' he ordered, thrusting it at me.

I did as I was told, hands shaking, coughing as it scorched a path down my throat. But it was sharp and clean – a welcome relief from the terrible stink of the sick rooms.

Cross swigged from the bottle, swilling it round his mouth before swallowing. 'Better?'

I nodded weakly.

He studied me with bloodshot eyes, half-curious, half-suspicious. 'What the hell are you doing here, Hawkins?'

I took another drink. 'God's work.'

Cross sputtered his drink on to the cobbles. 'Well, then,' he said, when he'd recovered. 'He must fucking hate you, mustn't He, sir? Any more meat, Mr Jenings?'

The nightwatchman was carrying a body wrapped in stinking rags out of the women's ward. It seemed too thin, too light to be human. He laid the bundle gently on the ground next to the others. 'Just these seven, Joseph.'

Just these seven. My God. No wonder the man was afraid of ghosts.

There was a roll of thunder. The men looked up at the sky as Cross walked slowly from corpse to corpse, eyes narrowed. 'Five men, two women.' He nudged the nearest one with his boot. 'Gaol fever by the looks of it.'

'Bollocks,' Jakes muttered in my ear. 'Starved to death, most of them.'

It started to rain.

Chapman brought a prisoner out from the sick ward, a shaking, sweating skeleton of a man and only a day or two from death himself. Chapman was careful not to touch him – just prodded him forward with his club. The man stared at the row of bodies, no doubt seeing his own future laid out in the dirt before him.

'Any of these have family?' Cross asked.

The prisoner nodded. He was shivering hard – feverish.

'Show me.'

He pointed a grimy finger. Four of them.

'Right,' Cross frowned and gestured to a small hut set close to the Common wall. 'Sling them in the Strong Room with the others.'

I flinched. 'Others? There are others?'

'Can't release the bodies until the family pays the fee. Governor's rules.' Cross took another long swig from his bottle and added, idly, 'Jack Carter's still in there.'

'What's this?' Woodburn cried, startled. He had been quiet all this time but now he seized Cross' arm. 'There must be some mistake. I gave Benjamin the money to release him.'

The trusties opened up the rest of the wards while Woodburn and Cross argued loudly over Jack's corpse and whether or not it was paid for. It was raining hard now, and lightning flickered in the east over Bermondsey, but the prisoners still streamed out into the open air, desperate to escape their cells at last. The yard was soon crowded with thin, dazed figures. Some were in a better state than others – the porters and servants who had secured jobs on the Master's Side and could afford to sleep in one of the better wards. Others looked like walking versions of the corpses laid out on the cobbles.

As I looked about me, stunned with the horror of it all, a young woman stumbled past, tears streaming silently down her face. She would have been pretty once but now her skin was covered in weeping sores, as if a hundred hungry mouths had burst out of her flesh. There were a few children running out into the yard now too, half-naked, scalps red and bloody from scratching at the lice crawling in their filthy, matted hair. The youngest, a boy no older than Acton's son, tottered over to me, holding a tiny scrap of pink silk. He waved it at me shyly.

I turned to Jakes, a hard lump in my throat. We stared at each other for a long moment, the rain soaking us both to the bone.

'Have another drink,' he said. 'Then we'll get started.'

He strode off through the crowds and into one of the wards. The trusties had finished moving the fresh corpses into the Strong Room. They covered the three without family in old, stained sheets and left them out by the wall. Then they scrambled back to the Master's Side as fast as they could.

Woodburn hurried over. 'Mr Hawkins, can you start the rounds without me? I must go with Cross and sort out this business with Jack's body – it really should have been taken away yesterday.' He leaned closer. 'Tell Captain Anderson we'll bring the food round to the begging grates at six o'clock tonight. Acton will be too busy collecting rent to notice.' He paused and looked deep into my face, eyes filled with concern. 'You've had a shock. One forgets.' He patted my arm. 'You've held up well, sir. I fainted the first time.'

'But you came back.'

Woodburn sighed. 'This is my flock. How can I abandon them?' He bowed and hurried away.

I felt a tug on my jacket. The little boy with the scrap of silk had edged close enough to reach me. 'Bread,' he pleaded, thrusting the cloth towards me as if it were money.

I shook my head. I couldn't speak.

He began to sob, held the scrap higher in his tiny fist. '*Hungry . . .*'

An elderly woman limped over and smacked the boy hard across the head. 'Sorry, sir,' she said, dragging him away, blackened nails digging into his arm. 'You won't tell the governor, will you?'

'They're only allowed to beg at the grates,' Jakes said, making me jump. I hadn't heard him approach. 'Come on. I've found someone who'll talk.'

Captain Ralph Anderson was prowling the ward like a wild animal. Even Jakes looked wary of him. A wide, badly healed scar cut down his left cheek into his lip – an old wound won in a battle or a brawl (either way I wasn't about to ask). It would have disfigured a better-looking man but it suited Anderson's wild, craggy face. There was a look in his eye I'd seen in old fighting bears as they were led out into the ring. *Oh, this again. Very well.*

Anderson was constable of his ward – the leader of a group of thirty men who shared a room not much bigger than Belle Isle. As we entered the cell two men staggered past with a large, sloshing barrel reeking of piss.

'Once you've tipped that out tell Harry Mitchell I want him,' Anderson bellowed after them.

This was the best ward on the Common Side, with six beds and a few hammocks slung from the wall. The room was empty now, and the scent of a thin beef stew bubbling in the hearth covered the worst of the Common Side stench. It was clean too – Anderson again, I thought, running the place like a barracks. He still wore his old blue coat from his days in the army, 3rd Dragoons, Jakes said. He'd fought at Ramillies twenty years back. The coat would have paid for a few decent meals but he'd kept it all this time.

He gestured for us to sit with him by the fire. Jakes chose to stand by the window instead – mainly, I think, because the chair he'd been offered was so ancient and worm-eaten it would have collapsed beneath him.

'So you're looking for Roberts' killer,' Anderson said, frowning at me as I perched cautiously on my own creaking chair. 'What's in it for my ward?'

A trade for information? Fair enough. 'I'm a friend of Charles Buckley, Sir Philip's chaplain. I'll make sure Sir Philip hears of any . . . complaints,' I ended, feebly.

Anderson shot me a withering look.

'You said you knew something?' Jakes called impatiently from the window.

Anderson leaned back in his chair. 'Nothing's free in this world, Jakes. You know that. Try again, Mr Hawkins.'

'I can put your case to Mr Gilbourne,' I said, thinking quickly. 'He's a decent man, he'll want to help. And he already knows of my investigation.' I stopped. Anderson was staring at me, open-mouthed with horror.

'*Gilbourne* knows?' He smacked his hand to his forehead. '*Perfect.*'

I frowned, puzzled. 'Is he not to be trusted? He seems an honourable gentleman.'

'Oh, aye, I'm sure that's how he *seems* . . .' Jakes snorted. 'Gilbourne can *seem* whatever he likes, cunning bastard. The man's a snake.'

'It's worse than that,' Anderson groaned. 'It was *Gilbourne* killed Roberts.'

Fourteen

The rain had turned to hail, clattering against the roof as if a thousand dice were being hurled down from heaven. Men from the ward hurried inside looking for shelter only to be ordered back out into the storm again. 'Private meeting,' Anderson growled as they retreated hurriedly from his ill-temper. 'And where the devil is Mitchell?'

'On his way. Working . . . other side,' one of the men wheezed, then bent double in a coughing fit, disease rattling in his lungs.

I'd asked Anderson questions, of course. *How do you know Gilbourne killed Roberts? Why did he do it? How did he do it? Why did you say nothing about it?* He ignored me. Jakes looked furious. I could see him weighing up his chances if it came to beating the story out of the old soldier. I wondered if it were possible to keep my dignity while hiding under the bed.

After a long, tense wait Harry Mitchell appeared, sluicing the rain from his tattered clothes. He was a stocky man of about forty, with a dark complexion — Cornish, I thought, or Welsh. He looked fit enough for the Common Side, but tired from over-work. I thought he looked familiar, and then I realised he was a porter on the Master's Side. He'd brought Trim his supper on my first night.

'You asked to see me, sir?' Cornish. Standing to attention as if Anderson really were his commanding officer.

Anderson gazed at him levelly and said one word. 'Gilbourne.'

Mitchell flinched. His eyes darted to Jakes, and then to me. 'Trustworthy, are they?'

Jakes put a wide, scarred hand to his heart. 'Upon my soul.'

'And mine,' I added hurriedly, touching my mother's cross.

Mitchell breathed heavily through his nose, and said nothing.

'Oh, for Gawd's sake,' Jakes muttered, and threw him a tuppenny piece.

Mitchell snatched it from the air and smiled at me, suddenly convinced. A miracle. He sat down on the bed nearest the fire, resting his hands upon his knees. 'Well, then. *Edward Gilbourne.*' Mr Mitchell had an unexpected flair for the dramatic. 'He killed the captain, didn't he?'

'Harry was Roberts' servant,' Anderson explained.

'Cooked his meals,' Mitchell nodded. 'Cleaned his clothes, his sheets. Errands and messages. Fourpence a week. First week, he apologises. Says he's not good for it. I says, "Don't you worry, Captain, I know you're an honourable gentleman, you'll pay me when you have it. Now how about some of this mutton broth?" Once he'd finished it right to the bottom of the bowl, I says to him, "Oh, and by the way, Captain. Forgot to mention. I pissed in that. And so will any servant you fancy hiring from the Common Side from now on. Unless you have that fourpence by any chance." He took it in good part, rest his soul. And he never played me after that. He was a rogue, but—'

'Harry . . .' Anderson prompted, exasperated. '*Gilbourne . . .?*'

'A week before he was murdered,' Mitchell continued, unruffled, 'the captain grabs a hold of me and says, "Harry, here's a tale for you. I'll be leaving the Marshalsea in a few days. So you must find yourself a new position." I just laughed – he was always talking nonsense.'

Jakes chuckled quietly. 'True enough. John spent half his life dreaming up ways to make money. Never came to nothing.'

'That's what I thought, Mr Jakes,' Mitchell called over from the bed. 'Just another one of the captain's stories. But he says, "Just you wait, Harry. I've got something on Gilbourne that'll finish him. I'll squeeze every last farthing from him."' Mitchell grabbed the edge of his greying, stained shirt and twisted it sharply.

'Blackmail,' Jakes grunted. He didn't look surprised by his old friend's behaviour.

A roll of thunder grumbled its way across the sky. 'What had Gilbourne done?' I asked Mitchell.

'The captain said it was best I didn't know. But it was wicked, he said. Truly wicked. Enough to destroy Gilbourne's reputation.' He paused. 'You won't . . . you won't tell anyone I told you this, will you?' he asked anxiously. 'I haven't dared say nothing until now. I don't want to get my throat cut . . .'

'Who would cut your throat?' I frowned.

Mitchell stared at me. '*Gilbourne*, of course.'

I laughed, incredulous. The thought of Edward Gilbourne slitting someone's throat . . . it was ridiculous.

Anderson looked at me sharply. 'You don't believe us?'

'Well . . . look.' I hesitated, wondering how to reply without offending Anderson, or implying that Mitchell wasn't being entirely honest. 'I didn't know Roberts, but by all accounts he was a liar and a cheat. Even his best friend admits that,' I added, shrugging at Jakes. 'But I *have* met Edward Gilbourne. He doesn't strike me as a killer.'

'And why's that, damn you?' Anderson cried, suddenly angry. 'Because he rides a fine horse? Because you like the way he ties his cravat?' He leapt from his chair and flung it hard against the wall. To stop himself throwing me, I thought, shrinking back. It broke into pieces and clattered to the floor.

'Ralph,' Jakes said, mildly, but we all heard the warning in his voice.

The two men faced each other across the room. Another roll of thunder. A stutter of lightning. I watched them both, worried. Jakes could beat the older man in a fair fight. But there were three hundred prisoners locked on this side of the wall with us — quite enough to tear us limb from limb if Anderson asked them to.

'Captain Anderson,' I said, holding up my hands. 'Forgive me, I meant no offence. I can see you are a man of honour. If you tell me Mr Gilbourne is not to be trusted, then I must believe you.'

Anderson studied me for a long moment, then sighed. He found himself another chair. 'Pour us all a drink, Harry.'

Mitchell brought out some cheap beer. Across the room Jakes relaxed, rolling his shoulders and unclenching his fists. He caught my eye and winked his approval.

'To Edward Gilbourne . . .' Anderson said, raising his mug of beer.

'. . . May he rot in hell,' Mitchell finished, cheerfully. 'We should tell him about the charity money,' he added, pointing to a spot on the wall close to where Anderson had thrown his chair. 'He'll believe us then.' I could just make out the remnants of what looked like an old shelf, with iron brackets screwed into the wood. They seemed to have been bent back with some force.

Captain Anderson shifted gloomily in his seat. 'Jakes — you tell him. I can't face it.'

Jakes poured himself some more beer and wandered over to the broken shelf. He touched the bracket, rubbed smears of dark orange rust from his fingers. 'The Common Side has six wards. Each ward has a constable, a leader.' He gestured at Anderson. 'Then there's a steward. The prisoners elect him to represent their interests and distribute donations. Food, money, clothes, medicine. The last steward was a man called Matthew Pugh. He wasn't a prisoner himself but he was on their side. Had a cousin who died in here, I think, or a friend.' Jakes waved his hand. 'Well — either way. He promised the prisoners he would petition the governor and Sir Philip for better conditions.'

'A good man,' Anderson declared, lighting a pipe. 'Only good man to work in this stinking place.'

'This all started, what . . . five years ago?' Jakes said.

'Aye,' Anderson scowled. 'Acton was chief turnkey back in those days. What Cross is today but worse if you can imagine it. Striding about as if he were lord of the manor, even then. "Keep the choice cuts on the Master's Side and throw the shit over the wall, lads."'

Jakes frowned. 'Pugh began to suspect something was wrong with the charity donations.'

I leaned forward. 'How so?'

'There weren't any,' Mitchell and Anderson answered in unison.

'Stolen?' I guessed.

Jakes nodded. 'The steward was supposed to have his own special seal – it proved to the charities that the money was reaching the prisoners and not just lining the governor's pockets. But Acton and Darby, the old governor, had stolen it. They took the money and divided up the donations between them.' He held my gaze. 'One hundred and fifteen pounds a year.'

My mouth dropped.

'More than that!' Anderson cried, flinging his pipe to the floor. It bounced and clattered into the hearth, broken in two. 'Twice that much, I'd bet my life on it! Those bastards stole the money, Mr Hawkins – and let the prisoners starve to death. Day after day, week after week. Hundreds of them!'

'Strange, eh?' Jakes gave a bitter laugh. 'Kill a man in the street and they hang you at Tyburn. Kill a hundred debtors in prison and they make you governor. Pugh spent three years fighting for justice. He tried asking Gilbourne first . . .'

Mitchell stretched himself on tiptoes, pretended to fuss over his filthy shirt cuffs. '"Oh, Mr Pugh, if only I could help!" he sighed, in a passable impression of Gilbourne – if the Palace clerk were fifteen years older and a foot shorter. '"Alas, my hands are tied! Ah, sir, it pains me how little I can do for you."

'He tried Sir Philip, too,' Anderson said, waving at Mitchell to stop. 'Begged an audience for three years and was refused every time. Then Mr Buckley joined the household.'

Charles. I looked up, startled. Oh, no, please God – if they told me Charles was involved in this scheme I couldn't bear it. I turned to Jakes. 'He knows of this?'

Jakes took a swig of beer. 'Pugh wrote to him asking for help. He persuaded Sir Philip to order a new charity seal.' He glanced at Anderson, eyebrow raised. 'Pugh wasn't the *only* good man in all this, Ralph.'

'Buckley's not so bad, I suppose,' Anderson conceded. 'Only reason I'm talking to *you*,' he added, glowering at me. 'But what difference did it make, eh?'

The room fell silent, rain clattering softly on the roof. The beef stew mumbled to itself in the pot. The storm had drowned out any sound beyond our own voices, but now it was passing I could hear prisoners calling to one another in the yard. I felt a sudden urge to jump up and leave – to run to the wall and bang on the door until I was let back on to the Master's Side. This story was not going to end well. 'What happened?'

Anderson stirred as if from a dream. 'Once we had the new seal, Pugh began collecting the charity money himself. We decided to keep it here, on the Common Side, where we could defend it. Pugh had a chest built with seven locks, one key for each constable and a seventh for the steward. We fixed the chest to the wall over there,' his eyes flickered to the broken hinges, 'and we all swore an oath to use the money fairly, for the good of the whole gaol. It worked. For a few weeks. No one starved. Acton was *furious*. Do you remember, Mitchell? Storming and raging about the gaol. Cursing us for stealing his money. *His* money!'

'And then?'

'And then?' Anderson snorted. 'He complained to the Court. And what do you think, Mr Hawkins? This time the deputy prothonotary found his hands *weren't* tied. Not one little bit.'

Mitchell muttered something in Cornish. It didn't sound friendly.

Anderson got to his feet and pulled a battered, rusty old box from under his bed, the lid scraping as he lifted it free. He plucked out a letter and handed it to me. It was from the office of the deputy prothonotary, dated July 1725 and marked with the Court's seal.

Upon information given to this Court by the Keeper that one Matthew Pugh has very often behaved himself very turbulently in the Prison, frequently occasioning disturbances amongst the Prisoners, and because of this impudent Behaviour, as well in this Court as the Office of Prothonotary, it is this Day ordered that the said Matthew Pugh be no longer permitted to have Access to the Prison of this Court, and that the prisoners be at Liberty to appoint another Person to receive the Gifts and Legacies belonging to them.
By the Court
  Edward Gilbourne
  Deputy Prothonotary

I shook my head. 'But why would Gilbourne help Acton? He loathes him.' And then I remembered Fleet's Law. '*Money.*'

'The next time Pugh came to the prison he was attacked by five of Acton's men. They grabbed the charity seal and tossed him out into the street.' Anderson slumped in his chair. 'That poor bastard spent three years fighting for us and they kicked him out the gate like a dog. He was coughing blood for a week.'

I read Gilbourne's note again. 'It says here that the prisoners have the right to appoint a new steward.'

Anderson gave a dry laugh. 'Oh, yes. Acton *gave us liberty* to vote for Mr Grace. You've met him?'

I thought of Acton's clerk at supper, scraping a line through a man's name. It had seemed cruel last night, but now I had witnessed first hand where he was sending them, it seemed crueller still. A thin shiver ran down my spine. 'I've met him.'

'We refused to give him the keys to the charity chest. So Acton stormed in with twenty men, ripped the chest from that wall over there and carried it away on his shoulders, laughing. "Mr Gilbourne's orders," he said. A year later he'd saved up enough funds to buy the position of keeper from Darby. And Gilbourne had a fine stallion to ride in to Court.'

I stared at the Court letter in my hands, at the large, confident signature at the bottom. Signed with a flourish – no doubt, no hesitation – though Gilbourne must have known he was signing a death warrant for countless men and women starving on the Common Side. I felt sick. How easily he'd fooled me with his flattery and charm! All those empty, cunning, worthless words. Of course he had his fingers in the pie; why should that be surprising? I'd admired his horse and his fine clothes, I'd seen the way the lawyers fawned about him. I'd always prided myself on reading a man's lies in his face but he had played me like a boy fresh in from the country. 'Damn him. I should have seen it.'

Mitchell patted my shoulder. 'You're not the first he's fooled,' he said, kindly. 'He acts the gentleman on the Master's Side, you see. I've seen him. He'll be whatever you want him to be. But it's all lies. A mask he hides behind. He'd fuck his own grandmother if he had to,' he asserted, with an air of authority.

I folded the court order. 'Perhaps *that's* what Roberts had on him.'

Mitchell cackled. 'Hah! Perhaps! Well, one thing I do know, sir. Whatever Gilbourne was up to, it had nothing to do with the Common Side. No one gives a damn what happens in here. We could all die tonight – each and every one of us – and they'd just shrug and find another three hundred wretches to take our place.'

True enough. I wondered what Roberts had discovered. An affair, perhaps. Would that be scandalous enough? I remembered the first time I'd seen Gilbourne, talking with Catherine Roberts out in the yard. I had wondered then if they could be lovers. Was that it? Was Roberts prepared to ruin his own wife's reputation to escape prison? Catherine said he'd never forgiven her for persuading him to give up their son. Perhaps there were other things he couldn't forgive. Perhaps he'd decided to take revenge on Gilbourne and Catherine together . . .

'I told the captain to be careful,' Mitchell sighed. 'I *told* him Gilbourne was dangerous. He wouldn't listen. "I don't care, Harry," he says. "I'll take that risk if it gets me out of this wretched hole. One last gamble."' He paused. 'Then a few days later they found him hanging in the Strong Room. Poor bugger.'

'Maybe he was lucky,' Anderson muttered. 'A quick death.'

Jakes frowned, and peered out of the window. 'The rain's stopped. We'd best head back before Mr Woodburn starts to worry.'

'Oh!' I exclaimed, remembering Woodburn's message. I told Anderson that the food would be sent round to the begging grate that evening.

Anderson sighed with relief. 'Thank God.'

'I heard a rumour of this,' Jakes said. 'Woodburn said he'd been given money in secret. A friend of the Common Side — that's all he'd tell me. I thought it might be Matthew Pugh.'

Anderson shook his head. 'Pugh doesn't have that sort of money to spare.'

'How much was it?' I asked.

'Five pounds,' Anderson replied. 'But we daren't keep it in here. Acton would sniff it out in a flash. Mr Woodburn buys food and medicine and slips it through the begging grate once a week. Should last us the rest of the year, if we're careful. Save a few people from starving, at least.' He gripped my arm and pulled me close. 'Swear you won't breathe a word.'

'I swear!' I said, wincing. Anderson was even stronger than he looked. He let go, satisfied. 'Would Acton really steal *food* from the Common Side?' I asked, rubbing my arm. 'Surely there's no profit in that?'

Anderson dipped his finger in the beef stew to taste. Pulled a face. 'He likes to keep us hungry, Mr Hawkins. We're easier to control that way. And the worse it is in here, the more he can charge over on *your* side of the wall. Why do you think the Tap Room looks out over the Common Side? He wants all you gents and ladies to see us, doesn't he? Living in the filth. Sick and starving. You take one look at us and you'll pay Acton *anything* to avoid the same fate. Did you know there are five wards over here standing empty? There's no need to pack us in like animals. But the more of us die in here, the more rent men like you will pay. Clever, eh?'

It was all true, I was sure of it. And the horror of it was – it worked. I would give just about anything, *do* just about anything, to avoid being thrown in here. I could still taste the vomit in the back of my throat. 'Perhaps things will change. If I talk to Sir Philip. If I can *prove* that Acton or Gilbourne killed Captain Roberts . . .'

'Fuck all the saints!' Anderson cursed. 'You don't let him talk like that on the Master's Side, do you, Jakes? If the governor heard him . . .' He paused, looked me dead in the eye. 'Last summer they chained a man to a corpse in the Strong Room for three days, for daring to stand up to Acton. I saw him when they pulled him out again. They took off his chains but it made no difference. He could still feel the corpse flesh against his skin. Scratched a hole in his arm the size of a hen's egg. He said he was trying to gouge out the dead man's touch.'

Jakes cleared his throat. 'No need to frighten him.'

Anderson looked at him. 'Isn't there?'

Jakes frowned and moved to the doorway, scouting the yard with a hand on his sword. Anderson pulled me back. 'Hawkins,' he hissed in my ear. 'Take my advice. Find another way out of here. You'll get yourself murdered, boy.' He released me back into the yard with a friendly shove and lumbered back into his ward.

Jakes and I pushed our way through the crowds of feverish, list-less prisoners, back towards the wall. Inside, in the ward, we had been under Anderson's protection. But now we were vulnerable – two men against three hundred desperate souls. They snatched at our clothes as we passed, thin fingers poking into pockets, under shirts, snaking and grasping and pulling. I clasped my mother's cross hard against my chest, afraid it might be ripped from my neck.

When we reached the door there was no one on the other side of the wall to let us through, and we passed an anxious few minutes knocking and calling to be released. Joseph Cross, having his revenge on us both. While Jakes slammed on the door with his club I pushed another grabbing hand from my arm only to discover it belonged to Harry Mitchell. He leaned in close, breathing stale beer breath into my face. 'I know Gilbourne's secret,' he said. 'The *blackmail*. I'll tell you for a price.'

I would have seized him by the throat and shaken the truth out of him if I could, but there were too many people pushing and shoving around us. I didn't want to be ripped to pieces for throt-tling Harry Mitchell. 'How much?' I muttered, reluctantly.

'Freedom. Same as you.'

The door swung open and Cross poked his head through. 'Come on, then, come on!'

Mitchell clung to me, suddenly desperate. 'Gilbourne'll kill me if he finds out I told. Get me out of here, Mr Hawkins. Settle it with Sir Philip. I swear I'll tell you everything.'

I pushed him away. 'I'll see.'

He fell back into the crowds. Jakes shoved me back through the wall while Cross closed and bolted the door again as fast as if he were barring the gates to hell. I suppose he was. I had never felt so glad to take three paces in my life. Back on the Master's Side. And alive! I could have kissed the cobbles with relief.

Fifteen

The storm had passed as quickly as it had come, the sky a clear, bright blue, as if the rain had washed it clean. The cobbles were slippery and the whole prison smelled mossy and damp, but the air was fresher, the east wind bundling the Common Side stench away with it. For the first time in a long while I wished I had stayed safe in the country, leaping over silver puddles, mud spattering my stockings as I made my way home to the vicarage. A safe, quiet, peaceful world. My father's world. And then a stray, traitorous thought – perhaps he had been right, all along. Perhaps I should never have left . . .

'So I'll return on Monday,' Jakes said again, waving a hand in front of my face. Tomorrow was Sunday. 'Can you stay alive until then, do you think?'

I nodded absently and he left, unconvinced. Losing Jakes was like losing a blade or a full purse. I would miss his protection. But I could not expect him to stay locked up in gaol with me. He had his own life out in the Borough – a wife and two young daughters. He would never in his life have brought them into the Marshalsea. I wondered briefly what his girls looked like and had an image of two miniature Misses Jakes in skirts, with squashed noses, scarred brows and meaty arms.

I pulled out Fleet's watch from a hidden pocket, marvelling that it hadn't been plucked from me in the scrabble by the wall.

Two o'clock. No wonder my stomach was rumbling – I hadn't eaten all day. With Jakes gone, I decided to find Fleet and tell him everything in the hope we could puzzle it all out together. Preferably over dinner. It was a dangerous strategy, trusting him with the truth. Trusting him with anything. But I needed his help. I realised now that Fleet had suspected Gilbourne all along. He'd known Gilbourne would be dining at Acton's when he dressed me up in Roberts' clothes. And thinking back, I remembered he'd been interested in Gilbourne's reaction in particular.

What else had he been keeping from me?

I was just about to start looking for him when I heard a commotion coming from the Lodge. *Walk away, Tom. Not your business.*

The Reverend Andrew Woodburn's voice – sharp and shrill with fury. 'Miserable, wicked boy! How could you? How *could* you?'

Oh well, maybe just a *quick* look? Before I had taken another step Benjamin Carter flew out of the Lodge door and into the Park, tripping and falling to his knees in his haste to escape. As he fell he dropped a couple of wooden boxes he'd been carrying under his arm. They clattered to the cobbles, landing at my feet. I picked one up, curious, and shook it. A handful of coins rattled and bounced against the sides. A few debtors gathered nearby turned my way, attracted by the music.

Ben was on his feet in a moment. 'Give it back,' he snarled, tearing it from my hands and hugging it to his chest. As he turned to pick up the second box Mr Woodburn rushed out into the yard, wheezing with the effort. Gilbert Hand sauntered behind, hands in his pockets.

'Do leave the boy alone, Woodburn,' he suggested, mildly.

The chaplain raised his ebony cane and for one astonishing moment I thought he might actually dash Hand's brains out. But then he caught my eye, and collected himself. 'Well, Mr

Hawkins,' he said, limping over to me. 'Here is an evil business.'

'But it is *business*,' Hand pointed out. 'You can't blame Benjamin for trying to earn an honest penny.'

'*Honest?*' Woodburn's eyes bulged so hard I thought they might pop from his head and roll across the cobbles. 'Stealing from a charity box? *Honest?*'

'Well now.' Hand rocked back on his heels. '*Stealing* is a strong word. What would you say, Hawkins? Young Mr Carter here,' he squeezed the boy's lean shoulder, 'has paid the governor a shilling for the right to beg charity round the Borough. And for that *honourable* work he is allowed to keep one tenth of what he earns. Would you begrudge him that?'

Woodburn tapped his cane irritably. 'And the rest, Mr Hand. Where does *that* go, pray?'

Hand affected an innocent look. 'Why, it goes to the Common Side, of course.'

'It does no such thing!' Woodburn cried, outraged. 'It goes straight into Acton's purse. And yours too, Mr Hand,' he added, jabbing a finger towards the ranger's waistcoat pocket. 'I know all about the deal you've made with him.'

'That is quite an accusation,' Hand observed. 'Slanderous, I'd say. I wonder what Mr Acton would make of it?'

Woodburn grabbed Benjamin's arm and wrenched him away from Hand's side, as if he were hauling him back from the edge of a cliff. He bent down so he could stare right into the boy's face. 'I gave you that shilling for Jack. To release his body. Benjamin . . . he's still lying there in the Strong Room with all the . . .' He paused, shook his head, unable to say the words. 'He's still lying there *because of you*.'

A guilty shadow crossed Ben's face. But then it passed. 'Jack's dead,' he said in a flat, sullen voice. 'I'm alive. I have to look after myself.'

'Oh, Benjamin,' Woodburn sighed. 'The *Lord* will look after you, if you trust in Him.'

Ben scowled. 'He didn't look after Jack, did He? Didn't look after my mother, neither. I *won't* end up like them.' He tore himself from the chaplain's grasp and sped off back towards the Lodge.

Woodburn watched him go, then turned and rubbed the tears from his eyes.

'You did your best, sir,' I said, while Hand smirked at me.

Woodburn sighed and trudged away without a word, head bowed. He looked wretched, as if his house had collapsed about his ears.

'Oh dear, oh dear. Poor Woodburn,' Hand said, smiling broadly. 'He *will* keep putting his faith in the wrong people.' He gave me a sly look and wandered off.

Fleet was not on his bench by the Lodge so I headed upstairs to the Tap Room. Mary was at the bar with Mack and a few other admirers. The singing and laughter was as loud as ever, holding the room in a drunken bubble. No doubt or worry or regret allowed in here; not until later when the bubble burst and all that was left was the grubby truth, men crying into their last drink and wondering how they had lost money yet again to the warden and his wife. I smiled at Mary and she glared at me then whispered something in Mack's ear. He slid off his chair and weaved his way towards the door.

'Trouble, Hawkins,' he murmured as he passed. 'I'm sorry.'

My heart sank. Could I not get five minutes of peace in this damned place? How on earth had I managed to offend Mary? I'd danced with her, hadn't I? At least I hadn't trodden on her foot like Mack.

It took me a moment to find Fleet – he was not sitting at his usual seat by the window but huddled in a dark corner with a companion, who had his back turned to the room. Fleet was also fully dressed, and in clothes that fitted him for once. His journal was open on the table between them and they were deep in conversation; so deep I was only a couple of feet away when Fleet spied me. He closed the journal with a slam and signalled to the other man with his eyes.

'Hawkins,' he said. His gaze slid from me to the stranger, but he didn't introduce us, and the man didn't turn round or show his face.

'Fleet. I must speak with you. I have news.'

He leaned back and smiled at me. 'Of course you have news. You *always* have news. You are a veritable *magnet* of news. Have you dined? Let me finish my business with Mr . . . *Smith* here and I will join you at Bradshaw's.'

'I'm banned from Bradshaw's because of you, sir. I am universally *hated* because of you. Mrs Bradshaw, Mrs Roberts, Mrs Acton . . . even Kitty Sparks has turned against me.'

'Four queens!' Fleet exclaimed. 'Now there's a hand. But I can't take the credit for all of them.' He tilted his head. 'Is there a chance you may have upset Kitty all by yourself?'

'I'll wait for you in Belle Isle. It's a *most pressing* matter, Mr Fleet.'

Fleet nodded, then shooed me away with a little flick of his hand. I gritted my teeth and turned to leave. As I walked away, I heard Fleet's companion mutter, in a gruff tone, 'That boy's trouble, Sam.'

'I know,' Fleet replied. He sounded pleased.

There was a sense of relief about the prisoners in the yard; people stood around laughing and chatting. It reminded me of the atmosphere at college after exams, or outside my father's church after one of his more thunderous sermons; a sort of giddy joy at having survived, for now. The same could not be said of the men and women queueing on the stairs leading up into the Palace Court, most of whom stood with eyes fixed firmly to the ground, lost in melancholy thoughts. Husbands and wives clutched one another tight, shuffling together as the queue moved up the stairs. A man pulled out his coins and counted them over and over, as if hoping they might multiply in his hand.

'The weekly rent,' said a voice behind me.

I turned and dipped a short bow. 'Mrs Roberts.'

She rolled back her veil. 'John and I would stand in that queue together,' she said quietly, her eyes on the slow march of debtors trudging their way into the Court. 'He would hold my hand so tight. Even if we had the money, we were always afraid . . . Mr Grace is a demon at finding new fees, new debts, if Mr Acton demands it. There is so much fear in this place sometimes I think it has seeped into the walls.' She put a gloved hand upon my arm. 'I owe you an apology, sir. Mr Fleet told me it was his idea to put you in John's clothes. He also said . . .' she bit her lip '. . . you know the truth about the ghost.' She put her hands to her face. 'What must you think of me?'

'Does my opinion matter to you, madam?'

She lowered her hands. 'Very much,' she whispered. 'Would you walk with me, sir?'

'If you wish.'

She slipped her arm through mine, leading me across the yard. 'You are angry with me.'

'You used me, Mrs Roberts. If you had come to me honestly, I would have been glad to help you.'

We passed Gilbert Hand, smoking a pipe by the lamppost. He grinned as we passed, and nodded his head.

'You are right,' she sighed, once we were beyond earshot. 'But I was desperate and I have . . . I have lost the capacity to trust. It's easy for people to dismiss Mr Jenings and Mrs Carey. And they could only catch a glimpse of the ghost – they both knew John too well to be fooled by . . . But if you saw it. If you saw his face and swore it looked just like his portrait . . . I think people might have listened.'

'And what of Ben Carter? You scared the boy out of his wits.'

She blushed. 'That was ill done of me, I know. But he is a sharp, clever lad; I knew he would recover. Oh!' she cried, gripping my arm tight. 'How to explain . . . just how desperate I have become? To discover the truth and be free of this place at last. To hold my son in my arms again. I believe I would do almost anything for that.' She shivered.

We walked on for a while in silence, until we reached the tree by Acton's lodgings. 'This is where you slapped me,' I said.

She stopped and touched a hand to the bark. 'It is also where I saw you dressed in John's clothes. I almost died of fright.'

'What a strange muddle we have made of things.'

She laughed. 'Perhaps we should begin again, Mr Hawkins.'

We turned and headed back towards Belle Isle. When we reached the entrance to the block she slid her arm from mine. 'So. Are we friends?'

I hesitated for a moment, then nodded. She smiled, grey eyes sparkling with relief and pleasure. Yesterday it would have made my heart race; today I was wiser. If Acton or Gilbert Hand or anyone else learned that she had invented the ghost that had caused so much fear and unrest around the prison, she would be thrown out of the gate in disgrace. She needed my friendship more than she wanted it. In short, I was still being played, but I didn't really mind. I understood her motives, even if her methods were a little *naughty*, as Moll might say. And who was I to judge anyone, after all?

'One thing I don't understand. How did your ghost slip out of the prison?'

She smiled. 'Poor Mr Simmons. He's an old gambling friend of John's. I offered to pay his debts if he would help me. He's an actor. Not a very good one, I'm afraid. But he knew how to play the part. The white face was his idea. Flour, I believe.'

'But where did he go? We searched every corner of the gaol.'

'Mr Fleet asked me the same thing. He was quite insistent.' She pursed her lips. '*Must* you share a room with him, Mr

Hawkins? His reputation is very wild. Are you not afraid he will corrupt you?'

'Mrs Roberts,' I warned, sternly. '*Catherine*. Tell me. How did Mr Simmons escape?'

'Oh, very well,' she said with a frown. 'But you must promise not to breathe a word.' She glanced about her to be sure no one was looking, then tapped her foot on the ground. 'The store cellar.'

I pressed my toes against the wooden trap door at our feet. Acton kept all the Tap Room drinks in the cellar; it was packed to the ceiling with crates of wine and barrels of cheap ale that he sold for thrice their worth. 'But we searched down there last night,' I protested. 'We didn't find a soul.' I didn't tell her that Jenings had been so frightened he'd nearly dropped his torch and set the whole place alight. Or that I'd managed to smuggle out three bottles of wine beneath my coat.

'There's another door at the far end that leads out onto Axe and Bottle Yard. No one knows it's there; it's been sealed up for years. It's so dark in the cellar, and no one has ever thought to look . . .' She caught my expression and stopped. 'Don't ask me.'

'I could escape. Tonight, if you'd help me.'

'I don't hold the key. And where would you go, Mr Hawkins? You know Acton would be held responsible for your debt if you escaped; he would hunt you down and . . .' The tears sprang in her eyes. If she was acting, she was far better than Mr Simmons.

What would Moll pay for information like this, I wondered? She could find someone to pick that lock in a flash. Free, secret access in and out of the Marshalsea? Oh, that had to be worth a great deal.

'Please,' Catherine whispered. 'Promise you won't tell a soul. Swear it!'

'Who loans you the key?'

She groaned. 'If I tell you, will you swear?'

'Very well.'

She leaned closer and put her lips to my ear. 'Edward Gilbourne.'

She left me then, gathering her skirts and whisking away towards the Palace Court and her room in the Oak ward. The transaction was done after all – my silence for her information. *Gilbourne*. Of course. He was at the black heart of everything in this prison, perhaps more than Acton himself. He must have been handing her the cellar key when I spied them from the window yesterday. Thinking back, there had been something odd in Gilbourne's expression when he talked to her. He looked at her the way I might look at a good hand at cards: possessive, secretive. Sly.

So: Roberts was intent on blackmailing Gilbourne. And Gilbourne had secret access to the prison, able to slip in and out any time he pleased. I blinked. There it was. Solved! And without Fleet's help, damn him. Gilbourne murdered Roberts to silence him – and in the bargain made a widow of Catherine Roberts. Now he was slowly, assiduously wooing her, helping her with all this foolish nonsense with the ghost to earn her gratitude and place her in his debt. And all the while knowing that Mr Simmons would never scare the murderer into revealing himself. Because he was the killer.

There must have been a second man, of course; Gilbourne couldn't have carried the captain's dead weight across the Park and over to the Strong Room on his own. Someone with a key to the Common Side, I supposed. My money was on Joseph Cross. Well, they could press Gilbourne for that if need be. There were ways of squeezing the truth out of a man.

I must send a letter to Charles at once. But who could I trust to send it? Jakes was gone until Monday and Gilbert Hand would read the contents. Mr Jenings, perhaps? I was still standing at the trap door considering all of this when Sarah Bradshaw cantered down the yard towards me. 'Oh! Mr Hawkins, sir! Oh, can you ever forgive me?' she gasped, clutching my hand and pressing it to her heaving bosom. 'I should have known it was all Mr Fleet's doing, dressing you up like that. The devil! Come and let me fix you dinner on the house. No, no, I insist!' she said, though she hadn't given me time to refuse her. 'You poor dear, what a time you've had. What must you think of us?'

I followed in her wake. At the Palace Court the rent queue had dwindled away. A man I recognised from the Tap Room was the last in line, turning his hat round and round in his hand.

'Sit yourself down, sir,' Mrs Bradshaw commanded, pushing me into the coffeehouse and clearing a table by the window. Kitty was at the hearth and a few prisoners were playing backgammon in one corner. Madame Migault was at her usual table, pecking at a dinner of calf's head and salad. A large bowl of punch lay half-finished at her side; she seemed to have drunk it by herself, though where she had put it on that sparrow-frame of hers I couldn't say. She looked cheerful. It didn't suit her.

Mrs Bradshaw ordered a knuckle of veal and a belly piece of pork from Titty Doll's and told Kitty to make me a fresh pot of coffee. Kitty still seemed out of sorts from our fight this morning and would not catch my eye – but I was too busy writing my note to Charles to pay her much mind. If the letter reached him soon enough, perhaps he could secure my release tonight. The thought made my heart leap. Charles had promised to help me in any way he could once I was free. Well, I had learned my lesson. I would start afresh, find a good, respectable job. Or one that paid well, at least. I took another piece of pork. Perhaps I could take Gilbourne's position, once he was arrested. I could reinstate . . . what was his name? *Matthew Pugh* to handle the charity money – for a small fee, of course. Thomas Hawkins, deputy prothonotary . . .

No, that didn't sound well at all. A glorified clerk? Oh, something would turn up, I supposed.

'Madame Migault. You tell fortunes, do you not?' I took a coin out of my pocket. 'Would you read mine?'

She squinted at me for a moment then beckoned me over. '*Rien à payer*,' she said as I sat down opposite her. She popped a calf's eyeball in her mouth with a festive air, rolling it from cheek to cheek before chewing down hard. Now I was this close her breath confirmed that she had most certainly not shared the punch bowl. She gripped my hand in both talons and turned it palm upwards, scraping her nails across the skin. 'Kitty,' she shrieked, making the coffeehouse flinch. 'Translate.'

'I speak French, madame.'

'Kitty!' she shrieked again, ignoring me.

'Ooh, a reading!' Mrs Bradshaw cried, clapping her hands and squeezing her way over to madame's table. 'I thought you didn't approve of such things, Mr Hawkins? Kitty, come here and translate for me, my love.'

Kitty turned from the fire. 'I don't want to,' she whispered, wrapping her arms about her waist.

'Come along, sweetheart,' Mrs Bradshaw trilled, but there was a sharp edge behind the request.

Kitty shuffled slowly towards us, her face deathly white.

I frowned with concern. We may have fought this morning but I missed her temper. This new mood was not like her. 'Are you not well, Kitty?'

She bit her lip. 'I'm well. Thank you, sir,' she whispered. It was the first time she had called me sir and meant it.

'I see your future . . .' Madame Migault crooned, scraping her long, blue-white fingernails against my palm. '*Oui . . . très clair . . .*' Her eyes rolled back and she stared into the distance, as if in a trance.

You old fraud, I thought.

'She's possessed,' Mrs Bradshaw whispered in awe. 'Ooh, Lord, I will die of fright.' She prodded Kitty eagerly. 'What's she saying?'

Kitty lowered herself down slowly into the chair between the madame and me and began translating in a shaky voice, her hands twisting her apron back and forth.

'I see your family,' Madame Migault claimed in a high, sing-song voice. 'They live in the country . . . your father . . . he is a man of faith, yes?'

I smiled. 'Easy enough to discover that, madame.'

'You betrayed him. *Lied* to him. He has not forgiven you. And he never will.' Her eyes snapped fast to mine. 'You will not see him again in this lifetime, monsieur.'

Mrs Bradshaw, who was standing behind me, gave my shoulder a squeeze. 'Oh, I am sorry to hear that, sir. Perhaps you can change that, now you've been warned.'

'*Non!*' Madame Migault smiled, triumphant. 'The future will not change.' She closed her eyes and continued. 'You have a friend . . . He wants to help you but it is too late. Your secret has been discovered.' Her eyes flung open. 'Betrayed!' she shrieked. And then, much lower. 'By someone close to you. Very close . . .' She began to chuckle, strange little hiccups, her shoulders jerking up and down.

Kitty translated, her eyes on the floor, her voice no more than a broken whisper. When she'd finished, Mrs Bradshaw gave a little squeal. 'What can it mean? Oh, it sends a shiver down my spine. Can't you find something more cheerful, Miggy? A wedding . . . ? A fortune . . . ?'

'No wedding. No fortune,' Madame Migault announced glee-fully. 'All your plans will fail. All your dreams will die. And you will die with them. Tonight!' She laughed, and poured herself another glass of punch.

'Well.' I drummed my fingers lightly on the table. 'I hope you're not expecting a tip.'

To my astonishment Kitty burst into tears, sobbing into her apron. I touched her arm. 'Come now, Kitty. It's just a silly game.'

'No game!' Madame Migault cackled into her glass. '*Pauvre monsieur*. Tonight you die.'

'*Madame!*' Mrs Bradshaw yelped. 'You mustn't say such things! Oh, Mr Hawkins, I don't know what to say! She's never like this as a rule. She told me I'd get a little dog before the new year.' She looked away, dreamily.

Kitty jumped up and ran from the room. Her feet pounded up the stairs, and then a door slammed somewhere above our heads in the Oak ward.

Mrs Bradshaw began to giggle and nudged me in the ribs, her elbow pushing hard on a bruise. I gritted my teeth at the pain.

'Oh dear,' she sniggered. 'I'm afraid you've sent her a bit topsy-turvy. She took a bit of a shine to you, not that she'd admit it. Must have been those *fine calves* of yours. Then she heard you telling Mrs Roberts you didn't care a fig for her. I said of *course* he doesn't, you silly jade. He's a proper gentleman! He won't have given you a moment's thought, why on earth should he? But she will go listening in and getting herself muddled up in things she's no place to . . . Her father was a doctor, I'll grant you, but her mother. *Well*. I blame Mr Fleet, filling her head with giddy ideas.'

Before I could even think of how to respond to this gurgling stream of gossip, Mr Grace entered the room, clutching the Black Book to his chest. 'Mr Hawkins. You did not come to be assessed.' He drummed his thin, maggot-white fingers on the book's cover.

'You know full well my rent is paid,' I said, indignant. 'Mr Fleet gave you the money himself.'

He gave a haughty little sniff. 'There are rules, Hawkins. You're not above them even with your *powerful* friends. You must come and explain yourself to the governor. At once.'

'Very well.' I stood up wearily. My letter to Charles was still in my pocket; I had most likely missed my chance to reach him before nightfall. Despite my best efforts, I would spend another night in this wretched place.

As I left the coffeehouse Madame Migault cackled into her hands, her eyes glittering with malice. 'Tonight, monsieur,' she crowed. 'I promise you. Tonight!'

Sixteen

A s I climbed the stairs to see the governor, I tried my best to
remain cheerful. It was not an easy task. John Grace walked
stiffly ahead of me as if I were being led to the executioner's
block. I told myself that I didn't believe in fortune tellers, particularly old baggages like Madame Migault. But her prediction,
followed so swiftly by a summons from Acton, was unsettling.

Grace led me into a long, low room that ran beneath the main
Court Room. A quiet place for the judges and lawyers to retire,
untroubled by poor debtors or their pleading, desperate families. Their robes of ceremony hung on pegs like sloughed-off
skins. There were no windows.

Acton sat behind a table at the far end of the room. Cross
stood to one side with a stretch of chains slung over his shoulder,
flanked by Chapman and Wills, another turnkey. My mouth
turned dry. So many guards, just to settle the rent? Behind them,
three prisoners drooped in a sad little huddle: a man and his wife
clutching one another and weeping quietly while the third – the
gentleman I'd seen with Gilbert Hand on my first day – seemed
struck dumb with shock. He clutched his battered old tricorn,
staring blindly at the floor.

It was a long walk to the table. Acton watched me approach
without a word, hands clasped in front of him, bright blue eyes
cold and unblinking.

I bowed. 'Mr Acton.'

'You're late.'

I glanced at the men behind him. Cross caught my eye then looked away over my head. 'My apologies.'

'The book, Mr Grace.'

Grace stepped forward and placed the Black Book open in front of the governor. He tapped a line then stepped back again. Acton made a play of studying it for a moment, then shook his head. 'You have not paid your rent, Hawkins.'

'I assure you I am paid up for the whole of next week.' I frowned. 'Mr Grace will vouch for that.'

Acton glanced at his clerk in mock surprise. 'Have you made a mistake, Mr Grace? That will go ill for you, sir. I don't tolerate mistakes in my gaol.'

Grace's pale lips drew into a nasty smile. 'I think it is the *prisoner* who is mistaken, Governor.'

My heart sank. This was no game. Something evil was happening here. 'Mr Acton. I fear there has been some confusion. Mr Fleet paid my rent to Mr Grace on Thursday afternoon – the day I first arrived here. If we could call Mr Fleet to explain . . .'

Acton slammed his fist on the table. 'I run this prison, not Fleet!' he yelled, voice booming off the walls. He curled his lip. 'And not Charles Buckley.' He watched as the fear took hold, eyes glittering with the power of secret knowledge. 'Well, Hawkins?'

I swallowed hard. 'I swear to you, sir, upon my life. Fleet paid the money to Mr Grace.'

Grace gave a cough. 'And you have a receipt for this transaction?'

I glared at him. 'You know I do not.'

Acton gave a nod. Cross and Chapman grabbed hold of me and pinned back my arms, wrenching my shoulders as I struggled against them.

Acton walked over, slowly. He raised his fist and punched me hard in the jaw. I sank to my knees, head reeling.

'Pull him up, Mr Cross,' Acton ordered, rubbing his knuckles.

They yanked me from the ground and held me firm.

'You can't do this!' I cried hoarsely, spitting blood on to the floor. 'I have paid—'

He hit me hard, again, and I stumbled back. The trusties pulled me back to my feet. 'I can do whatever I damn well please,' Acton said softly. He brought his face close to mine. 'This is *my* Castle. No one keeps secrets from me.' He put one large, calloused hand about my throat and began to squeeze. 'Poor Mr Hawkins. Strutting about, making trouble.' He squeezed harder. I started to choke. 'You're just a little mouse, aren't you? A little mouse trapped in a lion's paw.'

Blood roared in my ears. The room darkened.

'Governor.' Cross' voice, coming from far away. A warning.

He threw me to the floor.

I lay there for a moment half-stunned, lungs burning, taking in deep, grateful gulps of air. Chapman kicked me to my feet. I stared about the room wildly, at Cross and Wills and the other prisoners. And Grace, watching me with smug satisfaction in his cold eyes. I cursed and took a half-step towards him but Chapman grabbed me and held me fast.

Acton had returned to his desk. He smiled, as if nothing in the world had happened, and held up a letter.

My stomach lurched. It was the note Charles had sent the day before, charging me with my task. How had it fallen into Acton's hands? Where had I left it? I closed my eyes and groaned, remembering. I'd tucked it in Captain Roberts' waistcoat pocket. The waistcoat I'd thrown to the floor in Belle Isle last night.

This was Fleet's work, yet again. That was why he'd been so keen to leave the room this morning. A new game to play – and no matter the price I would have to pay for it. How could I have been such a fool?

'I've run the Marshalsea for a long time, Mr Hawkins,' Acton said. 'Long before I was governor. I make the rules. I decide who lives. And who dies.'

'Mr Acton,' I said, my voice a thin rasp in my bruised throat. I could taste blood in my mouth. 'If I might explain . . .'

At a gesture from Acton, Cross punched me hard in the stomach.

Acton laced his fingers together. 'You have falsely accused Mr Grace of bribery. A serious offence, sir. Mr Grace is a loyal and trusted official of the gaol. Chief clerk to the governor. Elected steward of the Common Side prisoners. He would *never* dishonour his position.'

Grace gave an obsequious little nod.

'I will not let this go unpunished,' Acton continued, leaning back in his chair. 'Mr Cross. Chain the prisoner and throw him in the Strong Room. Use the skull cap and collar. Fix him tight.'

Cross locked a pair of manacles upon my wrists, cold and heavy. 'Gagged?'

'No, no. Let him scream with the rest of them.' He chuckled. 'And no food – be sure of it. I don't want those scum over the wall taking pity on him.'

'How long for, Governor?'

Acton narrowed his eyes and considered me as if I were a piece of meat waiting to be hung. 'As long as it takes.' He picked up Grace's quill and dipped it in the ink. 'I shall scratch this one out for you, Mr Grace.'

He dragged a thick line through my name. It felt like a knife scraping across my throat.

Grace watched, unmoved. He gestured to the three prisoners huddled in the corner. 'And those, sir? The Common Side . . . ?'

Acton considered them for a moment, as if seeing them for the first time. 'No. They'll keep for another week.' He rose and patted the woman's shoulder. 'I'm a generous man.' He dismissed them with a wave and they hurried away before he changed his mind. Not one of them looked me in the eye as they passed.

Cross and Wills led me down into the yard while Chapman ran to the Pound to collect the skull cap and collar. We could have sheltered in the porch beneath the Palace Court but Cross wanted his revenge and he took it. He pulled me right out into the middle of the Park, displaying me like a piece of livestock at Smithfield market. Shocked, excited faces peered from windows, while those standing out in the yard gathered in groups to gossip and stare.

My mind raced, trying to think of some way to stop this – to stay on the right side of the wall. But I was too shocked to think straight. They were locking me in the Strong Room – where Roberts and Jack Carter died. Where they stored the dead. My knees buckled. 'Come on, Hawkins, be a man,' Cross said cheerfully, grabbing me before I slid to the ground. 'I gave you a week, didn't I?' he murmured in my ear. 'Might need to revise that one.'

Gilbert Hand was standing with Mack by the lamppost a few paces away. 'Bad luck, Hawkins,' he called, without a glimmer of fellow feeling. Mack gave me a distant nod. Neither drew any closer. I was no longer part of their world.

Only Trim came to my aid. 'For God's sake,' he said, staring in horror as Chapman returned with the heavy iron skull cap and collar under his arm. 'You can't mean to use those on him?'

Cross began pulling me towards the Common Side wall. 'Governor's orders.'

Trim trailed after us. 'Let me see to his injuries first. What's happened to his throat? He looks half-strangled! Damn it, Cross, where's your conscience?'

'Can't afford one.' He gestured at Wills to unlock the door.

'Trim,' I called out. He came closer and I managed to slip my letter to Charles beneath his jacket. 'Tell him what's happened. I beg you, tell him—'

Cross cuffed me hard across the head. 'No messages.' He pushed a finger in Trim's chest. 'Watch yourself, barber. Do you want to be thrown in with him?' He grabbed my shoulder and was pushing me through the door when Fleet jumped out on to the Tap Room balcony.

'Tom! What's this? What's happened?'

I glared at him, hatred burning like a furnace in my chest. I would have torn him to pieces if I could.

Trim ran towards the balcony. 'What have you *done*, Fleet? They're taking him to the Strong Room!'

Fleet turned pale, stunned into silence. And then he swung over the balcony and clambered two storey to the ground, agile as a cat. 'Wait! Mr Cross. I have money!'

Too late. Chapman shoved me through the door. I fell to my knees in the dirt. The door slammed and a key turned in the lock.

For a few moments I could hear Fleet's voice faintly through the wall, calling my name. He might as well have been calling from another country. And then a cry went up around the Common Side, drowning out any noise from the other side of the wall. They shouted down from cracked windows and came from every corner of the yard to gather round me, eager to see what fresh meat had been thrown into the pot. Chapman and Wills drew their clubs and kept them at bay.

'He's back.'

'Couldn't keep away.'

Roars of laughter. As they pressed closer I caught the stench of rotting, unwashed bodies. I flung my arm about my mouth.

'Ahh, do we offend you, sir? You'll be as bad as us in a few days,' a woman with rotting gums called out, and they all roared again. 'Even gentlemen stink in here.'

Cross raised his club. They stepped back, mute and sullen, but I could feel the tension pulsing in the air between us.

Chapman kicked me in the ribs. 'Get up.'

I staggered to my feet. A few of the stronger men had started to creep closer again, watching me keenly. I could feel their eyes upon my shoes, my clothes, the gold cross about my neck.

'Oh, they like the look of you,' Cross snorted. He spied the dagger tucked in my jacket and pulled it out, weighed it approvingly. 'Who gave you this? Jakes?' he asked, grunting when he saw he'd guessed correctly. He held the blade to my throat. 'Not so brave on your own, eh?' He pushed the tip harder and a trickle of blood slid down my skin. 'If I were a merciful man, I'd slit your throat right here.'

'Mr Cross . . .' I began to shake, despite myself.

'Oh, it's *Mister* now, is it . . . ?' Cross smiled. He traced a line across my throat, playing with me. The tip of the blade caught against the cross around my neck. He hesitated, then lowered the dagger, slipping it into his belt. 'Lock him up.'

Wills and Chapman grabbed my arms and dragged me across the yard. For a brief moment I saw Captain Anderson standing in the doorway of his ward. Our eyes met; then he stepped back into the shadows, shaking his head.

The Strong Room was a rough wooden hut squeezed in the furthest corner of the yard. As we drew closer the hot, putrid stench of the common shore caught in our throats, making us gag. The rain had turned the shit and piss into a slimy, mustard-yellow slop and sluiced it out into the yard, mixing with the rubbish and the mud. Fat flies buzzed low over the mess.

An old man lay with his back against the door of the hut, indifferent to the stink. He looked feverish, and was scratching at a livid rash running across his chest.

'Gaol fever,' Wills muttered.

Cross stepped back. 'Move him out of the way.'

Wills scowled. 'I'm not touching him. Let *him* do it.'

I backed away but they pushed me forward with their blades. What could I do? I couldn't fight them and I couldn't run. I might as well have been on the cart to the gallows for all the choice I had. I kneeled down and pulled him out of the way as best I could with my hands chained. As I settled him by the wall he grabbed my wrist. His skin was hot. 'Am I dead?' he whispered, voice slurred with delirium. 'Am I dead, sir?'

I pulled myself free and staggered back. As I did so I heard a splashing sound, followed by a loud, angry squeal. *Rats*. The narrow gap between the hut and the Common wall was teeming with them, splashing in a pool of stagnant water, fighting and scrabbling across each other's backs.

'Oh, God,' I cried. The men laughed and pushed me into the hut.

I stared about me, trembling softly. The stench was terrible. Rotten meat. Death. There were rats here too – I could hear them scuffling in the shadows. This was where Jack Carter had died. Where his body now lay, somewhere in the dark. I sank to my knees.

Cross lit a torch and entered the room, holding a cloth to his mouth. I could see the bodies now, wrapped in old sheets and piled in the far corner like pieces of kindling. The rats were swarming over them, squealing and biting, tearing the cloth. Tearing and shredding.

Oh, please God, no.

'Chain him up, Chapman,' Cross snapped, kicking the rats away with his boot. 'Fix him tight.'

Chapman tore off my wig and shoved the iron skull cap hard on to my head. The weight of it – twelve pounds or more – was pain enough on its own. But then he fastened the screws and the metal bit into my skull, squeezing until I was sure it would crack. I begged them to stop but they just laughed again, pushing me to the ground until my back slammed hard against the cold, dank wall.

'You can't do this,' I cried. 'You can't leave me in here. Cross! For God's sake, have mercy!'

They fixed the back of the cap to the wall, screwing it firmly until I was held fast and couldn't move my head. Then they set the collar around my neck, squeezing it tight. My throat was already bruised and swollen where Acton had choked me, and the rough iron bit deep into my skin. I began to panic, fighting to breathe as Cross checked my chains, cloth still pressed to his mouth. He nodded, satisfied, and rose to leave. The other men had already fled the room.

'Cross, please, I beg you. I will choke to death.' I clutched desperately at his jacket, all pride gone. The collar cut deeper as I tried to lean forward. 'Would you murder me, sir?'

He hesitated. Then he reached out and loosened the collar by a few precious breaths. I was about to thank him when he poked his fingers into my jacket and pulled out all of my coins, down to the last farthing, and the silver watch Fleet had given me. He picked up the torch and moved to the door.

'Have pity, sir!' I called. 'Leave me the light.'

'*Have pity, sir!*' he mimicked in a high, whining voice. And then he slammed the door, plunging me into darkness.

For a while I lay in a daze of pain and disbelief. It had all been so swift and so brutal; no time to defend myself or bargain my way out of trouble. My head pounded from the iron cap that gripped my skull like a vice; even the smallest movement would gouge my skin until the blood ran down my face. My body, battered and bruised enough from my beating in St Giles, ached and throbbed against the cold, rotten floorboards.

I could barely see in the gloom, but I could sense the corpses in the shadows, just a few feet away. The rats were creeping back; I could hear them moving in the darkness. One scrabbled across my legs. I kicked it away, kept kicking even when it was long gone back to the other side, back to the corpses. Easier meat. I tucked my legs beneath me and began to weep, silently.

Slowly, my eyes adjusted to the gloom. There were no windows, but there was a narrow gap above the door and a few holes in the roof that let in the last of the day's fading light. If I could just stay calm . . . I set my mind free; tried to imagine myself far away . . . but it was no use, the stench and the damp and the horror of the place held me pinned to the room just as tightly as the iron collar around my throat.

So this was where Captain Roberts had been found, hanging from a beam, his body shattered and broken. I prayed for his sake that he was already dead when they dragged him here.

The rats squealed, pouring over the corpses in a frenzy. I heard one of the bundles tumble from the stack, landing with a dull thud. The rats swarmed over it, and the cloth slid free. I saw an arm, grey-white and bloodless. Was it Jack Carter? Perhaps. It was hard to say for sure in the half-light. But I knew he was there, and I could hear the rats. I knew what they were doing only a few paces away.

I screamed, then. I screamed and cursed and howled at them to let me out. Screamed loud enough for the whole prison to hear me.

No one came.

In the end the fight left me and I lay back, exhausted and numb. As the sun set and the room sank into blackness my mind turned in upon itself, thoughts spinning and colliding. I thought of Gilbourne and Fleet, of Catherine Roberts, of all the mistakes I had made since I'd come to the Marshalsea. Later, I heard the nightly lamentation of the Common Side rise up into the night sky and I joined my voice with them, the other damned and wretched souls trapped in this hell on earth.

'You fool. You fool,' I whispered to the dark. For it didn't matter how I railed against Acton, and the cutpurses who attacked me in St Giles, I knew where the fault lay. My father had predicted it, long before that witch Madame Migault. *The path you have chosen leads but one way, Thomas.*

At some point, perhaps around midnight, the light from a lantern shone through the hole above the door and a voice called out softly. 'God save you, Mr Hawkins.' Mr Jenings, on night-watch. By the time I could think to reply, the light had gone.

IV) *SUNDAY. THE FOURTH DAY.*

Seventeen

I learned about despair that night. Its cold, deathless fingers wrapped about my heart until I was beyond fear and pain – beyond all feeling. The damp and rotten floor chilling my bones; my skin crawling with pests; the collar fixed about my throat; the rats fighting in the shadows; the festering corpses; the knowledge that I would join them soon enough . . . at some point I surrendered to it all and the night rolled on, inch by inch, moment by moment.

I closed my eyes and when I opened them Captain Roberts was hanging from a beam in front of me. But then I saw it was my face and I began to choke, the noose rough and tight about my throat, and I was twisting on the end of the rope, legs kicking, fighting to breathe. The rope snapped and I fell to the floor but I was cold, death-white, and the rats were pouring down from the walls, hundreds and hundreds of them, screaming as they clambered over me, teeth like daggers and eyes red like the furnaces of hell. Teeth slicing into flesh. Someone was banging on the door but they were too late, there was nothing left, nothing but bones and gobbets of blood.

'Open this door!'

Charles.

I opened my eyes and the dream dissolved away. Daylight streamed through the tiny gap above the door.

A scuffle; raised voices. A moment later the door flew open. I squinted, dazzled by the light.

'My God. What have you done to him?'

'Wait, Mr Buckley, don't poison yourself.' Woodburn's voice. 'Let Chapman pull him out of there.'

Another scuffle and then Charles was kneeling in front of me, coughing into a sweet-scented cloth held to his mouth and nose. He loosened the screws of my collar with trembling fingers. The collar fell free and he began unscrewing the heavy skull cap, eyes on mine. 'You're safe, Tom. I'm here,' he said softly. 'You, there!' he turned and shouted, voice muffled behind the cloth. 'Unlock his chains, damn you.' He pulled the skull cap free and rested my head on his chest while Chapman unchained me.

Charles grabbed my hand. 'My God, he's frozen to the bone! Tom, listen.' He touched my face. I couldn't stop shivering. 'Try to stand. I'll help you.'

He put his shoulder under my arm and I staggered to my feet, the room lurching and spinning about me. Trim was waiting outside with Woodburn. The chaplain gaped at me, horrified. 'Lord help the poor boy. He's half-dead.'

Trim rushed forward and helped Charles carry me out into the yard. I cringed and shrank back as the sun hit my eyes.

'He needs heat and a bath, and quick; or we'll lose him,' Trim said.

'Do you see, Buckley?' Woodburn cried, trailing after us. 'Do you see what is being done in Sir Philip's name?'

'Run ahead, sir!' Charles snapped. 'Call for hot water and plenty of it.'

I sank to my knees, wrapping my arms about me. I could still feel the weight of the skull cap pressing down on my head. I touched my fingers to my temples. They were sticky with blood. I began to shake again, more violently. I was still not sure if this was a dream. Perhaps I would wake again, still chained to the wall.

Across the yard they were opening up the wards and pulling out the bodies. Only three today. Trim and Charles turned away and began to retch.

They opened Anderson's ward last. The men had been banging on the door and shouting furiously, screaming to be let out, so Wills had left them until last out of spite. When he opened the door all the prisoners spilt out from the ward as if there were a wild animal trapped in with them. Anderson was the last one out. He was pulling something along the ground. Another body, trailing blood along the cobbles.

'Which one of you did it?' he yelled in a fury at his ward mates, spraying spittle in the air. 'Which one of you bastards murdered him?'

He laid the body out in the yard just a few paces away. Harry Mitchell. My stomach lurched. He'd been stabbed through the heart, his eyes fixed in a final moment of horror. I stared at his white, lifeless face and the walls began to press in, squeezing closer and closer. Trim kneeled down and put a hand on my shoulder. 'Breathe,' he whispered. 'Just breathe.'

'This is your fault, boy.'

I looked up at Anderson, looming over me, his face flushed red with anger. And I knew he was right. Mitchell had offered to help me – for a price – and now he was dead. 'I'm sorry.'

Anderson spat at my feet. 'I swear if you ever come over here again, they'll be pulling *your* body out into the yard. Do you understand?'

Wills was walking down the line of bodies. He reached Mitchell, studied the gaping wound in the dead man's chest, the twist of pain on his lips, the long trail of blood stretching back towards the ward entrance. He scratched his jaw. 'Gaol fever,' he announced. 'There's family in the Borough will pay for him. Sling him in the Strong Room with the rest.'

Up in Trim's room, Kitty was building up the fire. As I stumbled into the room she gave a cry and ran towards me.

'Wait outside, Kitty,' Trim ordered, pushing her out of the door as the porters began to arrive, pouring bucketfuls of steaming hot water into the iron tub set by the hearth. 'I'll bring you his clothes in a moment. You must have them burned at once, do you understand?'

With Kitty gone Trim bustled Charles away to work on the fire then stripped off my damp, infested clothes. I stood, staring at nothing, dazed with horror. I could still smell the stench of the corpses on my skin, as if it had leeched into every pore. 'I smell of death,' I said. The room began to spin. Trim grabbed me and lowered me gently into the bath. I shuddered, the heat stinging my wounds. He poured bowl after bowl of water over me, scouring my skin clean, washing away the filth and the lice. When he was satisfied he rubbed fresh balm into my cuts and bruises and dressed them. Then he wrapped me in a clean banyan, threw a blanket over my shoulders and settled me down by the hearth.

'Will you eat?' he asked, softly.

I shook my head, staring into the fire.

He touched my shoulder. 'Then I'll leave you to rest. Take good care of him, Mr Buckley. He needs peace and quiet.'

Charles nodded, brow furrowed. 'I'm so sorry, Tom,' he whispered, when Trim had left. 'I never meant to put you in danger like this.'

I sighed, and held up my hand. I didn't blame Charles. But I was too tired, too broken by what had happened to respond. So we sat in silence for a while, watching the flames dance and flicker, and the warmth came back to my bones, though the night still clung to me somehow. I wished I could walk through the fire and scorch it from my skin.

'Tom, forgive me. I must leave you now,' Charles said, breaking my thoughts. 'I have a sermon to give in an hour. I will speak with Acton before I leave,' he added, clenching his fists tight.

I waited until the door closed then rose and dragged myself over to the bed. The sheets were fresh, and smelled of lavender.

I pulled the blankets over me and tucked my knees into my chest, fingers touching the cross at my throat. For a second I heard Fleet's voice in the room below. And then Charles, much louder. *'Have you not done enough? Stay away from him, damn you.'*

I closed my eyes and fell into a deep sleep.

I woke to the sound of Jenings ringing a bell and calling out for afternoon service. I felt weak as a newborn lamb, and my head was pounding, but unlike poor Mitchell I was alive. I should go to chapel and thank God for it. I inched myself from the bed, trembling with the effort. Trim had left a change of clothes folded neatly on a chair; I dressed slowly in front of the mirror, shivering now that the fire had died. New bruises bloomed across my chest and stomach and my lip was split. Worst of all was my throat, scraped raw from the collar with deep gouges where it had bit hard in the night. It was swollen, too, and mottled with bruises from Acton's choking grip.

I covered it carefully with a fresh linen cravat, staring at the stranger in the mirror as I wound the linen round and round. The night had changed me. I was older, somehow, and harder. Some part of what I had seen had been trapped in my eyes, like a fly in amber.

The Park was almost deserted when I stepped out of the door and turned towards the chapel. By habit I glanced over at Fleet's bench and there he was. He sprang up when he saw me and waved his red velvet cap. I turned away and headed up to the chapel, knowing he wouldn't follow me. Fleet was many things, but he was not a hypocrite.

The same could not be said for Cross. There he sat, second pew from the front, head bowed, the very picture of a good Christian. John Grace sat next to him, back straight and narrow. Head clerk and head turnkey – my God, there wasn't a priest in the land who could wash their souls clean. The service had already begun, so I slipped on to a bench at the back. Catherine

Roberts was seated in the front pew with Mary Acton, while Henry squirmed on Kitty's lap a few rows behind them. Trim was there, sitting with Mack and Gilbert Hand. Jenings, standing to one side of the altar, had transformed from nightwatchman to church warden; he glanced up as I entered and smiled with relief to see me alive. Only Acton and Gilbourne were missing.

I closed my eyes as the old familiar words of worship passed over me. It was soothing to hear them again. I had not attended a full service since the day my stepbrother had spoken out against me in church. Church was no longer a place of comfort and peace – it was the place where I had been betrayed and humiliated. Where my father had lost faith in me for ever.

I couldn't take in much of the service; my mind kept wandering back over the wall to the other side of the prison. I stared at my unchained hands, clasped in prayer, and thought of those bundles of rags, discarded like rubbish on the Strong Room floor. My head began to pound, as though the weight of the iron cap had returned, pressing down upon my skull. I rubbed the sweat from my brow and took a deep breath, steadying myself again.

'Some call this prison a hell on earth,' Woodburn said sternly, gazing out at his congregation. 'But that is not so! Remember the prodigal son. Only when he had lost everything, when he was a poor, wretched beggar, walking naked upon the earth, did his blood cool, his sinful lusts abate. And only then did he repent, and find salvation with the Lord.' He paused, smiled benevolently. 'And so are you poor debtors stripped of your luxuries here in this prison; stripped of the distractions and temptations that lead men straight into the fiery embrace of the devil. The countless cruelties you endure in this wretched place; the violent punishing of your bodies; *these* will be the saving of your souls, in the great and terrible day of the Lord!' He paused, loosening his white neckerchief a little to relieve the bulging flesh beneath. 'Pain,' he continued and caught my eye. 'Pain is remedy. Pain is the lesson God sends us to bring us back to the path of the righteous.' He held up his hands. 'Rejoice then, in this holy gift you have been given! Rejoice in the pain! Rejoice in the humiliation! And praise God that he has brought you here to suffer and to repent on earth, and so find your path to heaven. Amen.'

The congregation coughed and muttered their amens back.

I glared at the ground, and said nothing. Woodburn had visited the Common Side that very morning. How dare he suggest those poor souls should thank God for letting them rot to death? Was Acton to be praised for creating such a *spiritual* and *inspiring* setting? Did Woodburn really think God looked down upon the Marshalsea and was pleased with what He saw? I pulled myself to my feet and stumbled from the chapel in disgust.

Fleet was waiting for me in the yard. 'Seven minutes,' he said, holding up his silver watch. He must have bought it back from Cross. 'Well, you lasted longer than I ever did. Which one was it? Praise the Lord for the purging power of pain? I'd like to show that blustering hypocrite the true meaning of pain.' His eyes gleamed with venom.

I ignored him, limping across the yard towards the Tap Room. If I had been strong enough, I would have beaten him to the ground.

'Tom, wait!' he called. 'Are you hurt?' When I didn't stop he ran after me. 'Let me pay for a doctor.'

I halted, and closed my eyes for a moment, every bone in my body aching. 'Did you take the letter?'

Fleet looked away shiftily, then cleared his throat. 'I confess I *borrowed* it. Madame Migault wanted to play a trick on you so I gave it to her to read. I thought it would be . . . diverting. I never dreamed the old witch would sell the letter to Acton.'

'When I am well enough,' I said, quietly, 'I think I will kill you.'

He tilted his head, fixed his black eyes on mine. 'You almost mean it,' he said, fascinated. I began to turn away and he touched a hand to my chest, blocking my way. 'I only read the first page.

I swear, if I had known it was so dangerous . . .' He frowned. 'And really, Tom, what on earth were you thinking, leaving it in your pocket for anyone to take? If you're to become a decent spy you really must learn to . . .'

I glared at him.

He stopped, and moved his hand from my chest to his own, placing it over his heart. He looked as serious as I had ever seen him. 'Forgive me. It was badly played on my part. Are we friends again?'

I shook my head. 'We were never friends, Mr Fleet.'

He dropped his hand. For a moment I saw a flicker of disappointment in his eyes – but then it passed. 'Very well.' He gave a short bow and turned to leave.

'Hey there, you two!' Chapman stamped towards us from the Lodge, swaggering with his own importance. On reaching us he thrust his thumbs into his pocket and planted his feet wide, glowering at us both. On Acton it would have been alarming. On Chapman it just seemed . . . a little silly.

'Governor wants to see you. Right away.'

Acton was dining in the Crown, so we must go to him. I was free of the prison for the first time in three days, but I was too busy bracing myself for another confrontation with the governor to enjoy my few brief moments out on the street. I thought of all the things I might say to him – all the things I might do. Weak as I was, I reckoned I still might have the strength to throttle him for what he'd done to me. I would enjoy the look of shock and surprise on that broad, ruby face of his.

And what would it achieve? A moment's satisfaction before I was pulled away by Chapman and thrown in chains again. Charles wouldn't arrive in time to save me again – Acton would make sure of that. I would die in that Strong Room with the rats swarming about me.

The pavement shifted under my feet and I half-stumbled. I would have fallen to my knees if Fleet hadn't leapt forward and grabbed hold of me. I bent double and retched, but my stomach was empty. I spat out a thin trail of bile into a clump of weeds.

'Hurry up,' Chapman growled. 'The governor's waiting.'

Fleet rounded on him. 'He's sick, for God's sake.'

I pushed him away, wiped my mouth with a trembling hand. 'I'm well enough.' I didn't want Samuel Fleet's pity.

Acton was dining alone in the Crown, tucked away in a private room upstairs. Chapman stayed at the bar while the landlady, Mrs Speed, escorted us up the stairs, chattering about the weather. I trailed behind, stomach rolling with nausea.

The room was small and oppressive, the walls hung with hunting scenes and the cracked skull of an old stag with a broken antler. Acton sat in front of a large window, the sun dazzling like gold at his back. In front of him, the table was laden with rich, half-demolished dishes: a boiled leg of mutton and greens; a pigeon pie; cod with oysters and enough bread and cheese to feed the Common Side for a week. There was a bottle of claret, too, and raspberry brandy. A fire blazed in the stove, heating the room to boiling point.

'Gentlemen.' Acton slurped back an oyster, wiped a glittering slug trail along his sleeve. He beckoned for us to join him. Fleet sat down at once at Acton's right hand, helping himself to a thick slice of the pie and a glass of claret. I remained in the doorway, the room tilting queasily beneath my feet.

Acton took a swig of brandy. 'So, Hawkins, here you are, alive and well. No hard feelings, eh?' His ice-blue eyes fixed on mine, daring me to contradict him.

'What do you want of me, sir?'

He cut himself a slice of bread and built it high with cheese. 'It seems Roberts was murdered after all,' he said, lips smacking noisily. 'Mitchell too, I hear. I won't have prisoners murdered in my Castle.'

'Not without your blessing, at least.'

Fleet froze, waiting for the explosion. But Acton just laughed, slapping his thigh as if I had made a fine joke. 'Well, well. Has my Strong Room made a man out of you, Hawkins?' He settled back in his seat and pulled out Charles' letter, dropping it on the table. 'Buckley spoke to me this morning. He says you suspect Gilbourne.' He smiled. 'I can live with that.'

'He feels the same about you, Mr Acton.'

'Does he indeed.' The smile faded. 'Fleet.' He kicked him under the table. 'What do you make of this?'

Fleet, who was busy reading Charles' letter, frowned absently. 'It was Gilbourne,' he said, as if he were talking of spilt milk, not murder.

Acton grunted and rubbed his jaw, considering me for a moment. 'Trouble on two legs, you are.' He scowled at Fleet. 'No wonder *he* likes you. The sooner you're out of my gaol the better; in a coffin or a carriage – makes no difference to me.' He struck the table with his palm. 'Here's my offer, sir. Pin this on Gilbourne and I'll gladly march you out through the Lodge myself.'

I stood a little straighter. 'That's no offer, and you know it.' I had lost my fear, I realised – left it somewhere in the dark last night. 'Sir Philip has already promised to release me if I discover the killer.'

A flicker of respect in Acton's eyes. 'Well then, sir, what is it you want?'

'No more beatings, no bullying. And keep your trusties on a leash. Especially Cross.'

He took another bite of bread and cheese. 'Anything else?'

'I must be allowed out of the gaol to investigate whenever necessary. Jakes will act as my guard,' I added, before he could protest. 'And the bodies in the Strong Room must be released for burial at once.'

Acton belched, set his shoulders. 'No, no – not that. The families haven't paid the fees.'

'Then pay it from your own fat pocket, you greedy son of a cunt.'

'*Tom . . .*' Fleet warned, softly.

I rounded on him. 'There are five bodies turning green in there – enough to breed a plague. I heard the rats feasting on—'

'Oh, very well!' Acton interrupted irritably. He waved at Fleet, who was tucking into a custard tart, quite unmoved by my little speech. 'You'll have to help him. He's not sharp enough to work it out on his own.'

I bristled. 'I would rather work alone, sir.'

'I don't give a damn what you would rather, *sir*.' He poured himself another glass of brandy.

'And what if *he* killed Roberts? Half the prison thinks it.'

Acton slid his gaze over my roommate. 'Well. That is a fair question,' he conceded. 'Did you kill the captain, you wretched little dog?'

Fleet put down his spoon and looked at Acton. The room fell silent, save for the flames crackling and popping in the stove.

'Answer me, damn you,' Acton snapped at last. 'Or I'll have the truth beaten out of you.'

Fleet smiled, very slowly. A chill ran down my spine, though I was standing several paces away with the door at my back. 'I would not advise that,' he said.

Acton leaned closer, pointed a finger hard in Fleet's face. 'Do not threaten me, sir. I will not have it. I don't care how much you pay me.'

Fleet laughed in Acton's face. 'Very well, Governor. I will keep my five guineas a month and you can chain me to your Strong Room and have Cross beat me as he beat that poor boy over there. Let him break my neck for all I care – leave my corpse for the rats and have done. And when the men who threw me in gaol decide they have need of my skills again . . . do you think they will reward you for it?' He tilted his head. 'What will you tell them?'

'I am not afraid of them,' Acton snarled. 'I have my own connections—'

'And then there is my brother,' Fleet continued calmly, taking up his spoon again. 'I'm not sure how he would react. He is only my *half*-brother, of course. Perhaps he would only cut out *half* your heart. He's most precise with a blade.'

Acton had pulled back in shock. 'He was transported,' he whispered hoarsely. 'They said so in the papers.'

'A remarkable ocean, the Atlantic,' Fleet said, waving his spoon back and forth. 'One can sail it both ways. Now – are we done with this tedious cock fight, Mr Acton?'

Acton seized the spoon from Fleet's hand and flung it to the floor, where it gleamed dully in the firelight. 'Your brother is in America,' he decided, with a firm tone. 'And he wouldn't give a damn about you even if he *were* back. He'd spit on your grave like the rest of us. I want this business with Captain Roberts finished, Fleet – do you understand me? I've had enough of it. I'll give you two days – after that I'll swear blind you confessed to it yourself and have you hanged for it. And as for you, Hawkins, I'll sling you back in the Strong Room faster than you can piss yourself. Now bugger off, the pair of you.'

We walked back without speaking, Chapman following behind with his face stuffed in a glass of ale he'd liberated from the tavern. The confrontation with Acton seemed to have pleased Fleet enormously and he hummed to himself all the way back to the gaol, pipe lodged between his teeth.

I cursed him silently, furious that Acton had forced us together again. I was still angry with Fleet for betraying me with Charles' letter – and I was angry with myself for not having the wit to keep it away from his thieving fingers. Why had I not destroyed it? I'd been too busy scolding Fleet for dressing me in Roberts' clothes, of course. The man was a trickster and a cheat, confusing and unsettling everyone around him for his own amusement and gain. Thank God I'd never met him at the gaming tables.

Another part of me knew I should swallow my pride and accept his help. For all his faults, Fleet was clever and cunning – and as it was now in his own interest to find the killer, he might just stop playing games long enough to uncover the truth. Acton had only granted us two days; I should not squander any of that time in sulking.

'How long do you intend to punish me, Tom?' Fleet enquired politely as we walked up the stairs to Belle Isle. He had an uncanny knack for reading my thoughts.

I ignored him and called down for a late dinner from Titty Doll's. Fleet could damn well pay for it, after all the trouble he'd brought me. I waited for it by the window, while he lay on the bed and smoked another pipe. I could feel his eyes on my back, could hear the light *tick tick tick* of the silver watch in his pocket. How *had* he retrieved that from Cross? And where was his journal? I wondered, then cursed myself for caring. This was the way he drew you in, like a fisherman setting his bait then waiting patiently for a bite. Or impatiently, in Fleet's case; I could tell from the sharp way he sucked on his pipe that I infuriated him as much by my silence as he had infuriated me by his thoughtless betrayal. *Good*, I thought, then shook my head. I had only known him three days and already we were like an old married couple.

A door creaked open in the building next door and Mr Woodburn emerged into the yard, round belly first. He patted his hat down upon his long wig and leaned upon his walking stick, surveying his flock. I called down to him, in the main because I knew it would annoy my roommate. The chaplain glanced up in surprise, holding a hand to his eyes to shield them from the sun.

'Mr Hawkins!' he cried. 'You are recovered!'

'Of course he's not, you old fool,' Fleet muttered behind me from the bed.

'Much recovered, sir, I thank you. I enjoyed your sermon this afternoon.'

A choking cough from the bed. '*Perjury!*'

Woodburn smiled and stood straighter, rocking back on his heels. 'I'm delighted to hear it.' He craned his neck and called a little louder. 'I'm sorry Mr Fleet was unable to attend service today. But then I've often observed that those who most need the Church's instruction are the ones who most obstinately refuse it . . .'

'Well, Mr Woodburn,' I said, tilting my head and giving him my most pious look, 'you will be pleased to learn that Mr Fleet owns a copy of one of your sermons . . .'

'. . . which I use to wipe my arse . . .'

'. . . which he reads each night for solace.'

'Is that so?' Woodburn's face crinkled as he tried to take in this astonishing fact. 'Well, well. I am glad to hear my words bring him some comfort.' He stepped closer. 'And what of the *other matter*, sir?' he asked in a stage whisper. 'Your *investigation*? I suppose the governor has put a stop to it?'

'No indeed, sir,' I said, lowering my voice. 'He's just now given us leave to continue our search.'

Woodburn looked taken aback. 'Indeed? And you are working with Mr Fleet, you say?'

I was about to confirm this when Fleet leapt from the bed and slammed the window shut. 'For heaven's sake,' he hissed. 'Should I find you a trumpet to herald the news across the Borough?'

I rounded on him. 'The whole prison already knows what I'm about, thanks to you. If you hadn't stolen that letter my investigation would have remained a secret.'

'Hah!' He plucked the letter from his coat pocket and waved it in my face. 'If you'd only confided in me I would have *burned* it before it fell into the wrong hands.'

'Meaning *yours*,' I snarled, snatching it from him and tossing it on the fire. 'I was *going* to tell you everything in the Tap Room yesterday, but you shooed me away like a dog. What was that business about, by the way? Who was that man you were speaking with?'

'A family matter,' Fleet said, airily. He paused. 'We appear to be talking again.'

I folded my arms. 'I haven't forgiven you.'

'Of course you have. You just haven't noticed it yet.' He held out his hand.

I knew I shouldn't take it. I'd only be cursing him again tomorrow – if I lived that long. He *was* a devil – there was no question of it. I should have Mrs Bradshaw embroider 'Do Not Trust Samuel Fleet' upon my handkerchief and pin it to my chest. But the truth was, I needed him. And worse than that, the gambler in me was whispering intently in my ear. *Take his hand. Take the risk.* Because for all the dangers of his company, there were rewards to be had and not just silver watches and rent money. Life was – quite simply – more interesting. A good deal shorter too, no doubt – but interesting.

'I suppose it is safer to be your friend than your enemy.'

'Not necessarily.'

I took his hand.

'Excellent!' he cried, seizing it and shaking it vigorously, the sleeves of his banyan slipping down over his knuckles. 'I was sure you would sulk for another hour at least. Let's order a bowl of punch,' he added hurriedly, catching my expression. 'It will help us concentrate.'

I dined lightly on toasted bread and butter with poached eggs, though it was hard to eat much with my bruised and swollen throat. I was still out of sorts from the night before. I tried not to think of the putrid fumes I'd breathed into my lungs all night. The thought alone was enough to turn my stomach.

Fleet drank most of the punch.

When I'd finished we settled by the fire and smoked our pipes. The food and the tobacco had gone some way to restore my nerves, the horrors of my beating and imprisonment beginning to fade at last. I yawned and stretched, as much as I could bear with all my cuts and bruises.

Fleet propped his hand upon his chin. 'Tell me. Why do you suspect Gilbourne?'

I told him of Mrs Roberts' confession about the trap door into the prison, and how her actor friend Mr Simmons had slipped in and out of the gaol thanks to Gilbourne's key. Fleet listened carefully, fingers steepled, black eyes gleaming like polished jade. 'So Gilbourne could have stolen into the yard without being seen, even by the turnkeys. And you're certain he holds the only key?'

I nodded. 'He must have had an accomplice, though – don't you agree? Someone with a key to this ward, and to the Common Side. Someone strong enough to help him carry the body across the yard. My money's on Cross.'

Fleet chuckled. 'Of course it is – and wouldn't you love to see him hang for it. But why would Cross kill Roberts? They barely knew each other.'

'Money. It's always about money; you said so yourself.'

'Well, I can't always be right about *everything* . . .' He trailed away, unconvinced by his own argument.

'Gilbert Hand told me to ask the ghost *what happened to the money*,' I persisted, but Fleet dismissed this irrelevance with a wave of his hand. 'Harry Mitchell said—'

'Harry Mitchell?' Fleet interrupted sharply. 'The *recently murdered* Harry Mitchell? You spoke with him? When?'

'Yesterday morning on the Common Side.'

'*Yesterday morning on the Common Side*. Of course. How foolish of me. So what did Mitchell tell you? When I questioned him he told me *he didn't know nothing*.' A frown. 'I paid him half a shilling for that astonishing revelation.'

'Well, he told me for free that Captain Roberts was planning to blackmail Gilbourne.'

Fleet sighed, and put his head in his hands. He sat like that for a long while, rubbing his fingers across his eyes as if he were tired beyond all expression. I had never seen him so . . . defeated. It was the shock of it, I realised later. Fleet prided himself on expecting the worst of people but he had not prepared himself for this. 'Roberts,' he whispered at last. 'You fool. You damned fool.'

'Mitchell said he knew what Gilbourne had done. He offered to tell me if I could secure his freedom. He was too scared to tell me anything while he was still trapped in gaol. He was afraid Gilbourne would have him killed. And now he's dead.'

A door slammed on the next landing and footsteps thudded across the floor above, the boards groaning and creaking. Trim, returning to his room. Fleet peered up at the ceiling with a worried frown. 'Mitchell was right to be cautious,' he said. 'We can't risk talking in here.'

'I suppose you're right,' I said, gazing up at the ceiling. 'Though I'm sure we can trust Trim.' I pointed to a damp patch near the window, where the boards were split and sagging. 'It's a wonder he doesn't fall through and break his neck, it's so rotten there.'

Fleet put a finger to his lips. 'It's rotten everywhere,' he muttered.

Eighteen

Fleet refused to say another word until we were safely out of Belle Isle. Even then he would not be drawn, except to acknowledge he had something pressing he wished to discuss, and that we must leave the gaol to do so.

'Then we must find Jakes,' I pointed out. Acton had agreed we could leave the prison to investigate but only under guard.

'Jakes will be in *church*,' Fleet said, sniffing with disapproval. 'Probably spends all day on his knees. And not in any useful fashion.' He coughed back a laugh. 'Why don't we take Cross or Chapman?'

'I don't trust them.' *And I don't trust you.* The thought of Cross and Fleet working together was quite disturbing.

He frowned. 'It will take too long.'

'He only lives a few streets away.'

Fleet planted his feet and opened his mouth to argue . . . then caught the expression on my face. It must have been dark because even he looked taken aback. He held up his hands in defeat then went in search of one of Hand's boys to send out a message. I sat down on an ale barrel by the door and closed my eyes. And there I was, back in the Strong Room in the dead of night . . .

'Mr Hawkins.' A soft whisper in my ear.

I opened one eye, and then the other. 'Kitty.'

She was dressed in her good Sunday clothes – a powder-blue gown tied with ribbons and a fresh white kerchief about her shoulders. Her hair was half-loose, copper ringlets falling about her face, and her chest was heaving; she must have run all the way across the yard to catch me. She put a hand to her stomacher as she caught her breath.

'How pretty you look,' I said, without even thinking.

She blinked, taken aback. 'You look rotten,' she said, then touched her fingers to my temple, where the skull cap had bitten deep. Her eyes shone with tears. 'There's something you must know—'

'*Catherine Sparks.*' Fleet had returned. He looked angry – dangerously so.

Most girls of eighteen would have squealed in fright, but not Kitty. She stood taller, put her hands on her hips. 'I'll speak with him if I wish,' she said, tilting her chin in defiance. 'You're not my father.'

I waited for the caustic reply, but none came. His shoulders sank. 'True enough.'

Kitty ran to him, dismayed, and threw her arms about his neck. He whispered something in her ear and she shook her head. 'It's not *fair*,' she pouted.

Fleet glanced at me and rolled his eyes. 'We'll discuss this later, Kitty.'

She stamped her foot. Fleet giggled and she punched him hard in the arm, then hugged him again before running back into the yard.

I watched her go, baffled by the whole performance. 'That girl changes faster than the weather.'

He raised an eyebrow. 'Now why might that be, Tom?'

I held my hands up in protest. 'I've done nothing to encourage her.'

'Handsome young men of twenty-five don't have to *do* anything. Here.' He handed me the dagger Cross had stolen from me the night before. 'We're free to leave once Jakes bothers to turn up.'

'What do you have against Jakes? He's a good man.'

'Precisely.'

I slipped the blade in my belt. 'I'm glad to have him with us. I can't afford to lose another fight. It's all very well for *you*, but I have my looks to consider.'

Fleet laughed and scratched his bristles. He was more grizzled than ever, if that were possible. Another bad night's sleep, no doubt. Perhaps he'd felt guilty for betraying me. But if it were guilt that kept Samuel Fleet awake, then he must have done something truly devilish. I'd not caught him sleeping once since I'd arrived. 'We mustn't discuss things in front of Jakes.'

'Why ever not? You don't suspect *him*, do you?'

'Of killing Roberts . . . ?' Fleet trailed away, contemplating the idea. His lips parted into a smile. 'You know, he could have done it. He has access to the turnkeys' room and all the keys. And he could have carried Roberts over to the Strong Room on one shoulder.' He clapped his hands. 'Excellent! Jakes it is.'

'Well, here he is now.' I nodded towards the Lodge. Jakes was barrelling down the corridor. 'Would you like the honour of arresting him? Or perhaps he could arrest himself, as the warrant officer?'

I thought that might curb his tongue. I should have known better.

'Good day to you, sir!' he cried as Jakes reached us. 'Tell me, did you murder Captain Roberts?'

Jakes stared at him, dumbfounded. 'What did you say?' he breathed, when he'd recovered his voice.

'We were just debating the possibility. Tom thinks not, but then he is a very trusting fellow.' He tapped my arm. 'We must knock that out of you.'

Jakes balled his hands into fists. 'How dare you!' he thundered. 'How *dare* you accuse me! Captain Roberts was my friend. My brother! You think I would kill the man who saved my life? I've spent the last three months trying to prove he was murdered. What have you done in that time, you sly dog? You've sat on your arse and done nothing – *nothing* – to defend your reputation. While the whole prison calls you guilty.' He grabbed Fleet by the collar and pulled him close. 'Tell me, Mr Fleet. Did *you* murder Captain Roberts?'

Fleet looked Jakes right in the eye. 'And what would you do, sir,' he asked, calmly, 'if I confessed . . . ?'

Jakes raised his fist.

'For pity's sake!' I snapped, stepping between them and stopping Jakes' fist with my hand. He glared at me for a moment, then lowered his arm slowly, eyes never leaving Fleet. 'We don't have time to spare for this! If you want to tear each other apart then you'll have to wait until we find the *true* killer. I need his brains,' I said to Jakes. 'They're no good to me smashed all over the yard.'

As we stepped into the bustle of the High Street again my heart lifted with joy. The Marshalsea was like an island, set in its own time and space. In the three days since I had been locked away I had almost forgotten there was a world outside of it – and I had been too distracted on my way to and from the Crown to appreciate those brief moments of freedom.

The street was packed with visitors who had crossed the river eager to enjoy Southwark's disreputable pleasures: bear fights and cock fights; theatre and gambling; acrobats and fortune tellers; cheap beer and even cheaper Flemish whores. It was probably not quite what the good Lord had in mind for His day of rest. Fleet looked almost dizzy with happiness.

'If we ran off in opposite directions,' he asked Jakes, brows raised in curiosity, 'who would you chase?'

'Look at all these people,' I sighed, watching the Southwark street boys darting between the wheels of carriages; the chairmen weaving in and out of the traffic; the women parading in their Sunday best. 'Do they know how lucky they are?'

'Don't pontificate, Tom.' Fleet tugged Jakes' jacket. 'I'm quite serious – who would you run after?'

Jakes clapped a hand on Fleet's shoulder and squeezed hard. 'Acton has cronies in every tavern. If either of you run, *they'll* chase you. And when they find you . . .' He squeezed harder. Tears of pain sprang in Fleet's eyes. 'Well. They're not *gentle* like me.' He let go.

Fleet rubbed his shoulder theatrically then winked at me.

'Speaking of taverns . . .' I said. 'The George?'

Fleet shook his head. 'You heard him. They're full of Acton's spies. No better than the Marshalsea. We need somewhere quiet, where we can't be overheard. Snows Fields will be empty.'

Jakes grunted his approval.

Fleet stared at him in alarm. 'Good God, are we in agreement, Mr Jakes? Now that *is* worrying.'

We turned right into Axe and Bottle Yard, which ran along the north wall of the Marshalsea. We passed the cobblers I'd heard from the other side of the wall, closed for the day; an apothecary and a confectioner's, and a grocer's. Somewhere along this wall was the hidden door to the cellar, where Mrs Roberts' *ghost* had slipped in and out of the gaol. It must have been well disguised as I couldn't see it. Further down the yard I caught the warm, tantalising scent of freshly baked bread and stopped dead, stomach rumbling.

Jakes pointed to the baker's up ahead. 'Nehemiah Whittaker's. Best bread in Southwark,' he said as we walked over. Then he leaned down and whispered in my ear. 'A friend of the governor's. Mind what you say.'

I bought myself a couple of rolls and ate them on the spot with a bowl of chocolate while Jakes chatted to Nehemiah's wife. Back in the yard Fleet strolled back the way we had come.

Jakes touched his sword. 'If you're thinking of running, Mr Fleet . . .'

'I'm thinking of picnicking, Mr Jakes,' Fleet said, heading into the grocer's.

At the end of the alley we clambered over a low wooden gate into a deserted field. I paused and gazed out at the wide acres of Snows Fields, a vast common space that reached all the way to Bermondsey. Ahead of us were orchards and little vegetable plots, some well-kept while others had grown wild and boggy. In the distance I could make out a tenter ground, its large squares of cloth pegged and stretched out to dry in the late afternoon sun.

As I turned into the field I tripped and almost lost my footing. The open ground was uneven, small humps of grass and earth undulating across the field. I looked about me. 'Is this a burial ground?'

Jakes blew out his cheeks. 'Looks like it, don't it? Mr Woodburn thinks so. He comes out here to practise his sermons.'

'He *practises*?' Fleet looked astonished.

The sun was low against our backs and cast long shadows across the grass. Jakes settled down beneath an old oak tree and leaned against its trunk. The tree was gnarled with age, scarred and weather-worn. One of its thickest branches stretched further than the rest, as if pointing at something far in the distance, in warning or in accusation.

'You could hang a man on that,' I said.

Fleet shot me a sidelong glance – the appraising look of a doctor whose patient has just revealed an alarming new symptom. 'Let's walk further out,' he said, wrapping his fingers about my arm and leading me away.

'I'll be watching you, Fleet,' Jakes warned.

'How delightful for you.'

When we reached a flatter patch of ground Fleet threw down the grey wool blanket he had been carrying under his arm and stretched himself out upon it. He put his hands behind his head. 'It is good to see the sky unfettered,' he said, quietly.

I sat down next to him and ate an apple. 'What was that business with Kitty?'

Fleet watched the clouds drift by, and said nothing. The birds chirped and called to each other in the branches above our heads, the wind ruffled its fingers through the grass. We could be anywhere, if we did not turn and look back towards the Borough, towards the gaol. I set my gaze straight ahead. Perhaps those white squares far in the distance weren't stretches of cloth drying on the tenter ground but the great sails of a fine fleet of ships. I could race to the shoreline and watch them glide past, silent and majestic, as I did when I was a boy. And then the memory took me by the hand and I was running down to the coast at Orford, the sky infinite above my head, the taste of salt in the air, the roar of the waves, the gulls wheeling and soaring on the wind, higher and higher.

When I woke the sun was low and there was a chill in the air. Fleet still lay on his back, staring up at the sky. I sat up, feeling groggy but well-rested. 'You let me sleep?'

'You needed it. And your snoring helps me think.'

'What time is it?'

He passed me his silver watch. Almost six o'clock. When I tried to give the watch back he pushed my hand away.

'Have you ever been in love, Tom?'

Only Fleet would ask a man such a question, with no warning or apology. It was a clever trick; he could read the answer on my face the moment he asked it. There is a second, before the mask goes up, when you can read the truth in a man's eyes – but you must ask quickly when he is not expecting it, and accept that he may well punch you in the jaw straight after.

'Not truly. Not in earnest,' he murmured, answering for me. He was right, but I didn't give him the satisfaction of telling him so. He reached for the bottle of wine and took a long swig. 'Kitty's the daughter of an old friend of mine. Nathaniel Sparks. He died five years ago.' He rubbed the gold band on his wedding finger as if he were Aladdin, summoning a djinn.

It took me a moment to realise he was answering the question I had asked him almost an hour earlier. 'Kitty said her father was a doctor.'

'Yes. He was an excellent physician. And very rich from it. All gone now, I'm afraid.' He pulled up a handful of grass and scattered it to the wind.

'What happened?'

He laughed, sourly. 'Kitty's mother, Emma. Quite pretty as a girl, and not without charm. But she needed Nathaniel to keep her steady. When he knew he was dying he made me promise to take care of her and Kitty.' He paused, and bowed his head.

I'd never seen Fleet like this before; there was no play in him. This, I realised, was where it all stopped. I waited.

'Nathaniel was the very best of men. Brave and loyal.' He touched a small scar on his temple. 'He would have been content to live quietly, especially once Kitty was born. But Emma wouldn't leave London and I . . . I had to have him near me, you see. Selfish . . .' he muttered at the ground. 'I didn't own the print shop back then. I was . . .' He looked back to where Jakes was sitting under the tree.

'You were a spy,' I said. I'd gathered as much from his conversation with Acton, back in the Crown.

'And worse,' Fleet muttered. 'And I loved it, Tom. It was a game – dangerous and exhilarating. If I died playing it, so be it. *You* understand.'

I nodded.

'But I should never have taken Nathaniel down with me. He was not suited to it. I didn't realise . . . no, that's not true,' he corrected himself. 'I realised well enough. But I didn't *care*. I was not prepared to give up the game and so I took him with me. And he died.'

He fell silent, staring hard out into the distance.

'Grief will drag you to some dark places,' he said at last. 'But guilt is like a whip upon your back, urging you on. Nathaniel's death was my fault and so I ran off in search of my own. By the time I returned to London five years had passed. The house was sold and mother and daughter had disappeared. I found Emma easily enough, though I barely recognised her, she was so altered. She was selling herself for gin in St Giles.' He grimaced. 'I paid her rent, bought her some food and clothes. Any money would have gone down her throat.'

'And Kitty?'

'Run away. Years before. Emma could barely remember her name, let alone where she'd last seen her. I spent months searching to no avail. Then last February I was thrown in gaol for safe-keeping – until the men who hired me decided whether to use me or kill me. And there she was, like a miracle, in Sarah Bradshaw's coffeehouse. It was as if she'd been waiting for me all that time. And untouched – my God!' He rubbed a hand across his scalp.

A sparrow flew down from a nearby fence. I threw it some crumbs and it hopped a little closer. 'Perhaps her father's spirit was watching over her.'

'Bollocks.'

'I only meant—'

'You meant to excuse me for abandoning her. Well, don't,' he snarled. 'I deserted her, Tom. She survived through her own wit and courage and nothing else. Don't deny her the credit of it.'

The sparrow bounced across the grass and flew away. 'Is she yours, Fleet?' I asked, softly.

Fleet's dark brows furrowed. '*Mine?*'

I flushed. 'You talked of love, just now. I couldn't help but wonder . . .'

'Good God!' he exclaimed, black eyes wide with astonishment. 'What the devil are you thinking? I held her in my arms when she was but a few hours old! No, no, no! She is not *mine*. She is not *anybody's*.'

'Then what did you mean, about being in love?' I frowned in confusion. 'I don't understand.'

Fleet stared at me sadly. 'No matter.' He glanced back at Jakes, still dozing beneath his tree, and lowered his voice. 'Another time, perhaps. But I must tell you about Roberts and Gilbourne. Build yourself a pipe first. You'll need it.'

'Roberts was not a bad man,' Fleet began, once I had lit my pipe. 'A fine officer, by all accounts. Brave and not without honour.'

'He saved Jakes' life.'

'Well. Let us not hold that against him.' Fleet snatched up the second bottle of wine, pulled the cork out with his teeth. He took a swig then wiped his mouth on his sleeve. 'He was not a bad man, but he was a fool when it came to money. If he had two shillings in his pocket he'd speculate with three. He was quite certain that his fortune was waiting for him just around the corner, and then the next, and the next. Ridiculous, of course. The only things waiting round the corner for Captain Roberts were his creditors.'

The gambler's desperate faith in providence. I knew that well enough.

'It was the remorse I couldn't bear,' Fleet continued, rolling his eyes. 'All those wasted hours spent sobbing into his pillow. *Oh, what have I done, what have I done?* Hours on his knees in the chapel, wailing to the heavens. *Oh, forgive me, Lord! I swear I'll change! Give me one last chance, I beg of you!* Pffrr! I doubt the Lord in His infinite wisdom fancied the odds on *that* promise. I told him – Roberts, you have brought this upon yourself. Don't bother God with your racket, you will only vex Him.'

'That must have been a great comfort.'

Fleet chuckled. 'He was no different from most, I suppose,' he conceded. He jerked his thumb back towards the prison. 'There are men locked away in there who've been waiting ten years for their fortunes to turn. *I'll win my case tomorrow. My debts will clear tomorrow. Tomorrow Great Uncle Whatsisname will die and leave me his fortune and I will be free at last!*'

I sighed the smoke from my lungs, remembering what Moll had said to me, the night before I was thrown in gaol. *Always tomorrow with you, Tom.*

'Then tomorrow arrives, carrying *nothing* under its arm. Horror. Fury. Despair!' Fleet threw up his hands. 'After that, the poison. *Hope,* snaking its way into your veins. And so it begins all over again. It's a prison men make for themselves. Gilbourne understands that. A predator knows its prey better than it knows itself.'

'What did Gilbourne want with Roberts?'

'His wife.' He took another swig of wine. 'I came back to Belle Isle one day to find Roberts collapsed on the floor with his head in his hands. Gilbourne had made him a proposition. He would pay Roberts ten guineas — enough to secure his release. In return Roberts would grant Gilbourne access to his wife. A guinea a time.'

'My God,' I whispered. The cunning and cruelty of Gilbourne's offer took my breath away. Catherine could cry rape but without her husband's support, who would believe her? And Roberts could only defend her honour by admitting his own guilt.

Fleet tilted his head. 'I suppose it made perfect sense to Gilbourne. There he sits all day in his office, setting fees and making deals. A shilling for this, a guinea for that. Why not buy a man's wife, if he's willing?'

There was a long silence. Fleet was right: Gilbourne was used to buying his way through life. He would snatch the bread from a starving man's hand if it kept him in fine clothes. But was there not more to it than that? He had toyed with me that night at Acton's for his own amusement. All that flattery and feigned modesty, drawing me in. *Oh yes, Mr Hawkins, all this is foolish nonsense, but* we *see through it, don't we?* Fleet had called Gilbourne a predator, but he hunted for sport, not appetite.

I had thought myself a man of the world, but this was too much. And Roberts wanted to *blackmail* Gilbourne for it? Was that all? Why not run him through with his blade, for God's sake?

'Roberts asked me for guidance,' Fleet said, stirring me from my murderous thoughts. He smiled grimly. 'A sign of his desperation, I suppose. It was clever of Gilbourne, to use Catherine. Roberts blamed her for convincing him to give up their son. And that money from her father . . . just enough each month to pay the rent, no more, when he could afford to free them a thousand times over. Roberts was very good at blaming everyone but himself.'

'But you stopped him.'

'I told him he'd burn in hell. It seemed to work.' Fleet shrugged. 'He wasn't a sophisticated man.'

'And Catherine never learned the truth.'

Fleet shook his head. 'A few days later he was dead. I presumed Gilbourne killed him out of spite. But if Roberts tried to blackmail him, that would give him a better motive, eh? Poor Roberts. He really was an idiot. I've met a lot of dangerous men – Gilbourne is among the worst of them.' He paused, and I could see from his face that he was remembering old stories, narrow escapes. 'We must be on guard. If he suspects we know the truth, our lives will be at risk. We know that he can come and go as he pleases, and that he has an accomplice, someone who works in the prison. We must—'

A discreet cough, a few paces away. Fleet jumped up with surprising speed, pulling the blade from my side and raising it high. 'A pox on you, sir,' he growled, 'sneaking up like that.'

Jakes looked at the blade as though it was one of Mrs Bradshaw's sewing needles. 'I promised Cross I'd have you back by nightfall,' he said calmly.

Fleet relaxed. 'Well. We wouldn't want to disappoint Mr Cross, would we? Lead on, sir.'

Walking back down Axe and Bottle Yard, I asked Fleet whether we should warn Mrs Roberts about Gilbourne. 'I've tried,' he said. 'But it's hard to make her understand without revealing the whole story. I don't think she's ready to hear anything bad about her poor, saintly husband.'

We agreed that our next step must be to gather more evidence on Gilbourne before confronting him. Fleet's word would count for very little on its own. 'We must talk to Gilbert Hand,' he said. 'Roberts asked him for advice, too. That's why he told you to ask the ghost about the money.'

'He confided in *Gilbert Hand*?' I marvelled. 'It's a wonder the story hasn't reached the Americas by now.'

'Gilbert knows when to keep his mouth shut. He didn't want to be murdered in his bed like Roberts. And he was right, eh? Look at poor Mitchell.' He frowned. 'But he'll tell the truth if Acton promises to protect him. We'll have to pay him, of course.'

'Of course.'

'And none of this will secure my freedom,' he added, gloomily. He stole a glance at Jakes, who was walking a few paces ahead. 'Perhaps I should just knock him on the head and run.'

'You're not tall enough to reach.'

'You could lift me.'

'You'd never see Kitty again.'

'Ahh.' Fleet put a hand to his heart. 'That's true. She still has so much to learn. History, philosophy, anatomy . . .'

'. . . good manners?'

'Fie!' Fleet stuck out his tongue. 'What use are *they*? I've taught her how to curse in French; is that not manners enough?'

'*Anatomy?*'

'It's my *duty*, Tom.' He gave me his finest impression of sincerity. 'All girls should be taught anatomy. We don't send soldiers into battle without first teaching them how to fight.'

I laughed and shook my head. I couldn't decide whether Fleet was the worst guardian in the kingdom or the best. Both, perhaps. We were still laughing when we turned out of the yard and on to the High Street.

We had only walked a few paces when Fleet stopped dead and gave a low curse.

A tall, well-dressed man was riding towards the gaol on a glossy black stallion. Gilbourne. My heart sank. How unsettling it was to see him again, now his true nature was revealed! He had not changed in appearance; he was the same handsome, elegant figure I had dined with two nights before. But my perception of him was so reversed that it was a wonder to me now that I had not seen through the amiable manner and fashionable clothes in a heartbeat. He was like a poorly counterfeit coin that you pull from your pocket in consternation, astonished that it could have fooled you for a moment.

As he reached the narrow entrance to the gaol he spied us and raised his hat.

'*Bow* . . .' Fleet prompted, and somehow I persuaded my neck to bend. Gilbourne jumped down from his horse and approached me with his hand outstretched, friendship in his eyes. I shook his soft white hand with its perfectly shaped fingernails, feeling wretched.

'My dear fellow,' he said, his voice dripping with sincerity. 'This is a most fortunate meeting. I wish to apologise for doubting you, sir.' He glanced over my shoulder at Fleet. 'But is this not the scoundrel who dressed you in Captain Roberts' clothes?'

'The very same, sir,' Fleet acknowledged with a low bow.

Gilbourne gave Fleet a wary look, as if recognising a loathsome yet somehow worthy opponent. 'You have forgiven him, Mr Hawkins? I'm not sure that is wise.'

'I have, sir. Mr Fleet may act the rogue, but I believe his intentions are honourable.'

'A generous assessment,' Gilbourne murmured, narrowing his eyes.

'Much too generous,' Fleet agreed. 'Call me shrewd or cunning and I'll own it. But honourable? Honourable men die much too fast for my liking.' He smiled at Gilbourne. 'That's why there's so few of them, no doubt.'

We stepped between the two closed-up shops into the dead, dank alley that led to the Marshalsea. Gilbourne's horse snorted and stamped its feet, forcing its master to pull hard upon the reins. I couldn't blame the poor thing; I would have joined it if I could.

We had not quite reached the Lodge when the gate flew open and Ben Carter dashed out, followed closely by Gilbert Hand. They pushed past us, making Gilbourne's horse rear and buck furiously. We pressed ourselves tight to the wall, afraid we might be kicked to death.

'What the devil . . . !' Gilbourne cried, fighting to calm the beast.

Gilbert Hand had already reached the mouth of the alley. 'Fast as you can, boy!' he shouted down the street. 'His life depends on it!'

'Whose life?' Fleet asked quickly, still pinned to the wall. 'Mr Hand! In God's name, what's happened?'

Hand flinched, as if seeing us for the first time. His face was white as chalk and his shirt was covered in blood. 'Mr Woodburn. He's been stabbed.'

Nineteen

The gaol was in uproar, turnkeys fighting to lock everyone back in their wards while the prisoners shouted their protest. Acton's trusties arrived just as we did, wading into the chaos with whips and clubs, beating anyone unlucky or foolish enough to stand in their path. There were screams, and curses, and glasses being smashed in the Tap Room and beneath it all, the low, thunderous rumble of the Common Side rising up on the other side of the wall. Woodburn was one of the few men who spoke out for them. He smuggled in food and medicine from their secret benefactor. *They'll tear the wall down if Acton doesn't stop them*, I thought. I had a sudden urge to rush up to the Tap Room balcony and cheer them on, even took a few tentative steps across the yard. Jakes grabbed my arm and dragged me towards the safety of the Master's wards.

Gilbourne took one sharp look about him and flung himself back on his horse, forcing prisoners and trusties alike to jump out of his way as he galloped out of the gaol. At the same moment Acton rushed into the yard and threw himself into the fray, seizing prisoners and slinging them about like carcasses. He would have stuck them on meat hooks too if he could, I'm sure.

Fleet turned to me, his eyes glittering with excitement. 'It's a riot, Tom!' He picked up an abandoned club and twirled it in his hand. 'God bless the Reverend Andrew Woodburn! An achievement at last!' A prisoner staggered past him, bleeding heavily from a cut above his eye. Jakes led him to the shelter of the Court porch before fighting his way back to us.

A wild clamour rose from the other side of the wall. The riot was spreading. I heard a voice cry out above the rest. 'One and all! One and all against the Butcher!' Captain Anderson.

I stared about me in panic. I knew how to defend myself but I was still weak from the battering inflicted upon me the night before. I had just enough sense to pluck the short blade from my side and stand firm while Fleet cleared a path with his club and Jakes shielded us from behind. By the time we reached the entrance to Belle Isle the trusties were winning the fight on the Master's Side, and Acton was preparing his men to venture through the wall and deal with the rest. The trusties would win, I knew that much from my brief stint on the Common Side. What they lacked in numbers they made up for in strength. Easy enough to fight ten or twenty poxy skeletons when your own belly's full of mutton and good ale.

We collided with Chapman on the stairs. Fleet grabbed him and pressed him against the wall. 'Where's Woodburn?'

Chapman jerked his chin to the next landing, and Trim's room, before clattering out to join the fight. We ran up to the next floor and burst through the door.

Woodburn was lying on the bed I had slept on just a few hours before, recovering from my own injuries. Trim had stripped off the chaplain's shirt and was holding a cloth to his left shoulder to staunch the bleeding, Woodburn's fat chest juddering with each painful breath. A bowl lay on the floor beside them, full of discarded, bloody rags.

Kitty was at the stove boiling water. Fleet crossed over to her and she looked up, her face softening with relief to see him. She slid a long, vicious dagger from her apron pocket. It had been wiped clean but there were still a few dark smears of blood upon the blade. She handed it to Fleet, who ran his fingers along the steel.

'That's a soldier's blade,' Jakes said, pulling it from Fleet's hand and taking it to the window to examine more closely. Fleet rubbed the dried flakes of blood from his fingers.

'Trim found it by the altar,' Kitty said. 'Dropped in the fight. We didn't see anyone go by on the stairs.'

Fleet nodded, and squeezed her hand before hopping eagerly to the bed to inspect Woodburn's wounded shoulder. I might have missed that quiet, private gesture before, but now I knew their history I understood it at once. Fleet was not Kitty's guardian or teacher; it was more equable and more important than that. They were fellow mourners – and both understood, profoundly, what the other had lost. A different, better life.

'What happened?' Fleet asked the chaplain, from the foot of the bed.

Woodburn's eyes flickered open. Seeing Fleet, he groaned and shut them again.

'He was stabbed,' Trim said, twisting round to face us. His shirt was stained with Woodburn's blood.

'No, indeed?' Fleet muttered. He rapped Woodburn's foot. 'Who was it attacked you, sir? Did you get a fair look at him?'

Woodburn moaned and shuddered. 'I was praying . . . the chapel . . .' He winced, fingers grasping the bed linen.

Trim murmured something reassuring and put a cup to Woodburn's lips. 'Someone stole up behind him.'

'Will he live?' I asked quietly.

Trim rocked his hand back and forth. 'It's not deep, but it may fester. I've sent for Stephen Siddall – he's the best apothecary in the Borough.' He stood up and rubbed his forehead wearily. 'How can this have happened?' he asked the room. He dabbed a wet cloth to the blood stains on his shirt. 'Why would anyone want to hurt Mr Woodburn?'

'Perhaps they heard one of his sermons . . . ?' Fleet murmured.

Jakes had been standing at the window, watching the riot die down, but now he spun round in one fluid movement and without any warning punched Fleet once, very hard, in the face. Fleet's legs crumpled beneath him and he fell to the floor.

'Blasphemous dog!' Jakes cursed, sucking the blood from his knuckle. And before I could react he pulled the half-stunned Fleet to his feet and slung him over his shoulder like a sack of laundry.

'*Bâtard!*' Kitty cried, grabbing a poker from the hearth and smacking Jakes across the back and legs with vicious swipes.

Trim ran over and tried to wrestle the poker from her fist while Fleet – who seemed quite content to be carried down the stairs on Jakes' shoulder – shot her a look of affectionate pride. The four of them bundled down the stairs together and I found myself alone with Mr Woodburn. He was barely conscious now. The wound on his shoulder was still oozing blood, but the worst of the flow had stopped. Trim was right, it wasn't deep, but it was precise and most definitely a stab wound, not the light slash of a blade. An inch lower and the point would have pierced his heart.

I perched carefully on the edge of the bed, watching the chaplain's chest rise and fall fitfully. Was this how God rewarded an honest servant? Woodburn had dedicated his life to the poor debtors in this miserable place. He had done everything he could to save their souls and now here he lay, cut down cruelly for his efforts.

I glanced down and was startled to see Woodburn was in fact perfectly awake, his gaze resting upon my face. I picked up the cup and brought it to his lips. He drank gratefully, but then a look of abject horror flooded his face. 'Ohh!' he groaned. 'Oh Lord, have mercy.' He pointed to the corner of the room, where one of Trim's coats was hanging over a chair. 'Oh, forgive me, forgive me!' he cried in a cracked voice, his eyes filled with terror. 'Do you not see him, sir? Oh, God!'

'Mr Woodburn,' I said, shaking him softly. 'There is no one there.'

'I should have stopped him. Oh God, have mercy on my soul.' He cried out again then collapsed against the pillow. The wound in his chest had begun to bleed more freely.

'Stopped who? Mr Woodburn?' I could hear footsteps, someone running up the stairs, moments away. 'Stopped who?' I leaned closer and whispered in his ear. 'Gilbourne?'

He didn't answer, and for a moment I thought he hadn't heard. But then he reached out and gripped my wrist. 'I thought I could save him.'

Trim bustled into the room, followed by Siddall, the apothecary, carrying a large leather bag in the crook of his arm. He hurried over to his patient.

I moved aside, too stunned to say a word. Trim touched my arm. 'You've turned pale,' he said. 'Must be the blood. Why don't you rest? I'll join you for a drink later.' He gestured over to the bed, where Mr Siddall was examining Woodburn's shoulder. 'I think we've earned ourselves a debauch, don't you?'

Down in Belle Isle, Fleet was settled comfortably by the fire smoking a pipe, a pot of coffee in easy reach. The left side of his jaw was red and swollen from Jakes' punch, but apart from that he was the very picture of contentment. In truth I had never seen him so cheerful – the chaos of the riot and the puzzle of Woodburn's stabbing were like two whores arriving at once on Christmas Day; the only problem being he wasn't sure which one to fondle first.

Kitty was lying on my bed reading a book, her copper hair unpinned and flowing loose about her shoulders. She had not heard me enter and her eyes were cast down upon the page, so that she looked half-asleep. Her lips were curved into the softest smile and there was something so sweet and restful about her in that moment that I had the sudden desire to lie down at her side, my chest against her back, my arm about her waist, my face buried in that warm mass of curls.

'Samuel . . . ?' she said, eyes studiously upon the page.

'Yes, my dear?'

'Is it true that a man's prick looks like a white hog's pudding?'

Fleet coughed out a staccato of pipe smoke. 'Well . . . I suppose it does, in a manner of speaking.' He slid his gaze to mine. 'Why don't we ask Mr Hawkins for a practical demonstration?'

Kitty sat bolt upright, green eyes bright with alarm. When she spied me standing in the doorway she gave a scream of indignation and ran from the room, skirts whispering across my legs as she passed.

Fleet laid down his pipe, put his knuckles to his mouth, and laughed until the tears ran down his face. I picked up the book that had fallen to the floor and read the frontispiece:

THE SCHOOL OF *VENUS*
OR, THE LADIES' DELIGHT,
REDUCED INTO RULES OF PRACTICE.
Being the Translation of the *French*,
L'Ecole des Filles
By S. Fleet

I flicked idly through the pages and arrived upon a rather cheerful drawing of a couple fucking on an ottoman.

'All my own work,' Fleet called out proudly. 'And it's the full translation, mind – not like that scoundrel Curll. I fervently believe there is a special place in hell for booksellers who promise a volume crammed with filth and don't deliver on it.'

I dropped the book back on my bed for later. 'Mr Woodburn said something strange to me, after you'd left.'

'Well, that has certainly removed any *frisson* from the room,' Fleet observed, waving me to the chair opposite his. He steepled his fingers and narrowed his eyes while I relayed the chaplain's confession. '*Was* he talking of Gilbourne, do you think?' he asked, when I was done.

'Perhaps . . . But then why not give his name?' I shook my head. 'But it was more than that. I have a feeling . . .' I paused, hardly able to believe it. 'I think Woodburn saw something that night. I think he might . . . He had the look of a guilty man, Fleet. I cannot fathom it, but there it is.'

Fleet settled back and gazed up at the ceiling, deep in thought. 'I think Woodburn knew his attacker.' He placed his hand on his left shoulder, tapped his finger where the wound lay. 'There is no conceivable way he could have been stabbed from behind with a wound of that kind.' He took his pipe and mimed the blade's thrust. 'They must have been standing face to face. Woodburn would have looked straight into his eyes as the blade fell.'

A cold, thin feeling slid down my spine. 'Who was it, Fleet?'

He shook his head. 'Not you. Not me. Not Jakes,' he said, counting us off on his fingers. 'We were all returning from Snows Fields at the time.'

'And not Gilbourne,' I said miserably. 'He arrived when we did. *Acton*, then . . . ? Damn it. We're going about in circles!'

'Whoever it was, we shall not puzzle it out tonight,' Fleet reasoned. 'Gilbourne has fled, Acton's busy mopping up after the riot and if I know Simon Siddall he'll have given Woodburn a sleeping draught and charged him a guinea for it.'

'Well then, there is only one choice left to us, Mr Fleet.'

He raised an eyebrow. 'Punch?' he asked, hopefully.

I grinned. 'Punch.'

The Tap Room was closed, smashed and battered by the riot, but nothing stopped the flow of drink in the Marshalsea. There was too much profit in it, and anyway – who wanted to stay sober in here? Mrs Bradshaw and Mary Acton had joined forces and set up a makeshift bar in the long, low retiring room in the Palace Court. I had no desire to return to the place where I had been beaten and humiliated only the night before, so I ventured out into the yard to find a porter who would take my order and bring it over to Belle Isle.

The Park had settled back into an uneasy peace after that short, bright flare of violence. A few of the men – prisoners and trusties alike – were nursing cuts and bruises, but no one seemed to have been seriously injured, at least on this side of the wall. Mack had set up a game of Hazard under the Court porch, though it was growing dark now and there was a chill in the air. I smiled and nodded politely, but did not head over to greet him. I had grown less fond of Mack the more I knew him; he was Acton's man, when it came to it, and unlike Trim he had not lifted a finger to help me when I was dragged over to the Common Side.

Jenings was lighting the lantern in the middle of the Park; a fiddlesome task given its height. I strolled over to thank him for calling out a blessing when I was chained to the wall of the Strong Room. His words had been the one bright moment of comfort during that long and terrible night, and I had not forgotten it.

'I wish I might have done more, sir,' he said, glancing about him to be sure we were not overheard. 'If I were a different man I'd stand up against the lot of them.' He clenched his jaw. 'They are not Christianlike, Mr Hawkins. And now poor Mr Woodburn has been attacked in God's chapel. And on a Sunday!'

We both shook our heads at this. I feared that I myself was not as 'Christianlike' as Jenings wished to believe, but I agreed with him that the manner of Woodburn's attack was shocking. Stabbing a clergyman when he was at prayer in his own chapel – what kind of a man would dare commit such a sacrilegious act? But then, if a man were prepared to commit cold-blooded murder, what would he not do? I must speak with Woodburn again, as soon as he was recovered. It was his duty to confess the truth of it; something I would put to him as soon as he was strong enough to hear it. Tomorrow – it would have to be, the moment he was awake. There was no time to waste. I did not intend to be thrown back in the Strong Room.

I hailed a porter and ordered a four-shilling bowl of punch and some food. We had missed dinner, save for the bread and fruit we'd eaten out in Snows Fields, so I chose several dishes to share with Fleet and paid the man an extra penny to hurry it along. It was all Fleet's money, of course, but I didn't think he would mind. He had enough of it.

I was returning to Belle Isle when I felt a soft touch upon my shoulder. I spun round to discover Catherine gazing up at me, grey eyes bright with worry. She was wearing a charcoal-coloured riding cloak with the hood up, framing her face.

'Mrs Roberts.' I gave her a short bow.

She inclined her head, but her eyes darted up to the windows as if she feared we were being watched. 'I was troubled to hear of your ordeal last night.' She placed a gloved hand upon my arm. 'You are recovered, I trust?'

'Yes, thank you,' I replied, sparing her the truth. My fresh injuries – added to the beating I'd received in St Giles – would take many days to heal. And there was something more, beneath the physical hurt. I had no time to acknowledge it now, but I knew it was waiting for me, like a bailiff at the door. 'Were you caught in the riot?'

'I kept to my room,' she said, then lapsed into silence.

I waited, conscious of the wall that was growing up between us. I'd thought – for a little while – that she might have some affection for me. I had wanted to prove to her that I was more than what she saw, better than her husband. I might have changed my ways for her. Perhaps. *Perhaps*. In any case, she was not quite what she appeared. In truth, I did not really know Catherine Roberts at all. She had good reasons for everything she had done. And I felt sympathy for her troubles – even more so now I knew how close her husband had come to betraying her in the worst possible fashion. But I wasn't sure I could trust her.

By chance we had stopped right next to the trap door of the store cellar. There had been no more ghostly sightings since I'd grabbed a hold of the rather fleshy Mr Simmons two nights before, but I was sure Catherine was at work on a fresh plan to clear her husband's name. This much, at least, I believed – that she wished to remove the stain of suicide from Roberts' death and reclaim her son.

She took a deep breath and continued. 'Is it true you have been instructed to find my husband's killer?'

'Yes. By Sir Philip himself. And Mr Acton.'

A tiny smile of triumph. 'And do you . . . have you any suspicions?'

'None that I may speak of at present.'

She looked up, sharply. 'Even to his widow?'

I said nothing.

She hesitated, glancing over her shoulder before reaching a hand into her cloak. To my astonishment she pulled out the dagger I had seen not half an hour before in Trim's room. It had been cleaned more thoroughly since then but there was no question this was the blade used to stab Woodburn.

'Jakes passed it to me,' she said. 'He recognised it at once. It belonged to my husband.'

'Put it away, for God's sake,' I hissed, pushing her hands beneath the folds of her cloak. She had her back to the yard, but anyone looking out of the window would have seen her holding it.

'I keep it hidden in my room,' she said, tucking it back into her skirts. 'John always kept a blade under his pillow, so I thought I should do the same. It's one of the few things I have to remember him by. They played cards for his belongings, did you know that? That's why that . . . *devil* could dress you up in his clothes.' She gave a shudder of revulsion.

I did not have the spirit or the inclination to defend Fleet's actions two nights before. Though it struck me that if it hadn't been for that *devil*'s counsel, her beloved husband John might well have sold her to Gilbourne for ten guineas. 'Who could have taken it?'

She shook her head helplessly. 'You know how it is, Mr Hawkins. Servants and visitors coming in and out all day. It frightens me to think how easy it would be to kill someone in here – and never be discovered.'

'There are a hundred ways to die in here,' I said, surprised that this thought had never struck her before. 'Death slips in and out of this place whenever it pleases. With no need for a key.' I tapped my toe against the trap door. 'D'you know three more died just last night, as well as Mr Mitchell?'

She gasped in shock. 'Last night? How?'

'Starved to death, I suppose. Or gaol fever. Gilbert Hand says it's worse in the height of summer—'

'Oh, from the Common Side,' she said, waving her hand dismissively.

As if it were a far-distant land, and not fifty paces from where we stood. I took her hand and bowed, formally. It was a dismissal, and I saw from her expression that she felt it. Her lips parted in surprise, then drew into a hard, thin line. And then she turned and stalked away towards her room, grey cloak merging into the early-evening shadows.

I heard a low chuckle from the room above.

'It's bad form to listen to private conversations.'

Fleet leaned his arms on the window frame. 'No such thing as privacy in a prison. Mr Trim can hear you snoring from the next floor up. Isn't that right, sir?'

Trim poked his head out of the window and nodded vigorously. And then both men looked past my shoulder and grinned.

'Dinner!'

'Supper!'

A trio of porters strode by, one carrying a large bowl of punch, the others shouldering a tempting variety of dishes on large wooden trays. I checked Fleet's watch. A half past seven. Too late for dinner and a little too early for supper.

'Hurry up, Tom,' Fleet urged. 'Get those fine calves of yours up here at once.'

By the time I reached Belle Isle the porters had already set the dishes down upon the table, which Fleet and Trim had carried to the middle of the room. I had been hungry when I ordered, and was paying with another man's coin, which is to say I had perhaps gone a little *overboard*, but Fleet didn't seem to mind, in fact he was dancing about the table with anticipation, shooing the porters out of the way so that he could begin. It was a feast – as much as could be had in the Marshalsea: spit-turned shoulder of lamb with greens; beef broth; bologna sausage with thick slabs of bread and butter; stuffed veal fillet with salad and cucumbers; dressed salmon and a fine apple pudding.

Fleet ladled himself a glass of punch and set it next to a half-drunk glass of claret at his side. He considered them both tenderly for a moment, then tapped the punch bowl. 'You're sure this is a *four*-shilling bowl, Tom?'

I nodded happily. The fourth shilling paid for an extra half pint of raspberry brandy tipped into the mix. Trim took a sip and pulled a face. 'Not enough sugar,' he declared. 'I'll fetch some from my room.'

'How's Mr Woodburn?' I asked as he scurried to the door.

'Resting.' He pointed up at the ceiling, a flicker of concern crossing his face. 'We must be careful not to wake him.'

Fleet snorted. 'He's been dosed with Siddall's best sleeping draught. We could dance upon his bed and he wouldn't wake tonight. We must try that later, eh?' He tipped back his chair and watched Trim run up the stairs, then fixed me with a dark, warning look. 'Watch what you say in front of our good neighbour, Tom. And pile your plate while you have the chance,' he added, loading his own with enough food for three men. 'Trim eats like a hog. I have it on good authority his tailor has let out his waistcoat three times this year.'

'You don't trust Trim?' I asked, then answered my own question. 'You don't trust anyone.'

'I trust *you*,' Fleet said, shovelling food into his mouth, which was practically kissing his plate. 'But don't take that as a compliment.'

'I won't,' I said, then paused. 'Why not?'

'I trust *you* because beneath that thin, rakish veneer . . .' he waved his fork at my clothes '. . . you are a man of honour. Don't look so worried, I won't tell a soul,' he grinned, spiking himself a piece of veal. 'It's your parents' fault, of course. They must have poisoned you with talk of charity and honesty when you were a child. And see where it's brought you! You are not fit for public office of the lowest kind. The Edward Gilbournes of this world flourish and profit handsomely and always will. But men such as you . . . I'll bet you don't even cheat at cards, Tom. It's a wonder you've survived this long.'

I held up my hands in protest. 'I don't *need* to cheat at cards!'

'And is that the reason you don't?' he shot back.

I slumped against my chair and said nothing. It was true, I didn't like to cheat – in the main. Fleet had uncovered a truth I had kept hidden even from myself – a truth that lay at the very core of my being, hard and unpalatable as a peach stone. *Honour.* 'Perhaps I should have been a cleric after all,' I grumbled, pushing my food about my plate.

'Nonsense,' Fleet cried, holding his hands up as if to ward off something deadly. 'All those scheming, duplicitous bishops and archdeacons? They'd eat you for breakfast. No, no – you must not take your . . . *condition* so hard. We just need to find you an honest occupation, where a man's word counts for something.' He tilted his head. 'Do you ride well? You would make an excellent highwayman.'

Trim arrived with a pestle and mortar filled with ground sugar and some sweet-smelling herbs. 'My own recipe,' he smiled, tipping the contents into the punch bowl and swirling them into the brandy.

Fleet poured a fresh ladleful of Trim's new, improved blend. Then he handed it to me. 'Try this for me. I don't trust men bearing herbs.'

'Try it for yourself,' I cried, indignant. 'I'm not your taster.'

'What on earth are you talking about?' Trim asked, bewildered. 'You do not think I've poisoned it, surely?'

I was about to explain that Fleet had been drugged the night of Roberts' murder. Then Fleet looked at me. If looks were daggers, I would have been skewered to the far wall. 'Very well,' I muttered, taking a long gulp. And then another.

'Well, his wits seem fine to me,' Trim said, after a while.

Fleet looked dubious.

We ate and drank in contented silence for a time, though I found I could not eat much, despite my rumbling stomach. The bruises on my throat, hidden beneath my cravat, made it hard to swallow, though I did manage to finish two bowls of the broth. Trim, as Fleet had promised, did indeed have an extraordinary appetite but I did not begrudge him for it; he had shown me many kindnesses since my arrival at the Marshalsea, not least tending to my injuries that morning. If food was the fuel that made the stove of his heart burn brighter, so be it. And as I said: I was not paying for it.

I had settled the silver watch upon the table and remember it was showing a quarter past nine when we heard two pairs of footsteps upon the stairs. Cross entered first, cantankerous as ever and without knocking, kicking the half-closed door open with his heavy boot. 'Visitor,' he grunted, helping himself to a generous serving of punch while Fleet looked on, scandalised. A moment later Charles stepped into the room, smiling when he saw me at the table. I stood up and we embraced each other warmly.

'You look much better,' he said, holding me at arm's length. 'I was worried, this morning. Exceedingly worried.'

I smiled and did not correct him. And in truth I was better, except that my mind kept travelling back to the night before, and my head still ached where the iron cap had ground into my skull. Here among friends, the horror of the night seemed far away. But I was afraid what I would see when I blew out the candle and closed my eyes.

Seeing the punch was almost gone, Charles sent Cross for a fresh bowl; a gesture that transformed Fleet's opinion of my childhood friend in a flash.

'Most gentlemanlike of you, sir,' he beamed. 'You are welcome to take anything from the floor by way of thanks.'

Charles blinked at the mounds of rumpled clothes, the litter of obscene pamphlets, the ivory tusk, then picked his way over to a seat by the fire, empty-handed. I followed him there and we smoked a pipe together while Trim and Fleet scavenged their way through the last of the dishes.

Charles glanced over at Fleet, then leaned in close, lowering his voice. 'I'm surprised to see you have forgiven him, Tom. It's a miracle you survived the night. When I first came into the Strong Room this morning and saw you fixed to the wall . . . You were so pale. I thought . . .' He winced and shook his head.

I told Charles about Woodburn's rambling confession – of what, I wasn't sure. I also told him what I had learned about Gilbourne and the offer he had made to Captain Roberts: ten guineas for the use of his wife. Charles look sickened, wringing his hands and staring away into the fire. 'We must get you out of this damned place.'

'We'll interrogate Woodburn tomorrow morning,' I said, sounding more reasonable than I felt. 'If anyone can wheedle the truth out of a man it's Samuel Fleet. It's in his interest to help me now.'

Charles barely heard me. He was still staring into the fire. 'I wish I could do more to help you.'

'You have done far more than I deserve,' I said, feeling the truth of it for the first time. 'It's my own fault I've ended up in here, Charles. I must find my own way out.'

Cross arrived with the fresh bowl, slamming it down on the table. 'They're locking the front gate,' he said to Charles. 'You'd better come with me. Or would you like to spend the night here, sir?'

Charles picked up his hat and bid the room a good evening. I walked down to the yard with him, grabbing the last chance to step outside before they locked up the wards for the night. Charles touched my arm and smiled, but he looked worried. 'For God's sake, be careful, Tom. You know now how dangerous it is in here. I can't promise to arrive in time to save you on the next occasion. And keep an eye on Fleet – he's not—'

'Thank you, Charles,' I interrupted, clasping his hands. I couldn't face another lecture on the duplicity of Samuel Fleet, true as it may be.

Charles smiled, but he did not look happy. 'I'll pray for you.'

Cross, who had been leaning against the wall, gave a low chuckle as he stepped out of the shadows. 'Prayers won't do you any good, Mr Buckley,' he said, glancing up at the dim light glowing from Belle Isle's window. 'It's the devil runs things in here . . .'

I smoked another pipe as the turnkeys locked up the prison. The Common Side wailed its protest for another night.

'Mr Hawkins?'

It was Jenings with his lantern and keys, come to lock up my ward. Jakes stood behind him, his massive bulk shadowy in the dark. I threw my spent pipe to the ground and headed wearily for the door. Jakes followed me up to Belle Isle and checked the room while Jenings hovered outside with his keys.

'No hass . . . ash-assassins here,' Fleet declared, then giggled. He and Trim had settled hard into the second bowl.

I poured myself a glass, anxious to catch up, and offered one to Jakes. He shook his head.

'One of us should stay sober.'

'Good man!' Fleet cheered. He really *was* drunk.

'I'll stand watch downstairs tonight,' Jakes said. 'Any trouble, just call from the window.'

Jenings cleared his throat. 'Forgive me, gentlemen, but I'll need to lock you in now.'

Trim rose unsteadily and weaved his way to the door. He almost tripped when he reached the landing, and might have fallen down the stairs if Jenings hadn't grabbed his coat and pulled him back. Fleet watched him leave, then shook his head. 'Can't hold his liquor,' he said, then hiccuped.

Jakes frowned at me. 'As I said. Just call . . .'

I was pleased to see there were still a few servings of punch left in the bowl, despite Trim and Fleet's best efforts. Trim must have tipped the rest of his 'recipe' into the mix; it was more richly spiced than the first and stronger with it. All the better – my body still ached from its beating and nothing deadened the pain like a half pint of brandy.

I had intended to discuss plans for tomorrow with Fleet, but he was making little sense by this point and after two further glasses I was no better. At first I blamed the lack of food in my stomach, but when the room began to blur and I found I couldn't stand, I realised at last that something was wrong. I reached for Fleet, who had slumped against the table, his head resting heavy on his arm.

Slowly, with great effort, he lifted his head. And for the first time, I saw fear glittering in his eyes. 'Tom . . .' he groaned, his voice dredged from the deep. 'Drugged . . . Fetch help . . .' He gripped my hand and dug his nails into my palm, the bite of it waking me a little. Then his head dropped again and his hand slid from mine.

Somehow I pulled myself to my feet and staggered across the floor, legs heavy as iron. If I could just reach the window and call Jakes. But the room was spinning and the words stuck in my throat. I stumbled, and fell. Pulled myself up and fell again. After that – nothing.

V) *MONDAY. THE LAST DAY.*

Twenty

I woke. Head pounding, mouth dry.

The room was in shadow, that strange grey light that comes in the hour before dawn. I was lying across my bed, fully clothed. Had I dragged myself there or had someone carried me?

Not dead. Not murdered. I lay still for a moment, staring at the ceiling, relief washing through every cell of my body. Alive.

'Fleet.'

I could just make out the shape of him across the room. He was still sleeping. I sat up and groaned as the room swayed and settled again, took a deep breath as my head cleared. Fumbled for a candle, for the tinderbox buried deep in my coat pocket. Struck the flint against the steel till the sparks flew. Lit the candle.

'Fleet. Wake up.'

I picked up the candlestick and stumbled across the room. He was lying on his back, one arm stretched to the floor, the other over his heart. I held the candle higher.

His throat was cut. Red rivers across white skin.

Not Fleet. Please, God.

It wasn't real. The gaping wound. The blood-stained sheets. Black eyes wide open and lifeless, staring at nothing. It was a dream. I touched his hand. Cold.

I ran to the door but it was locked tight. I beat upon it with my fists, shouting for help, kicked it till the wood splintered and the lock smashed open. I staggered out on to the landing as Jakes pounded up the stairs, Jenings moments behind him, lantern held high.

'Mr Hawkins!' Jakes cried. 'What in God's name . . .' He looked into the room and froze. Then he turned and grabbed Jenings and pushed him towards the stairs. 'Call the alarm! Fleet's dead.'

The truth of it hit me like a fist. My legs crumpled and I slid slowly down the wall. I heard Jenings cry out across the yard; heard the prisoners yelling the news through the walls.

'Fleet's dead!'

'Murdered!'

'The devil's gone back to hell!'

A riotous clamour of shouts and jeers rumbled up through the gaol.

It sounded like applause.

'Mr Hawkins.' Jakes touched my shoulder and I flinched. He kneeled down, brought his lips to my ear. 'Did you kill him?'

I stared at him.

He jerked his chin towards Belle Isle. 'The door was locked. No one would blame you, if he struck first.'

I shook my head, rubbed my hand across my scalp.

'Then who . . . ?' Jakes frowned. 'I stood guard at the ward entrance all night. No one came past.'

I dropped my hands and rose wearily to my feet. We faced each other across the landing.

'You are sure of that?' I whispered. '*No one* came into the ward? Not a soul?'

'Upon my life.'

A cold chill ran through me. If no one had come into the ward from the yard in the night, then the killer must have been hiding in the ward all along, waiting for the best time to strike. He dosed the punch then stole up to Belle Isle once he knew it had taken effect. 'He must have picked the lock,' I said. I could hardly bear to think of the rest. I had lain there fast asleep while Fleet's killer had drawn his knife and . . .

Fleet's eyes had been open. Had he woken, in those last few moments? Had he cried out for help? I shuddered and rubbed my eyes. And then a thought struck me. I peered down the stairwell and then up to the landing above. 'Jakes. Has anyone *left* the ward this morning?'

He shook his head. 'The cells are still locked.'

I stared at him in alarm. 'Then he is still here. He's still on the ward. We must keep the whole building locked. And stand guard. We mustn't let him escape.'

Jakes was about to reply when there was a loud crash downstairs, followed by a short scuffle. Then a girl's voice cried out. 'Let me through! For God's sake let me through!'

Kitty. A moment later and she was on the stairs, followed closely by Acton himself. She shoved past me and flung herself towards the room. Jakes tried to grab her but she kicked him hard in the shin and slipped through his grasp. He sprang after her but I stopped him. 'Go back to the main door. He'll use the confusion to slip past us.'

Jakes nodded and pushed his way past Acton, pulling out his club as he ran down the stairs to the main entrance. I heard Kitty cry out, once, on the other side of the door – a low, terrible moan of grief. As Acton reached me I held out my hand, blocking his path. 'For shame, sir. Give her a moment.'

He started to protest then saw the look in my eyes and shrugged. 'Why not? A moment.'

The room was quiet. The early-morning light streamed through the unshuttered window, spilling on to Fleet's body. The candlelight had spared me the worst of it, but the sun was pitiless in its glare. There was blood everywhere: pooled beneath the bed; soaked into the bed sheets. The smell of it hung in the air. All that life, bled out and gone.

But it was the stillness I couldn't bear. Fleet was never still; he was always reaching for his pipe, or pacing the floor, or leaning forward to press his point home. Four days, I had known him. But I felt the loss as if I'd known him a lifetime, deep and hard in my chest like a knife.

Kitty was kneeling at his side, his cold white hand pressed to her cheek. Her petticoat was stained with his blood. She gathered herself up as I moved towards her, tears streaming down her face. I opened my arms and she collapsed into me, sobbing against my chest as I held her tight.

I led her gently from the room to Mrs Bradshaw, who was waiting on the landing. She shook her head at me as she bundled Kitty into her arms.

'Terrible business, Mr Hawkins,' she said, craning her neck to get a better view through the door. 'Quite terrible . . .'

I walked back inside, numb with shock. Acton was glaring down at the bed, fists balled on his waist. 'Well. What a mess,' he said, shaking his head slowly. 'We can't call that a suicide, can we? He's been bled like a pig.'

My hands clenched into fists, nails biting hard into my palms. 'It was someone on this ward. Had to be.'

'Is that so . . . ?' He frowned. 'Well, he'll pay for it, damn him. I squeezed a lot of money out of Samuel Fleet these past few months. Whoever killed him owes me a fortune.' He slapped a hand down hard upon my shoulder. 'It wasn't you, was it, Hawkins? Did he get a bit too *friendly* in the night?' He leered at me. 'Wouldn't put it past him. Wouldn't put anything past that whore's son.'

I shrugged his hand away. 'Fleet was murdered because he was hunting for Roberts' killer — and at your command. It's a wonder they didn't cut my throat, too.'

Acton snorted. 'No need, was there? Fleet was the clever one.' He pulled at the neck of Fleet's shirt and whistled in appreciation. 'Very neat,' he said, examining the wound.

I staggered to the window and opened it wide, taking deep breaths to fight back the sickness. It was no use. I had barely enough time to find a chamber pot before I threw up the contents of my stomach. The fine dinner I had shared with Fleet and Trim last night. The punch, dosed with a sleeping draught. Trim . . . and Woodburn! My God, I had forgotten – I *must* speak with him. But when I tried to stand I fell back to the floor, my head in my hands. It was pounding hard – the effects of the drugged punch, no doubt. I leaned back against the wall and felt despair wash over me. Acton was right – Fleet was the clever one. How would I ever survive in this cursed place without him?

'You done?' Acton asked, tipping his chin towards the chamber pot. He wiped the blood from his hands on to the bed sheets. 'I wonder what they'll think of this.'

I rubbed the sweat from my brow. 'Who . . .' My voice sounded cracked. 'Who do you mean?'

'The men he worked for. The men who locked him *in* here. "Too dangerous to live and too useful to die", that's what I heard. They won't like it, I reckon. I could be in trouble for this.' He glanced at me thoughtfully, then grinned. 'Maybe I'll tell them you did it.'

My stomach lurched. He would do it in a flash, I knew. 'I was drugged.'

'So you say.'

'You still need me,' I blurted, in desperation. 'I can solve Roberts' murder. I know it was Gilbourne, I just need to find the second man.'

Acton grunted in surprise. 'You think there's two of 'em?'

I gestured to the bed. 'Whoever killed Fleet also helped kill Roberts. Gilbourne couldn't have carried the body on his own.'

'True enough,' Acton muttered. 'That dandy-prat can barely lift his own cock to piss.' He narrowed his eyes. 'So who's this friend of his, eh?'

I have no idea, I thought, helplessly. Woodburn knew, I was sure of it, but he had been half-mad last night. 'I am almost certain. I just need more time to gather evidence. Give me a week—'

'Do you take me for a fool?' Acton growled. 'I gave you two days and you've had one. I'm losing patience, Mr Hawkins. Find this other man by lock-up tonight.' He gestured at Fleet's body. 'Or I swear you'll hang for this.'

He left and the room fell silent. Nothing felt right in here. Too still. I pulled myself to my feet and gathered the things I needed: the silver watch; my pipe and tobacco; my blade. A few sheets of paper. I threw a blanket over Fleet's body – the same square of grey-blue wool he had stretched out upon on Snows Fields just the day before. He would have laughed at such a foolish, irrational gesture. *Waste of a good blanket, Tom.*

I reached down and closed his eyes.

Twenty-One

O ut on the staircase I paused for a moment and took a deep, steadying breath. When I was calm enough, I leaned over the staircase and called down to Jakes, standing guard at the main door of the ward.

'Are they all locked up?' I shouted over the din. The prisoners were still calling out the news of Fleet's death all around the gaol.

Jakes turned his battle-scarred face up to mine. 'The whole prison. Governor's orders. Doesn't want another riot.'

I heard banging from the floor above. 'Is that you, Hawkins?' Mack bellowed. 'Tell them to let us out, damn it. I've a business to run!'

I hesitated on the landing, listening to my neighbours clamouring to be released, their voices raised in fear and outrage. One of them was dissembling. One of them had picked the lock and slipped into Belle Isle last night while I lay sleeping. Had they thought of murdering me too? Had they placed the blade to my throat? And if so — what had stopped their hand?

'Mr Hawkins?' Trim called down, banging on his locked door. 'Is it true? Is Fleet murdered?'

I took a few steps up towards his landing. 'Trim! Is Mr Woodburn awake?'

There was a short pause, then Trim's voice called again through the door. 'He wouldn't stay. I tried to stop him – he's much too sick to leave . . .'

I gave a shout of alarm and slipped down the stairs as fast as I could. Jakes unlocked the main ward door in time for me to catch sight of the round, shabby figure of Mr Woodburn, limping his way across the yard towards the Lodge, leaning heavily on Joseph Cross for support. I glared at Jakes. 'You let him out?'

'Didn't see any harm in it,' he said. His eyes were red from standing watch all night. 'He didn't kill Fleet, did he?'

'No – but I think he knows who did. He's running away.'

Jakes' jaw dropped. I raced down the yard, shouting for them to wait.

Woodburn turned as I reached them. He looked as if he had aged twenty years in the night. His eyes were glazed and unfocused and there were strange, fresh scratches on his hands as if an animal had torn at them. 'Oh! Thank God!' he cried, grabbing at my coat and bunching it weakly in his hands. 'You are safe.'

Cross began to pull him away. 'Come along, sir. Your chair is waiting.'

I glared at him. 'Leave him be! I must speak with him at once.'

'On whose orders?' Cross snarled.

'The governor's. Run and ask him if you wish.'

Cross pulled a sour face, then took a step back, folding his arms. 'Go on, then.'

I cursed under my breath. The last person I wanted standing over me now was Joseph Cross – but there was nothing I could do about it. Mr Woodburn still had hold of my coat.

'You're safe,' he mumbled, patting my chest. 'I couldn't save him. I tried but I was too late . . . too late. So much wickedness . . .'

'Mr Woodburn, please, I beg you.' I took hold of his shoulders and gave him a little shake. 'Do you know who killed Roberts?'

'Roberts . . .' he breathed, staring at a patch of air behind us. 'Roberts . . . who killed Roberts . . .' He swallowed hard. 'Do you see him?' he cried, of a sudden. 'Look! Do you see him with the noose about his neck?'

'He's raving,' Cross muttered.

'Mr Woodburn.' I tightened my grip on the chaplain's shoulders and he blinked, his eyes clearing for a moment. 'Please, just tell me the truth. It was Gilbourne, was it not?'

Woodburn's round, florid face crumpled in bewilderment. 'Gilbourne . . . no . . . although . . .' He looked away and then he started to nod eagerly. 'Yes! Yes! You are right, sir! He's to blame! Edward Gilbourne!'

My heart leapt – here was the truth at last. 'And the second man, sir. Who was it helped Gilbourne? Who killed Samuel Fleet last night?' I looked him deep in the eyes, trying to reach the kind, gentle man I had met on my first day in the gaol. The man who returned again and again to the Common Side and smuggled food to the prisoners – at the risk of his reputation and even his life. 'Sir. Who was it stabbed you yesterday? You saw him, did you not?'

Woodburn gave a start and backed away. His eyes darted wildly back to the prison wards and Belle Isle. He scratched anxiously at his hand, nails raking through the skin. 'I cannot say,' he whimpered. 'I cannot . . .'

I seized his jacket. 'You must!' I cried. 'My God, I will beat it from you if I must—'

'Leave him be!' Cross yelled, tearing us apart. He called for Wills and Chapman, who were drinking beer under the lamppost. I was shouting by now, screaming at the chaplain to tell me the truth. He covered his face with his hands, blood pouring from the deep scratches in his skin, and sobbed wretchedly.

'I stabbed myself!' he wailed. 'God forgive me!' He pulled his hands away, his face filled with horror and revulsion. 'I stabbed *myself.*'

There was a moment's shocked silence. Cross was the first to recover. 'Take the chaplain to his chair,' he ordered Wills and Chapman. They obeyed at once, leading Woodburn away through the Lodge while Cross held me back. I fought him as hard as I could but he was too strong, flinging me hard on to my hands and knees on the cobbles. By the time I had picked myself up Woodburn was gone.

'He *knew* Fleet's killer!' I screamed, voice shredded with despair. 'For God's sake bring him back.'

Cross held up a finger and tapped the small cut on his lip where I had hit him four days ago, the morning I had arrived in the Marshalsea. And then he turned, put his hands in his pockets and sauntered towards the Tap Room, whistling.

I must keep moving. If I stopped for a moment, the rage and the grief would knock me down. My body was feverish and my head felt heavy – some lingering taint from the sleeping draught, perhaps. No matter. I would work my way through it. Woodburn had given me one name at least. The second I would have to discover for myself – and before sunset.

Acton was back in the turnkeys' office in the Lodge, seated at his desk, running through the accounts. Grace leaned over his shoulder, pointing at some fresh soul marked for damnation.

'Mr Acton.'

Grace glared at me. 'The governor is busy.'

Acton leaned back on his chair and studied me for a moment. 'Still hunting, then? Glad to hear it.' He glanced at Grace, prodded the ledger. 'Murder's bad for business.'

'I need a room where I may work. Somewhere quiet.'

He scratched his jaw. 'My parlour's free this morning. Mary's busy tidying up the Tap Room.'

'Mr Hawkins,' Grace wheedled. 'Pray tell me. Who will pay your rent, sir, now Mr Fleet is dead? I will need assurances . . .'

'Damn you, sir, we're not brutes!' Acton roared, rounding on his clerk. He picked up the thick ledger and smacked it hard over

Grace's head. 'In any case, Mr Hawkins will be leaving us tonight.' He gave a slow, cruel smile. 'One way or another.'

Up in Acton's parlour, I ordered a fire to be lit and laid my paper upon a small writing table set in a corner by the window. I'd planned to write a short account of the night's events in the hope of discovering some fresh clue, but I couldn't settle. It seemed I had inherited Fleet's restlessness, but not his precision of mind. For the life of me I could not fathom why Woodburn would have stabbed himself. There was a chance he was lying – to protect himself or someone else. But he had seemed so distressed and shamed by his confession I doubted it.

Whatever the truth behind the stabbing, I was sure of one thing. Woodburn knew who had killed Captain Roberts. Had someone admitted his guilt to the chaplain, then regretted it? I groaned, furious with myself for letting Woodburn escape without pressing the truth from him.

I pushed open the window and called out to a porter for a pot of coffee and some raw milk and bread. Then I sat down, picked up one of Acton's quills, and dipped it in the ink.

Someone had tipped a sleeping draught into the punch last night. If I wrote down every possible suspect – no matter how improbable – perhaps the killer would reveal himself.

Mrs Bradshaw & Kitty prepared both bowls

A porter delivered the first bowl

I drank from the first bowl with Trim & Fleet

Joseph Cross took a glass from the first bowl

Cross delivered the second bowl, paid for by Charles

Trim, Fleet & I drank from the second bowl

Charles & Jakes were offered punch but neither accepted a glass

I dismissed *Kitty* at once, scratching out her name with the quill.

Fleet had not murdered himself, so his name was the next to go. The ink covered his name like soil over a coffin.

Could *Charles* have slipped a powder into the second bowl? Yes – it was just feasible. But for what possible purpose? And in any case he left the gaol before the front gate was locked. Whoever murdered Fleet must have stayed on the ward all night. Another name scratched.

The same was true of *Jakes* – he could have drugged the punch when no one was looking, and upon reflection he did refuse a glass from the second bowl. But then he knew he would be standing watch all night and would need his wits about him. And if he was the killer, why would he have encouraged me in my hunt for the truth? Fleet would have left Jakes uncrossed purely out of spite, but it did not make any rational sense. I drew a line through his name.

Mrs Bradshaw? She kept a supply of Mr Siddall's sleeping draught in the Oak; she'd given some to Catherine Roberts just the other night to calm her nerves. It was no secret that she mistrusted Fleet and thought him a dangerous influence on Kitty. She could have poured the draught into the bowl before sending it up to us. I hesitated, quill hovering over her name. But then how could she have slipped past Jakes, standing at the main door? She did not have the figure to slip past anyone, even under the cloak of night. And in any case, it was a very large step from disliking a man to slitting his throat.

The porter arrived with my breakfast. I watched him closely as he laid out my bread and milk and poured me a dish of coffee. He was from the Common Side – I could tell from his hollow cheeks and tattered clothes. Most of the porters came from over the wall, glad to earn a few extra farthings and breathe the fresher air on the Master's Side. No one gave them a moment's notice; not even Fleet. Servants came through Belle Isle every day for one reason or another – to deliver coal or clear the dishes or empty the chamber pots; the hundred little chores we all took for granted. I handed the man a farthing and he bowed and left.

It could have been the porter. No one paid them any heed. He could have hidden himself in one of the stairwells after delivering the first bowl, waited for the drug to take effect then stolen back up to Belle Isle when everyone was sleeping. No need to pass Jakes at the main door. And though porters didn't carry keys, I wagered many of them knew how to pick a lock in the dark. After that he could have returned to his hiding place and waited for the panic of discovery the next morning. No one would notice a porter slipping back out in those first chaotic moments.

I drew a ring about the porter's line, then hesitated. There was every reason to suspect him, but I knew, in my heart, this was not Fleet's killer. I closed my eyes, heard Fleet's voice at my ear as if his spirit were in the room with me. *Don't know it in your heart, Tom. Know it in your mind. Why* was he not the killer?

Because it was the *second* bowl contained the sleeping draught.

I opened my eyes. The draught only began to work after we drank deep from the second bowl. And Cross had taken a glass from the bottom of the first bowl, where the draught would have been strongest. Enough to make him feel out of sorts, had it been dosed.

I drew a line through the porter and considered the two names that remained.

Joseph Cross

Trim

Of the two men, I knew who I wanted it to be. But that did not make it the truth. A cold, unhappy thought stole into my mind, like a cloud across the sun.

A sharp rap at the door made me start from my seat. A moment later Edward Gilbourne entered the room, followed closely by Acton.

I leapt up, confounded. I was not ready to confront a man as clever as Gilbourne – not without clear proof of his guilt. I glared at Acton, silently signalling my alarm as Gilbourne removed his gloves and tossed his tricorn carelessly on to a chair. Acton ignored me, closing the door with a soft click and leaning his back against it, hands tucked in the pockets of his red waistcoat.

'Well, sirs,' Gilbourne said, settling himself by the hearth and running his fingers down his legs, caressing the fine, dark brown silk of his breeches. He seemed calm but it was an act, I could see it now. He had noted my expression when he arrived and now he was preparing himself for battle. 'I am glad to see you were not hurt in the riot.' He turned to me with an open, friendly expression that made the blood freeze in my veins. For a moment, I thought I could hear Fleet's voice, whispering in my head. *Careful with this one, Tom. Careful.*

'Mr Acton tells me you are close to solving the murder. I take it this means our good governor is not a suspect.' He shot me a knowing, complicitous smile. 'I would be obliged if you could explain why I have been summoned at such short notice. Am I here to order an arrest warrant? That would be fast work indeed. But you are a very capable man, of course.'

His flattery bounced off me like hail off a roof. I did not know what to do, or say. Should I confront him with Mr Woodburn's accusation? But what use were the ravings of an old man who had just confessed to stabbing himself in his fear and madness? Curse Acton for springing this upon me! At least he'd had the wits not to tell Gilbourne of my suspicions – he was so quick-minded he would have found a thousand answers on his walk from the Lodge gate to Acton's parlour. I crossed to the window, thinking hard. And then I realised there was one thing I could test him on. 'I'm afraid I'm not sure why you were summoned here, sir. But you should know that Mr Fleet was killed last night.'

Gilbourne sat back, startled. 'Good God!' he exclaimed. 'I am sorry to hear it. He was killed in the riot?'

I frowned. Gilbourne did seem genuinely surprised by the news. 'Someone cut his throat while he was sleeping.'

'Murdered in his bed! Poor devil.' Gilbourne shook his head. He twisted in his seat to look at Acton. 'But then, I suppose he did have many enemies. In and outside the prison . . .'

I couldn't bear the hypocrisy another moment. 'Yourself included, Mr Gilbourne.'

He laughed, feigning astonishment. 'Good heavens! You are not accusing *me*, surely? I was one of the few who defended him! My dear Mr Hawkins, forgive me. You seem a little frantic. I fear your grief is affecting your judgement.' He raised his eyebrows. 'Perhaps you liked Mr Fleet a little too well? I believe he had that effect on certain . . . *gentlemen.*'

I said nothing. What could I do? I needed Fleet's help to catch a snake such as Gilbourne. What use was I on my own?

'Well,' Gilbourne sighed, reaching for his gloves. 'This has all been most diverting. But if you would excuse me, gentlemen, I think I shall return to town. I'm meeting friends for dinner.'

Acton stepped forward and shoved him back into his chair, holding him firm. 'This is my Castle, Mr Gilbourne. I'll say when you can leave.'

Gilbourne's face darkened but he was no fool – he held still and waited.

When Acton was sure his point was made, he stepped back to guard the door again.

Gilbourne turned his gaze on me, cold and contemptuous. 'So. You wish me to defend my honour, is that it? A butcher and a failed rake. Very well, sirs. I could not have killed Mr Fleet last night. I was at a lodge meeting at the Anchor and Crown in Shorts Gardens until three, then took a room in a bagnio for the rest of the night. I have friends who will vouch for me. Powerful friends.'

I raised my hand to stop him. 'I know you did not kill Mr Fleet.'

Gilbourne blinked in surprise. 'Then what, *pray*, is all this nonsense?'

I hesitated. The room was stifling and I could hear the blood roaring in my ears.

'For God's sake, Hawkins,' Acton growled. 'Show your hand, you cork-brained fool. He says you murdered Captain Roberts, Gilbourne. And I swear to God if you're the reason my Castle's been in uproar these past months I'll hang you myself.'

For a second I caught a glimmer of fear in Gilbourne's eyes. And then he smiled and shuffled back in his seat, like a child waiting to be told a bedtime story. 'So, I murdered John Roberts, eh? Well, well – how astonishing. And why would I do such a thing?'

I rubbed the sweat from my brow, cursing Acton under my breath. There was nothing for it; I would have to accuse him and hope to God I could force him to confess. 'Mr Gilbourne. I know that you offered Captain Roberts a sum of ten guineas to rape his wife. When he refused, and threatened you with blackmail, you slipped into the prison through the cellar and killed him, with the help of an accomplice.'

And there it was. The simple, ugly truth.

'Son of a whore,' Acton whispered, though he was probably just thinking of the ten guineas. Gilbourne said nothing.

I leaned against the mantelpiece, mouth dry, sweat sticking my shirt to my back. 'Roberts told Fleet everything. You guessed that, but didn't care so long as he kept his mouth shut. But when you heard he was helping with my investigation you sent your accomplice to cut his throat.'

I waited. This was the moment for confession, for Gilbourne to break down. And then I would have him. But something was wrong; the moment was slipping away from me. I had expected rage, denial – violence, even. But Gilbourne seemed quite unmoved. He brushed a piece of dust from his breeches and gave me a thin, condescending smile. 'And you have proof of this?'

I stood a little straighter. 'Mr Woodburn accused you of it this morning, sir. In front of witnesses.'

'*Did* he?' Gilbourne frowned. 'How strange. Well, the fat old fool never did like me. He accused me of stealing charity money once, can you imagine that, Mr Acton . . . ?' He fiddled with a lace cuff. 'I suppose I stabbed poor Mr Woodburn, too?'

'No. He . . . stabbed himself.' I felt my face flush. It sounded ludicrous, even to me.

Gilbourne sniggered. 'He stabbed *himself* . . . ? Extraordinary!'

My heart sank. It was no use — Gilbourne had defeated me, without leaving his chair. I couldn't even avenge my friend's murder, unless I simply ran my blade through Gilbourne's black heart before he drew another breath. I confess, in that moment I considered it.

Gilbourne rested his chin on his hand. 'D'you know, I could almost pity you, Mr Hawkins.'

Acton was growing impatient, rocking back and forth on his heels. 'Is any of this true, Gilbourne? God knows you're capable of it.'

Gilbourne sneered at him. 'Oh, that is precious, coming from you . . . Yes. As it happens I *did* offer Captain Roberts ten guineas for his wife. What of it? It was a generous offer, I thought.' He smirked. '*Lady* Roberts, gliding about as if the whole world should kiss her feet. She's just a common slut who ran away with the first man who charmed her legs open. I thought it would be amusing to fuck some sense into her.'

This was too much, even for Acton. 'You planned to rape Mrs Roberts for sport?'

'It's hardly *rape*, sir, if the husband consents. Oh, he refused at first, I grant you. And he did try to blackmail me, poor fool — but once I explained to him it would be his word against mine, and how many of my friends were lawyers, and magistrates . . . he soon had a change of heart. A man will do just about anything to stay alive. The trick is knowing his price, isn't that so, Mr Acton?'

Acton shrugged his agreement.

Gilbourne stood up and stretched, considered his reflection in the glass and began adjusting his cravat. He caught my eye in the mirror and smiled. 'Roberts sold his only son to escape the

Common Side. Why not sell his wife to buy his freedom? So we shook upon it and I paid him the five guineas in advance. Unfortunately someone murdered him that same night and stole the money.' He picked up his hat and gloves. 'If you ever do find the real killer, I'd be *most obliged* if you could return it. I have my eye on a new pair of boots for the winter. Or perhaps you might explain to Mrs Roberts that her husband has sold her to me for a guinea a fuck?'

I could take no more. I drew my dagger and held it across his throat, pushing him back to the mantelpiece.

'Acton!' Gilbourne cried. 'For God's sake pull him off me!'

Acton chuckled. 'Let him murder you, what should I care? They'll hang him and I'll be done with the pair of you.'

I lowered the blade slowly, keeping the tip at Gilbourne's chest. Acton's words had struck home. This man was not worth hanging for. 'Why did you help Catherine with her ghost?'

Gilbourne raised an eyebrow. 'Oh . . . you know of that?'

'What's this?' Acton asked sharply. 'What do you know about Roberts' ghost, damn you?'

Gilbourne rolled his eyes. 'There is no ghost. It was all a foolish hoax, plotted by Mrs Roberts. I helped her, Mr Hawkins, because she *paid* me to. And she is so *very* grateful. I must confess I have laughed long and hard about that.'

I dropped the dagger, sickened by every word. My shoulders sagged. What more could I do?

'*Ohhh*,' Gilbourne simpered. 'Am I free to go, sir? You're too kind.' And with that, he gave me a low, mocking bow, and left the room.

Acton considered me in silence for a moment. 'Idiot,' he muttered, and followed Gilbourne through the door.

I sank to the floor and put my head in my hands. What a fool. What a stupid fool. All my hopes, all my efforts . . . all my dreams of escape. Of avenging Fleet's death. Ruined by my own hand.

Gilbourne could never have beaten Fleet in such a humiliating fashion. His scorn was like acid; my whole body burned with the shame.

It must have been an hour or more before the sound of footsteps on the stairs roused me from my stupor. It was Charles, breathless and hot, come all the way from Mayfair to comfort me. Or so I thought.

'My God, Tom,' he said. 'I am not sure my spirits can stand another shock like this! How do you fare?' He squinted at me for a moment. 'Not well,' he decided. 'You're pale as ash.'

I told him of my meeting with Gilbourne. 'Good God! He admits it all?' Charles exclaimed, scandalised. 'Shameless devil. Sir Philip will know of this – once you are safely released, of course.'

'Released?' I laughed, bitterly. 'I doubt I shall ever escape this place. Not without Fleet's help.'

Charles didn't answer for a while. He wandered about the parlour, coming to rest in front of a rather pretty study of pink roses and lavender painted by Mary's father. 'This is not ill done . . .' he murmured.

'For God's sake, Charles. Whatever you wish to say, please say it before I'm sent mad with your pacing.'

He bit his lip; turned away from the painting. 'There is a way you might walk free within the hour,' he said, gesturing to the clock upon the mantelpiece. 'But you will not like it.' He put his arm on my shoulder and led me to the chair by the fireside. He settled himself on the other side of the hearth, in the same chair Gilbourne had sat in an hour before. The fire had died away to a few weak embers. 'You were fond of Mr Fleet.'

'I am not sure . . .'

'You were friends,' he persisted. 'By the end.' He shifted in his chair, drew out a pipe, then seemed to think better of it. He slipped it back in his coat pocket and linked his fingers together. 'There was a darker side to Samuel Fleet. Sir Philip has many powerful friends, in privileged positions. Fleet was known in those circles as a useful but dangerous man. He was a spy, Tom.' He paused. 'And an assassin. He killed countless men in his time.'

Of course. I did not doubt it for a moment. That quick, cunning mind. The ease with which he held a blade. Fleet himself had hinted that he knew too many secrets; that he was languishing in gaol for that very reason. 'Why tell me this?'

Charles looked grim. He never did like confronting trouble, even as a boy. But he liked half-finished business even less. 'I took a turn through the gaol just now. I spoke to the turnkeys and the trusties. The porters. Any prisoners that weren't locked up. Most of them are convinced that Fleet killed Captain Roberts. And they don't give a damn who killed Fleet. Sir Philip and Mr Acton are hoping for a quick end to the matter. Killing was Fleet's business. He was *in the room* the night Roberts was murdered. He might have done it.' He cleared his throat, looked away. 'Tell Acton that Fleet confessed to you. He'll be happy to believe it if it puts an end to the business. Tell him now and I promise you will be released at once.'

'No.'

'Tom . . .'

'*No!*' I glared at him. 'I will not accuse an innocent man.'

'He's *dead*,' Charles said, chopping his hand through the air as if it were an executioner's blade. 'What does it matter? He has no reputation, no kin. No one would suffer from this.'

'What of Kitty?'

He blinked. 'The *kitchen maid*? For God's sake, Tom! You will *die* in here. Look at you! Four days inside and already you're battered and bruised from head to foot. I know you – you'll pick a fight with the wrong man or wander into some trouble and then it will be your corpse they're carrying through the Lodge gate on a cart. Please, I beg of you – don't throw your life away because of some ill-placed loyalty to a man you barely knew! No one cares about Samuel Fleet.'

'You want me to lie. To destroy a man's reputation. And what of his soul, Charles? They'll bury him in unconsecrated ground—'

'God damn it, you're a stubborn fool,' he complained, through gritted teeth. 'You know what Fleet was, in your heart. At best, a rogue. At worst, an invert and a killer.' He caught my expression and held up his hand. 'Forgive me, but I must be blunt. Samuel Fleet is already burning in hell for what he's done. What is one more murder to add to his name?' He got to his feet. 'Come with me now and we will tell Acton together.'

I considered it for a moment. I owed Charles that much. But my thoughts couldn't travel far before hitting a wall as hard as iron, and there was no scaling over it. I would not, *could not* betray Fleet. It was not rational, but no less true for that. 'No. I'm sorry, Charles. No.'

He winced, and stared at the floor for a long moment. 'Then it is over,' he murmured, and rose from his chair. 'I will not stay and watch you die in here.' He gave a short, formal bow and turned to leave. At the door, he paused, and looked back. 'He would have betrayed *you* in a flash.'

I smiled sadly. 'I know.'

The clock upon the mantelpiece struck noon. I wandered over to the writing table and picked up the paper with the list of scratched-out names. Then I threw it upon the fire, pushing it deep into the coals until it caught light with a bright flash, the sudden heat scorching my face as the names burned away to nothing. The last name to burn was Trim's.

Twenty-Two

'Oh dear, oh dear, Mr Hawkins. You *are* in trouble.'

Gilbert Hand was sitting beneath his lamppost, legs stretched out, drinking a mug of beer. He grinned, presenting his teeth for inspection.

'You knew Roberts took the money.'

Hand shrugged in acknowledgement. 'A man needs to know when to keep his mouth shut, Mr Hawkins. I'm not a blabber.' He took a long swig of beer. 'Governor's furious with you. You made him look like a fool in front of Gilbourne. Surprised he didn't throw you in the Hole for a few days. He hasn't tried you in there yet, has he? The hole under the stairs? It's like being buried alive, they say . . .'

'What *else* do you know, sir?'

He gestured across the Park. 'I know I don't want to go out of this world like that.' I followed his gaze to the prison wards. Two porters were carrying Fleet's body out on a stretcher, wrapped in an old sheet. Jakes — still standing sentinel — pulled off his hat as they passed and bowed his head.

'Where are you taking him?' I called out.

'Coroner,' one of the porters said without stopping. They carried the stretcher towards a cart that had just turned in through the Lodge. A crow flew down and perched on a wheel, watching intently as they loaded Fleet's body on to the back. The driver shooed it away.

Acton stood by Fleet's bench, fists on his hips, and watched the cart rumble past. For a moment our eyes met across the yard. I knew that he would be happy to see me leave the gaol the same way, preferably before the day was over.

Jakes strode to meet me. 'They've let everyone out. Acton's orders. I saved your things.' He pointed through the door to a small bundle of possessions tied in a sheet. 'They've been gambling for the rest up in Belle Isle. It'll be stripped bare by now.'

I ran up the stairs, two at a time, and burst through the door. The room was empty. The old, cracked mirror had been pulled from the wall. Books, blankets, pots, pans and clothes, all the raggle-taggle of Fleet's life had gone. Even the coal had been pinched from the bucket. Only the bed frames remained, like skeletons picked of meat. Kitty stood at the window, clutching Fleet's red velvet banyan to her chest. She'd mopped up the pool of blood from the floor, but it had left a large, dark stain on the boards. Something to give the next occupants nightmares.

'I won this for you,' Kitty said, holding out the banyan.

I folded it carefully and placed it at the end of my bed. 'Did you keep nothing for yourself, Kitty?'

She reached into her apron and pulled out the gold ring Fleet used to wear. 'It's a poesy ring. It belonged to my father.'

I held it up to the window light and read the inscription hidden on the inside of the band.

I Cannot Show the Love I Owe.

'It won't fit,' she said. 'It slides off my finger.'

'Here.' I unhooked the clasp of my mother's chain and tucked the cross into my waistcoat pocket. I slipped the ring on to the chain and fastened it about her neck, fingers brushing against her cool, freckled skin. So smooth; the finest silk. After all that had happened, this . . . this was what I needed. I couldn't help myself. My fingers whispered slowly down the nape of her neck. She shivered and turned to face me, eyes wide and serious. And then she rose on tiptoe and touched her lips to mine, gently at first and then deeper, wrapping her arms about my neck. I lost myself in that kiss, so sudden and unexpected. No one had ever kissed me like that, not in all my life. The room melted away, all my debts, all the horror, the whole prison was gone in a heartbeat. I was set free. I slid my arms around her waist and drew her close, as close as I could, pressing my hips against hers. I could feel the pulse of her heart thrumming against my chest.

'Let her go!' Catherine Roberts stood in the doorway, gaping at us in fury.

We jumped and stepped back, the moment broken like fine china on the floor.

Mrs Roberts' gloved hands balled into fists. 'You *scoundrel*!' Her voice echoed about the empty room.

I saw the kiss from her eyes now, how it must seem. Taking advantage of a grieving girl. And after I'd promised – *vowed* I wouldn't touch her. I wanted to explain but there weren't words – and she would never have understood.

I took another small step away from Kitty. Felt the gap between us again. 'What is it you want of me, Mrs Roberts?'

'You betrayed my secret. I've been ordered to leave the prison at once.'

I closed my eyes for a moment. My heart was still beating hard and it took me a moment to understand or even care what she was saying. 'Yes. Forgive me. I told Acton about the ghost. I'm afraid I had no choice. I was trying to discover your husband's killer, madam.'

'What's this about the ghost?' Kitty asked.

'Mrs Roberts hired an actor to sneak into the prison.'

'You *promised* not to tell!' she said, glowering. 'How am I to discover John's killer now I'm banished from the gaol? I have lost my *son* because of you! I will never see him again!' She broke off, sobbing into her hand, shoulders shaking.

Kitty glared at her. 'It was all a trick? You sent an actor to frighten Ben Carter – when his brother lay dying?'

Mrs Roberts dropped her hand, rubbing the tears from her cheeks as she composed herself. She gave Kitty a cold, regal glare. 'How dare you speak to me in such a pert fashion! Do you think one kiss from a gentleman makes you a lady?'

'I think you should leave, madam,' I said quietly. A day or two ago I might have called her Catherine – but not now.

She rounded on me. 'Mr Acton told me of the vile accusations you made about my husband and Mr Gilbourne.' She put a hand to her throat. 'John would never, *never* agree to such a foul thing. He was a *true* gentleman.'

I sighed but said nothing. She would never accept the sordid truth: that she had given up her family, her reputation and her heart to a man who would have sold her body and soul for ten guineas. Who could blame her for denying it?

'Kitty.' She held out her hand. 'Come here, child.'

'I'm not going anywhere,' Kitty declared, tossing her head.

'You poor girl.' Mrs Roberts laughed. 'Do you think he will care tuppence for you, once he has taken what he wants? Come. If I'm to leave this place I might as well take you with me. A lady's maid is a good position, Kitty – don't ruin yourself for something so worthless. I'll pay you a fair wage.'

'I'm obliged to you for your kind offer, Mrs Roberts. Kitty replied slowly and with great deliberation, 'But I'd rather suck Mr Woodburn's cock.'

Mrs Roberts flinched. And then she drew herself up, winter-grey eyes cold with disapproval. 'You will end up like your mother, child. A common whore, selling herself in a stinking alley for a glass of cheap gin.' She pulled her hood over her face and glided away from us down the stairs.

Kitty set her jaw, defiant as always. But I was close enough to see the shimmer of tears in her eyes. I wished that I could take us back to those few precious moments, before Mrs Roberts had torn us apart. I thought about taking her in my arms again. But the walls were back in place and we could both feel it.

'So,' I said carefully. 'What now, Kitty?' *Tell me to kiss you again and I'll do it.*

She glanced at the dark stain by Fleet's bed and shuddered. 'I shan't stay here. I'll cut my hair and join the army.'

'You'll do no such thing,' Jakes growled from the doorway. He stared about him, taking in the plundered kingdom of Belle Isle. 'Is there nothing left? Bloody locusts.'

Kitty picked up her broom, propped against the wall. 'At least I can sweep the floor properly,' she sighed. She dragged the broom across the floor, sending up a cloud of dust. 'I haven't seen it in months. Not since the captain died, now I think of it.'

'What do you mean?' I asked, coughing as the dirt caught in my throat.

She paused, tucked a lock of hair behind her ear. 'The room was swept clean, just here.' She gestured at the area that ran from my bed to the door. 'I tried to tell Samuel but he was in one of his dark moods. He wasn't always the way you saw him.' She slid the broom beneath my bed, sweeping out thick grey clumps of dust.

I frowned at the empty boards. 'Why would they sweep the floor?'

'To clear a path through all the junk?' Jakes suggested. 'A man could trip and break his neck on it in the dark.'

Something caught my eye: a glint of silver in the dust. I stayed Kitty's arm. 'Perhaps they dropped something.' I stooped down and plucked a coin from the dirt. A silver crown. I blew away the dust and held it out in my palm for them to see. A rust-brown mark covered the old king's face. I scraped at it with my thumbnail. Blood. 'They killed him, then swept up all the money.' I turned the coin over in my palm, thinking hard. 'Gilbourne paid Roberts five guineas – that's a fair sum in here.'

'It will be long spent by now,' Jakes said with a frown, rubbing the scar that cut through his brow.

A loud creak from the floorboards above broke the silence. I peered up at the ceiling. Trim was still in his room. I glanced at Jakes, then lowered my voice. 'Ask about – in the gaol and in the Borough. Who was flush, after Roberts' death? Who paid off an old debt, or stood a round in the Tap Room? There's a chance *someone* will remember.' I touched his shoulder as he passed, brought my lips to his ear. 'Ask about Trim. And Cross.'

Jakes blinked in surprise, then shrugged, as if to say, *I would believe anything, of anyone, in here*. 'Will you be safe, on your own? I promised Mr Buckley I'd look after you, sir.'

I touched the hilt of my blade. 'I'm not the man I was four days ago.'

'Aye.' He nodded slowly. 'It changes people, this place. Or perhaps it strips them back to what they really are. Never quite worked that one out.' He gave a short bow. 'I'll be back by candlelight.'

I grabbed his arm. 'Sooner if you can, Mr Jakes. If I don't have an answer for Acton by sunset he plans to arrest me for Fleet's murder.'

'No!' Kitty cried in horror. 'No – I won't let him.'

'The devil take him,' Jakes muttered. 'He would do it, too, I'm sure. But you'd never hang for it – the jury would see you're an honest gentleman.'

Kitty slipped her hand in mine. 'I'd speak up for you, Tom,' she said softly. 'We both would.'

Jakes nodded his agreement. I smiled at them, touched by their loyalty and their faith in me – but loyalty and faith would not save me now. Acton could fool the whole court if he chose. How simple it would be. Fleet murdered Captain Roberts and I murdered Fleet. He could line up his trusties one by one and they would say whatever he told them to say. I doubted Cross or Wills or Chapman would care about perjuring themselves. That is if I survived long enough to stand trial. It wasn't hard to kill a man in gaol, poor old Mitchell was proof of that. *Mitchell*. I had almost forgotten about him. Easy to forget, over on this side of the wall. Perhaps that was a mistake. Perhaps there was something to be learned from his murder . . .

'Tom?' Kitty squeezed my hand, returning me to the world.

I blinked then rubbed my eyes. My head was spinning with questions about money and murder and motives. Jakes had left the room — I could hear his heavy boots stomping down the stairs. I should leave too; I had already wasted too much time here. I looked down at Kitty and she smiled, eyes bright. No, not wasted. I touched a stray lock of her bright red hair, then tucked it behind her ear.

'I must go,' I said. I'd be no good to her swinging from a rope at Tyburn.

She opened her mouth to protest then thought better of it. 'But we will talk, later?' she asked, anxiously. 'Do you promise?'

Oh, yes . . . *talking*. The unfortunate penalty for kissing. 'Of course. If you wish.' *If I'm still alive*. I leaned down and touched her lips. And even with the threat of the noose I could have stayed just a little longer.

'Go,' she said, then giggled as I pulled her closer. 'Go, for heaven's sake, Tom. I'll wait for you.' She pushed me away. 'Just this once.'

There is no easy way to tell a man you suspect him of murder. On another day and in a better state of mind I might have found a more gentlemanly way to raise the matter, but there it is.

'God in heaven!' Trim gasped, staring in alarm at the blade pressed to his heart. 'Are you mad, sir?'

I shoved him hard against the wall. 'I'm losing patience. Tell me. Did you kill Fleet?'

He shrank back. '*No!* I swear it!'

I let the blade travel from heart to throat. 'And Roberts . . . ?'

'No,' he whimpered, holding very still. A bead of sweat slid down his face. 'I swear . . .'

I held the dagger against his throat for a long, still moment. He was hiding something; I could see it in his eyes. I stepped back, lowered my blade. Ordered him to sit.

He did as he was commanded, stumbling over to the little table where we had eaten supper together on my first night in prison. 'Mr Acton will know of this,' he sniffed.

I ignored him and poured us both a glass of wine. 'Who killed Roberts?'

He took the glass, cradling it in both hands as if it were a prayer book.

I stood over him. 'Did you help carry his body to the Strong Room?'

'Why do you ask me these questions?' he asked, his light brown eyes filled with hurt. 'I have only ever been kind and civil to you, sir.'

'Which is why I have not slit your throat. Someone tampered with the punch last night. I saw you put something in the bowl.'

Trim's mouth opened and closed in shock. 'Cinnamon and nutmeg,' he stammered, when he'd regained his voice. 'A little sugar – we drank it together, Mr Hawkins! I was knocked out cold all night, the same as you! I'm still groggy from it, I think.' He rubbed his forehead.

'You bought a sleeping draught from Mr Siddall.'

'To aid Mr Woodburn!' he cried, exasperated. 'Here, it must still be on my shelf. Let me show you.' He jumped up and began searching along his medicine shelf, reaching on tiptoes to study the higher shelves. 'I only gave him a spoonful,' he called, back turned as he shuffled through his collection of glass and stone bottles.

Trim ran a neat, well-ordered business, with everything easily to hand. He should have found it at once. He continued searching frantically for a few moments, then cursed under his breath. 'Someone must have stolen it.'

'I doubt the governor will see it that way.'

He blanched. 'What are you saying, sir?'

I motioned for him to sit down again. 'You live one flight up from Belle Isle. You can make no account of the sleeping draught you bought from Mr Siddall.' I paused. 'And you knew Captain Roberts planned to sell his wife for ten guineas.'

He gave a jolt, tried to protest. I cut him dead.

'The walls are thin here. Voices carry to other rooms.' I tapped the floor with my foot. 'Fleet said he used to hide up here with you when the captain and Mrs Roberts fought, but you could still hear them. Every word.'

'Yes, that's true enough,' Trim nodded. 'Fleet would shout down the scores, like a boxing match. Poor Fleet. I wish he were here.' He scowled at me. 'For all his faults, *he* was always a gentleman.'

I gestured to the bed at the other end of the room. 'I heard Fleet arguing with Charles yesterday morning, when I was resting up here. I couldn't make out every word, but then I was in the far corner.' I walked over to the window, where a chair rested on an old rug; I moved them back to reveal the ancient, rotten floorboards hidden beneath. They were so ruined I could see down into Belle Isle through the cracks. 'If I'd been standing here, I think I would have heard everything.'

I raised my boot and smashed it hard into the board, stamping down again and again as the wood splintered and cracked. Trim watched in dismay, but said nothing. I put all my rage into it, and when I was done there was a large, gaping hole – wide enough for a man to pass through. 'There!' I cried. 'Is that not better? The next time a man is murdered in Belle Isle you will be able to see as well as hear it all.'

Trim groaned, and covered his face with his hands.

'I am losing patience, sir,' I warned. 'What did you hear?'

'I cannot say,' he sobbed, his voice muffled by his hands.

'Damn you!' I cried, bearing down upon him. 'I can break your head as easily as these boards.' I shoved the table out of the way and pulled him to his feet, shaking him hard. 'Fleet died because you said nothing! How many more deaths will your conscience carry?' And with that I threw him to the floor in a fury.

He landed badly, crying out in pain and terror. He was close to confessing now, I could see it. Trim did not hoard secrets for profit. He'd kept quiet because he was afraid. I just had to make him believe it was more dangerous to say nothing.

'Tell me. Or I will let Gilbert Hand know that you heard everything. It will fly round the prison by nightfall. How long will it take, do you think, before they come for you, like they came for Fleet?'

'Very well,' he sobbed. 'Very well.' He dragged himself to his feet, wincing as he put his weight on a twisted ankle. He poured himself a fresh glass of wine then hobbled slowly to the chair by the fire. He gave a long, weary sigh, and rubbed his eyes. 'Has it never occurred to you that Captain Roberts *deserved* to die?' He stared into the fire. 'He sold his wife for ten guineas. Such a man should be hanged, wouldn't you say?'

'I don't give a damn about that.' I paced the room, still clutching my dagger. *'What did you hear?'*

He scowled, and took a fortifying swig of wine. 'They came for him at midnight,' he said, at last. 'I didn't hear them enter the ward. They must have crossed the yard like ghosts, crept up the stairs and picked the lock. They pulled him from his bed to his knees – that's what woke me. The thud as he hit the floor.' He shuddered.

'What next?'

He closed his eyes. 'Coins, scattering and rolling across the boards. Lots of them. And then one of the men . . .' He opened his eyes, took a deep breath. 'One of them said, "D'you think this will save you?" The captain must have thrown the money at them

– the five guineas Gilbourne had paid him in advance. But they hadn't come for the money, Mr Hawkins.'

'They'd come to punish him.'

'No!' Trim shook his head vigorously. 'They'd come to save him.'

I frowned. '*Save* him? By murdering him?'

'Save his *soul*. Roberts had changed, in those last few weeks – after he lost his son. He went to chapel every day. Prayed in his room for hours. Perhaps he thought it would bring Matthew back, somehow.' Tears sprang in his eyes. 'It was my fault he died. I heard Gilbourne come up to Belle Isle and pay Roberts the money. The captain would have left the gaol the next day and Mrs Roberts . . . D'you know what Gilbourne said, when he gave Roberts the money? "*I'll be doing you a favour, Roberts. She'll be quiet and cringing as a mouse by the time I've done with her.*" I couldn't . . . I *couldn't* stand back and let that happen.'

'Who did you tell?' Though I could guess, now.

He swallowed hard. Leaned forward a little in his chair and whispered the name.

Woodburn.

Twenty-Three

Mid-afternoon and the shadows were growing longer in the Marshalsea yard. Another day was ending — leaving men with more debts to pay and less hope to live by. I felt like Captain Roberts' ghost, drifting past the other prisoners. They looked at me as if I were a ghost too — as if I had the mark of death about me.

I hurried towards the chapel, left unlocked in all the chaos of the riot the day before. I lit the candles and sat down on a pew near the front, took my mother's cross from my pocket and bowed my head. Fleet was dead; Charles had abandoned me; my family and friends were beyond my reach. When the sun set tonight I would be accused of murder. I closed my eyes, and asked for guidance, comfort — anything. A cold, bleak silence grew around me.

I opened my eyes. I was wasting time. I should act, before it was too late. But my head felt as if it were back in that damned skull cap, and I was feverish, my shirt slick with sweat, my body flushing hot then cold. The effects of the sleeping draught, perhaps — and all the other trials of the day. But thinking back, I realised I had felt out of sorts ever since Charles and Trim had dragged me from the Strong Room. Hardly surprising — the very air had been poison; and I had breathed it in all that night.

There was a small patch of Woodburn's blood left unscrubbed by the altar. Trim had confirmed the strange truth that the chaplain had stabbed himself with Captain Roberts' blade; he'd stumbled upon him in the act, and wrestled the knife away before Kitty arrived. Woodburn had never intended to kill himself, I was sure of it. Trim had agreed with me.

'The wound was deep but it missed the heart. The shoulder is a good place to cut if you aim to recover. But still – to stab himself . . . what madness! I can scarce believe it, though I saw it with my own eyes.'

'Not madness, Trim. Cunning. He wanted to deflect attention. Why would we suspect him, if he were a victim himself?' Woodburn had dissembled from the beginning, offering to help me in my search for the truth while pointing me towards Acton, then Gilbourne, knowing all along that they were innocent of this one crime at least. I could see how he would have squared it with his conscience; they were cruel, wicked men, whereas he had been doing God's work, saving Captain Roberts from committing an unforgivable sin. What was it Woodburn had said to me, when we first met? *There's so much good work to be done here. So many souls to save.*

'There are other ways to play the victim, without stabbing yourself,' Trim remarked. 'I fear his guilt is sending him mad. He was raving about ghosts when I found him. He's convinced that Roberts is haunting him.'

'The ghost wasn't real.'

Trim tapped his head. 'I think he's conjured up his own spirit, Mr Hawkins.'

That was true enough. Woodburn had seemed half-mad this morning. It was his own conscience that had summoned up a ghost to plague him. 'Well, I pray it haunts him to his grave.' I paused. 'Could *he* have killed Fleet?'

'No, no. We gave him Siddall's strongest sleeping draught. The same one *we* drank, I suppose. He only woke when I did. We heard you banging on the door and he said . . . He said, *Oh, merciful God. He's killed again.*'

And for all of this, I was still no closer to learning who 'he' was. Trim only heard Woodburn's voice on the night of the murder – the beating must have taken place in the Strong Room as the men had only stayed in Belle Isle for a few minutes. After Woodburn stabbed himself, Trim begged him to confess everything but Woodburn had refused. He kept saying it was his fault, that he was to blame for it all, and that they had never meant to hurt Captain Roberts – just frighten him. But when Trim asked him who the other man was, Woodburn had looked frightened and said Harry Mitchell had died for knowing less. And so they both kept quiet – and Fleet had paid for their cowardice.

I slipped my mother's cross back into my pocket. As I did so my fingers brushed against the silver crown I'd plucked from the dust in Belle Isle. I took it out and held it in my palm. Woodburn had swept up the money that night while his companion removed the body and now he was distributing it among the sick and starving of the Marshalsea Common Side. Five pounds. The missing crown would have made it five guineas. The only time Gilbourne had ever given his money to charity – albeit unwittingly.

If only I had managed to force the truth from Woodburn. Perhaps I could persuade Acton to come with me to interrogate him again. The sight of the governor might just frighten the chaplain into giving up the name. That is if he had not lost his wits entirely. But I doubted Acton would agree to it. There was no time, damn it. No time.

There was a soft rustle behind me, like feathers.

'*Monsieur.*'

Madame Migault, in her old black silks, her white hair a nest for yellowing ivory combs and faded ribbons. I had not heard her come in.

'*Madame.*'

She studied me with those beady eyes of hers, a smile playing across her thin, cracked lips. 'You are sick.' Triumphant – as though she had brewed the infection herself.

I tried to step past her but she blocked my path, clutching at my arm with gnarled fingers. 'I know what you are,' she hissed. 'I've watched you from the shadows. Nothing but a boy in a man's clothes.'

I remembered my first night in the gaol and the low, mocking laughter I'd heard in the darkness of the yard. I'd thought it was a ghost, back then. What a credulous fool I'd been. I pulled my arm free.

'You cannot have her,' she spat. 'She is *mine*. She works for *me* now. *Le diable est mort, et Kitty est à moi.*'

'Kitty?' Anger burned in my chest. 'What do you want with her?'

'Sharp eyes, quick hands. She brings me secrets. Steals things I can use . . .' Something cruel gleamed in her eyes. 'How do you think your letter fell into my hands? Did it drop from the sky, perhaps?' She fluttered her fingers.

'Fleet stole it from me. He confessed it.'

'Ahh . . . *le diable*!' she cackled. 'Even he has a weakness! *Non, non*. He was protecting his dear little Kitty. She stole your letter and brought it to *me*.'

'I don't believe you,' I said, dismayed.

She laughed in delight. 'I told you, monsieur. She is mine. And you will not take her from me.'

Out in the yard, Mack was letting Acton win at shuttlecock while Cross looked on with a sly grin. Cross had played no part in Roberts' death: I was certain of that now. If it had been about money, or revenge, then I could have believed it of him a thousand times over. But Cross was not interested in saving a man's soul. And if Cross had been involved, Gilbourne's money would never have reached the Common Side. Whoever killed Captain Roberts

– whoever dragged his body across the yard and hanged him from a rafter in the Strong Room – had believed he had God on his side.

In the middle of the Park, Jenings was lighting the lamp as the afternoon drifted towards twilight. The large ring of keys at his belt jangled as he worked. I was about to approach him when the door to the coffeehouse swung open and Kitty emerged, hitching up her skirts and smiling as she ran towards me. As she came closer she faltered and slowed her pace. Her smile dissolved. 'Tom. You're so pale. What ails you?'

I stared down at her. She'd betrayed me – and I'd nearly died because of it. I should hate her. I forced myself to hate her. 'You stole the letter.'

I wanted her to deny it – more than anything. But I could see the guilt burning in her eyes. 'I . . . I wanted to explain before,' she stammered. 'Samuel wouldn't let me.' She paused at the mention of Fleet's name, then took a deep breath and continued. 'He took the blame for me . . .'

'There is no need to explain, Kitty.'

'Oh, Tom! I'm so glad! Madame Migault caught me reading it and she snatched it from me – to play a game, she said. I'd only read the first few lines – I'd no idea any harm would come of it. When they sent you to the Strong Room I almost *died*. I only thieved it as a game – to pay you back for calling me *a little servant girl* to Mrs Roberts.' She bit her lip at the memory. 'As if I were nothing. Worthless.'

I smiled. 'Well, that was wrong of me. You are much more than a servant girl.'

She smiled a heartbreaking smile and reached for my hand. 'Am I?'

'Naturally.' I pulled my arm away. 'You are also a fine thief and an excellent liar. And I'm sure that soon enough you will learn to spread your legs and make a decent whore as well.'

She flinched, as if I'd struck her. Then she squared her shoulders and lifted her chin. 'Do you think you are the first man to say such things to me?' She looked me up and down, and it was as if her sharp green eyes were taking in every inch of me, from my borrowed clothes to my empty pocket, right to my very core. 'I thought better of you,' she said. 'So did Samuel.' And then she turned and walked away.

I thought of running after her. I thought of catching her in my arms and telling her the truth – that I had forgiven her the moment Madame Migault had told me. In a heartbeat. And the fact that I had forgiven her so easily terrified me. I could lie and swear it was the fever burning in my blood that made me cruel. In truth I had wanted to hurt her. Her theft – her *betrayal* – had given me the excuse I had been looking for to push her away, like a boat nudged out from the shore to float out and disappear to the horizon. I had tasted what Kitty wanted from me when we kissed, though she'd tried to hide it. More than I could give. More than I could *afford* to give a servant girl. A kitchen maid.

Acton had it right. I was an idiot.

I pulled out Fleet's silver watch. It was almost five o'clock. I had so little time left to save myself – and yet I could almost feel the truth ahead of me, just beyond my grasp. Who was Woodburn's accomplice? Not Cross. Not Trim. Then who? How had he killed Fleet – and Mitchell for that matter? They had both died the same way: murdered in a locked room while others slept about them. *Oh, God.* The cobbles danced and spun before my eyes as I realised what I must do.

I had to speak with Captain Anderson. I had to go back over the wall.

A few minutes later I held the key to the Common Side door tight in my palm. Gilbert Hand had a key for everything but there was suspicion in his copper eyes when he pulled this one out for me. 'You want to go back over there? What for? Not gone mad, have you, Hawkins? I hear old Woodburn's half a step from Bedlam . . .'

I couldn't afford to pay him anything for the loan of the key. The only coin I had left was the silver crown I'd found in the dust of Belle Isle – but I needed that as evidence. And I was damned if I would give him Fleet's watch. So I traded in the only other currency Hand understood – information. I told him everything I knew about Roberts' murder apart from Trim's involvement, and promised more once I'd spoken with Anderson.

'Anderson?' Hand frowned and scratched beneath his brown wig. 'He's chained up in the Strong Room for starting the riot.' He grabbed my sleeve. 'Ten minutes, no more. And if they catch you, I'll say you stole it from me.'

So now I stood within the shadow of the wall, just as I had the first time I'd stepped into the prison yard. It felt as if twenty years had passed since then, not four days. A soft breeze blew through the Park, bringing with it the scent of tobacco. Without thinking I glanced up towards the Tap Room balcony. Fleet was not there, nor ever would be. There was no one to pull me back from the wall, to clap an arm about me and drag me upstairs for a glass of punch. And there was no one to see me slot the key into the lock, or slip through the door and into the Common Side.

I closed the door as quietly as I could and rested my back against the dank wall. I could hardly breathe, the weight of terror pressing on my chest as if a house had collapsed on me. I was risking my life in here. If Acton found me breaking into the Common Side he would beat me to death in front of the whole gaol.

Fortunately for me the yard was empty, the prisoners still locked in their wards as punishment for the riot. I crept down the wall towards the Strong Room, stealing glances at the Tap Room balcony in case someone should step out and see me – a solitary figure in the empty yard. I inched my way forward, the sweat trickling down my back. As I drew closer a dozen rats rushed squealing from the stinking water that ran between the wall and the Strong Room, as if they remembered my scent. I kicked at them as they scrabbled about my feet, then hurried to the door.

I'd thought it would be locked – that I would have to call to Anderson through the small hole carved above it. But it swung free when I pushed it, letting out a familiar warm stink of death and decay. I shrank back, my arm across my nose and mouth, fighting the instinct to turn and run.

Anderson was chained to the wall just as I had been two nights before, the iron cap screwed tight to his skull and the collar biting into his thick neck. Rain had seeped through the roof in the night and the ground about him was churned to a soupish mud. His face was crusted with blood and he had two black eyes, but he seemed calm as I approached, as if resigned to whatever Fate might fling at him next.

'Hawkins,' he growled, then coughed, spitting an oyster of phlegm into the darkness. 'I told you not to come back here.'

'Who killed Harry Mitchell?'

Anderson closed his eyes for a moment and gave a short, dry laugh. 'Suppose I knew. Why should I tell you?'

'Acton has given me until sunset to discover the truth. He wants me to fail.' I squatted down and looked him in the eye. 'You could help me to disappoint him.'

He smiled briefly. He'd lost a tooth in the fight – the gum was raw and bloody. 'What'll he do to you? If you do fail?'

'He'll charge me with Fleet's murder. And Fleet will be blamed for Roberts' death.'

He grunted. 'So it's true, then? The old devil's dead.' His eyes flickered to the door. 'I heard them shouting this morning but I didn't believe it.'

'Someone cut his throat. The same man who stabbed Mitchell through the heart.'

Anderson's brows knotted. 'No. We took care of Harry's killer yesterday. Slipped a blade between his ribs.' He shifted as much as he could beneath his chains, then sighed. 'Riot's a good distraction if you want to murder a man.'

'But then . . .' I stood up and rubbed the sweat from my face. I'd thought Mitchell's death had been connected to my investigation. Had it been a coincidence after all? 'Who was it?'

'Fred Owen. Been on the ward with me for three years . . . Wasn't a bad man, not really. Just desperate.' He grimaced. 'Someone slipped five shillings through the begging grate. Said if he killed Harry there'd be ten more. Owen had a daughter on the streets. Nine years old.' Anderson fell silent.

'Did he see who it was?'

'It was dark. Can't see much through the grates.'

'And the voice? Did Owen tell you *anything*?'

'He was too busy dying, Mr Hawkins.' He paused. 'But I know why Mitchell was killed.'

I waited. 'Well?'

'What's it worth?'

I cursed under my breath. I had no time for bargaining. 'I have nothing left, sir. You'll stop an innocent man from being sent to the gallows, is that not enough?'

'Not really.'

I groaned, looking about me as if the damp, squalid hut might suddenly bring forth a treasure hoard or a dozen willing maids with dimples in their cheeks. And then I remembered how it had felt to be chained against the wall, the iron collar pressing hard against my throat. 'I could loosen those screws,' I said.

A desperate, eager look flashed in Anderson's eyes before he could stop it. We had a deal, it seemed. I found an old piece of metal and got to work as Anderson talked. The metal was jagged and sharp and cut my hands but I hardly noticed.

'Mitchell confessed everything to me the night before he died,' Anderson said. 'Said he was going to tell you – that you'd promised to get him out of here in exchange. He knew blabbing to you was dangerous so he thought someone on this side should know the truth. It was Harry that tipped the sleeping draught into Fleet's punch the night Roberts got it. He was hired the same as Owen – someone came to the begging grate and paid him a few shillings. Harry thought they was going to rob Fleet, that's all. Then the next morning they found the captain swinging from the beams up there.' He glanced up at the ceiling. 'Bad way to die. And now his soul's trapped in here with all the corpses till judgement day.'

I shivered. 'Did Mitchell recognise the man who came to the grate?'

'No. Voice was muffled. But he said it was familiar somehow. He was sure it was someone from the gaol.'

I loosened the last of the screws. 'Could it have been Woodburn?'

Anderson stretched his neck, then shot me a puzzled look. 'Mr Woodburn? Nah, Harry would have known him at once, even in the shadows. He's the only fat man in the gaol . . . But why would Woodburn . . .' He trailed away, confused. 'He's the one swore it was murder not suicide.'

'I think it was an accident.' I gazed about me, at the old blood stains on the floor, the rats scrabbling over the rotting bodies heaped in a corner. 'Roberts had agreed to something terrible – something *damnable*. They wanted to stop him so they brought him here where it was quiet and they tried to persuade him against it.'

'With their fists. Two against one.' Anderson looked savage. 'Bloody cowards.'

'Woodburn knew if the coroner called it suicide, Roberts would lose his right to a Christian burial. He couldn't bear the thought of it. Bad enough to kill a man, but to put his soul at risk . . .'

'*Noble*,' Anderson muttered sarcastically. 'So why hang him up there in the first place?'

I rubbed my eyes. 'I don't know.'

• • •

And there was my trouble: I didn't know. I didn't know who the second man was. I didn't know why he'd hanged Roberts up in the Strong Room. I didn't know how he'd snuck into Belle Isle last night and slit Fleet's throat. All I did know was that I needed to discover the answers before sunset – and that was just one hour away.

Twenty-Four

Somehow I was able to return to the Master's Side without being seen. It helped that no one ever chose to look at the wall, so by the time I had stepped away from the door it appeared as though I was simply taking a turn about the yard.

I returned the key to Gilbert Hand and told him what I'd learned, saving the part about Owen's murder. Captain Anderson was in enough trouble as it was. It was a good trade for Hand — he'd risked very little and now knew as much as I did about Roberts' death. He patted his stomach as if I'd just fed him a feast, which I suppose I had, in a way.

'Are you well, Mr Hawkins? You seem a little feverish.'

I was about to reply when the door to Acton's lodgings swung open and the governor emerged. 'Hawkins!' he called across the yard, then beckoned me with the crook of his finger.

Hand, scenting trouble, melted away.

I trod slowly towards Acton, praying he would grant me more time. Even a day might be enough. A tall, slim figure slipped out of the governor's lodgings to stand beside him. Gilbourne. He put his hands in his pockets and gave a wide, mocking smile as I approached.

'Well, Hawkins?' Acton looked me up and down. 'Do you have a name for me?'

My mind whirled. Mitchell had thought he recognised the voice at the begging grate. It was someone who knew the gaol well and could come and go easily. Chapman? Cross? One of Hand's boys, or Gilbert Hand himself, for that matter? Or one of the porters, perhaps? But it was no use – I did not have enough proof to accuse any one of them. 'I do, sir.' I took a deep breath. 'Mr Woodburn.'

The two men started in surprise. Then Gilbourne let out a peal of laughter and clapped his hands together. 'Oh! This is too rich, sir! The Reverend Andrew Woodburn, no less. The gentleman you say accused me of the same crime this morning? I suppose this is why . . . why he *stabbed himself* yesterday?' He broke into a fit of giggles.

Acton slid his new ally a look of ill-disguised loathing. 'This is all you have to say to me, Hawkins?' He snorted. 'No wonder you're sweating like a hog. Well – no matter. We have another name for you, don't we, Mr Gilbourne?'

Gilbourne stopped laughing and stood a little straighter. 'We do indeed, sir. Fleet killed Roberts. He confessed it to me the day before he died. I'm afraid in all the confusion of the riot I *quite* put it from my mind.'

I glared at him. 'That is a lie, sir.'

'*Is* it?' Gilbourne grinned. 'Well, sadly he's not alive to defend himself, is he? It's a shame you killed him.'

My heart lurched. 'Mr Acton. Give me one more day. I beg you.'

'No, no. I like this story better, I think,' Acton replied. 'Fleet killed Roberts and you killed Fleet. We'd best lock him up, eh, Gilbourne?' He wrapped a hand about my arm and began dragging me towards the Lodge.

I stumbled forward in a daze. I had to stop this somehow. If I could get a message to Charles . . .

Gilbourne strolled after us. 'Do you have your whip, sir? He may resist arrest . . .'

'Mr Acton,' I said quietly. 'Would you break your word?'

He stopped dead, still gripping my arm. 'What did you say?'

'You gave me your word I would have till sunset.' I looked up at the sky. 'It is still light.'

Acton hesitated. 'That is true.'

'Oh, throw him in the Pound, for heaven's sake,' Gilbourne snapped, impatient.

Acton let go of my arm and rounded on Gilbourne. 'This is my Castle,' he said, poking a thick finger in Gilbourne's chest. 'You tell me what to do again and I'll break your neck.' He took a watch out of his pocket and consulted it closely. 'I'm a man of my word, Mr Hawkins. Half an hour. Use it wisely.' He shrugged. 'Or fuck Mrs Bradshaw for all I care. Mr Gilbourne. We have business to discuss.' He put a hand on Gilbourne's back and pushed him towards the Tap Room.

I staggered over to Fleet's bench and collapsed, shaking with shock and relief. But what now? What could I possibly achieve in half an hour?

A large shadow fell across the bench. I looked up to find Mr Jakes standing over me, a loop of chains wrapped over his shoulder. Thank God. As I pulled myself back on to my feet my head began to spin and for a moment I thought I might faint. Jakes caught hold of me, eyes filled with concern.

'What's happened, sir? You look half-dead with fright.'

I waved him away. 'I'm well enough, thank you.'

Jakes frowned, unconvinced. 'I asked about the Borough. The only Marshalsea man with spare coin in his pocket after Roberts' death was Acton.'

'I know, I'm sorry – I've wasted your time. Woodburn gave the money away.'

'Woodburn?' Jakes wrinkled his brow.

I explained quickly what I had learned.

'*Woodburn*,' Jakes muttered again to himself. He curled his fist around the hilt of his club. 'And the other man?'

'I don't know.' My head felt as if it were splitting in two and I was pouring with sweat. 'I thought perhaps it was Trim, but he's terrified. He's locked himself in his room and says he won't come out until we've discovered the truth. Jakes, we must find Woodburn without delay. I'm sure you can persuade him to confess.'

'That's what I came to tell you. He sent this to the Lodge.' He pulled a note from his pocket. 'It sounds . . . strange. Stranger still now I know what he did. Thought I should bring these with me.' He shifted the weight of the chains slung over his shoulder.

I unfolded the note.

Mister Jakes

  I beg of you to come at once to Snows Fields where I must confess something of great Import. Bring Hawkins for I fear his Life depends on it.

  God help us all.

  Rev'd Andrew Woodburn

I read it again, a plan forming. I glanced up towards the Tap Room, where Acton and Gilbourne were drinking. I must be quick.

'It's growing dark,' Jakes said, peering anxiously at the sky. 'If we're to meet with him we should leave now before the light fails.'

And before Acton locks me up for murder. I read the note again. 'It sounds like a trap.'

'You may be right, Mr Hawkins.' Jakes grinned. He put a hand in his coat to show me the long sword hidden beneath. 'Let's walk into it with our eyes open and our blades high, eh?'

I did my best to seem calm as we walked towards the Lodge gate but the truth was I could barely breathe with fear. At any moment I expected someone to shout my name, for a half dozen trusties to seize me and drag me back in front of Acton. We reached the turnkeys' room. Cross was seated with his feet upon the desk, drinking as usual. My heart was beating so hard I was sure he must be able to hear it ten paces away.

'Open the gate, Joseph,' Jakes said.

Cross narrowed his eyes. With every moment that passed I was sure he would call the alarm. *Hawkins is trying to escape!* They would rip me to pieces like dogs. Cross slammed his glass upon the table and stood up slowly. 'It's too late,' he said.

My heart sank. But when I looked in his eyes I realised he didn't know what Acton and Gilbourne had planned for me. He only meant it would be dark soon. 'I have an appointment with Mr Woodburn,' I said hurriedly. 'I've squared it with Mr Acton. Ask him if you wish, sir . . . but I should warn you, he's in a foul mood.'

Cross scowled and pulled out his keys. 'Keep an eye on him,' he said to Jakes as he let us out.

The door slammed behind us. Jakes shot me a sidelong glance. I could see he was puzzled by my behaviour, but I didn't dare tell him what I'd planned. He could lose his job for this. I smiled, hoping the guilt didn't show upon my face. 'Let's go.'

We did not take the path down Axe and Bottle Yard to Snows Fields as we had the day before. Instead we turned left, and left again, into Mermaid Court, which backed on to the Common Side wards. A row of tiny, barred windows had been cut into the thick stone wall overlooking the dank, shaded alley. These were the begging grates; the only way to pass food and money into the gaol without Acton seizing it for himself. But Mermaid Court was not a thoroughfare, and few men came this way by chance. The Common Side stench leaked into the alley; too many bodies trapped together with no air, no food, no water to clean themselves.

They must have heard our footsteps echoing down the alley-way. Grubby fingers poked through the bars, desperate faces pressed hard against the iron grates. Some dangled strings out attached to small begging bowls, like fishermen hoping for a catch.

'*Have mercy, sir.*'

'*We starve! Send food, for pity's sake!*'

I paused, took the bloodied silver crown from my pocket and thrust it through the bars into the first hand I touched. No need to keep it for evidence now. 'God bless you, sir,' a voice cried. 'May your prick and your purse never fail you!' The beggar's benediction. The hand drew back and I heard a scuffle break out, shouts of anger as they fought for the prize.

Jakes watched all this, eyebrow raised.

'Lead on, damn it,' I said, and pulled my dagger from my coat.

At the bottom of the alley, a high gate marked the boundary to Snows Fields. Jakes pushed on it with one hand and it swung free. I turned and looked down Mermaid Court and the high wall of the Marshalsea. Whatever happened on Snows Fields, I would not return to the gaol. If Woodburn confessed everything I would send Jakes back to give the word to Acton and return to town, devil take the consequences. If not – I would run. And pray to God Jakes didn't do his job and chase after me.

I still had Fleet's watch; that would give me enough capital to flee London. Once I was safe I would write to Charles and hope he could clear my name. I wasn't sure where I would hide – in truth I could barely think straight, my head was pounding so hard. All I knew was that I could never go back.

I stepped through the gate.

Jakes was already halfway down the narrow, muddy track that cut through the high meadow grass. I hurried after him, glancing back to be sure we were not followed. The grass rustled and whispered in the breeze and my heart began to pound in alarm. A dozen men could be hiding in the long, tangled grass and we wouldn't know it.

At last we escaped the meadow into low, scrubby ground. Jakes was heading for the patch of grass where Fleet and I had sat the day before. He would have loved this; running headfirst into danger. And there *was* a thrill to it – I'd grant him that. To learn the truth at last, no matter the cost.

It was dusk, the tenter fields a dim grey mass in the distance. There was just enough light to see out to the edges of the field; the old oak tree a black silhouette, its gallow branch thin and sharp against the darkening sky. A dozen crows had clustered together in a fractious squabble up ahead, cawing at one another as they prepared to roost for the night. Jakes kicked out at them with his boot and a couple flapped reluctantly into the air, landing a few feet away on the nearest burial mound.

I gazed about me in the fading light. There was no one here. Just me, Jakes and the crows. And in that moment, I understood at last – no one else was coming.

This was my place of execution. There was no cart, no cheering crowds, but I would die here. Time slowed as the truth settled about me; the crows silent and watchful, the wind still.

Jakes watched, calmly, as I raised my dagger. And then he smiled; a tinge of regret in his eyes.

I remembered the first day we'd met, riding the river to Southwark. He'd confessed then, if I'd only listened. *I've seen better corpses on a battlefield.* He'd seen the captain's body. He had been there, that night.

'You killed him,' I said, backing away. 'Your best friend. The man who saved your life.'

Jakes gazed at me evenly. 'He saved my life, yes. And I saved his soul. I'd call that even, wouldn't you?'

I could run – but he would never let me go. He was a sword's reach away – but I was weak; feverish. He would run me through with his own blade in a flash. I would have to distract him somehow. I swallowed hard.

'How could you do it? My God, Jakes – you're a – a good, honourable man.' Even as I spoke the words, I could not believe what he had done.

'Because I loved him,' Jakes said quietly, almost to himself. 'He was my captain and my brother. I never knew a braver man on the field. But when it came to the battle for his *soul* . . . he was a coward. He always gave in to his cravings – for drink and women and gambling.'

'You have just described half the men in England, Mr Jakes. It doesn't give you the right to murder them.' I stepped back, trying to put some space between me and his blade. The longer we talked, the more chance someone would pass by and call the alarm.

No one will come, Tom. You must fight this alone. Fleet's voice, clear and urgent in my head.

'He would have sold his wife for ten guineas,' Jakes said, circling me warily. 'I couldn't let that happen. The stain on his soul . . . he would never have washed it clean. We never meant for him to die. We just wanted to show him where he was heading. John was a man of action, not words. You couldn't describe hell to him. But you could *show* it to him.' Jakes winced. 'I chained him to a wall and I beat him, God help me. I showed him the corpses and the rats. And Woodburn told him how much worse it would be for him – an eternity in hell.'

I had slipped a few feet further from him as he spoke. If I could run towards the tenter grounds I might be able to lose him. It was almost dark. 'It was an act of mercy, then?'

'Aye!' he snarled angrily. 'Mock all you wish but it *was* merciful. I stopped him from damning himself. I risked my own soul for his – with a glad heart. John repented at the end, I know he did.'

'Before you murdered him.'

'It was an accident!' Jakes cried – and I could see the torment in his eyes. 'He'd promised to give back the money but Woodburn said to beat him again, just once more, so he would never forget.

I don't know . . . I don't know what happened. I hit him and he fell back. And then . . .' Tears streamed down his face. 'He just lay there. I didn't mean to kill him, I swear.'

'And now he lies in an unconsecrated grave – for all your talk of saving him! Why the devil did you hang him? Why make it look like suicide except to hide your own guilt?'

Jakes rubbed the tears from his face. 'I'd meant to leave him on the ground but the rats . . . They eat the eyes first, did you know that? I couldn't . . .' He swallowed. 'I hanged him out of reach. He deserved that much.'

I said nothing, marvelling at a man who could kill his best friend, but was too squeamish to leave his corpse for the rats to feast on. Took another step back. 'And what of Fleet? Did he *deserve* to be murdered in his bed?'

'Samuel Fleet?' Jakes spat. 'I shall not lose a moment's sleep for that black-hearted demon. Mitchell, I confess . . . that was a hard choice. But he would have died soon enough in that hell hole.' He sighed, then gave a soft shrug. 'He's at peace now.'

'And of course he can't accuse you of murder from the grave.'

'No. I suppose not.' Jakes took a step forward.

I stumbled back, holding my blade high. 'But why kill again? Why risk your *soul* for me? Let me run to the Mint and you will never hear of me again.'

'You're dying, Mr Hawkins. Gaol fever.' He pointed with the tip of his blade to my chest, where my shirt had come loose.

I glanced down, then pulled at my shirt. My heart lurched. A dull red rash was spreading up from my stomach like an invading army. I knew what it meant. Fever. Delirium. Death. No need for Acton to send me to the gallows. I closed my shirt with trembling hands. 'Then . . .' I swallowed hard. 'Then why kill a dying man?'

'Because you have nothing to lose. You will tell them everything. And they will believe you.'

With that he lunged without warning. I parried, just in time, our blades clanging as they met. He swung a second time, the blow tearing the dagger almost from my grasp. I staggered back and he struck again, raining blow after blow as I parried weakly with my shorter blade. I did my best, fighting hard to defend myself – but I was no match for him. He swung again, harder this time, a shattering blow that almost threw me off my feet. The dagger flew from my hand. He punched me hard in the stomach and I fell to my knees.

He loomed above me, sword raised. I had no strength left; the sweat was pouring down my back and the world was spinning around me like a merry-go-round. The sky blazed red, caught in the last moments of sunset.

'Have mercy,' I said.

He brought the hilt down hard and I crumpled to the ground, barely conscious. He pulled me to my feet and slung me over his shoulder, carrying me as he must have carried Roberts, as if I weighed nothing at all. Ten, twenty, thirty paces, never breaking his stride. I was too stunned, too sick to comprehend what was happening. He flung me down then started dragging me across the ground towards the oak tree as if I were already a corpse. I felt the earth slide away beneath my feet and then I was falling, tumbling into a hole. I landed hard on my back, wind knocked from my lungs. Loose earth spattered over my face, in my mouth.

I was in a grave. He had dug a grave ready for me.

I spat the soil from my mouth. The earth was cold and dank beneath my fingers. The grave was deep – four feet at least. He must have spent hours on it. All this afternoon, when I'd thought he was out in the Borough. No need for him to ask people about the money; he already knew where it had been spent. All this time he'd stayed close, pretending to help, when really he was just making sure I never uncovered the truth.

'I'll say you ran off,' Jakes said, softly, as I struggled and scrabbled to pull myself up. 'They won't come looking for you here.

No blood on the grass. Not a sign of a struggle. I'm sorry, Mr Hawkins, truly. I'll come and pray for you, when I can.'

'Wait!' I begged. I could have stood the blade at my throat but not this. Not to lie in an unmarked grave, never found, never mourned. I pulled my mother's cross from my pocket, felt its familiar shape against my fingers. 'Pray with me first, for pity's sake.'

He hesitated, then nodded, as I knew he would. He thought of himself as a good Christian, after all.

'Our Father, who art in heaven . . .' How many times had I said those words? They poured from my fevered lips, little more than a whisper. Jakes bowed his head, murmuring the words to himself. As his gaze slid from mine I gathered the last of my strength and pulled myself from the grave, heaving myself over the lip and dragging myself free. I staggered to my feet and ran blindly towards the trees ahead.

Jakes cursed and chased after me, boots pounding the earth. I stumbled into the small copse, heart racing. He was only a few paces behind, I could hear him crashing through the bushes. I ducked behind a broad ash tree and held still, chest heaving.

'You can't hide for ever,' he called. 'I will find you!'

If I ran, he would hear me. If I stayed, he would find me. The bark was sharp against my sweat-soaked back, the air fresh and sweet. Perhaps this was not such a bad place to die after all. Better than rotting in gaol. I pushed away from the tree and started to run.

A gunshot rang out – loud and hard as a thunderclap.

I stopped, and turned, dizzy with fear and exhaustion. Lantern light glinted through the trees. I fumbled desperately towards it, branches tearing at my skin, calling for help – and ran straight into Joseph Cross. He held the lantern up to my face.

'Hawkins. Bloody hell. You look like Death.'

'It was Jakes,' I panted, clutching his coat. 'He murdered them all.'

Cross snorted. 'He won't be doing that no more.' He gestured towards the small clearing up ahead. I let go of his jacket and dragged myself forward, grabbing at branches to keep myself from falling.

The clearing was like a stage, lit silver by the rising moon. Jakes lay in the middle on his back, groaning in agony. His hands clutched feebly at a gaping wound in his stomach, blood streaming through his fingers. And standing over him . . .

The breath caught in my throat.

Standing over him was Kitty, Fleet's pistol in her hand.

Our eyes met briefly across the clearing. Then she looked away, pouring a fresh measure of powder down the barrel with a steady hand. I stumbled a few more paces towards her, Cross following, the lantern casting its soft light upon the bloody scene. Kitty finished reloading in silence then turned back to Jakes.

'No,' Jakes whispered hoarsely. 'I'm not ready. I beg you . . . Send for a priest . . .'

She raised the pistol, aimed it at his head. Cocked the hammer. 'Give my regards to the devil, Mr Jakes.'

Fired.

A haze of gunsmoke drifted slowly up into the sky.

'Fucking hell,' Cross muttered.

She dropped the pistol and strode towards me. 'Tom. You're safe.'

I held out my hand to stop her. 'Keep away. I'm sick. Gaol fever.' But then, I had kissed her, only a few hours before, up in Belle Isle. Lips pressed hard against mine.

The fever had taken over. I could feel myself falling. Dying, perhaps. It felt like dying. I slid to my knees, then to the ground. Darkness rushed towards me like the roaring waters of the Thames and I was lost.

PART THREE

LIFE AND DEATH

Twenty-Five

I woke in a small, cramped cell.

I was lying on my back on a narrow bed, the cloth mattress damp and reeking with sweat. The shutters were closed but a candle stub flickered and sputtered on the table beside me. A wooden cross hung on the wall. I rubbed my face and scalp, long bristles rasping against my fingers. I must have been here for days.

Memories slipped in and out of reach. The fever had been the worst of it, burning through my body, heat like the furnaces of hell. A sharp, heavy pain in my head as if my skull were back in the iron cap. Delirium. Days melting into each other. Anxious voices, faces covered with scented cloths hovering over mine. Prayers chanted in another room. A soft, cool hand holding mine.

Stay, Thomas. Please stay with me.

I had been a whisper away from death. I could feel it in my bones.

Peeling myself from the sheets I sat up slowly, head spinning. The air smelled faintly of piss and vomit, mingled with lavender. Someone had tied a fresh sprig to the bed. I crushed the leaves between my fingers and breathed in the thick, warm scent.

I swung my legs to the floor, shuffling over to the window like an old dog. The room faced out on to a busy street – I could hear the clop of horses, the whisk of carriage wheels, shouts and laughter. I pulled back the shutters and sunlight poured into the room, half-blinding me. With a few hard shoves I opened the old casement window and peered down into the bustling high street. Tradesmen rattled carts along the cobbles to market; a farmer guided a small, skittering flock of sheep towards the bridge. Across the road, two girls of the town lay stretched out on the brothel steps, wiggling their toes and basking in the autumn sunlight.

Dawn in the Borough and I was alive. My heart lifted.

On the pavement below my window, Charles and Trim were arguing with one another. Charles gestured to a hackney carriage waiting nearby. Trim shook his head, hands planted firmly on his hips.

'Charles.' My voice was hoarse, broken. I cleared my throat and tried again.

He looked up, then grinned and ran into the house, thumping up the stairs. A moment later he bounded into the room, Trim following close behind. I almost wept upon his shoulder, I was so grateful to be alive. But the simple act of walking to the window had left me dizzy. I swayed upon my feet and would have fallen if Trim had not seized hold of me.

'Settle him down,' he said to Charles, before heading to the door to call for a jug of small beer.

Charles ushered me slowly back to the bed. As we sat together, side by side, he explained that this was a sponging house owned by one of Acton's cronies. If the Marshalsea was hell, then this was purgatory – where debtors with just enough capital to stay out of prison were kept under the watchful eye of the bailiffs. Some marshalled enough money to return home, the rest were squeezed of their last pennies then thrown into prison. A place of lost causes and low odds.

'What do you remember?' he asked.

I tried to think back but the fever had left me weak and confused and I had not eaten in many days. It was only later that I remembered it all: the chase through the trees, Kitty in the clearing with a gun in her hands and Jakes, clutching the gaping wound in his stomach. Perhaps my mind was trying to spare me from the memories, until I was well enough to endure them. 'Jakes . . .' I whispered, through cracked lips. 'It was Jakes.' I began to shake violently.

Charles put an arm about my shoulder. 'You're safe now, Tom.'

Trim returned and poured me a mug of beer. 'Slowly,' he warned, placing it between my trembling hands.

'Who brought me here?' I asked.

Charles explained that I had been carried from Snows Fields back to the Marshalsea. Acton had taken one look at the fever tearing through me and refused to take me in, for fear I would poison the Master's Side and ruin his profits. 'We'll sling him over the Common Side if you like,' he'd said. It had been Cross, strangely enough, who had reminded Acton of Sir Philip's promise of freedom. Acton's compromise had been to send me here, where I could sweat the fever out or die from it – and I could guess which outcome he would have preferred.

I could not understand then why Cross had spoken for me. He gave me his reasons later, the last time I saw him – said he didn't want me poisoning the Common Side with my sickness. It was Cross, after all, who had to pull the bodies out each morning, not Acton. Some days I think there was more to it than that – a moment's charity, perhaps. On other days I think he just wanted me gone from the prison.

'How long have I been here?'

Charles smiled grimly. His eyes were bloodshot, shadowed with dark grey circles. 'Almost a week. It's Sunday today, the first of October.' He paused. 'You were very sick. Trim has been tending you these last few days – he's had the fever before so it was safe for him. We didn't think . . .' He swallowed hard.

'They administered the last rites just three days ago. I wasn't allowed in the room for fear of infection.' He glanced at me curious. 'Do you not remember?'

I closed my eyes. Yes; there had been voices in the darkness. Words of comfort and peace. I had drifted away upon them, glad to be free at last. Something had brought me back. Something sharp and bright. Something worth fighting for . . .

'Tom?'

. . . A dream, perhaps. The memory faded. I opened my eyes, shook my head.

'Well. Perhaps that's for the best,' Charles said, glancing carefully at Trim. 'Let's talk of more cheerful matters. I have some excellent news.' He paused, then smiled. 'Sir Philip has paid off all your debts.'

It took me a moment to understand what this meant. I clasped his arm. 'All of them? I'm free?'

He grinned. 'As promised, Tom.'

'And Jakes? Woodburn?'

Trim cleared his throat. Charles gave him a sharp look, and shook his head. 'Sir Philip has dealt with everything. Don't let it concern you.'

A servant arrived with tea and breakfast. I watched hungrily as he laid out the dishes but when I sat down to eat I could barely finish half a roll.

Trim watched me with a worried expression. 'D'you see now, Mr Buckley? He's not well enough to travel yet.'

Charles frowned. 'What choice do we have? If he stays another day in this hole he's liable to catch another contagion.'

'Then we should find him a good, clean room in the Borough,' Trim argued. 'They'll take him at the George now his fever's passed.'

'The George?' I looked up from my roll with renewed interest. 'Should we go there now?'

'Yes, *thank you* for that suggestion, Mr Trim.' Charles glared at the barber. 'But as you know Sir Philip has invited Tom to stay at his lodge in Richmond while he recovers.' He turned to me. 'There's a carriage waiting to take us to the river.'

'Could we . . .' I thought of the two whores sunning themselves on the steps outside. 'Might we go tomorrow? I am a *little* tired.'

Charles placed a hand on my shoulder. 'Tom, please, I beg you. You need peace and rest. Let me take care of you. When you are well we will hit the taverns together, I promise.'

I nodded my consent. I had missed Charles these past few months – and he had saved me from prison. If this was what he wanted, I would go with him.

'Good. We should leave at once, as soon as you are dressed. There are fresh clothes on the chair here.' He pulled out his purse and tipped a stream of coins into his palm. 'Mr Trim, sir, would you be kind enough to pay the bill? You may keep the change.'

'It's just Trim,' he muttered irritably, but he took the coins. 'Take care, Mr Hawkins.' He gave a short bow and left before I had a chance to thank him.

I would like to say it was the effects of the fever, or the speed with which Charles scooped me up from my sick bed and bundled me into the waiting hackney coach that made me forget. Perhaps it *was* these things, or perhaps it was just that I did not care to think deeply enough. Whatever the reason, we had almost reached the river and Tooley stairs when I realised what I had forgotten.

'Charles, wait. We must turn back.'

He stuck his head out of the carriage to peer down the street. 'We're almost at the river.'

'Charles!' I clutched his arm, pulling him round to face me. 'I must find Kitty. She saved my life. I can't leave without seeing her.'

Charles said nothing, just stared at me sadly, his body swaying as the carriage swung round a corner.

'We must go back,' I called to the driver. I knew something was wrong. I could see it in Charles' face. But I refused to understand. I clambered from my seat and grabbed the driver by the shoulder. 'Stop, damn you!'

The hackney pulled to a violent halt, half-flinging me from the carriage. The driver turned and glared at me. 'Grab me again and I'll break your jaw, you bloody fool.'

'Turn around at once! Take us to the Marshalsea.'

'Tom,' Charles said, softly.

I shrank back against the carriage seat. 'Don't say it. Charles, don't say it, I beg you.'

He placed a hand on my shoulder. 'I'm sorry, Tom. She's dead.'

She's dead. She's dead. I don't remember the rest of the journey to the Thames, just those words turning round and round with the wheels of the carriage. It wasn't possible. Not Kitty. She'd saved me. She'd killed Jakes for me. She was my reward for everything I'd been through. Wasn't she? She couldn't be dead. What plans could I make without her? What life could I possibly have worth living?

Sir Philip had sent his own personal yacht from Richmond to collect us. His daughters Mary and Constance had sailed down with a picnic, no doubt curious to see Mr Buckley's infamous friend. They were met with a hollow wreck of a man, bludgeoned with grief.

'I'm afraid Mr Hawkins has just received some bad news,' Charles said, gripping me tightly and steering me on to the boat.

To their credit the young Misses Meadows seemed honestly concerned for my welfare and found me a quiet, shaded corner to rest. 'Cushions,' Mary said firmly, as if they were a remedy for all misfortunes, from disease and death to the apocalypse.

I lay down and covered my face with my hand. I could not weep, not here, as much as I wanted to. Charles sat down next to me. I dropped my hand. 'How did she die?'

'Let's talk of this later, Tom. You must rest.' Beneath the concern I caught the faintest hint of impatience. No one else would have heard it, but I knew Charles too well.

'Was it the fever that took her?'

He sighed, then nodded.

My heart sank still further. I thought of her lips pressed against mine, her hands around my neck. 'I killed her with a kiss.'

Charles looked away, and said nothing. I had made him uncomfortable. All this fuss over a kitchen maid.

The boat hit a swell, rising then dropping swiftly with a sharp splash. The jolt of it brought me to my senses. What sort of a man was I, lying on velvet cushions and whimpering to myself? Not the man Kitty had wanted. I pulled myself to my feet and found a seat near the prow. A servant brought me a glass of wine and a pipe.

Constance, seeing I had rallied, skipped over and settled down next to me, fanning herself vigorously. She was a pretty girl with a lively manner and in other circumstances I would have enjoyed her company. 'Mr Hawkins, sir.' She lowered her voice. 'Mary and I were thrilled to hear of your adventures in gaol. Do you promise to tell us your story? When you are recovered, of course.'

I opened my mouth to reply, but could not think what to say. How could I sit at supper and describe what I had witnessed to a pair of innocent young ladies? A boy of thirteen beaten to death; rotting corpses teeming with rats; waking to find my friend with his throat cut, the life stolen from his bright black eyes. How could I weave that into a pretty story to amuse Sir Philip's daughters? And worse, knowing that their father had sat back and let it all happen? I smiled vaguely and took a sip of wine.

Constance leaned closer, whispering behind her fan. 'Charles made us promise not to ask, but I must know . . . is it true you shot the killer right through the heart?'

I stared at her. 'I didn't kill anyone, Miss Constance.'

She frowned. 'But you *must* have! Papa said so. Mr Buckley said you were very brave.'

'No, madam. Kitty Sparks shot Mr Jakes.' Once in the stomach and once right between the eyes.

'Kitty Sparks . . . ?' She closed her fan with a sharp snap, then sat back and studied me narrowly. 'A *girl*?'

'A kitchen maid.' I paused. 'I loved her.'

She stared at me for a long moment, eyes wide. Then she blinked, and laughed, and tapped her fan playfully on my arm. 'You are teasing me, sir. How wicked of you.' She jumped up, twirling her fine blue silk skirts as she danced away from me to join her sister. I remembered Kitty running across the yard, picking up her skirts. A flash of dainty ankles. Charles, who had been standing close enough to hear, shook his head slowly and turned away.

The boat sailed on up river, the sun glinting on the water. I looked back towards Southwark, but we had turned a bend and it had slid from view some time ago. I'd left it behind without noticing.

The next few days passed like a dream. Sir Philip's hunting lodge was vast, with servants standing ready to answer every possible whim. I had been given a suite of rooms close to Charles' quarters, with my own valet, who watched me from the corner of his eyes as if I might strike him or steal something small and valuable. Why not? I had killed a man, apparently.

Only Charles and Joseph Cross knew the truth. They had decided between them to hide it. Kitty had shot Jakes in cold blood. If the world discovered it, her reputation would be ruined for ever. At worst, she could have been transported or hanged. So Cross pulled the pistol from her hand and told everyone that I'd shot Jakes. I was half-dead anyway – what did it matter? Kitty protested, but no one believed her, apart from Charles. He knew I was not capable of it.

So Kitty was free to stay and watch over me. I remembered her now. She'd held my hand and pulled me back from the brink of death. And then the fever had taken her instead.

There was talk of a trial, in the days after I recovered. But I was a gentleman, and Jakes was not. Sir Philip had friends, and influence. The talk died away.

And Mr Woodburn? Charles muttered something about the Church protecting its own. 'He's locked away somewhere. Or sent abroad perhaps. He should probably hang for what he did . . .'

'No,' I sighed. Mr Woodburn hadn't escaped punishment – his own conscience would see to that. 'Let him live, wherever he is. He was a fool. A dangerous fool. But he didn't kill Roberts – or anyone else. In his own muddle-headed way he truly thought he was doing good.' I shook my head at the idiocy of it all.

As time passed I grew stronger, and my appetite returned, but my spirits remained low. I found that I could not stay indoors for long, and took to exploring the grounds alone for hours. I liked to walk about the lake close to the house, where the horses sheltered beneath the trees, then head deep into the woods, kicking up the autumn leaves as if I might find answers beneath them. When it grew dark Sir Philip's wife, Lady Dorothy, would send men out with lanterns to find me. I would return to my rooms to find a warm bath by the fire, and fresh clothes.

At night I dreamed I was back in the grave on Snows Fields and would wake with a cry of terror and the taste of soil in my mouth.

Twenty-Six

'*You had no right, Charles! No right at all!*'

We were in Sir Philip's library; unread books stretching high to the ceiling. The rain had been falling hard since breakfast, and I had retreated here to spend a peaceful morning roaming the shelves. I liked this room; it smelled of old leather and pipe smoke and the family rarely used it.

It was over a week since I had arrived at the lodge. Long walks, fresh air and good food had revived my strength, but a darkness still lingered. It rose to claim me in the dead of night: a dense, endless fog of dread and anxiety. Hour after hour I lay awake, my thoughts twisting and coiling upon themselves in a hopeless tangle.

I should have felt glad to be alive and free. I still grieved for Kitty and Fleet, but their deaths were like sharp blades in my heart – clean, honest wounds that I could understand. It was something else that kept me awake at night; something more insidious than grief. I couldn't see it and I couldn't name it but I knew, deep in my soul, that it was there.

I was reading an old copy of the *Gazette* when Charles entered the room. I was glad to see him; I had not spent much time with him these past few days. He worked long hours with Sir Philip, but the whole family had set off for London that morning to prepare for the coronation. Mary was a maid of honour to the queen and would be near the head of the procession tomorrow.

'Charles!' I grinned. 'Are you free at last? Let's call for a bottle of wine and play some cards. You will have to lend me some money.' Sir Philip had cleared my old debts, but I had no fresh funds in my pocket. I was penniless. Again.

He gave a regretful smile. 'I have a sermon to write. But here – this arrived for you this morning.' He held up a letter, then added, carefully, 'It's from your father.'

I shrank back. 'How did he find me?'

'I wrote to him.'

I glared at him in fury as he slid the letter from the envelope. 'You had no right, Charles! No right at all!'

'If you would just read it. I think it may surprise you.'

I tore it from his hand and flung it into the hearth.

Charles sprang forward and grabbed it before it caught light, knocking the glowing embers away with his fingers. 'Tom, please. For my sake. It is just one page.'

'Oh, very well,' I sulked. 'Hand it here if you must.' I opened it out, steeling myself for the words of rebuke and triumph.

My Dear Child

I have just received the News this morning of your recent Troubles and write to you in all Haste. My boy – I beg you to come Home to your Family to rest and recover. I have enclosed three pounds to help with your Journey and pray you would come at once.

My Dearest Son, why did you not write to me? Did you think I had forgotten you? I have missed you, Thomas, every day – and prayed for you. Charles tells me you have grown up to be a good man and a true Friend, and that you have performed a great Service to Sir Philip Meadows. I am sure with the support of such a noble patron, your youthful transgressions will be forgiven. I shall write to the Bishop of Norfolk on your behalf, the moment I hear from you.

My boy. We are both Stubborn, but I am old now — too old to be governed by Pride. Come home to your Family, who love you, and take over my Duties here in the parish. This is your true calling, my Son, and the dearest wish of your beloved Mother. Pray to God and He will show you your rightful Path.

Your Loving and Affectionate Father

I read it again. Three times. Held it out at arm's length to confirm the handwriting.

Charles was smiling. 'D'you see, Tom? You're saved!'

I shook my head, mystified.

The rain had stopped. It was a mild, grey October afternoon; a day to make mild, grey decisions. I walked down to the lake and sat beneath the large weeping willow at the water's edge. The grass was dry beneath its branches, which hung down like bed curtains. My own secret chapel of contemplation, hidden from the world.

I pulled the letter from my pocket and read it over once more. *My dearest son?* My father had never spoken of me in such affectionate terms. Edmund, my stepbrother, had always been his favourite. At least, that is what I had always thought. Had I been wrong, all this time?

I could go home. Leave all my struggles and cares behind me and start afresh. And why not? What was left for me in London? More gambling, more debauches, more debts. How long before I found myself thrown in gaol again? How long before I fucked the wrong whore and caught the pox? There could have been another path for me, if Kitty had lived. A riotous, disreputable life, to be sure, but my God it would have been worth it. But she was dead and that path was closed to me now.

I leaned back against the willow's trunk, and allowed myself to think of home for the first time in three long years. Not the last angry days and the arguments, but happier times. I thought about the life I could lead; the life I had studied and prepared for since I was a child. The Reverend Thomas Hawkins. A well-conducted, respectable gentleman. A vicarage, two hundred pounds per annum, a hundred acres of land. Servants. A pretty, dutiful wife to run the farm while I sat at my father's old desk and wrote sermons. Respectful neighbours. The simple pleasures of shooting and fishing and long walks down to the coast. No need to follow the high fashions and low habits of the town. Peace, health. A long, contented life.

Was *this* my path, after all? Had I been running away from the one thing I truly wanted?

My father had told me to ask God for guidance. I closed my eyes and prayed.

You'd die of boredom, Tom.

A gust of wind. A rustle of leaves. I opened my eyes and swore I caught a flash of red velvet through the branches. I blinked, and it was gone. I'd been dreaming.

I'd been dreaming, but now I was awake.

I sprang up and pushed my way free from the willow, running back towards the house. I grabbed hold of a passing servant and ordered him to find a boat to take me back to the city. My father was right; it was time to go home. Home to London.

I gathered up my few possessions then went in search of Charles. His room was empty, his trunk packed ready to join the family in town for the coronation. I smiled at the neat piles of books and carefully folded clothes. I hadn't been here since my first night; we'd sat by the fire, talking for hours. I'd thought there would be more time to reminisce, but I had barely seen him since then. And it was then that a sudden doubt leapt out and seized me. The strange, formless anxiety I had felt ever since I'd arrived at the lodge sharpened to one question.

Had Charles been avoiding me?

I'd spent more time with Lady Dorothy and her daughters than with my old friend this past week. I had not given it a moment's clear thought, but now I began to wonder. Charles had always been ambitious. Not everyone could see it but I had always known what lay hidden beneath his quiet, friendly manner; the iron core every man needs to advance in the world.

Was that why he had written to my father? To be rid of me, now I had served my purpose? No, no – that was wrong. Unkind. Charles had been a good, loyal, patient friend. If it weren't for him I would still be rotting in prison.

But I could not ignore the chill, creeping suspicion that something didn't add up. It was the same feeling I had at cards, when I was sure someone had cheated but couldn't prove it.

I paced the room, thinking hard. It wasn't true. I was mistaken. But the more I thought, the more I doubted. Sir Philip and Lady Dorothy adored Charles; he was like another son to them. Why did he not beg Sir Philip to release me, when he knew my life was in danger? And why had he kept his distance these past few days? Now I thought about it carefully, his behaviour struck me as strange; almost furtive. As if he were afraid that if I spent too much time with him . . .

. . . I would guess his secret.

I stopped still, in the middle of the room, understanding at last. Stripping away sentiment, my sense of obligation and loyalty, it all became clear. Charles had not helped me in the Marshalsea. He had *used* me.

If Charles had begged my case, Sir Philip would have listened; I was sure of it. But it suited them both to have me locked up in gaol; their own personal investigator, desperate to uncover the truth. Charles had left me there even when I had been chained and beaten and thrown in the Strong Room. And see how obliging I'd been! There would be no more talk of ghosts. No riots. No bothersome letters from a grieving widow. No loss of profit.

I'd intended to wait and talk to Charles – perhaps persuade him to sail up to London with me. Now I knew I had to leave at once. I was afraid I might see the truth confirmed in his eyes: that he was not my friend; had not been for a long time. Perhaps it was that day I had called out to him in the street in front of his patron, bottle in hand. Or even before that – in some ruthless, clear-eyed moment when he realised he didn't need me any more. The boy he had once admired, who had protected him at school, was sinking, while he was rising far beyond reach.

Oh, yes, Charles. Much better to pack me off to Suffolk, far away and out of trouble. And have me believe it was a kindness, too.

I sat down at his writing table, feeling hollow and light-headed. I would write him a note, explaining I had left for the town. I owed him that much, and then we were done. There was no paper left out so I opened a drawer and reached inside. My fingers closed on a soft leather pouch. I pulled it out.

My purse. Stolen from me in a stinking alley in St Giles. I weighed it in my hands, the coins clinking together softly. Still full.

How could it possibly be here, now, in this room? Something hard pressed down upon my heart. The heavy weight of a friend's betrayal.

A moment later the door opened and Charles strode in, smiling. 'Tom! What are you—' He stopped, seeing the purse in my hand. His mouth opened in shock. Then he glanced away in a shifty fashion, smoothing his black silk waistcoat. 'I hear you've called for a boat. I think you should see if it's ready.'

I rose from my chair, blood pounding in my ears. I held the purse out in front of me, wishing it would somehow vanish. Perhaps I was mistaken. Please God, let this all be some foolish misunderstanding. 'This purse was stolen from me.'

He frowned impatiently. 'The money is all there. Take it and go.'

I stared at him, barely able to breathe as the truth struck home. 'What did you do, Charles?' I whispered. 'My God. What did you do to me?'

'What did *I* do?' He gave a sharp, incredulous laugh. 'You think to blame me for all your troubles? I have worked without cease for years to attain all this.' He gestured about him. 'Do you have any notion how hard it is to secure a patron when you have no family, no connections? I have sacrificed everything for this position. But you cannot begin to understand that, can you? You were born with every conceivable privilege. Money. Good health. A good *family*. And see what you have achieved with these fine gifts! You have drunk and gambled and fucked away every penny you've ever owned. Wandered through life as if the whole world owes you a living. Well, here's the truth of the matter, Tom Hawkins. The world doesn't give a damn about you.'

Pain burned in my chest. How could he say these things to me — my oldest, dearest friend? I stared at him, hoping that he would suddenly laugh and tell me this was all a joke. But the mild-tempered, amiable boy I had always loved had vanished and a stranger stood in his place. 'You *helped* me. You gave me all your savings.'

'No. Not all of them. Not even close. Just enough to keep you from starving in prison.' Charles paused, deliberating for a moment. He lifted his chin and looked me straight in the eye. 'I will be honest with you. You might as well know the whole truth. You might even learn something from it. The night you came to me and asked for my help, I had known for days that you were destined for the Marshalsea. I'd seen your name on the list of arrest warrants.'

'No.' I sat down heavily, clasping the arm of the chair. 'I don't believe you.'

He clasped his hands behind his back and crossed to the window, staring down upon the neatly landscaped garden below. The sun shone through the pane, casting his face half in light, half in shadow. 'We all have masters, Tom. The only free men in this

world are idiots and fools. It is Sir Philip's duty to keep the prison
running well. And it is my duty to aid him in that task. To be of
value to him. No matter the personal cost.' He bowed his head.
'Catherine Roberts was drawing too much attention to the
Marshalsea, with all her talk of ghosts and murder. Sir Philip
wanted . . . *needed* things returned to normal. Acton refused to
investigate, even with the gaol teetering upon the brink of revolt.
In truth we half-suspected him of the murder. When I saw your
name on the list I knew God had placed it there for a reason. Do
you not see, Tom? You were already destined for gaol and we
needed a man we could trust. What harm was there in that? You
would help me. I would help Sir Philip. Sir Philip would help us
both. This is the way the world works. Where would we be without it? Without Sir Philip's patronage, what would I be? A poor
country curate scrimping a living on a few pounds a year.' He
paused. 'You know, he is very grateful to us both. Mrs Roberts is
content and the gaol is running smoothly again. This could still
go very well for you, Tom, if you could just . . . if you would only
think *straight* for once.'

My hand squeezed tight about my purse, the edges of the coins
digging into my palm. 'I had enough money to save myself.'

He bit his lip. 'Yes. And for that . . . for that I am sorry, Tom.
But don't you see? It was too late. I'd already promised Sir Philip
that you would help us. I could not afford to let him down – I had
vowed to resolve the matter for him before the coronation. Sir
Philip is a kind and generous patron, but he does not take well to
failure. I would have lost my position – and he would have made
sure all of his friends and allies shunned me as well. I would have
been ruined.'

'So . . . You paid men to rob me.'

Charles turned from the window. 'I had to – don't you see? I
needed you in the gaol. I never thought you'd win at the gaming
tables! I spent half the night pacing about outside, praying to
God you'd lose.' He gestured to the purse. 'Half the money was

mine to begin with. All I did was call upon a few cutpurses to get it back.'

'They nearly killed me, Charles!'

'No, no – I swear it! I would never . . . Their chief had worked for us before. He only struck you because you were damned foolish enough to fight back.'

'This was my freedom!' I shouted, clutching my purse tight. 'And you stole it from me.' I swallowed hard, fighting back the tears of bitterness and rage. 'You wrote that damned note to Fletcher, didn't you? Just to be sure. My God, Charles – are you not ashamed of yourself? Do you not feel *any* guilt for what you've done?'

He coloured. 'How can I make you understand? Will you not try to see things from my side? You think because you don't want this life it is not worth having! But I have worked damned hard these past years while you sat drinking in poxy taverns, squandering all the gifts God gave you. If there is any shame or guilt to be felt, it is on *your* side, not mine.'

I put my head in my hands. All the beatings I had endured, in St Giles and in the Marshalsea. Even the night in the Strong Room. Nothing had hurt me as much as this – nothing but Kitty's death. 'You've broken my heart,' I said.

'Oh, *Tom*,' Charles said, and laughed. He didn't believe me – because he did not want to. He turned to leave, then paused. 'It was only a matter of time before you were thrown in gaol. All I did was nudge you back on to a path you were always destined to follow. I looked after you well enough – did I not? Now you have a full purse and a chance to start your life afresh. How many men can say the same?' He smiled down at me. 'When you have calmed down and considered the facts, you will understand. In fact I think you'll realise you would have done just the same in my position.'

Anger and bitterness surged inside of me. I rose to my feet. 'No. I would not. I would *never* betray a friend.'

He rolled his eyes as if I were a naive child. 'And that's why *I* will be Bishop of London one day. Whereas you . . .' He looked me up and down, and gave a little smirk. 'What will *you* be, Tom?'

I considered this for a moment. And then I punched him hard in the face. He collapsed to his knees, eyes streaming, blood gushing from his nostrils all over his fine silk rug.

'What will I be?' I stared down at him in disgust, cradling my bloodied fist as he sobbed on the floor in pain and fury. 'I'll be the man who broke the Bishop of London's nose.'

Twenty-Seven

I never thought I would return to the Marshalsea, but here I was at the Lodge gate. I banged my fist against the door before I could change my mind. The grate slid open and a familiar pair of bloodshot eyes glared at me through the gap.

'*Oh, for God's* . . .' But he opened the door and let me pass.

My plan on fleeing Richmond had been to head straight for Moll's, buy a pipe, a girl and a bowl of punch, and forget all about Charles and his betrayal. But the Thames had other ideas. The river was crammed with visitors pouring into the city for the coronation, with long queues to all the stairs on the north side. Fights were breaking out between the watermen and two boats had already capsized, flinging their passengers into the dark, filthy waters.

My boatman considered the chaos for a moment before steering us decisively towards the south bank. 'I'll drop you at Tooley stairs,' he said. 'Safer to walk back across the bridge today.'

The boat bumped up hard against the same worn, greasy steps I had taken with Jakes that first day, laden down with chains. I took it as a sign; one last visit to the place that had almost killed me, but this time as a free man.

The Park was packed with prisoners taking the air while they could. There were a few new debtors I didn't recognise; a reminder that prison life rolled on and always would. A young whore was hard at work consoling an old, drunk gentleman on Fleet's bench. She winked at me as I passed, one hand busy in his breeches while the other slipped into his pocket.

Acton and Gilbourne were nowhere to be seen, thank God. I would have turned on my heel and left if I'd seen them. I spied Mary Acton frowning down at me from the parlour window, Henry at her hip trying to eat her hair. I raised my hat and gave her a deep, theatrical bow. She pursed her lips and disappeared from view.

Gilbert Hand was in his usual spot by the lamppost. I nodded to him but didn't stop; I didn't have the time or the inclination to feed any wriggling worms of gossip into the Ranger's eager beak.

I'd forgotten how badly the whole place stank; I'd grown accustomed to the fresh Richmond air and the contrast was almost unbearable. I bought a nosegay from a young gypsy girl in the yard to mask the stench, then dropped by the chandler's shop where I bought tobacco, candles, a pound of butter and a few other little parcels. And then I crossed over to my old ward, up the familiar, worn-down stairs to Belle Isle – but Fleet's empire of mischief and disorder had vanished. It was just a tatty old room with rotten floorboards and five new occupants crammed into two beds. Acton was getting his money's worth, as ever.

But it was Trim I had come to see, and he was at home, brewing a pot of tea. I poked my head round the door and he leapt up in astonishment.

'Tom! Well, I never! I hardly recognised you in your fine clothes. That is . . . you were very sick, the last time I saw you,' he added hurriedly as I stepped into the room.

I stared at myself in the looking glass near the fire, seeing myself with fresh eyes. I was still dressed in the snuff-coloured suit Lady Dorothy had given me, and a new short wig tied with a black silk ribbon. I had the straight, confident posture of a man with money in his pocket: three pounds from my father and the ten Charles had stolen from me. I looked . . . respectable.

We shook hands and I presented him with the parcel of goods I'd bought.

'Very good of you, sir,' he said, opening up the tobacco and building himself a pipe.

'You were very good to *me*, Trim. I doubt I would have survived without your help. And . . . well, consider it a small apology for accusing you of murder.' I paused. 'And threatening to kill you.'

'It was my own fault,' he said quietly. He put down his pipe and crossed to the window. The old floorboards had been mended since I'd stamped my foot through them. 'I should have spoken out. I should at least have told Fleet what I'd heard that night. Perhaps he would still be alive . . .' He bowed his head.

'It was *not* your fault, don't speak such nonsense. Blame Woodburn and Jakes. Blame Gilbourne for tempting Roberts in such a foul way. Blame Roberts himself! He should never have taken the money.'

He smiled, but I could see in his eyes that he would always feel some guilt for what had happened. Far more than Gilbourne ever would, damn him. Jakes and Roberts were dead, and I doubted Woodburn would ever fully regain his sanity. But Edward Gilbourne had survived without a scratch on that smooth skin of his, without the faintest stain upon his reputation. Well, he had escaped justice in this world, and there was nothing I could do about it. This was not an Italian opera where all ended well. A shame, really – I would happily pay to see Gilbourne on the stage. As a castrato.

Trim handed me a cup of tea and nodded towards the door. 'Mr Buckley's not with you, then?'

'We had a fight.'

'Indeed?' He shot me an appraising look. 'A bad one, I think.'

He betrayed me. My oldest friend. I could still scarcely believe it. All those years of friendship, all those happy memories – destroyed by his treachery. I could not even begin to explain this to Trim. I sat down, turned my face to the fire. 'He was not the friend I thought he was.'

'Ambition and friendship are poor bedfellows,' Trim observed, joining me by the fire and resting his tea on the small bulge of his stomach. 'I think perhaps Mr Buckley would see loyalty as a weakness.'

I warmed my hands against my cup of tea. 'Strange. I only knew Fleet for a few days, but he was a better friend to me than Charles ever was.'

'Easy to mistake good humour for good character. And what of Mr Jakes, eh? He seemed such a decent, Christianlike man.'

'I think he was, in many ways. He'd lost his way, of course. In fact I think he was quite mad, at the end. But he truly believed that he was doing God's work.'

'Then we must pray that God forgives him.' Trim paused. 'I've been praying for Mr Fleet these last few days. Though it's hard to know where to *start*.' He chuckled for a moment then fell silent, and took a long draw on his pipe. 'May he rest in peace.'

I smiled at this, and sent my own private prayer to the heavens. I doubted Fleet had ever enjoyed much peace or rest in his life – but perhaps that was how he preferred it. 'There is something I wished to ask you,' I said, after a while. 'Charles rushed me away from the sponging house before I had the chance.'

He sat up straight. 'Kitty?'

I nodded, tears springing in my eyes. I brushed them away, surprised at their sudden return. I'd learned to hide my grief in Richmond – no one wanted to see it there. Trim, though, would understand.

'You wish to know where she is.'

'Where she's buried, yes.'

'*Buried?*' Trim spluttered out a long stream of smoke. His tea slopped over its cup and he cursed, setting it to the floor. 'What in heaven do you mean?'

'Charles said . . .' I stared at him, eyes wide. A flicker of hope flared in my chest. 'He told me she died of the fever. That she caught it from me.'

'No! No, indeed!' Trim cried, horrified. 'Kitty's alive and well, I swear it! She never caught the fever.'

I leapt from my seat. 'My God! Then where is she? Is she here, in the gaol?'

His shoulders slumped. 'No. She's gone. Ran off ten days ago, when she heard you'd left for Richmond. No one's heard from her since, not even Mrs Bradshaw.' He frowned. 'She's vanished.'

I asked about the prison – half-frantic with joy at the news and panic that I would not find her. Kitty knew how to disappear without trace when she wanted; Fleet had spent months searching for her before stumbling upon her in the Marshalsea. I could not wait that long, damn it. But no one had the faintest idea where she might be.

'She's not in the Borough,' Mrs Bradshaw declared. 'Mr Hand sent Ben out to hunt for her. We even sent a message to Mrs Roberts but she's left the city. Now there's a thing.' She drew closer. 'She's reconciled with her father, would you believe. Now poor Captain Roberts is no longer . . . *a suicide*,' she mouthed, 'they couldn't use that against her in court. She's returned home to her son. Now.You *must* tell me.' She seized my arm. 'Is it true Mr Gilbourne was planning to *use her terribly*?' Her eyes gleamed with excitement.

'Please, Mrs Bradshaw. I must find Kitty.'

'*Elle est morte!*' A thin, piercing voice cut through the coffee-house. Madame Migault was in her usual corner, reading evil in the tea leaves. 'I've seen her! Dead in a ditch. *Murdered.*' She ran a finger across her throat.

'Shut your mouth, you poisonous old baggage!' Mrs Bradshaw cried.

I left them fighting, their voices carrying out across the Park.

• • •

'Hawkins!'

I had almost reached the Lodge when Acton stormed into the yard with Grace and two guards at his back. He was drunk and holding his whip in his hand, just as he had been the first time I'd seen him. 'What the devil d'you think you're doing swanning about the place? Get out before I kick you out.'

I held his gaze. 'One day the world will know about you, Acton. About what you do in this place.'

He gave a contemptuous laugh and spat at my feet. 'The world doesn't care, Mr Hawkins. Not one damned farthing. Mr Grace.' He turned to his clerk. 'Have Mr Gilbourne write an Order of Court. I will not have troublemakers in my Castle.'

And so that was my last trip to the Marshalsea. The letter with its Court seal arrived care of Tom King's coffeehouse the next day, signed in Gilbourne's hand, banishing me from the gaol for my impudent behaviour and for spreading malicious gossip about the esteemed head keeper and the Palace Court's deputy protho-notary. I burned it.

The last person I saw as I left the prison was Joseph Cross, standing at the Lodge door, swigging from a bottle of wine. It struck me, for the first time, that he must have been hand-some once, before the drink and hard living caught up with him.

'What are you staring at?'

I put my hands in my pockets and rocked back upon my heels. 'And a good day to *you*, Mr Cross.'

'You run out of money, then? Am I locking you up again?'

'Not at all. I hear you stopped Acton from sending me over to the Common Side when I was sick with fever.'

He glanced down the corridor towards the Park. Acton was standing at the yard door, a black silhouette with the sun at his back. 'Didn't want you fouling the place,' he muttered. 'It's all well and good for the governor – he don't have to deal with all the stinking corpses, does he?'

I smiled. Cross would sooner die than admit he wanted to help. 'Well, I am grateful to you, sir.'

Cross look disgusted. 'Grateful won't buy me a round in the Tap Room, will it?'

A fair point. I pulled out a guinea and dropped it in his palm. 'For saving my life.'

His hand snapped shut faster than a dog's jaw about a rabbit's neck. 'Not sure your life's worth *that* much, Mr Hawkins.' But then he grinned, and tilted his head towards the open door. 'Go on, then. Fuck off before I lock you up for sport. Lucky bastard.'

I crossed the bridge, glad to be home at last. Kitty was alive and waiting for me somewhere amidst the bustle and swagger of these streets. Charles had wanted to keep her from me. I'm sure he thought he was doing me a good turn – saving me from a disgraceful match to a common kitchen maid. Well, he'd failed, thank God. I would find her and I would disgrace myself as soon as possible. As often as she would let me. I strolled through the city, enjoying the press of the crowds, everything on display, everything for sale. How could I have thought of leaving it for a moment? So what if there were thieves lurking in the shadows; fights spilling out from every tavern; lice, vermin, the pox; foul air and poisoned water? London quickened my pulse and made my blood sing in my veins – and for that I would forgive it anything.

I bought a new walking cane with a silver top; a tinderbox and a chain for my mother's cross. Ordered a pair of shoes from a cobbler off the Strand. And as the sun set I made my way back to Moll's.

'Tom Hawkins! Here you are at last!' she cried, striding across the room. She kissed me full on the lips. 'Word is you killed a man.'

I grabbed her by the waist and pressed my lips to her ear. 'I haven't killed a soul. But don't you dare tell anyone.'

She gave a wicked smile. 'Your reputation is safe with me, sweetheart.'

It was the night before the coronation and I had never seen the coffeehouse so packed. It seemed as though half of London was crammed inside, waiting to catch a glimpse of the king tomorrow.

Moll found me a quiet corner then slipped away into the crowds, promising she would be back soon. 'Someone I think you should meet.' I ordered a bowl of punch from Betty, smoked a pipe and wrote a short note to my father, thanking him for his kindness and forgiveness. I'd thought it would be a hard letter to write – but the words flowed easily and my heart felt lighter when I had finished. He would be disappointed by my decision, but there it was. The Church was his vocation. London was mine.

I had just finished writing when a shadow fell across the table. I glanced up and the breath caught in my throat.

Fleet.

I blinked, startled, and the spell was broken.

The stranger in front of me wasn't Fleet. He was younger – thirty at most – with a darker complexion and a stronger build. He didn't move like Fleet. He moved like a soldier, steady, serious and full of purpose as he sat down opposite me. But those black eyes under heavy brows; the shape of his jaw . . . they had been enough to fool me, for a moment.

I remembered Fleet's meeting in the Tap Room, the day before he died, and the stranger who never turned round to face me. *A family affair*, Fleet had said. 'Are you his brother?'

'Half.'

I peered at him in the candlelight. 'On which side, sir? Your mother's or the devil's?'

His face remained still, but his eyes glittered with amusement. 'You don't recognise me.' He pulled a dagger from his side and laid it on the table between us, fingers caressing the hilt. 'D'you remember this? I held it to your throat.'

The hairs rose on my neck. This was the man who had robbed me in St Giles. I poured myself a glass of punch and knocked it back, trying to keep my hands from shaking. 'I should challenge you to a fight, I suppose.'

'That would be unwise.' He drummed his fingers lightly across the blade. My blade.

'I was thrown in gaol because of you.'

'Shouldn't walk down black alleys with a full purse.' He rubbed his jaw. Clean-shaven; another difference.

'But you asked your brother to keep an eye on me,' I guessed. 'You felt guilty.'

'No,' he said flatly. 'Curious. Wanted to learn why a man would refuse to hand over his purse, even when his life is at stake.' His lips curled into a half-smile. 'Useful to know in my business.' He plucked a note from his pocket and slid it across the table.

I held the note up to the candlelight, squinting at Fleet's impossible scrawl. It was dated the day before he was killed.

My Dear Brother

Thank you for my Gift; he is keeping me most Amused in this wretched Hell Hole. How he has stayed alive without my aid these past five and twenty years is a Mystery. In Three Days he has been Beaten, Tortured and Chained to a Wall; fallen in Love (twice); fought in a Riot and wrestled a Ghost. He also snores like the Devil.

You asked if I might Discover why he Refused to give up his Purse to you when you had gone to the Trouble of holding a Knife to his Throat. Given that he is not a Lunatick (so far as I can tell), here follow my Conclusions, after Three Days of Close Study:

i) He is a man of Instinct more than Reason

ii) He is drawn to Trouble — or perhaps it is fairer to say, Trouble is drawn to him

iii) He believes — at heart — that God will Protect him

An Unfortunate Recipe for Disaster, you will agree — but it is the last point I fear the most. A man of true Faith in this City is like a Naked Man running into Battle, believing himself fully Armed. Diverting and alarming in Equal measure.

In other Circumstances I would propose we Shipwreck him upon a Remote Island like Robinson Crusoe before he does himself an Injury. But here is the Strangest Truth of all. I would miss him. He has awoke me from myself, James; awoke me from a deep slumber. I'm not sure How or Why, but there it is. Perhaps it is his Youth, his Curiosity. I Suspect it may be his Legs.

Whatever the Truth may be — I Thank you, dear Brother, from the Bottom of my Black Heart, for Placing him in my Path. I am much Obliged and remain, Sir, your Obedient Servant, etc

S.

I folded the note, shaking my head. He'd captured me well enough.

Fleet's brother gestured for me to keep it. 'There is something I would like to know. You found him. His body . . .' He leaned forward. 'How did he die?'

I remembered the blood upon the walls. The ugly slash of red across Fleet's throat. 'With his eyes open.'

He breathed in sharply, and bit the corner of his lip. '*With his eyes open,*' he murmured, at last. 'That's good.' He nodded to himself then studied me for a long moment, black eyes as unreadable as his brother's. 'Word is you killed Jakes. But I don't see the mark of death on you.'

'No.' I lowered my voice. 'It was Kitty. Kitty Sparks.'

He blinked in surprise. 'Nat's daughter?'

'Shot him right between the eyes. With Fleet's pistol.'

He sat back, a slow, satisfied smile spreading across his face. '*With Sam's pistol.* He would have liked that. I am indebted to you, Mr Hawkins, for this information. Perhaps I might perform some small service in return?' He picked up my dagger and trailed the tip slowly across the table. 'The man who paid me to rob you, for instance?'

'No need. I broke his nose this afternoon.'

He chuckled, and slid the dagger towards me. 'Here. In case you run into someone in a dark alley.'

I tucked it away. 'But I wonder if you might help me with another matter, sir. Kitty vanished from the Marshalsea ten days ago. No one knows where she is. Perhaps some of your friends could ask around town.' And saying that, I remembered his son, the link boy. *Sam Fleet*. Named for his uncle.

'My *friends* can find anything or anyone, Mr Hawkins. But that won't be necessary in this case.' He stood up, then beckoned me to follow him. Samuel would have weaved and danced his way across the room, quick as a fox. James Fleet cut a clean, straight path, and men drew back to let him pass.

As we came closer to the hearth he clapped a hand upon my shoulder, and pointed to a low, battered leather armchair set by the fire. A pale, slender hand rested against the arm, clutching a pipe. Fleet's journal lay on a table close by. 'There, sir.' He disappeared back into the crowds.

'Kitty?'

She turned her face from the fire then rose slowly to her feet. For a moment I thought James had been mistaken, she seemed so altered. She wore a black hat, tilted jauntily over one eye, and her plain servant's clothes were gone, replaced with an emerald silk gown, trimmed with lace and tied with black velvet ribbons. But the change was deeper than her fine clothes; she seemed older, somehow, and more sure of herself. Then again, she had killed a man.

'Well. Mr Hawkins.' She gazed at me steadily, green eyes offering no clue to her thoughts.

I hesitated. Since learning she was still alive I had imagined what I might say and do in this moment. I'd thought I might sweep her into my arms. But then I had also dared imagine she would be pleased to see me. 'Kitty . . .'

She pursed her lips. '*Miss Sparks*. Well; and I suppose you've heard of my change in fortune at last? Samuel left me everything in his will. And now here you are. What a *queer* coincidence. Am I good enough for your company now I'm a lady and not some common slut?'

I stared at her in consternation. 'I had no idea, I assure you.'

She laughed at me. 'Do you think I'm a fool? I saved your life. Nursed you when you lay dying. I risked my life and my *soul* for you, Tom Hawkins. And how did you repay me? The moment you were free you abandoned me without a moment's thought.' She clenched her teeth, fighting back the anger. 'I saw you in Sir Philip's yacht, flirting with his daughters. I watched you from the riverbank as you sailed away down the Thames. And I vowed I would never let a man betray me again. *Never*.'

I sighed, remembering the pain I'd felt that day; the dull weight of loss that had oppressed my spirits ever since. 'I was not flirting, Kitty,' I said, quietly.

'Well, that's how it seemed to me. All those cushions.' She frowned at the floor, skirts bunched tight in her fists. Even in her fury, she knew this sounded ridiculous. 'Perhaps you were not flirting,' she relented. 'But you cannot deny that you left me. Well, I'm glad of it. You taught me a valuable lesson and now I'm free of you.' She narrowed her eyes. 'I will not be fooled again, Mr Hawkins.'

'Charles told me you were dead.'

She froze, hand pressed to her heart. 'Oh,' she breathed, the blood draining from her face. '*Tom*.'

'I thought I'd lost you.'

Her eyes welled with tears. She blinked them away. 'I see.' Her fingers trailed across the soft silk of her gown. 'So, you didn't know about the will?'

'No.'

'But you still came looking for me?'

'Yes. As soon as I knew you were alive. Trim told me this afternoon.'

'Well, that's . . .' She shook her head. '*Well*.'

And that is the closest I have ever seen Kitty Sparks come to admitting she was wrong, about anything.

I kissed her then, as many times as she'd let me. This was the life I thought I'd lost; I would not let it slip through my fingers again. And then Moll appeared and fell into a deep, involved discussion with Kitty about business. Covent Garden's most notorious coffeehouse and London's most disreputable print shop – there was a great deal to talk about. I ordered a bowl of punch and drew up a chair by the fire and before I knew it I had dozed off.

Kitty nudged me awake at midnight. 'You were snoring,' she said. She tucked her feet up beneath her and smiled at me.

'God save the king!' someone shouted.

'God save Moll King!' someone called back – and everyone laughed.

Kitty watched Betty pour a fresh pot of coffee with a soft expression. 'A new king,' she murmured, then shot me a bright smile. 'A new day.'

I stretched and yawned. 'I suppose I should find myself an occupation. A place to live . . .'

Kitty smiled and nudged her toe against my thigh. 'Why, don't you want to live with me, Tom?'

I propped my hand against my chin in a vain attempt to appear nonchalant. 'What about your reputation?'

'I'm rich. I don't need a reputation.'

I cleared my throat. 'How rich, exactly . . . ?'

'*Very*.'

I leaned forward and took her hand in mine. 'I will make an honest woman of you, Kitty Sparks.'

She grinned. 'Don't you dare.'

We left Moll's at dawn, crossing the piazza to Russell Street. Kitty wrapped an arm about my waist and I pulled her close, touching my lips to her cheek. The buildings grew more tatty and disreputable the further we went, private homes and smart coffeehouses making way for an apothecary, then a grocer's shop, a rundown tavern, a gin shop. A brothel. The stink of piss and rotting food wafted up from the gutters. Kitty slipped her arm free and held her skirts up out of the filth. 'Home,' she said.

And then I saw it, from the corner of my eye: a small, dark building, shrunk back from its neighbours as if it were sulking. The windows on the lower floor were piled high with a confusion of books and maps and engravings all tossed together in an impossible jumble. The shop sign sported a cocked pistol, set at an indecent angle.

I cupped my hand and peered through the dirt-smeared window.

'It all needs sorting,' Kitty said. 'I haven't had the heart these last few days.'

'I can help.'

She raised an eyebrow. '*Indeed?* You'll roll up your sleeves and scrub the floor, will you?'

'I meant the books and pamphlets. The sketches. I'd be happy to read through them . . .'

She laughed. 'I'm sure you would, you dog.' She stepped closer and kissed me.

'Tomorrow?'

'Tomorrow,' she agreed. And then she took my hand and pulled me through the door.

THE HISTORY BEHIND
THE DEVIL IN THE MARSHALSEA

This novel was in part inspired by actual events and many of the characters are either real or based loosely on real people. All of the conditions described are taken from first-hand accounts – if anything the reality was even worse. The anonymous debtor and writer of the poem 'The Marshalsea, or, Hell in Epitome' (1718) described prisoners being chained to rotting corpses as punishment.

Many of the details of the prison come from John Grano's contemporary diary of his life in the Marshalsea from 1728 to 1729. (See the note on real characters for more information.) I also drew extensively from the Gaols Committee report of 1729 and the reports of William Acton's murder trial from August 1729.

Much of Mr Woodburn's lecture comes from a real sermon given to debtors in Ludgate prison in 1725. One can almost hear them shuffling and sighing in their seats nearly three hundred years later. The descriptions of turnkeys having to knock back cups of liquor before they opened up the prison wards is based on evidence from *The State of the Gaols in London* by William Smith, MD (1776 – which shows just how little conditions had improved in fifty years). Corpses were left to rot until grieving families could pay for their release. Mary Acton loved to dance – and Acton hated it. And there was a room called Belle Isle on the Master's Side.

Real people in the novel

Many of the characters in the novel are based (to a greater or lesser degree) on real people, living and working in the Marshalsea and around the Borough in 1727. Much of this information was drawn from the prison diary of John Grano, a debtor in the Marshalsea between 1728 and 1729.

I'm indebted to John Ginger who, as well as editing Grano's diary, compiled a biographical list of prisoners, trusties and key characters in the Borough. Many of the biographical details listed here come from that source.

William Acton

Former butcher. A turnkey in the Marshalsea from at least the early 1720s. Chief turnkey from 1726 and deputy warden from March 1727. Married to Mary Acton, whose father James Wilson was a painter and formerly a prisoner on the Common Side. William and Mary had one son, Henry, born December 1724. In August 1729 Acton was put on trial for the murder of four prisoners. (We would have called it manslaughter – the prisoners had either been beaten or treated so badly that they had died of their wounds or related illness.) Acton was found not guilty – but his reputation was severely damaged once the truth about his brutal regime became known around the Borough. He left the prison shortly after and ran a pub called the Greyhound until his death in 1748. He left a decent fortune to his wife and only son.

Captain Ralph Anderson

In prison on the Common Side. He makes a brief appearance in Grano's diary and there is a reference to an Anderson starting a riot in 1729 – according to Grano he attacked Acton with a knife.

Betty

A young black woman called Betty worked at Moll's and appears in sketches of the coffeehouse. Betty was often used as a generic name for a young maidservant, so this was probably not her real name.

Sarah Bradshaw

Owned the coffeehouse in the Marshalsea. A prisoner from August 1721 owing £50. Voluntary resident from 1729.

Henry Chapman

Barman or 'tapster' in the Marshalsea from 1724. Voluntary after 1729. Owed £110, which seems a lot for a former 'slop seller of St Giles'. (Slop sellers were merchants of work clothes, such as butcher's aprons.) He was a witness for the defence in Acton's trial.

Joseph Cross

Turnkey and former bricklayer of Wardour Street. One of Acton's trusties.

The 'Ghost'

This was inspired by a story in the Gaols Committee of a ghost that appeared to a prisoner held in the Strong Room of the Fleet prison. It was even illustrated in the report, alongside drawings of instruments of torture and starving prisoners in the sick wards.

Edward Gilbourne

Gilbourne was deputy prothonotary of the Marshalsea Court. He wrote the order stripping Matthew Pugh of his position as steward and banning him from the prison (quoted verbatim in the novel). In the Gaols Committee report (which includes Gilbourne's note as an appendix), Acton claimed it was Gilbourne who told him to take the charity cabinet. Gilbourne denied this. Pugh mentions Gilbourne again in a broadside of 1729 as a corrupt man who should be brought to justice. An Edward Gilbourne bought a house in Kensington in 1735, and there's a will at the National Archives for an Edward Gilbourne of Kensington who died in 1756.

John Grace

Briefly mentioned by Grano. The Committee report confirms that he helped tear down the charity cabinet and was imposed as steward until Acton abolished the post. Witness for the defence at Acton's trial.

Gilbert Hand

Known as 'the Ranger of the Park', Hand was an Acton trusty but also ran errands for prisoners. Previously a farmer.

Jenings

Jenings, the watchman, was the only one of Acton's trusties who spoke out against him at the trial.

Moll King

Moll was an infamous figure who managed to dodge the law most of her life. With her husband Tom she ran the most notorious coffeehouse in London (and there were about six hundred of these). The coffeehouse features in several satirical prints and paintings of the Covent Garden piazza including Hogarth's *Morning*. When Tom King died the coffeehouse changed its name to Moll King's. It was a real den of iniquity, rowdy, open all night and prone to rioting. Moll did end up in prison for a short spell later in life, but she died rich, with property in Hampstead, and passed the coffeehouse on to her son William.

Richard 'Mack' McDonnell and wife (first name unknown)

They ran the chophouse, the memorably named Titty Doll's. Mack was an Irish painter living in St Giles before ending up in prison in 1726, owing £46.

Sir Philip and Lady Dorothy Meadows

Sir Philip was Knight Marshal and ultimately responsible for the Marshalsea. It has been argued that one of the reasons Acton was found not guilty at his murder trial was because it would have reflected badly upon Sir Philip and by extension the court and the government. (Sir Philip had turned a blind eye to the illegal subletting of the position of keeper from Darby, the old governor, to Acton.) His daughter Mary was a lady-in-waiting to Queen Caroline, the wife of George II.

Madame Mary Migault

Mary Migault (née Valence) was a widow and had been in prison since June 1727. She had several run ins with John Grano.

Matthew Pugh

The old Common Side steward continued to seek justice for prisoners after Acton's trial collapsed. In a world that shrugged its shoulders over corruption and inequality, Pugh fought valiantly for justice – but sadly to no avail.

Trim

Not much is known about Trim except that he was a prisoner and acted as the Master's Side barber.

Nehemiah Whittaker the baker and Stephen Siddall the apothecary were working in the Borough at the time.

Select Bibliography

This is a small selection of works I found particularly useful – and fascinating - during my research. Hogarth's pictures were also an immeasurably valuable resource in terms of clothes, household objects, street scenes and, well . . . *everything*.

If I had to recommend just one book from this list I would suggest Lord Hervey's memoirs. Hours of malicious, scandalous fun. But I don't have to, so would recommend them all.

Contemporary sources

–, *A Report from the Committee Appointed to Enquire into the State of the Gaols of this Kingdom. With the Resolutions and Orders of the House of Commons thereupon*, 1729.

–, *The Tryal of William Acton, Friday 1 and Saturday 2 August 1729*

Defoe, Daniel, *A Tour through the Whole Island of Great Britain*

Ginger, John (ed.), *Handel's Trumpeter – The Diary of John Grano, 1728–9*

Mudge, Bradford K. (ed.), *When Flesh Becomes Word: An Anthology of Early Eighteenth-Century Libertine Literature*

de Saussure, César, *A Foreign View of England in the Reigns of George I & George II*

Sedgwick, Romney (ed.), *Lord Hervey's Memoirs*

Secondary sources

Borman, Tracy, *Henrietta Howard*

Buck, Anne, *Dress in Eighteenth-Century England*

Cruickshank, Dan, *The Secret History of Georgian London*

George, M. Dorothy, *London Life in the Eighteenth Century*

Moore, Lucy, *Amphibious Thing: The Life of a Georgian Rake*

Moore, Lucy, *Con Men and Cutpurses: Scenes from the Hogarthian Underworld*

Peakman, Julie, *Lascivious Bodies: a Sexual History of the Eighteenth Century*

Porter, Roy, *English Society in the Eighteenth Century*

Porter, Roy, *Enlightenment*

Stead, Jennifer, *Georgian Cookery (English Heritage series)*

Styles, John, *The Dress of the People*

Vickery, Amanda, *Behind Closed Doors: At Home in Georgian England*

Worsley, Lucy, *Courtiers: The Secret History of Kensington Palace*

ACKNOWLEDGEMENTS

Firstly I would like to thank both Jo Unwin and Clare Conville for their brilliant encouragement and help. Big thanks to Carrie Plitt and to everyone at Conville & Walsh – especially Jake Smith-Bosanquet, Henna Silvennoinen and Alexandra McNicoll.

Joint firstly (this is allowed, I've decided) – thanks to my publisher Nick Sayers for his tireless support and brilliant editorial guidance. Also to Laura Macdougall, Alasdair Oliver, Kerry Hood, Ellen Wood and the whole team at Hodder for everything.

My US publisher Andrea Schulz provided thoughtful and perceptive notes that really made a difference – I am very grateful both to her and her team at Houghton Mifflin Harcourt.

Thanks to the staff at the British Library – especially for not looking at me in a funny way when I ordered up a multi-volume collection of eighteenth-century erotica. It was for research. It was for research. It was for research. (What I tell you three times is true.)

Thanks to Richard Beswick for being a thoroughly bene cove. To David Shelley for his support and good humour. To Luigi Bonomi for his very useful and thoughtful advice. To Ant, Vic and the Kirstys for their fine company and kindness. To Jo Dickinson, Harrie Evans, Lance Fitzgerald, John O'Connell and Andrew Wille for friendship and wise counsel. Very special thanks to

Rowena and Ian for all this and their incredible hospitality. And a low bow with a flourish to my parents and my sisters Kay, Michelle and Debbie.

I'm grateful to everyone at Little, Brown for their encouragement — especially Ursula Mackenzie, Cath Burke, Hannah Boursnell, Sean Garrehy, Clare Smith and Adam Strange.

Finally, thanks and eternal gratitude to my very dear friend Ursula Doyle for her loyalty, generosity and regular trips to the tavern.